Haddie's Tangled Web

ML Space

ISBN: 0989013537
ISBN: 978-0-9890135-3-6

Cover Design by Jeff Fielder

To My Mother

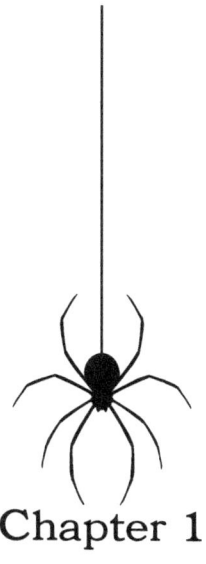

Chapter 1

DAVID JUMPED FROM THE TAXI AND RACED TO THE HOSPITAL ENTRANCE AS they pulled his wife out of the ambulance. Haddie lay on the stretcher beneath a white sheet, her hand reaching for his, her flaming red hair matted with blood. He wondered how bad it was under the sheet.

"Haddie, you're going to be OK."

She slowly shook her head back and forth. Her eyelids fluttered. David gulped for air as she gripped his trembling hand. He heard the paramedics barking orders, the wheels squeaking as they rushed the gurney up the concrete ramp into the hospital.

Lights flooded the entry. David ran his hand through his thinning hair. Voices, instrument traps, and whirring machines filled the corridor. The gurney stopped. Doctors and nurses surrounded them. David watched the light in Haddie's eyes brighten and fade like a failing lantern. Her lips moved, as if trying to form words, providing brief glimpses of shattered teeth. He moved closer, turned his ear to her, and looked up at the ceiling, praying for the first time in his life. He stroked her hair. It was rough and sticky. He pulled his hand back and stared at his blood-stained palm. He closed his eyes and pressed his forehead against hers. How bad was it under that sheet? Hit and run? Had the car only grazed her? Why did she always work so late? He looked down the length of the sheet that covered her body, and then back up to her face. He wanted to speak, to say something reassuring, but only stared. Her eyes dimmed and he sensed she did not have long. Judging by her pained look, he thought she knew too.

"It's going to be OK," he said, holding her hand.

The tears welled in his eyes. She stared back at him, her grip weakened on his hand, her eyes half-closed. She gurgled with each rise and fall of her chest. Without saying a word, she told him that she really screwed up this time. She was so engrossed in her case and tomorrow's deposition that she failed to look both ways before stepping into the street. She never saw the car. And the car hadn't just grazed her.

The gurney moved again.

A man spoke. "We're taking her to surgery now, Mr. East. You'll have to wait out here."

David heard him but held onto his wife's hand. Haddie's eyes widened, darting from one nurse and doctor to the next. Her grip on David's hand tightened.

"Promise me," she whispered. Her voice gurgled.

David looked into her eyes. "I promise."

"To your dying breath."

This time he could not hear her voice. He read her lips.

"To my dying breath."

Her hand went limp. He let go and watched his wife disappear through the metal double doors. He exhaled and his body deflated. His legs shook. He leaned against the wall and stared. The antiseptic air made him dizzy. A man moaned on a stretcher. A breathless woman in labor gripped her swollen abdomen as she was wheeled around a corner. Life saving devices ran full tilt. It was a busy night.

The waiting area was empty except for an elderly couple huddled together on a vinyl couch. David dropped onto a chair and rubbed his eyes. Thirty minutes ago he was at his office, working late in the heat of the tax season. He had just saved his client a significant sum of money and had opened a calculator to confirm the results when the phone rang.

"Your wife has been in an accident. She's being taken to Placer Hospital."

He remembered asking what happened. He remembered asking if she was all right.

"Hit and run, Mr. East. It's very serious. Please hurry."

He sat on the couch, shaking uncontrollably, so light-headed he thought he would pass out. His mind reeled back to this morning; kissing her good-bye, sipping coffee in bed, and a hundred other scenes. Visions of their years together; in her wedding dress, gathering firewood at their Adirondack cabin, her walking out of their apartment twelve hours ago with her overstuffed briefcase, and now her blood-stained hair...

David looked at the elderly couple. They held hands, sitting still as stones. Their prominent veins intertwined like blue roots across their pale hands. The blue roots seemed to bind them, snaking upwards and disappearing into their shirts. He couldn't take his eyes off those hands, holding tightly, anchored in stone. Then an overwhelming realization came over him. He would never grow old with Haddie. Although the elderly couple sat with faces drawn, leaving no doubt there was tragedy awaiting them behind those double metal doors, they at least had each other. He was alone.

He was gazing at an end table covered with wrinkled dog-eared magazines when out of the corner of his eye he saw a surgeon pulling his mask down and plodding forward. His head was bowed. David sprang out of his seat, praying that the doctor was coming to address the elderly couple.

The surgeon appeared to look through David and when he spoke it was in monotone devoid of emotion. His voice was well-tempered, like a fine sword, honed by decades of reporting bad news.

"We did everything we could, Mr. East. She's gone."

David felt his body turn cold. He dropped back to the chair. He would never touch her again. Never speak to her again. He could hear people talking to him, but the shock included a loud ringing in his ears, and the voices seemed to call from a great distance. He gripped his chair and bent over. The tears flowed as the agony of losing his Haddie settled in.

Her eyes had told him it was bad. There was no time even to say good-bye. Her bewildered look just before she disappeared behind the metal doors burned into his brain. Every time he thought of her that image would appear first. Maybe just for a second, before something more pleasant took its place, but it would always appear first. And it was completely unlike her. She never looked bewildered. Except on death's door. She knew she was not coming out alive.

Promise me.

I promise.

But promise what? He had no idea what he had promised.

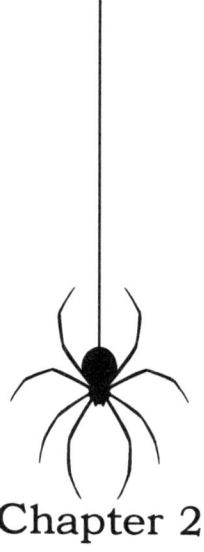

Chapter 2

DAVID HELD FLOWERS AT HIS WIFE'S FRESH GRAVE. THE MOURNERS WERE gone. He had watched them as they passed by the casket, surprised by how many he didn't know. He scratched an itch along his side, feeling his middle-aged paunch jiggle under his touch. He was alone. Haddie was all he had. She was his sole companion and the love of his life. He felt as if he had just pushed off from the top of a long steep slide with a bottom to nowhere.

David was an only child. He barely remembered his mother, and his father passed away not long after David finished college. Haddie's family was small, too. Her parents preceded her as well, but if they hadn't, David suspected they wouldn't have been much comfort. How could she marry an accountant when there were so many lawyers, doctors, and Wall Street whizzes in Manhattan? And no children? Haddie said it wasn't so, but David expected they blamed him for being childless.

They married right out of college and had been comfortable together for twenty years. They tried hard to have children. After a few years with no success, they went to a fertility clinic, where he discovered that he had an extremely low sperm count. They joked about it and tried to beat the statistics, to no avail. Over time they immersed themselves more and more into their work. The intimacy diminished and their lives became work centered. She became a partner in her law firm. He crunched numbers for one of the Big Five accounting firms. They made good money, enough to have a comfortable lower Manhattan apartment. They took a yearly vacation. Went out to nice restaurants. But they gave up on having a family.

Haddie still had a sister living in San Diego. She didn't come, but David received a nice vase of flowers from her yesterday, with a note that read, "We miss her terribly." He accidentally left them out on the terrace overnight and they froze.

He never thought he could feel worse than when his father died, but this was worse, much worse. David closed his eyes. He had walked through the funeral like a shell-shocked soldier. There was a big turnout from his office. Although he felt some comfort surrounded by people, it left him cold. They couldn't feel about Haddie as he did.

He was glad Gil came. Gil was a friend. He was fairly new to his firm and still had life in his eyes. And unlike everyone else, he didn't ask how he was feeling.

"I'm so sorry. If there's anything I can do for you, let me know," Gil had said, hunched so his face was level with David's.

Catherine was clearly in despair. Although she never looked directly at him, David felt she was watching him. She was Haddie's longtime assistant. Dressed in black with black-framed glasses, she was a few years younger than him, and reminded David of a librarian but with something simmering just beneath the surface. He knew little of her, but she was fiercely loyal to Haddie. Haddie had said many times she didn't know what she would do without Cat. David always felt a bit jealous when she said that.

The biggest turnout came from Haddie's law firm. They were easy to spot in their expensive clothes. Haddie was a partner and with her unexpected passing there was now a void at the firm. Even with his intense grief, he felt a tension among them. Perhaps it was just his imagination. He shook his head and then looked out at the bare trees. He was thinking too much. It wasn't healthy to dwell within one's own thoughts. At least not for him. *Overactive imagination,* the doctors had told him. That was after his father's death. After the dreams invaded his mind, tossing his sanity around like a rag doll.

There was one other man clearly in grief. David didn't see him arrive or leave, but only as he stood on the other side, head bowed. He couldn't say now what the man wore, but he recognized the face. Perhaps it was because it most closely resembled his own; sullen and lifeless. He even forgot himself for a moment and felt empathy for *him*. The man looked familiar, but left without speaking to him or shaking his hand. How could David not know someone who appeared to grieve so deeply for his wife of twenty years? Though he felt he should have confronted the intruder, he had neither the will nor the desire.

He just wanted Haddie back. That's all that mattered. He would never be the same without her.

David stared at the frost weighing down the first grass blades of spring. Tree limbs hung in despair, the spring buds dormant and closed tight. It was the coldest March he could remember. He stared at the tombstone and thought that forever more this was the closest he would be to her, separated by six feet of cold earth. He wished he had said something more to her as she disappeared into the emergency room. Something to calm her. Her eyes, those reaching hands. It all happened so fast.

He took a deep breath. His exposed hands burned from the cold. He looked down at the pansies in the pot. Purple, pink, and yellow petals with black faces on them. He set the pot down and knelt near the headstone. Ignoring the cold, he dug a trowel into the partially frozen dirt, the disturbance releasing a faint organic odor. When the hole was about a half-foot deep, he tipped the pot over and the pansies fell out, their root ball exposed, the fine root hairs intertwined like a web, holding the soil together. He placed the plants into the hole and backfilled with dirt, compacting it with his hands. The ground felt hard and cold through his pants, the frost melting on his knees. He felt the wind against his face and hands and knew it would be well below freezing again tonight, and the flowers, cold-hardy as they were, would be dead by morning.

He stood and gazed at the hundreds of other headstones about him. Would he come back here, every year, or every month, to "visit"? To talk to her? He thought he would. The wind picked up and penetrated his overcoat. He shivered, turned, and walked toward the parking lot to his BMW.

During the weeks that followed, David worked more than ever. He was obsessed with numbers. He understood them. They were predictable and responded consistently to manipulation. Now, more than ever, he immersed himself into his work. He felt like a machine. He bore the greatest caseload of anyone in the office. It kept his brain busy. When he was alone he had too much time to think. His apartment had become a form of solitary confinement where he could not conjure any pleasant thoughts to ease his mourning.

David rubbed his chin and felt a thick sliver of fat, as if a large slug had taken residence under his skin. He hated to cook, so the long hours at his desk coupled with the endless pizza and fast food had turned him from a pear-shaped middle-aged man to a beach ball in little over a month. He sat up and looked at his calendar on the far side of his cubicle. April 17th. He stretched his hands. His carpal tunnel seemed to be getting worse. His backaches, headaches, that damn second toe on his right foot...

Gil appeared at his cubicle. "Hey, Dave. How about getting out of here a while and grabbing some lunch?"

David looked up. David never could figure out Gil's hair. It always poked up on top, like he was constantly sticking his finger in a light socket.

"No thanks. I brought some pizza from home."

Gil sighed, rubbed his large hooked nose, and leaned against the cubicle frame. "Dave, you've been saying 'no' for five weeks. You're starting to give me a complex." Gil towered over the cubicles. "Come on. It'll be good for you to get out. You're here every morning when I walk in, you're here when I leave. What, do you sleep here, too?"

"No. I go home to eat pizza." David crossed his arms and forced a smile that froze on his face.

Gil stared at David's ample belly. "You look like shit, Dave. Come on, take a break. Maybe we should skip lunch and just go for a walk."

David tapped his pencil against the desk. Walking seemed like such an effort these days. But, Gil had a point. And Gil was the only person that he really liked around the office. He didn't want to alienate him.

"OK."

Gil raised his eyebrows and smiled. "Atta boy. I'll grab my jacket."

They took the elevator, walked through the lobby and out onto the street. It was cold and the wind whipped down the man-made canyon filled with cars and buses. David thought that the smell of car exhaust might be less noticeable today, but it wasn't so. He guessed that if it whipped the exhaust away from this street, it probably just brought in exhaust from another.

As they walked down the sidewalk, they looked a little like Laurel and Hardy minus the bowler hats. Gil cast him sidelong glances. David kept a quick pace as he tried to think of something to say. They gravitated toward a small park. David coughed as his heavy breathing cleared his lungs. He fixed the top button on his overcoat as they passed the bare tree branches. They followed a concrete path that circled the park, past the squirrels, pigeons, bare trees, and sickly bushes.

"So, how are you?"

"Wonderful," David replied.

Gil looked down at his feet as he walked. "We've been worried about you."

David didn't break stride. "Oh? Who is we?"

"The guys at work. Even Bill."

"Our fearless office manager? What's he worried about? I've made him more money in our division in the last month than probably anyone in the history of the company. Shit, I thought he'd want everyone to ditch their spouses."

Gil forced a laugh. "It's not your productivity. It's your... state of mind. You're not acting like yourself."

David glanced at him and then looked away. Didn't he know his wife had just died? Should he be wandering the hallways telling jokes? He *never* did that, not even during his happiest days. But Gil's accusation left him paranoid. David felt he was handling Haddie's loss as best he could, and better than when he lost his father. But, Gil had no way of knowing that his father's death led to a stay at Tippingdale. That was a long time ago, though it probably was buried in employment records somewhere.

"I understand how horrible it must be for you, believe me," Gil said quickly. "But, you took no time off after … you know. What I'm saying is, maybe you should take a break."

David winced and rubbed his face. "And do what? Sit in my apartment and watch TV? Visit the in-laws? Go to Bermuda?"

Gil sighed. "Mourn."

"I feel better at work. There are people around. It makes me feel better, even if I don't talk to them. And I stay busy, working."

They had almost finished a circuit around the small park. David watched a mother and her two children play on a swing set. She wore a wedding band. Her husband was probably at work. David felt a shot of envy course through him. They would meet at the dinner table tonight and talk about the day's insignificant events. He shook his head. He was breathing hard. He could feel the sweat freeze on his forehead like little pebbles stuck to his skin. They started a second circuit.

"OK. We're just worried about you. You don't have to go through this all alone. I guess that's all I'm saying."

David nodded. They fell silent as they circled the small park. When they finished their second circuit, David led them back onto the street and back toward the office in grim quiet.

David came home from work, exhausted. He lay in his king-sized bed and turned and stared at where she used to sleep, now bare except for her pillows. He burped and his chest burned. He knew he shouldn't eat double cheeseburgers and french fries right before bed. When Haddie was here, they often ate late because of their long hours. Several years ago when he first woke in the middle of the night from heartburn he thought he was having a massive coronary. He had a panic attack and was ready to call 911 before Haddie calmed him down. She teased him for three days about freaking out over a little acid reflux.

The pain in his chest intensified. He grabbed several pillows and elevated his upper body. Maybe this time it was a heart attack. He almost welcomed it. He sunk his face into her pillow and he could smell her, but just barely. It was fading and soon would be gone forever. He closed his eyes, and after quite a time, fell asleep.

"Hello, David."

David sat up. Haddie was seated at the foot of his bed. It was dark, but David knew her voice and silhouette; the full-bodied shoulder-length hair, the straight nose that turned up slightly at the tip, the strong chin and smooth neck. There was melancholy in her voice. A hollowness, like the echo off canyon walls.

The dreams are back. Stay calm. Talk to her.

David took a deep breath. "I'm horrible, Haddie. I miss you." David stared at the outline of her red hair and squinted to discern her fine features. He remembered when they first started dating, his few college friends ribbed him how her eyes were too far apart, but that was one of the things he loved about her. And with age she grew into that face. "How are you?" As soon as the words left his mouth, he wished he could've taken them back.

"Well," she sighed, "I've been better. I'm dead."

David stared at her. He tried to stay calm. He wanted to say something to reassure her. Dammit. He felt guilty for the last month for not saying a reassuring word as she disappeared behind the metal doors, and yet he never actually tried to think of what he would say if he could go back in time. If he had, he could repeat it to her right now, and maybe it would resolve the guilt, melt it away, far away from him. But all he could think of was her torn dirty clothing, her bloody head, and all those bright lights.

Haddie sighed. "I'm sorry, it was my fault. I walked right out into traffic. Oh, I could kick myself."

"It's OK. I'm sorry it happened. Are you OK?"

David couldn't quite tell, but it looked like Haddie rolled her eyes. He wasn't making her feel better.

"David, I'm dead. Of course I'm not all right. I never even saw the car that hit me—"

"Haddie, I'm sorry. It's just that this is kinda weird—"

"Like when your dad died?"

David's pulse quickened. "Yeah."

She looked away, wrung her hands in front of her body, creating a silhouette against the wall, like playing a game of casting hand shadows. "I don't know. It feels like I'm in a waiting room."

David sat transfixed, watching her.

"I feel like the jury is out and I'm waiting for a verdict. And, I stepped out of the waiting room." Haddie looked over her shoulder and then back at him. "You have not lived up to your promise."

David frowned. "What promise?"

"The promise you made."

David thought back. Yes, the promise. He had wondered whether she was delirious, or all she meant was "carry on without me, soldier," or something like that. "You never told me what I was promising."

Haddie thought a moment, and David knew she was thinking back to her last moments with him. She sighed. "To your dying breath. To publish my novel, David."

David knew this was just a "normal" dream now. "Haddie. Come on. You don't even like to read."

"That's not nice. I'm not kidding. You promised."

David's face burned. She actually had written a novel? "Are you talking a real novel? I mean, when did you have time?"

"It took me five years." She began wringing her hands again. "Listen, David, I don't have a lot of time. It's all in the apartment. Please."

Five years? He rubbed the back of his neck. "Why didn't you tell me?"

She glanced around. "I don't have time..."

"Haddie, you should have told me."

"Well, it's embarrassing. I didn't know if it would be any good... and you're so critical."

David grimaced, his face turning red. He took a deep breath. "Why is this such a big deal? I'm sorry, but you're dead. What difference does it make now?"

Haddie looked up at the ceiling and groaned. "There's not much I can do about it myself, now is there? I don't want to be remembered only as a shark lawyer—"

"You were a damn good one."

"Yes, yes, yes." She waved her hand. "Listen. You promised me on my deathbed. Doesn't that mean anything to you?"

David rubbed his gut. "Yes, it does." He looked and saw the pleading look on her face despite the darkness. "OK. Of course I will."

"Thanks, honey." She blew him a kiss. "And take care of yourself. You're starting to look like Pudgie." She smiled and was gone.

David raised an eyebrow. Then he looked down. His gut lay bare in front of him in all its cellulite glory. He thought of Pudgie, their corgi. He got fat in his old age, some kind of hormonal problem. They loved Pudgie. Haddie. She had a wicked sense of humor. Though she always had a way of teasing him that never made him mad. A smile and a twinkle. She was one of a kind. And if she wrote a book, he was going to get it published if it took ... well, to his final breath.

Why hadn't she told him she was writing a book? Was he really that critical of her? She never said that to him before. He settled back into the sheets and pillows, the fabric folding around his head and body. Haddie wrote a book. He didn't feel upset at what she said. In fact, he felt a new life inside him, and for the first time since she died, a purpose. He now had something to live for.

David woke to a gray light. He sat up quickly and examined the place where Haddie sat. The blankets crumpled around her spot. But they crumpled in many other spots, too. What a dream. It seemed so real, like he was having an actual conversation with her. Her scent now seemed to permeate the room. She always had a fresh scent. It didn't matter if it was first thing in the morning, late in the evening, or after a sweaty workout. She smelled of rain, mixed with that skin lotion she always used. He knew that scent.

"Not again," he moaned.

His overactive imagination. At least that's what the psychiatrist at Tippingdale had told him. And it was dreams just like this one. It had been many years ago, when Haddie and he were dating, that his father died. The psychiatrist told him he couldn't let go, so that was why he dreamed of his dad. It was his way of keeping him alive. The dreams seemed real. They felt normal, usually with them sitting in the kitchen over coffee and chatting. And when he woke he could smell the cigars his father smoked. Olfactory delusions, the psychiatrist said, quite common. David was cooperative at Tippingdale and the dreams passed after several months. He was only hospitalized because he had stopped eating and going to work. Haddie lived nearby, drove him there, and checked him in. He had to hand it to her; she stuck by him through it all.

His stay was voluntary. He only had to deal with guards and the rules for a short time, and he released himself from Tippingdale. And he believed what the psychiatrist told him. It was the only thing that made sense.

David rose from his bed and poured himself a cup of coffee. Somehow, talking to Haddie, even though he knew it was only a dream, made him feel a little better. Like an addict, he got a fix. It wouldn't last long, but it was at least something. He thought of ol' Pudgie. What an obnoxious little dog. He barked constantly and tried to bite the mailman. And at the end, he looked like a football with stubby legs. They both cried when Pudgie died.

But he knew those dream "fixes" came at a price. He grew dependent on those dreams with his dad. He thought of nothing else. He needed Tippingdale. The psychiatrist pulled him out of it. He told him that life was for the living. He warned that the subconscious is strange. It doesn't always know what's best for its host.

That conversation with Haddie felt real. He spoke to her and she spoke to him, just like old times. He even had thoughts that seemed real, like, why didn't she tell him about the book? And when he woke her smell permeated the room. He smiled and thought to himself that he was thinking too much. His overactive imagination raising its ugly head, probably because he loved her so much. Just like his father. He didn't want to let go. Her book wasn't real; it was too unlike Haddie. It was just a figment of his imagination. It was just a dream.

It was time to focus on his real life. He sat in front of his computer and checked his e-mail for new messages from existing clients. There was nothing, just as he expected. He checked his watch. It was only 6:00 a.m. He stood and went to the shower.

He ran the soap over his body. The soap rolled over the lumpy fat like a roller coaster. He looked down and grimaced. He couldn't see his feet. Haddie was right. He was a lardo. That's it, no more donuts for breakfast. And he'd start walking at lunchtime, too. He stepped out of the shower, toweled off, and walked into the closet. He pulled out a pair of gray slacks, white shirt, black tie, and gray jacket. As he piled these into his arms, he noticed an umbrella in the top cubby. He had looked for that umbrella several times over the last couple of weeks because of all the rain. He stood on his toes, his clothes in one hand and with the other reached for the umbrella. His fingers brushed the shelf. He dropped his head and grunted, pushing himself as high as possible. Two fingers closed on the umbrella fabric. He pulled and it dropped over the shelf to the floor, dragging along a white package.

He grabbed the umbrella and gazed at the white cardboard protector held together by a thick rubber band. David caught his breath and felt his heart thump in his chest. He took off the rubber band and pulled out a manuscript, feeling its heft. The title page read, "A Kiss During Mourning", *by Hadraniel East.*

"I'll be damned. She did write a book."

David looked up and pursed his lips, thinking that he might have actually talked to his dead wife. But, he knew better. He knew that although he had not known the book was there, he must have known she had written a novel, and had stored that information in his subconscious. Maybe … he thought back to the hospital the night Haddie died. Had she told him everything, and he just forgot? Maybe so. He probably felt guilty, deep down inside, about not doing what he had promised. So, his dream brought it to the forefront, to a place he could grasp and act upon.

He carried the manuscript to the kitchen and set it on the table. He sat down in front of the computer, grabbed the mouse, and navigated through the directories. He saw a "Haddie" folder. He had seen but never opened it before. He never had a reason. He clicked and it brought up dozens of folders. He recognized many of them immediately as titles of her clients; "Mossrup and Dunn," "Paltons Cosmetics," "Young, Earle, and Watson." These were names she had mentioned at dinner. Dry explanations, or curses, or celebration, all depending on their stage or outcome.

He could see her freckled rosy cheeks now, her vibrant red hair pulled back, holding a glass of red wine, telling one of her stories at the dinner table. She had brought a grown man to tears on the witness stand. She was ruthless in the courtroom. And she had smelled blood with him. His story did not add up, and she tore him apart like a shark tearing up a fur seal. She won the case. The shark lady won the case, and she sat with David at dinner, her smile overtaking everything but her freckled rosy cheeks and sparkling green eyes, drinking her red wine.

He perused the folder list and one caught his eye. "Novel."

"Ah," he said.

David double clicked the folder. There were two files. One was ""A Kiss During Mourning."" He opened the file and stared at the title page, called, unsurprisingly, just like the hard copy, "A Kiss During Mourning."

David sat back, folded his hands and rested them on his big belly. He looked at the bottom of the file. It was 389 pages. A real novel. Why hadn't she told him? This wasn't a new dress or a pair of shoes, which she bought on the sly because she didn't want him to think she was wasting money. This was a big part of her life. And she kept it from him.

He rubbed his face. He always gave her privacy, assuming that she would always tell him the things that were important to her, important to them. Did she only reveal to him things that were convenient? What else hadn't she told him?

He shook his head and emptied the thought.

He clicked back on the folder. The second file was titled, "Synopsis." He clicked on it and saw it was a short one-page file; a summary of the work.

Hannah Coss is playing a deadly game. Her husband of twenty years died of a heart attack while in the arms of another woman. Facing her grief and betrayal, there is an awakening deep inside her. An awakening that must be satisfied. She abandons her career and embarks on a voyage of discovery. She jets to Europe, races bareback through the Mongolian steppes, caravans through deepest, darkest Africa, jeeps through the Australian outback, and sails up the Amazon. Is there a man that can tame her? Is there a man who can deliver the perfect kiss? For him, the reward will be her uninhibited desires. For the others, a gift of cyanide-laced wine. Will Hannah be satisfied? Or will she leave a trail of dead lovers as revenge for the sins of the man who wronged her?

David was open-mouthed. He shook his head, rubbed his eyes, and sat back, staring at the document. He had seen these paperback books grouped on cheap metal racks with flowery titles, women exposing their cleavage, and men showing off six-pack abs.

"Oh my God," David whispered, "my wife is a romance novelist."

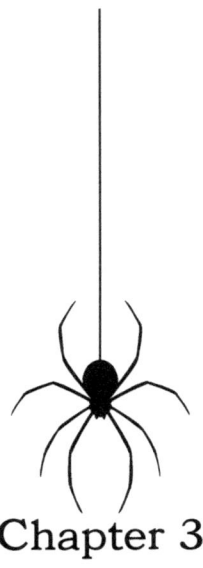

Chapter 3

MY SHARK LADY? MY HADDIE? THE ONE WHO BROUGHT LARGE CORPORATIONS to their knees in wrongful death lawsuits? Whether full-grown men, half-grown women, fragile paraplegics, no jugular was safe with her in the courtroom. Romance?

He stared at the synopsis again. Wait. "Cyanide-laced wine." Ah. Poison. Death. A trail of pretty boys hoping for a piece of action, only to have their erections rudely interrupted by stupor and death. He had read about cyanide before. It disrupts cellular respiration. If you're lucky, you may smell almonds before falling into a coma.

He rose from his chair and stood over the manuscript resting on the kitchen table. He flipped through some pages and let it come to rest. Maybe this won't be so bad.

David looked at his watch. He usually left for the office about now. He grabbed his cup and poured more coffee, picked up his cell phone and sat back down. The book lay in front of him. A gift from Haddie. The gift of her imagination, untethered, and poured onto this paper. This day was for her.

"Hello, Judy? This is David East. I won't be in the office today."

"Mr. East. Is everything OK?"

She sounded worried.

David eyed the novel in front of him. "We'll see."

David straightened out the manuscript. He flipped the title page and began to read.

Rojo took Hannah into his arms and kissed her. She succumbed to his strength, her face up, flaming red hair falling down her back. She finally broke away, breathing hard, and placed her hands onto his bare tanned chest. She let her fingers brush his skin as she stepped away, his arms reaching out to her.

She smiled. "Sit down and relax. We have all night."

He lay back on the lounge, the tropical air blowing through the open window.

David cringed and crossed his arms. *This is repulsive. Haddie wrote this? Maybe she was delusional.*

She turned and the smile melted from her face. Better than the biker in Brussels, but not as good as the surfer in Sydney, she thought. And the surfer was not good enough. There was a table in front of her, on it resting a bottle of Chianti and two glasses.

Rojo watched her from the lounge. He was mesmerized by the long flowing hair, demure body, her easy gait.

He burned for her.

Hannah turned with two full wine glasses in her hand. She handed one to Rojo.

"It relaxes me," she purred.

Rojo smiled. "I don't need wine to make love to you."

Hannah pouted. "Oh, please. I hate to drink alone."

Rojo bared his teeth. "As you wish."

He took a long drink. His eyes widened and he grabbed his head with both hands. As he struggled to stand, his body shuddered, and he tripped into convulsions. He looked up at her, pleading, and then collapsed onto the tile floor.

Hannah finished her drink before he hit the floor. "Cyanide acts so quickly."

She watched him until she was sure he would move no more. Then, she grabbed her bag and left the room.

David pursed his lips. Now, *that* read like something Haddie would write. He wondered if that was how people really died from cyanide poisoning. Knowing Haddie, he was sure she had done her homework before setting up that scene.

As he sunk deeper into the story, he couldn't help but notice the similarities between Hannah and Haddie. Similar name and flaming red hair. But, it went beyond the physical resemblance. When David read the synopsis he interpreted it as a search for true love; perhaps a bit morbid, but certainly a reasonable "romance novel" topic. But, as he read more and more he realized it didn't appear to be that at all. It wasn't even a sexual journey. It was downright predatory. Hannah seemed to leave a swath of six-pack abs in her wake as she jetted around the world. It was a revenge tale. He could imagine his shark lady gleefully dispatching her victims around the globe as she typed at the computer, but could he imagine the romance novel crowd reading this thing? He had deduced that this was the intended reader audience, and confirmed it by reading her one letter to agents that stated the genre she targeted.

After many hours and several cups of coffee, David reached the novel's midway point. He had just read a passage that gave him pause.

Hannah lounged at the pool, the sun glistening off her tanned, well-oiled body. The Mediterranean resort was one of the most expensive in the country, but she was willing to pay the price for her next prize. As her mother said, "You can just as easily fall in love with a rich man as a poor man, so why conduct your search through tawdry back alleys?"

Poolside was deserted, so Hannah bided her time with a frozen daiquiri and the latest Nora Roberts novel. Then, a young couple appeared with a small child. She watched the little girl for some time, splashing in the pool and drifting along with inflatable rings around her arms. After a while, Hannah lost her appetite for the task at hand and retreated alone to her room.

David sat back, reminded of their failed attempts to produce a child of their own. Perhaps it was divine destiny; that the power that be thought them unfit. The passage reminded him of a specific incident. One that occurred when they were in the throes of trying to become parents. Haddie's sister and husband came to visit, and they brought their three-year-old son. David and Haddie offered to watch the tyke overnight so the couple could get some alone time, and David and she could "practice being parents." As soon as his parents left, the child became an unbearable tyrant. No matter what they tried, the boy threw tantrum after tantrum.

Finally, the next morning, after a night with little sleep, David took the monster to a local swimming pool. The water seemed to calm the boy, and as he was a very good swimmer, David kicked back in a lounge chair next to the pool edge. He dozed briefly, only to awaken with the little tyke tugging on his big toe.

"I need to go potty," the little boy said.

David, fighting to stay conscious, remembered what the kids did at the local public pool he went to as a kid. The kids just peed in the water as they swam around in the pool. The chlorine took care of the rest. It seemed like a great idea at the moment.

"Just pee in the water."

The boy's eyes widened. David just nodded, and fell back to sleep.

The yells and screams roused him out of his slumber. He awoke to the commotion, lifeguards running around, and looked to see the boy standing by the side of the pool, his trunks around his ankles and wee wee exposed, a stream of urine flowing, spelling his name in the water.

Maybe he wasn't fit to be a dad.

David read for a while longer and then decided he had read enough for one day. Although he was no writing critic, read only the occasional new best seller, and never romance, his untrained eye thought this was good. Really good. She brought Hannah to life. And the way she brought the pretty boys to death was so real he swore he could smell almonds as he read those scenes. It was descriptive, it was alive, it was … *full*. It surprised him. She surprised him. The shark lady was artistic. She certainly looked like an artist. The petite body, long slim hands and fingers. It belied her brutal attacks in the courtroom. How many hostile witnesses, even hearing of her abilities prior to taking the stand, had been falsely put at ease when they first saw her in the courtroom? And how could he, married to her for twenty years, know her as the shark lady and never have a clue of her artistic talents?

David looked down at the manuscript. Her writing brought him closer to her in a new way. It certainly made him miss her more than ever. He felt the tears, but they froze like stalactites somewhere in the recesses of his head. He rose from his chair and walked over to the refrigerator. As he peered inside at the stale pizzas and french fries, he thought of Pudgie. He patted his belly and closed the door.

David went back to the computer and opened Haddie's files again. She had written ten query letters to ten different agents, trying to sell them on her book. David knew that an agent was necessary to sell a book to a large publisher and assumed that these letters had not yet been sent. For the rest of the afternoon, he modified them, explaining that she had died and he was her husband who promised to publish his wife's only work. He also printed out her book, running out of paper after printing five copies. So, he decided he would send out just the five that day, and contact the other five agents if necessary.

Freshly showered with the manuscripts in a box under one arm, David walked out into the wet April street. The rain was cold and the wind drove it sideways, chilling him and negating the umbrella he held red-knuckled in his free hand. It was not yet afternoon rush hour, so the streets were fairly empty as he made his way to the post office. On the way, he paused outside a pub. Haddie's law firm had thrown a party for her there when she made partner. He had never seen her so happy. Her face shone while employees gathered to congratulate her. And it seemed everyone at the firm showed up at some point during the party. After a while, she sat on a high bar stool, like a queen on a throne, while worker after worker came to her. He joked with her for several days after that she had looked like some mob boss, and all the monkeys came to kiss her ring. She got mad at that, so he stopped.

He continued to the post office and mailed the packages. All the agents were right here in New York. He could have just dropped them all off in person. But he didn't. There was no rush. They would get the packages soon enough. As he stepped out of the post office back into the cold rain, he looked up at the small square of sky between the skyscrapers and squinted to stop the rain from blinding him.

"There you go, Haddie. Good luck."

David went back to work the next day. He thought about staying home and reading the second half of Haddie's novel, but in the end he thought it would be best to get out of the apartment. And, it was a romance novel, after all. It wasn't exactly the kind of book he sought out, though it was interesting to read *her* craft. For the next week, he spent long hours behind his desk, making money for the company with his mathematical mind and quick pencil and computer key strokes.

He also made some decisive health changes. He cut out the fast food and processed crap, at least for most meals. He stuck with whole foods, and if he ate out, it was to get sushi or a salad. His only real weakness was the chocolate éclairs sold at the local bakery. And he took walks with Gil to get some exercise and fresh air. Or as good as fresh air gets in downtown Manhattan. The changes made him feel better both physically and mentally. He didn't get the sugar highs and crashes, and he felt like the weight was slowly coming off.

On one of his walks with Gil, they decided to take a taxi to Central Park and walk the southern portion. It was chilly for late April, but the wind was not blowing too hard and the sun was out.

David and Gil entered at Columbus Circle. David stared up and thought maybe he saw a hint of spring green on a willow tree. He had on a comfortable pair of walking shoes and could feel the blood surging through his forty-year-old body as they walked north past the carousel.

"Are you in a hurry?" Gil asked, as he stepped up the pace to keep up.

"I have a meeting at two o'clock and I'd like to get at least to

Jackie's Pond and see if the turtles are out." David breathed hard in and out. He was barely of medium height, and his torso was long relative to his legs. He had to take almost two strides for each of Gil's.

A few joggers passed them, talking casually and disappearing around a bend. David watched them enviously. When he was in college, he jogged some and even did some races. Maybe he would start up again, if his knees didn't scream at him too much.

"You're looking better, Dave."

He shot a glance at Gil. "Shit. I still waddle when I walk."

"Yeah, for sure. But you got some color now. And you look like you lost a little weight."

"Thanks. I guess I'm feeling a little better."

David wondered why he felt better. Time is supposed to heal all wounds. Yet, it was more than that. Maybe it was partially because he had gotten Haddie's novel out into the world. That was part of it. But not all of it. He knew why his life had brightened. He felt it ever since his dream with Haddie. Since that dream he felt better. When she took him to task that he had not kept his promise, she had loaded him with a responsibility, but had also lightened his grief. He felt a little lighter on his feet; he slept better. He *knew* it was just a dream. And yet, finding her manuscript the next morning was weird. When he had dreams of his father, they never directly led to actions while he was awake. Of course, his father didn't seem to have any regrets, and certainly didn't leave behind an unpublished novel.

"I dreamed about Haddie a month ago." David blurted it out after strongly inhaling the smell of freshly cut grass at the ball field.

"Oh man, I'm sorry."

"Sorry for what?" David asked.

Gil glanced at him, then looked away. "I don't know ... I—"

"It was a good dream."

"Oh," Gil said quickly. "That's good."

"Did you know she wrote a novel?"

Gil's face creased. "Haddie wrote a novel?"

"Yeah, a romance. I didn't know either."

Gil stopped. "A romance? No way."

David kept walking and Gil had to trot to catch up.

"That's what I thought. But, it has quite a bit of gruesome killing in it. At least in the part I read."

Gil shrugged. "That sounds a bit more like Haddie."

"I promised her I'd get it published." David said it quietly. He wasn't sure how much he wanted to tell Gil.

"I had no idea. When did you promise her? How could you, and not even know she wrote it?"

"She asked me the night she died. I didn't remember her asking me until the dream."

They entered a small wooded area. David decided to finish his story.

"I had the dream. She reminded me of my promise."

Gil gave David a sidelong glance but said nothing.

"Sure enough, the next morning, I woke up and found it in the closet. Isn't it funny how the subconscious works?"

David could hear Gil's labored breathing. He picked up the pace. Robins bounced along the grass, their heads tilting this way and that, listening for worms.

"Hey, wait a minute. Are you trying to say that you talked with your deceased wife?"

David responded quickly. "Of course not. Obviously, at some point I saw the novel in the closet, and it just didn't register at the time. I must not have remembered what I had promised Haddie in the hospital either. It was a stressful time. The dream brought it out of my subconscious, that's all."

Gil looked at him guardedly. "Oh. OK."

David patted Gil on the back. "Don't worry. You know I'm not religious or superstitious. When you're dead, you're dead."

Though, he thought, maybe some people are more dead than others.

April turned to May. David sat in furry slippers and a sweater and listened to the morning news one morning, nodding in agreement as the weatherman said it was the coldest spring since 1888. The leaves were budding out everywhere in defiance, but David wasn't so sure if they were going to win the day.

After work one day he checked his mailbox on the way up to his apartment and found a package. He saw it was addressed to him in his own handwriting. It was a response from one of the literary agents. He ran upstairs, unlocked his apartment, threw off his jacket, and opened the package. It contained a rejection letter and the manuscript.

David frowned. He couldn't imagine anyone turning down her work. He set the letter down. Well, it was at least a pleasant rejection and he still had four more out there. Over the next several evenings, three more form rejections dribbled in. Each time he opened a package, adrenaline shot through his system, followed by disappointment. It reminded him when he tried to get into several good schools, including Cornell, Brown, Penn State, and Tulane. Over the late spring and summer he ran down to the mailbox each day, sometimes even waiting for the mailman. And when each letter came, he felt the shot of adrenaline, followed by disappointment. He ended up going to NYU, got good grades and a decent job, but the college rejections always gnawed at him. Now, these agents were opening old wounds, and it got personal. They weren't rejecting him, they were rejecting his wife's work. He felt very protective of her, and angrier and angrier with the agents.

There was one query still out there. David walked over to his computer and looked up the remaining agents on Haddie's list. He prepared letters for four of them and then came up with an idea. He looked up the remaining agent that had not yet responded to his inquiry. Her name was Margot Beasley and her office was located in midtown Manhattan. David had heard that a writer should never make a personal appearance to plead their case with an agent. But, he felt if he could talk to one, they would surely understand his wife's passion. Maybe it would make a difference. He decided he would take a taxi to her office tomorrow. It was Friday, so maybe by the afternoon Margot Beasley wouldn't mind a break from reading all the crappy would-be novels she received.

David mailed the four additional queries on his way to work the next morning. While sitting at his desk, and in between devising tax shelters and charitable strategies for clients, he thought about what he would say to Ms. Beasley. First, he had to actually talk to her. She probably had desperate, starving writers coming to her office every day trying to convince her they were the next John Irving. How could he come across as not being crazy, and get her to consider Haddie's work seriously? He wasn't going to convince her with his looks. Although he wasn't as fat as he once was, he still had a paunch. When he walked into a room, his presence and personality didn't exactly scream I'M HERE. And ever since the sixth grade when Tommy Mazika said he had an hourglass head, even though Haddie insisted it wasn't so, he was convinced of it himself. He looked up at the clock. He had been watching it all day. It was one thirty. Close enough. He turned off his computer, picked up his bag, and took the stairs to the lobby.

As he sat in the taxi thinking about what he was going to say, he kept seeing Haddie's pleading eyes. *Promise me.*

"OK, Haddie," he thought. "I'm going to give it the old college try."

The taxi stopped in front of a brownstone on a quiet side street. David stepped out, paid the driver, absentmindedly ran his hand through his thinning hair, and walked through the door. There was a well-lit foyer that opened into a large lobby. At the far end, behind a dark wood desk, sat a stern young lady with her black hair pulled back in a bun. David took a deep breath and strode over to her. She watched him through her glasses, her face frozen and smooth. As he approached, the edges of her mouth rose, but he didn't think it looked like a smile.

"May I help you?" she asked. She seemed to be looking right through him.

She knows. She knows I don't have an appointment, and she is going to stop me from meeting with Margot Beasley.

"I'm here to see Ms. Beasley," he said, smiling courteously. Her name tag read "Stephanie," but he felt calling her by her name would not help the situation.

Stephanie's mouth became a straight line and the muscles on her neck tightened. She looked like she was trying to swallow something sour. She reached for a black leather-bound book and as she flipped it open, asked, "Do you have an appointment, Mr.—"

David saw someone enter from a side hallway as he answered. "East. David East. And no, I do not have an appointment."

Stephanie raised an eyebrow and closed the book like it was time for her to go home. And she looked like she still had not swallowed the sour thing. "What is this regarding?"

"Well, I sent in a romance novel my wife wrote—"

He thought he saw Stephanie glance at the person standing near her desk, but he wasn't sure. "I'm sorry, Mr. East, but her appointment book is full. Ms. Beasley is a very busy woman."

"You're Mr. East?"

David looked away from the sour woman and at the woman who addressed him. She wore a gray high-collared shirt. Her face and hands were deeply lined from decades of smoking. She had a hardened face that might have been pretty 500,000 cigarettes ago.

"Yes, I am."

"Your wife is Haddie?"

"Yes."

She walked to him and held out her hand. "I'm Margot Beasley." David shook her bony hand.

The wrinkled lady looked at Stephanie. "Ms. Weeks, would you hold my calls for a few minutes?" She looked at David. "Come with me, Mr. East."

Margot Beasley turned and led David to her office in silence. The office smelled of cigarettes and alcohol. It was brightly lit from the sun shining through several lightly curtained windows. Margot sat behind her desk and offered David a seat with a wave of her hand.

"I'm sorry to hear about your wife, Mr. East." Her eyes seemed to melt a little when she said that.

"Thank you, Ms. Beasley." David wasn't quite sure why she called him in here. Perhaps she felt sorry for him.

"My company worked with her law firm. Although I never worked with Haddie, we all knew her. She didn't specialize in copyright law. Sometimes I wish she had. We could've used her."

David stared at the full ashtray on her desk. Her hands were shaking, but he wasn't sure if it was because she was in need of a cigarette or a stiff drink.

"I read her work, Mr. East. It is very good. Actually, it's better than that. Unfortunately, I can't help you."

David's hopes rose and fell like a roller coaster. He tried to speak but could not think of what to say.

"I manage careers, Mr. East. Your lovely wife has passed away. One book is not a career." She shrugged. "It's too bad. She could have had a career in romance."

David cleared his throat and shifted in his seat. The smell of her office was nauseating, and the bright light was making him sweat. "Can you recommend anyone, or another track I can try?"

Margot Beasley stood. "I don't recommend other agents to anyone. I doubt if anyone would help you, because again, one book is not a career. Have you thought about self publishing? It's not the vanity publishing it once was. For a relatively small fee, you can have the book on Amazon where the world can see it."

David wiped the sweat off his forehead. "I don't think that's what she had in mind."

She picked up the manuscript and handed it to him. "Thank you for sending it to me. I enjoyed reading it. If she were living and planned on writing more, I would have loved to take her on."

The sun reflected off the white paper and nearly blinded him. He squinted and took the manuscript. "Thank you for your time, Ms. Beasley."

David shook her bony hand again and walked out. He stepped into the bright sunlight, the shade tree leaves shimmering in the breeze. He walked to the corner and looked for a taxi. As one approached, he decidedly stepped back, threw his jacket over his shoulder, and instead began the trek back to his apartment. He stepped purposefully, like on his lunchtime walks with Gil. What had Beasley said? Basically, no agent would represent a dead woman's novel. That's what she said.

Promise me, David.

He promised her. And he wasn't going to go the self-publishing route, either. Although it did not have the stigma it used to have, he was sure Haddie wouldn't want that. No, that wouldn't do. Not for Haddie's novel. He promised her. It was their last communication (not counting dreams). It was his last real connection to her. It gave him purpose. And he felt if he could do this, properly publish her book, he could go on with life. It wouldn't be the same as when Haddie was in his life, but he could carry on. Just having the goal made him feel better. He had lost weight, he was socializing a bit, at lunch anyway. He had to find a way. He now knew that the four queries he sent this morning would come back rejections.

No agent will represent a dead woman. Agents develop careers.

In his dream Haddie said that she wrote the book because she didn't want to be remembered as a shark lawyer. Remembered by whom? Him? The New York population? Is that why she wanted to be published? She liked money. Just like him. Did she want to show she could make money at something besides bringing witnesses to tears? Or did she just want to share her art with the world?

David crossed the street and made his way through the quietest neighborhoods he knew as he continued downtown. When they were in their twenties, just starting their careers, he and Haddie walked these streets. Some of the neighborhoods weren't very walkable then, especially at night. But during the day, on a sunny afternoon, they would explore the island, drink coffee, and occasionally hand a quarter to someone in need. They certainly were idealists then. They thought they could change the world and make it a better place.

He felt like that now. He could make the world a better place by sharing Haddie's work. He had to find a way.

David walked briskly the four miles back to his apartment. He was tired. Tired from actual physical activity for a change. Why didn't he walk like that more often? Why did he and Haddie stop taking their walks around the island? When did they get so wrapped up in their careers that they stopped going to the cafés? While he cooked and ate dinner, he thought about that. It was their failure to have children. They became so obsessed with that, for years. When it was clear it wouldn't happen, they both retreated to their careers. They stopped dating each other. They stopped helping each other. It seemed the easiest thing to do.

David cleaned the kitchen and got ready for bed. He lay there in his bed and stared at the ceiling. He could hear the sounds of the city, alive with cars and lights.

Promise me.

He was going to help her. To his last breath if necessary. But how?

No agent will represent a dead woman.

Was it possible to find someone? Someone to represent her?

David smiled. He had an idea. Did it conflict with Haddie's wishes? Why did she write that novel? He believed he found his answer as he walked around Manhattan today. It harkened to an earlier time. One that did not hinge on money, power, and career. When the offer to make her a partner would have elicited a laugh and a wave of her hand. When the scene of a witness breaking down on the witness stand would have made her cringe. She wrote the book to show she still had soul. She didn't need her name in lights; she wanted to entertain and bring a smile to the faces of people who read it. To allow them to escape the very world in which she was operating, with the wood paneled halls, hyenas in suits, sour receptionists.

He jumped out of bed and turned on his computer. He found the remaining query letter to the agent that had not been sent. The letter was addressed to Mary Lamb.

"Jesus," he said. "I bet she was teased as a kid."

The first sentence read:

My name is David East and I am seeking representation for my late wife's romantic novel "A KISS DURING MOURNING."

He let out a deep breath. He looked up at the ceiling, the glow of the computer screen reflecting off his face.

"What do you think, Haddie? You think I'm doing the right thing?"

His eyes darted around the room, half expecting the window curtains to flutter, a glass to fall on the floor and shatter, the floorboards to creak. Something to tell him it was a good, or crazy, idea. But all was quiet. He sighed, placed his fingers on the keyboard, erased the first sentence and replaced it:

My name is David East and I am seeking representation for my romantic novel, "A KISS DURING MOURNING."

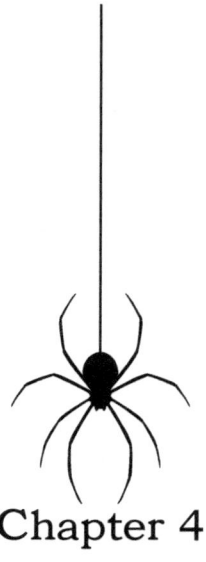

Chapter 4

AFTER BREAKFAST, DAVID TOOK A TAXI TO LAMB'S LITERARY. IT WAS IN a high-rise on the upper Eastside. He held the manuscript under his jacket to keep it dry as he slipped into the building and took the elevator to the seventh floor. He wandered the halls until he found her company. He tried the door but it was locked. He peeked through a window; the office was dark. He stepped back and noticed a slot in the door. He kissed the manila folder, slipped it through the slot, and heard it slap against the hard floor.

David stepped out of the building and into the rain. Rain and more rain. The early spring freeze had been replaced with a late spring soak, the wettest in years, causing flooding in low-lying areas across the Northeast. Instead of hailing a taxi, David ducked into a bookstore a few blocks away. He and Haddie had often gone there, before their careers mutated into ravenous beasts that consumed all their time. Although he walked under eaves and pulled the collar of his jacket up around his neck, the rain soaked his half-bald head by the time he reached the door.

He stomped his wet shoes as he crossed the threshold. The smell of fresh paper and bindings made him think of Haddie. He walked over to the café, grabbed several napkins, and dried his face and neck. A college kid behind the counter watched him.

"A cup of coffee, please." He tossed the napkins in a waste can.

He placed two dollars on the counter, took his coffee, and walked the aisles. He smiled as he passed the romance section, wondering if Haddie had many forays into this corner for writing ideas over the last five years. His eyes followed the colors of the rows of books along the shelves, the stacks on side wooden tables. He removed his jacket and slung it over his shoulder. He spied a table next to a window where he and Haddie liked to sit and make fun of the "serious businessmen" in suits stream by. It was ironic that they became part of that scene. How many times had he walked by a café these days on his way to work and a young couple made fun of him?

"David?"

It was Cat. Although the locals had traded in their winter black clothes for more varied colors, she was still in black, with black-framed glasses, her blonde hair pulled back into a ponytail. She looked beautiful, though David felt guilty thinking such a thing of Haddie's assistant.

"Oh, hi."

They hugged briefly. Cat did not seem to be a hugger-type, and he knew if they hadn't shared the mutual grief in Haddie's death, she may not have even said hello to him.

"How are you?" she asked, and cleared her throat.

"I'm OK." David noticed Cat carrying a book, but could not see the title. "What are you reading?"

Cat glanced down at her book and rolled her eyes. "Nothing. I'm just checking things out." She glanced at his coffee. "I'm going to get some." She hesitated. "Are you going to be here awhile?"

David looked out at the pouring rain. He felt her eyes watching him, and he felt a sudden urge to flee. He pushed it out of his mind and body. "Yes." He pointed over to the table. "I'll be right over there."

"Great." Cat smiled and walked to the café.

David watched as she walked away and hopped the steps to the counter. She was graceful. He hadn't noticed that about her before. Although she was indispensable to Haddie, David rarely saw her, so most of what he knew came from Haddie's stories about her. He walked over to the magazine rack and stooped to pick out a business magazine. A roll of fat around his midsection tightened its grip. He swore at his spare tire and stood, empty-handed except for the coffee, and walked over to the table. He had a clear view of the street and the Gothic buildings as people under umbrellas hustled by in the rain. His body felt damp from his walk but the coffee cup felt warm on his hands.

He shifted in his seat as Cat approached him and sat down. David smiled and took a sip of coffee. He felt her eyes bore into him, and felt so self-conscious that his hand shook. He set the cup down. Why did he feel this way? He knew. He was intimidated by her looks.

Cat took a sip out of her cup. "That's pretty good." Her legs were crossed, one foot pointed toward the window.

They sat quietly for a few minutes. He did not like the silence. "So. What have you been up to?"

She glanced downwards. "Not much. I worked for Ms. East so long that I'm not sure what to do with myself. It was very nice of her to remember me in her will. It's given me some time to think."

David knew that Haddie left her $50,000 as part of her life insurance policy. She had talked to him about that. David wondered what kind of life Cat lived. Although Haddie told stories about Cat, she hardly ever spoke about her personal life. About all he knew was that she was in her late thirties, single, and very efficient. What he didn't know but would find out later was that Cat had been married. She lost her husband in a car wreck just a few months before she met Haddie. He also didn't know she was a high school track athlete. She won the high school state championship in the 200 meters. David tried out, but never played sports in school. The closest he came was an intramural bowling team. And he wasn't very good.

"She thought very highly of you," David said.

Cat smiled and looked at her cup. The warmth of her smile made her skin glow. "Yes." She blushed and changed the subject. "And I do have some leads. There is a hotel upstate that's been calling me, but …" she rested her chin on her palm and looked out at the rain.

"It must have been very hectic working with Haddie. She never stopped."

Cat gazed at David, circling her hands around the coffee cup. "Yes, she kept me busy. You get used to that kind of thing. I still wake up at five thirty, expecting Ms. East to call me any second with another fire to put out."

David smiled. That was Haddie, especially over the last ten years. He also knew that Cat never called Haddie, Ms. East. "You can call her Haddie, Cat. Even though you and I didn't talk to each other very often, the way Haddie talked about you, it was like you were part of the family."

"OK," Cat said, and her green eyes flashed like stained glass. Her eyes pinched together somewhat on the outside, giving her eyes almost an Oriental look. Her eyes were not only green, they were bright spring green.

However, David suddenly saw something sad in her eyes. He couldn't put his finger on it, but her face turned sullen. Not defeated, but as if she had lived though tremendous loss. He felt a sudden urge to put his arm around her, to tell her everything was all right. David realized he was staring. He dropped his gaze and wondered how close she really was to Haddie. Did she know Haddie had written a novel? Perhaps. He weighed asking her, but would have been envious if she had known, while he hadn't. He enjoyed sitting here with her. He didn't want to ruin it.

Cat was now staring out the window.

"I don't think it's ever going to stop raining," she said.

David sat in his office that afternoon with his nose buried in an obscure section of the tax code. However, his mind was not focused on numbers. Instead, it was riveted on spring green eyes, a lithe body of well-defined long muscle under soft skin, blonde hair, her crossed leg, toe pointed toward him, welcoming him. They had talked for some time, and he found his concentration drifting from their conversation to her body and more primal thoughts. David did not understand the merits of Keats and Kingsolver, whoever the hell they were, but he did feel a physical urge that had not surfaced since his wife's death. And although the endorphin rush made him feel *good*, it knocked him for a loop. It was as if he had been clotheslined by one of man's most basic needs, and he responded with a somewhat abrupt parting with Cat.

So now he sat in his cubicle, a world away from the brief pleasure he shared with her, wondering what he was doing here. Why was he so hard on himself? Why did he practically run away from a pleasurable feeling?

His cell phone rang.

"Hello?"

"Mr. East?" It was a woman's voice.

"Yes." David put his finger where he had stopped reading, or had at least been trying to read.

"This is Mary Lamb. Did I catch you at a bad time?"

David caught his breath. Mary Lamb? She was calling him. That had to be a good sign. "No, not at all, Ms. Lamb. How can I help you?"

"Please call me Mary. I read your book and I just loved it."

David stared off across the cubicles. "Really? That's great."

"I did, Mr. East." Her voice was high-pitched and singsong. She sounded excited.

"Please call me David."

"OK." He heard the shuffling of papers. "I noticed you live here in Manhattan."

"Yes, downtown."

"Perhaps we could have lunch? I'd like to talk to you about representation. That is, if someone else has not already scarfed you up?"

Lunch? Do lunch? David could hardly believe his ears. It had been nearly three months since he lost Haddie. As Ms. Beasley had said, Haddie's work really was that good. The other queries, sent before he became the "ghost writer," had all come back with rejections. The only submittal he had not heard back on was his modified submittal to Mary Lamb. It really *was* about the writer's career.

"David? Did someone sign you already? David? Are you still there?"

David shook his head. "I'm still here. Yes, I mean, no, no one has signed me."

"Well, great. Can you meet for lunch at The Canal? How does your schedule look?"

"My schedule is great. I mean … I could meet today, if you want."

"OK. Eleven thirty? We'll beat the crowd."

David cleared his throat. "Yeah. Sure. Eleven thirty."

"Great. Bye-bye."

David lowered the phone. His forefinger was obediently stuck on the third paragraph of the tax code section. He removed it, snapped the book shut, tossed it on his desk, and glanced at the clock. It was after ten. An agent was interested in Haddie's work! He rubbed his face and looked down at his clothes. Slacks, white shirt, tie. Was that good enough for lunch with an agent? He stood up and paraded around the office, a full grin on his face. Haddie's legacy would not solely be as shark lady.

He passed a young lady intern and she stepped out of his way, pressing herself against a potted plant and giving him a wide berth. She had been told he was a little off his rocker ever since his wife died. And that grin! Slowly, faces with furrowed brows appeared above and around cubicle walls, watching the half-crazed accountant saunter up and down the aisles, that grin plastered on his face.

"David?"

David realized he might have been swinging his arms a little wildly and let them rest by his side as he wheeled around to face Gil. "I did it! I got an agent for Haddie's novel."

Gil's face broke out into a wide grin almost as big as Dave's. "Really? Cool!"

David grabbed Gil's shoulders. "Because agents were saying 'no' because Haddie had passed, so I sent it to a new agent as *my* novel. She loves it. Haddie might get published after all!"

David moved quickly down the wet streets, dodging puddles and pedestrians. It had stopped raining, and although it was still cloudy, the sky was not the thick gray blanket it had been for the last few weeks. He had decided to walk to the restaurant to burn off some of his restless energy. He carried a notepad and a pen ready in his pocket. His daily walks had become second nature, and the only irritating thing about them was the constant odor from the city streets; a mix of car exhaust, garbage, and dog piss. As he walked, he suddenly yearned to be out in the country. It had been so long he forgot what real outdoors smelled like.

He thought back to his honeymoon with Haddie. They had gone to the Adirondack Mountains and stayed at his cabin near Old Forge. There wasn't much of a night scene up there, unless you like black bears, but at that time they were their own nightlife. He could almost smell the pine trees nestled around the cabin as he turned the corner and arrived at The Canal.

When David told Gil he was going to The Canal, Gil had smiled and muttered, "That's the place for power lunches, buddy." David had never heard of it. He now stood outside, in his wrinkled slacks, unpolished black leather shoes, and shirt with the sleeves rolled up, exposing his hairy forearms. The restaurant was full of suits. A short, somewhat squat lady with a moonface framed by short brown hair and dressed in sharp edges approached him.

"David East?"

She had an easy smile and watchful eyes.

"Mary?"

"Yes." She stuck out her hand. She had a firm grip. "I got us a table over there."

David nodded and followed her to their table. He thought she looked as good as she could possibly get with the clothes she was wearing, some kind of black dress thing with a top that was like a sport coat for overweight women. He saw some gray hairs on the back of her head just before she turned to sit down.

"David," she said, emphasizing his name by briefly placing her hand on his forearm, "I just love your book. It's got power. I have never read a book, especially a romance book, where a woman took such control over her sexuality."

"Yes," he said, waving a hand in the air, "that's what I was going for."

"Well, you *succeeded*."

"What would you like to drink?"

The pair looked up and saw a young waitress with a pen and pad. They both ordered water. Mary ordered a salad with balsamic vinegar. Considering her weight, David was surprised by her choice. Perhaps she had some kind of hormonal problem. David ordered a sandwich. They made small talk for a short while and then Mary got back to the book.

"Her raison d'être. You captured it so well." She smiled and placed her napkin on her lap.

David raised an eyebrow. What was a *raison d'être*?

"You really understand women, David."

He thought he saw her flash her eyelids at him when she said that. Was she flirting? David wasn't used to that. He was always kind of pudgy and had that damned hourglass head. This was probably only the third time in his entire life a woman flirted with him. Haddie was one of the others. And some blind girl ...

"How long have you been an agent?" David asked. He felt he needed to break the mood. All this attention made him feel a pit in his stomach.

"Over ten years," she replied, then glanced over at an older lady at a nearby table. That woman was sharply dressed, statuesque with gray hair. "Listen," she said, "I represent three other romance authors. Together they have sold nearly 500,000 books. Women eat this stuff up. And your book is fresh. It's raw—"

"Your pastrami sandwich sir, and your salad, ma'am."

They both sat straight to make room for the food.

As he held the thick sandwich, David could feel Mary's gaze boring into him.

"How long have you been writing, David?"

He froze, his sandwich poised inches from his face. If she had waited a split second longer before asking him, he could have taken a big bite and gained a little time by having to swallow his food before answering. At this point, it would look very odd to chew off a slab of pastrami before speaking.

"Um, not very long, really." He smiled at her.

"Oh," she said, using her fork to shift some lettuce through a small puddle of balsamic vinegar. "So, you have a day job?"

"Yes," he said, still holding the sandwich in the ready position. "I'm an accountant."

Mary dropped her fork. She quickly looked down, picked it up, and cleared her throat. "Well. I didn't know accountants could be so sensuous."

David wrestled with what sensuous meant and how it applied to the book. He finally stated what he usually did when someone underestimated him. "I'm from upstate."

Mary smiled patiently. "I hardly ever say this because you never know in today's market, but, I can sell your book."

David had just taken a mouthful of meat. "Mmmpff," was all he could manage.

He was chewing vigorously to get the mass down his throat when she leaned forward and asked almost in a whisper, "I have to ask. It was such a beautiful, moving scene. What was her motivation with the pygmies?"

David stopped chewing and stared at Mary. The pygmies? He hadn't read that far. He really needed to finish the book. He managed to swallow the pastrami sandwich concoction. "What do you think it means?"

"Oh. It's different for everyone? I love it!" Her eyes shone at him.

It was at that moment that David understood the power of the pen. He had written … er, Haddie had written a book that moved Mary to be enamored of him. Or maybe it was the promise of big money. He wondered how she would have looked at Haddie, if she were alive and sitting here?

David smiled. She loved the book. She represented successful authors. He was happy. "How much do you charge?"

She never took her eyes off him. "Fifteen percent of domestic sales, 20 percent of foreign."

David had no idea whether that was a good deal, but he nodded approval. And he also discovered the secret behind her figure when she ordered for dessert the double decadent chocolate mousse cake covered with ice cream and topped with whipped cream.

The African Congo was no place for a woman. At least that's what Mr. Westerstreet told her just before Hannah slipped the cyanide into his shiny tin cup. But, she wasn't just any woman. She was on a mission. One that thus far had taken her through five continents, thousands of miles, dozens of men, and a pound of oxygen scavenging poison. But now she was alone in the jungle and there were men hiding in the darkness. She almost wished she was back in Kansas when the dark men emerged from the bush in their nose rings, tight curly hair, and piercing, lustful eyes; the tallest one didn't even reach her breasts.

"This is so weird," David said. He sat back and stretched. Hannah was running around the world, leaving her cyanide trail. But now, unknown to her, a man was following her. A private detective that had picked up her murderous scent in Romania. David fingered the pages he had left and compared them to the pages he had read. He was about three quarters through it now. He thought about what Mary had asked. "What was her motivation?"

Revenge. It's what he thought one hundred pages ago, and now, just past page three hundred, he still felt that way. Revenge for being mistreated by one man, she would take it out on all men. Yet, something was swimming around in the back of his head. It was an itch, and there was no way to reach it and scratch.

Revenge. Is that right? That's what it was to him. Like Mary said, was it different for everybody? And what was it to Haddie? What was Hannah's motivation in Haddie's eyes? Why would Haddie write a novel like this? About revenge? It seemed like Hannah was getting back at the world for being wronged by one man. Is that what Haddie wanted to convey? He knew her so well. Or, did he? How well did he know his wife? Hannah sounds miserable. Was Haddie miserable? Was she pouring out her thoughts and frustrations on the page?

David leaned forward, his face in his hands. He began to tremble. He shuddered in his loneliness. He looked up and on a shelf, half-hidden by a bronze plate celebrating ten years with his company, was a faded framed photograph. It was Haddie and him outside their cottage in the southern Adirondacks near Old Forge. He had quite a bit more hair then, and Haddie had finer crow's feet. They were both smiling into the camera. He remembered taking that photo with the auto shoot feature. It took four tries to get it right. The first two only captured their feet, and Haddie had her eyes closed in the third. Those three ended up in the wastebasket. This one captured the moment, when they were happy, before life got complicated. Their cottage sat on a lake, and they, along with several other cottage owners, sold out to a real estate company that turned them into rentals. They made a nice profit on that. Since then it seemed all they chased were profits and the next rung on the ladder. They worked twelve- to fourteen-hour days, often on weekends, completely lost to each other. And now, he had no idea why his deceased wife wrote a book and did not tell him. And he had no idea what Hannah's motivation might have been. He realized he did not know Haddie, and had not known her for a long time.

He buried his head in his hands and cried. He cried for losing his Haddie. But now he realized he did not lose her a few months ago. He lost her years ago.

David woke early, put on a robe, poured himself a cup of coffee and stood at a window, staring down at the street below. It was drizzling and dawn gray. There were cars parked along the quiet street. The bustle of morning had not yet started. He sat down in a chair and thought of yesterday. A wave of loneliness engulfed him. He stood and paced the room. Perhaps if he could just dream of Haddie again, it would give him some peace. He had felt better after he had the one dream with her. It was comforting. Maybe he could reconcile his grief through dreams.

Ultimately, that's what happened with his father. When his father died shortly after David graduated from college and he started having dreams, it was almost as if his father never passed. They always took place at the metal kitchen table, vinyl upholstery covered chairs resting on a chipped linoleum floor. The faint scent of kielbasa, cigars, and coffee. And they talked. They just talked about the family, his mother, his future, the passing of pets. And his father looked as he did before he died. And when David woke, he swore he could still smell the old kitchen. It was *that* real.

The dreams consumed him. He stopped eating, stopped getting

out of bed. Haddie stood by him. They were engaged when she drove him to Tippingdale. The land of men in white uniforms, soft classical music, goofy pills, and kaleidoscope skies. He wasn't going down that road again.

He needed to reconcile his feelings with Haddie. But maybe without the dreams. He needed to know more about what she thought these past ten years. But would it settle anything? Closure. It would bring closure. Reading her novel, he realized how little he knew her. If he could understand her, her motivations, desires, it would bring closure to her death and her life with him. Then he could move on.

But she was gone. How could he learn anything about her? He had the novel, but since he did not understand Haddie, he could not be sure he understood her novel. Her friends? She really didn't hang out with anyone. He couldn't imagine anyone at her office providing him with insight that he didn't already know.

Except Cat. Cat was with her most of the time. Haddie said she couldn't do without Cat. Maybe Cat could help. And she had been friendly to him at the bookstore. He would call her.

Who else? Haddie's sister in San Diego? Since their marriage, Haddie had only talked to her a few times a year. And it was always Haddie who called her. David strained to remember her name. Susan. That was it. Susan never called. David stared out the window and took a sip of coffee. It wouldn't hurt to talk to her.

What else? He set his empty cup down and walked to the bedroom. He opened the closet door and peered up at Haddie's side. On the top shelf was a shoebox filled with letters. He had never touched the shoebox before, and only knew there were letters in it because he had once seen Haddie with it on the bed as she placed a letter inside and returned it to the closet. He rubbed his chin, pulled the shoebox down, and sat on the bed.

He opened the box and it bulged with letters in their original envelopes. Some were plain white while others were of colored pastels or embossed with flowers and such. He pulled a few at random and looked at the postmark. After a few minutes it was clear that Haddie had organized these chronologically. The earliest coincided with her college days and the most recent was only a few months old.

David hesitated before opening an envelope. Would reading these really help him? These were not her writings, but the writings of others, at best responses to questions from those she had sent a letter. He held the first letter in his hand and tapped it against his palm. The letter had been in the box so long it had attracted moisture and the residual glue on the envelope had resealed itself. He sighed and placed it back into the shoebox, left it, and walked into the kitchen.

With two pieces of whole wheat bread in the toaster, David turned on his computer. He buttered his toast and sat down with a glass of orange juice. The front page news was the weather. There had been more rain in the city for the month of May than any other year on record. There was flooding along the Susquehanna, Delaware, and Hudson Rivers. The story covered several pages with pictures of homes half-buried in muddy water, boats plying up normally dry city streets, and residents on their roofs. Schools were closed because the streets were too unsafe for children to walk down. An old resident of one hamlet even said that it was worse than the flood of 1972. David remembered that one because he was living upstate at the time.

He was in the morning kindergarten class and met up with his buddy at the corner. He remembered walking down the middle of the deserted street to avoid the worst of the water draining along the curbs and sidewalks. Dressed in a yellow rubber raincoat, his canvas shoes squished water with each step. The school was empty when they arrived. They tried door after door but they were all locked. Finally, a custodian saw the boys through a window and told them the school was closed and to head back home. David lived on top of a hill so his home was fine, but he heard several stories of his relatives who lived along the river, watching the water rise above the bank, breaching the curb and sandbags, and pouring into their homes. As bad as the water was, it was the mud left behind that did the most damage.

When he finished breakfast, he set his dishes in the sink and strode to the bedroom. It wouldn't hurt to read a few, would it? He plucked the first letter from the shoebox. It was postmarked June 3, 1988. David recognized the flamboyant handwriting style of Haddie's mom, Elizabeth. He pulled the deeply creased letter out of the envelope and sat on the bed.

Haddie,

Your father and I are so proud of you! Straight As again. You are really spoiling us! We know you will do well in law school, just like your grandfather. Keep your nose to the grindstone.

David sounds nice. He loves numbers? Is he going to be a physicist? I hate to pry. Let's just hope he doesn't become an accountant! You can do better than that, dear.

David swallowed. He *did* become an accountant.

Not that there's anything wrong with accounting. They just don't make the money like doctors and lawyers. Speaking of lawyers, how's Jefferey? He was such a nice boy. Do you two still talk?

David's face burned as his grip tightened on the letter. Haddie had dated Jefferey prior to him. Jefferey. What an asshole. And pre-law. He was a corporate lawyer now in Albany or somewhere.

He folded the letter, put it in the envelope, and set it back in the shoebox. Elizabeth's letter was in a dingy brown envelope that resembled parchment. As he looked at the envelopes stuffed in the box, he noticed many dingy brown envelopes among the multitudes. It seemed that Haddie had saved every letter from her mom.

David stared at the shoebox and then slowly pulled the next letter out. It was postmarked August 18, 1988.

Haddie,

Well, I'm still recovering from last weekend. When are you coming to Hartford again? It was just like old times. And what I said before you left still goes. You're welcome to come live with me any time.

I know you're confused right now. But I meant what I said. I love you and always will.

Jefferey

P.S. You forgot your toothbrush.

As David mentally worked out the timeline, the pit in his stomach grew. He had been dating Haddie for three or four months before she went to see Jefferey. He looked at the letter with disgust, folded it and stuffed it back into the shoebox. He stood. His father once told him, "let sleeping dogs lie," and he realized opening the letters was a mistake. However, what was done was done, and there was no way to resolve it. She was gone. He searched his memory back to August 1988 to try to remember what was happening between them. How serious were they? He thought pretty serious. They got married in April 1990.

David tossed the shoebox back into the closet and got dressed to go for a walk and pick up an éclair from the local bakery. He had grown very fond of éclairs over the last several months, and they were his last food vice. As he stepped out into the light drizzle, he tried to push away the bad thoughts that kept rushing back in. His marriage with Haddie had been strong. There was no reason to doubt that. Or was there? What else hadn't she told him?

Then his insides turned to ice. The man at Haddie's funeral. The one who stood in grief. The one David actually felt empathy for. Jefferey. That's who it was. He had only met him a few times before, and that was over twenty years ago, so he hadn't recognized him. It seemed you always remembered people as they looked when you last saw them. It's sometimes a shock when you see someone after a long time. Jefferey was no different. He had aged, and it took those letters to jog his memory and make the connection. But, there was no doubt that was Jefferey in grief at Haddie's grave.

David got lost within himself and walked for a long time, the smell of car exhaust especially strong, occasionally broken by the smell of black soil and earthworms when he passed one of the small corner parks. With his head down, rain dripping down his face and neck, preoccupied with his Haddie, he wandered Manhattan in no purposeful direction, as if trying to get as lost on the island as he now felt within himself.

His cell phone buzzed in his pants pocket, and as he pulled it out, he was hoping it might be Cat.

"Mr. David East?"

"Yes," he responded.

"This is Detective O'Neill. How are you?"

"Um, fine." David reached back into his memory bank. Before the detective spoke again, David remembered him. He had spoken to him the day after Haddie died. Since she had been hit by a driver who then fled the scene, her death was treated as a homicide. David didn't think she was run over on purpose. He had been so filled with shock and grief that he never really got mad, though his heart raced now whenever taxis sped by him. A person is killed every day by a taxi in New York City. It was simply her time.

The detective confirmed what David thought. As he walked along, his shoes full of rainwater, his wet clothes feeling like lead on his body, he listened. They were closing the case. There were no witnesses, no leads, no tire tracks, no physical evidence. But he would keep David informed if anything came up, and told him to call him any time if he had any questions.

When the conversation was over, he found himself near his apartment building. He went inside and climbed the stairs to his home. He stepped into the kitchen and tossed his jacket over a chair. He slapped his forehead and swore. He forgot his éclair.

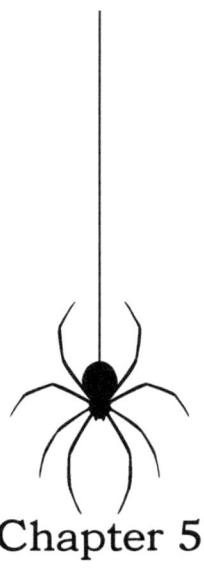

Chapter 5

DAVID REMAINED IN A FUNK FOR THE NEXT TWO WEEKS. THE DAYS WEREN'T so bad. He worked long hours, devoting his mind to actuary tables and questionable tax shelters. Gil left on vacation and everyone else just seemed to take his black mood in stride. "He's never been the same since Haddie died," they seemed to say when they looked at him. All of them. They continued to sidestep him in the hallways, as if he was infectious. He heard the whisperings that stopped when he entered the kitchen, the quick glances around the common room when he picked up his office mail.

The nights were bad. He had no further "Haddie" dreams and no escape from his thoughts. And his thoughts ran wild, dragging him along for the ride, an unwilling participant. They invaded the deepest recesses of his mind, and he began to wonder if his life with Haddie had ever been normal. Maybe it wasn't that they were so engrossed with their work that they didn't have time for each other. Maybe, it was only he who was engrossed with work, and she started to live without him.

Each night he would turn off the television, many times not remembering what show had been on. He would retire to his bed and lie in the dark. There were times when he could sense her, just out of reach, just of out of sight and earshot. Eventually he would fall asleep, get up in the morning, and do it all again.

He called Haddie's sister Susan but she wasn't much help. In fact, she acted very guarded, as if she had been warned of David's precarious psyche. He thought about asking her a lot of things, like why she never called Haddie, and why she didn't attend the funeral. Had there been an argument? But, in the end, he couldn't bring himself to ask her the tough questions. They mostly made small talk, and barely scratched Haddie's surface. The only statement that Susan made that gave David pause was when she asked about the Adirondack cabin he once owned. She had gone up there for several days when he and Haddie first got married.

"I never should have sold it," he said.

"I figured it was Haddie's idea," Susan said. "She always got what she wanted."

It was a Monday morning when the phone rang. David did not receive many phone calls anymore, so it startled him so much he dropped his toast on the floor.

"David? This is Mary Lamb," she said, sounding breathless. "I've got great news. Are you sitting down?"

David visualized her rubbing her hands together with glee, gazing into the phone with big bug eyes. He sat down in a kitchen chair and rested his elbows on the table. "Yes."

"Entropy Home bought your book! It would have been slated for next year during the summer, but another that was planned for an August launch has been pulled. Huge lawsuit. Now, get this. I sent your book over to Cynthia, a senior editor, and she read your book and loved it! She said it was so well written that ... and she never says that ... she said they'd send it over to a proofreader and "A Kiss During Mourning" would fill this summer's slot. That's record time, David! Record time."

David sat silently, trying to absorb that burst of information.

"So, Cynthia and I start negotiating, and of course, I get real coy about how your book was creating quite a buzz—"

"Buzz?"

"Interest. A lot of interest. So, anyway, I've got you a contract, a three-book deal, with an $800,000 advance."

Eight hundred thousand dollars! David dropped the phone. It bounced along the table and slipped off the edge. He dove for it, cupping it in his hands as his nose slammed onto the floor. Pain shot through his head. He rolled over onto his back, gasping, and brought the phone to his ear.

"David? Are you OK?" Her voice hardened. "You weren't sitting down, were you?"

"Oh, shit." David sat up, his nose pounding, blood dripping down onto his shirt. He heard a light buzzing in his ears and the room appeared to swim around him. Was it caused by his fall, or the news?

"David, you're moaning. What's happening?" Mary's voice seemed to pound through the receiver.

David wrapped his shirt bottom around his nose and said in a nasally voice, "Don't worry, I'm fine. Did you say $800,000?"

"Yes!"

David removed his shirt. It was soaked red. He held it for a few moments under his nose, waiting for the bleeding to stop. He placed his hand on the chair, grunted, and lifted himself to his feet. "Jesus. Unbelievable."

"This is my favorite part of the job. News like this always leaves my writers speechless. I'd love to celebrate with you, but I have to be in Jersey this afternoon."

David visualized her beaming, dollar signs in her eyes. What was 15 percent of $800,000? That was easy: $120,000. She deserved it. She sold it, and probably got him the best deal possible. He hated sales. He couldn't sell a rich man dying of thirst a glass of water.

"That's OK, Mary. Thanks for the great news. You did a great job."

"Well, thank you. And don't forget me in your acknowledgements."

David sat back in the kitchen chair. He held his bloody shirt in one hand and gripped his pounding head with the other. He gazed up at the ceiling, and then slowly all around him.

"We did it, Haddie."

We did it? She did it. It was her writing that sold the work. He was just a salesman. And he would get all the credit, all the money, and if it became a best seller, all the fame. His stomach felt queasy.

He stood, and the room spun a bit. He gripped the table for a moment and then walked to his room, tossing the shirt in a hamper. His cut was $680,000. Pre-tax, of course. Probably $400,000 after tax. He should be smiling; why did he feel so guilty? Old Margot said it herself. There was no way to get an agent for Haddie. No way. He had to do what he did. His heart was in the right place. That's all that mattered.

David leaned against the table. The pounding in his head eased. That was it. It was easy. After the book came out, he would tell everyone that Haddie wrote it. He would explain everything. And even better, he would write her into the acknowledgements in such a way that it would be obvious to any reader that once he announced the news she was the author, they should have known it all along. He rinsed the blood off his face in the sink, his nose stinging from the water and the soft brush of his hands. He grabbed a shirt out of the closet and slipped it on. As he buttoned it, his fingers slowed. Work? Today? Did he need to work? Taxes suddenly became decidedly boring.

His fingers began to speed up. No, work was still necessary. At least for the time being. But, he would treat himself and take a detour on the way to work and get a coffee. He looked at himself in the mirror. His nose was swollen and red. He grabbed a jacket and took the stairs to the sidewalk.

His steps felt light as he walked under partly cloudy skies and the oily sour smell of downtown. His emotions seesawed from glee to sorrow as his mind reeled from Haddie, to how he kept his promise, from the money, to his compromise. He knew the advance was special because he did not have to wait for the book to sell. He'd probably have it in his chubby little hands within a week or two. What should he do with it? What would Haddie do?

He stepped inside the café and looked for Cat, half expecting her to be sipping a cup near the window. The café was crowded with morning commuters, as people brushed by him. He wondered if she took the job upstate. The table by the window was empty. He bought a cup of black coffee and sat at his table. His mind wandered again as he stared at the empty chair in front of him. Haddie, the money … did he do the right thing?

A man coughed a few tables away. His face was lined and weighed by loss. The woman he sat with was probably a few years younger, but looked more like a decade younger. She had not experienced the things the man had. There is something about loss. Something that only is known to one who has experienced it. He thought of Cat and could almost see her, her long fingers wrapped around her cup of hot coffee. Those spring green eyes. He reached inside his jacket and pulled out his cell phone. He wasn't sure why, but he had her number memorized. She answered on the third ring.

"Hello?"

"Hi, Cat, it's me, David."

Her voice brightened. "David. How are you?"

"Good. I didn't wake you, did I?" David rubbed his swollen nose.

"My God, no," she answered.

David shifted in his seat. "I'm down at the café, and was wondering if you wanted to come down for a cup of coffee."

There was a short silence. "Oh, I'm sorry. I've got an interview uptown this morning."

David's stomach fell. Although he was only looking for companionship, he felt like he had just been rejected for a date.

The silence fell heavy on his ears. Asking her was a terrible mistake. He opened his mouth to speak.

"How about tomorrow morning?" she asked.

"Oh," David smiled. "OK. See you then."

The bar was busy. People jostled for position at the bar, and David was thankful that Gil and he had snatched a table away from most of the foot traffic. He stretched his legs in front of him and sighed. It had been hard sitting at his desk today. The book would be published in three months. The money would come in within a short few weeks and he would put it to good use. Perhaps a charity in Haddie's name. It eased his guilt on publishing the novel under his own name. He just wished he could have seen the look on Haddie's face when her book was published.

"So, whatcha gonna do with all that money, rich guy?"

David looked over at Gil, who was grinning from ear to ear. His hair was especially unruly today. It almost seemed to match his mood. "I've been thinking about that. I want to give at least some of it to charity. One that Haddie would have picked."

Gil laughed. "How about the poor fund for personal injury lawyers?"

David laughed, and felt his second beer going to his head. "Oh, yeah. That's one charity anyone could have sympathy for."

Gil watched two giggling women in skirts saunter by on their way to the bar. "Hey, five o'clock."

David started to look at his watch to argue, because it was nearly seven, and then turned his head to the right behind him. One of the girls stared at him, her big eyes looking like a deer caught in a car's headlights. David quickly turned back around and brought his feet up underneath him.

"She was checking you out."

"No, she wasn't," David said. Girls never looked at him.

Gil kept his eyes on the two women as he sipped his beer, and after a few minutes waved at them. David rolled his eyes and stared at his beer. His chest felt warm, his head even warmer, and after only two beers, he wondered if he might actually have to concentrate on his balance if he stood up.

"Did you get in a fight?"

David jumped and turned to see the blonde girl who had been staring at him from the bar, now bent over him just a foot from his face. Her face was scrunched in a look of wonderment and, perhaps, disgust. David reached up and touched his swollen nose.

"Yeah," Gil said. "He got into it with some brawler down the street. You think my buddy looks bad? You should see the other guy."

The girl's eyes widened. Her friend stepped around to get a better look.

"Oooh," she said. "Can I touch it?" She reached up and felt his nose with her thin fingers. Her fingernails came dangerously close to David's eyes.

"I didn't get into a fight. I fell in my kitchen this morning and smashed my nose on the floor." David was cross-eyed as he watched those fingernails. They quickly pulled away.

The girl gave Gil a sarcastic look and they both walked off. Gil spread his arms. "I set you up and you murdered it. Man, oh man." Gil shook his head and took a large gulp from his glass.

David smiled. "She was just a kid. Plus, I'm not ready for that."

"I keep forgetting what an old man you are," Gil said.

David laughed and gazed around the bar. Everybody seemed younger than him, except for a couple of really old codgers seated at the bar. He looked at Gil, who was several years younger. He had an air of irresponsibility that David envied. More important than age, Gil's head was in an entirely different place. He was single, never married, and had not experienced a loss like him. Gil noticed that David was staring at him.

Gil leaned over the table. "Now don't tell me the 'dark David' showed up tonight." He was smiling, except for his eyes.

"What do you mean?" he asked.

Gil hesitated and then pushed on. "At work everyone says there are two of you. One is the 'dark David,' the other is just 'abnormal David.' I was hoping that maybe a third version would show up tonight, like, 'Joker David,' or "Mass-murderer David.' Just for a little variety."

So the whispers and looks at work were not all in his imagination. It surprised him how quickly sympathy for his loss turned on him and his mourning became a statement on his constitution. Had people found out about his previous breakdown and thought he was going off again? He certainly didn't want to discuss that with Gil. At least not now. And Gil was trying to lighten the mood. The levity was not lost on David. He smiled. "I'm Batman tonight."

"Cool. We'll go for a drive later."

David sighed. He visualized Haddie walking through the bar entrance, her red hair framing her pink freckled face. When was the last time he had a drink with her out on the town? Five, maybe six years ago? Where was it? Probably Clifton's, uptown near the park. Celebrating a promotion? The outcome of a case, or a big bonus?

"David." Gil was looking at him with raised eyebrows. "You still there?"

"Sorry. I was thinking about Haddie."

Gil took a deep breath. "You had a lot of good years with her. As bad as you might feel, you really are lucky."

"Yeah I suppose so," David said, scratching his head. He thought of the letters, how she had not told him about the novel. "I just wonder how happy she was. I found a few letters in the closet—"

"Oh shit," Gil said. "Don't tell me you're going to start reconstructing your relationship with Haddie because of a few letters, or that she didn't let you in on her little secret about a book. I feel like I'm on Oprah." He spreads his arms like a conductor, his long arms sticking out just a bit too far through his sleeves. "Today on Oprah, women who dump their husbands by being run over by large vehicles."

David's jaw dropped and his face turned red. Gil bit his lip.

"Sorry, man," Gil said. "It was tragic. And you deserve to mourn and feel bad, and be 'dark David' and 'abnormal David.' But don't start down the road I think you're heading. It's a slippery slope."

David stared down at his beer. "Fair enough."

Gil waved his hand as if to erase the last several minutes of conversation. "Ah, forget the women tonight. We'll just get drunk."

David leaned back in his seat and finished his third beer. "Now, that sounds like a plan."

David woke fully clothed on his bed, head throbbing in time with his heartbeat. His mouth felt waxy and dry, his eyes half shut by goo. His clothing encrusted his body, his shirt stained with vomit. He remembered now. Driving the porcelain bus. His body retching and gushing. That hadn't happened in years, maybe decades. His body shook as he struggled to sit. He held his hands over his temples, wincing in pain as one hand bumped his swollen nose. His mind drifted to his college days, when this happened on a monthly if not weekly basis. A rite of passage, a college buddy had said.

He staggered to the bathroom and saw the remnants of his dinner and beer splashed on the underside of the toilet seat and a ring in the toilet bowl. He took a few sips of water from the bathroom sink, then peed, flushed, and staggered back to his bed, falling cross wise on it. There would be no going to work today.

Oh! *Cat.*

He shot a glance at his bedside clock. He had fifteen minutes to get to the coffee shop. David jumped up from the bed, and suddenly felt the room spin out of control. He landed face first and let out a yell as his nose hit the firm mattress. He pushed off the bed with his shaking arms, and walked unsteadily back into the bathroom. He ran some cold water over his face and brushed his teeth. He placed the toothbrush back in its holder as he glanced into the mirror.

"I look like shit."

He felt like it, too. He walked out into the living area and took a deep breath. He looked down at the carpet and felt like lying down, curling into a ball and falling asleep just like old Pudgie used to. He caught a glance at his cell phone and sighed. He picked it up off the kitchen counter and punched in Cat's number. However, before it began to ring, he closed it. Surprisingly, his desire to see her outweighed how crappy he felt and the effort it would take to meet her.

David was late and Cat was already seated at *their* table when he arrived. She was gazing out the window, mug in hand, oblivious to his approach. Her eyes reflected off the window, and David felt she was looking for something. Was she thinking of her husband, whose life had been cut so short by tragedy? She looked like she had lost something important, as if something had been taken away and left her empty, like a shell washed on the beach. David thought of a policeman friend of his, whom he knew during his early tax career. His friend said that he hated to go downtown to where the homeless drug users hung out near Battery Park. Because they had nothing. And there was no one more dangerous than a person with nothing to lose. Did he think this about her? His imagination was running overtime.

David wiped his brow and slowed as he came to the table. "Good morning, Cat." As he said this, he knew his nose would arouse interest or disgust. It had turned into a rainbow of color overnight, and now was varying shades of purple, red, and green.

Cat turned to him and her smile quickly faded. Her face was blank, though she stared at his bulbous black and blue nose. She raised her hands to her face. "What happened to you?"

David sat down. Concern? That was good. "Oh, I fell and hit my nose on the floor. It's all right." He waved it off like he slammed his nose onto tile floors once a week.

There was no morose fascination in Cat's look. "It looks like it hurts."

She stared at him and he became very conscious of his hourglass-shaped head. He lowered his gaze to his coffee and took a sip, but he still felt her stare. It made him feel as if his head was made of glass, with his memories and desires swirling around for all to see. She looked tired, and in a way, maybe worse than he looked after a night of drinking.

"Any luck finding a job?" he asked.

Cat crossed her legs and held her mug with both hands. "No. I decided not to go upstate. I just can't seem to leave here."

David enjoyed her spring green eyes for a moment. "Well, I'm glad you're here."

She smiled and her gaze intensified. He felt as if at any second she was going to reach into his skull and pull out something sacred. He shook his head and watched her hands. As he did, he began to sweat. He swore he smelled of stale beer and partially digested food. Cat did not seem to notice.

"You don't mind talking about Haddie, do you?" she asked.

"No," he said quickly. Actually, he did. He wanted to let his thoughts of Haddie lie quietly for a while.

"I feel funny about asking you this," she bit her lip, and her eyes cast downwards.

"Feel funny about what? Go ahead." David's body warmed even more, and he felt like the stale beer was going to start pouring out of him in buckets.

"Well," she started, a thin smile across her lips. "I love birds, and I gave Haddie a pin of a bird. An owl. Would you mind parting with it?"

"Not at all," David said. He did not remember the owl pin. He smiled at her. "I'll bring it by your place tomorrow after work. Just give me your address before we leave."

They talked pleasantly for a while and then went their separate ways. They mostly reminisced about Haddie. Too much, in David's opinion. He felt a wall between them, a sort of taboo, but at the same time, a desire. It might not be sexual desire, but it was an attraction of some sort. Perhaps it was because they were both lonely. They felt safe talking to each other. Whatever it was, David wanted to continue seeing her. As he walked out of the coffee shop, despite the sore nose, aching head, and gut-wrenched stomach, it was the happiest he had been in some time.

David's imagination started galloping again.

"*Find out more. All the truths are buried in Haddie's letters.*"

David sat on a sofa, his headache fading with the day. He did not want to listen to that voice in his head.

"*Don't you want to know the truth?*"

He looked toward his bedroom. He picked up the remote and turned on the television. An Alfred Hitchcock thriller was on. *Stranger on a Train*, about some guy who tries to kill his niece who completely trusted him. Or something like that. He was only half listening.

"*You can't live with your head buried in the sand. Come to the closet. Open it.*"

David rubbed his temples. He knew numbers. Understood numbers. Affairs of the heart were another matter. He had little understanding of other people's emotions. Maybe it was because he lacked confidence in himself. He could not see positive feelings thrown his way. He, with the hourglass head, the middle-aged spread, the mostly bald pate. At the rare parties he attended he always stood in a corner, glass in hand, almost daring someone to come say hello. Only Haddie understood him. Only Haddie loved him as a man. Screw the closet. If it held truths that burst that bubble, he didn't want to know about them.

"*Maybe it won't be that bad. Maybe she did love you, in spite of all your faults. Read the letters, David. They might have a big surprise for you.*"

That's what he was afraid of. Haddie was beautiful. She was a genius. She moved seamlessly through the old boy network and the café crowd. How could she have just been happy with him all these years? She lived for competition, cutting the throats of witnesses, tearing down the other lawyer's case. And on top of all that, she was an artist.

David shot a glance at his bedroom. Perhaps there was no tragedy waiting in those letters. If he read them, he would know for sure and could move on with his life.

"Atta boy, David. Now you're showing your true stripes. Go on in, the truth awaits."

He rose from the couch, walking reluctantly, yet feeling pushed toward the closet by a phantom tailwind. The bedroom was dark with the blinds closed and he shuffled through to the even darker closet. He turned on the light and pulled the shoebox down from the shelf. He peered down at the multitude of envelopes, neatly arranged in chronological order. He had inspected only a few. The rest would take him what was left of the day.

He found few new secrets in the shoebox. The news was trivial for the most part, slowly making his head hurt, not from over imbibing, but from the useless information that was fighting for space within his mathematical brain. One piece of information that was surprising was Haddie's mother's grudging respect for him before she died. He read that letter twice, wondering why Haddie never shared that with him.

Although most of the letters contained useless trivia, some did provide a perspective on Haddie's life, and chronicled events that would otherwise be forgotten with time. A letter from 1997 reminded him of when she had her wisdom teeth pulled. She looked like a red-headed chipmunk stocking up food for the winter, her cheeks swollen, drinking milkshakes he made for her from a blender he bought just for the occasion, and later, eating ice cream he bought from a creamery.

Or the brook trout. Haddie hated fishing, at least she said, but was always lucky when she wet a line. On one occasion she caught a three-pound brookie and they baked it for dinner. Her mom commented on it in a letter to her. So, Haddie must have been happy enough about catching it to include it in a letter to her mom.

He discovered the spiral-bound notebook when the end tip punctured his finger as he set the shoebox of letters back onto the shelf. The shelf was just high enough that he could not see a flat notebook resting all this time under the shoebox. He pulled his hand away and looked at it, expecting to see blood. However, there was just an indentation on his fingertip where the metal jabbed him. He shook his hand, reached up, pushed the shoebox aside, and grabbed the notebook.

It was a plain lined notebook with a wrinkled, red cardboard cover. The sharp metal spiral stuck out from the bottom. He opened the cover and flipped through the pages. The pages were covered in writing. He imagined Haddie carrying this with her, folded up and shoved in her purse. He remembered the purse. She always carried a big purse. He opened the notebook to the first page.

It was recipes. Recipes for cyanide-laced wine. Arsenic brownies. Rat poison pie. With notes. "Lemon to mask the bite." "Sugar to cover the bitterness." Each page had a new recipe. A new way to kill. The writing was neat and measured. The notes were functional. It was the workings of a logical, methodical mind. It fit Haddie in a morbid kind of way. But as he held the notebook, he felt something else. An absence of emotion. Not in himself, but within the pages of the notebook. It was hard and matter of fact. It was utilitarian. It was to be used.

David's hands shook and the bottom half of the notebook fell away, the pages hanging down. A loose page fell out. It fell face down on the closet floor, but David could see handwritten ink shining through from the other side. He put the notebook back on the shelf, thinking that soon he would throw it, and all the letters in the shoebox, into the wastebasket. He would do it soon. He could still see the sharp spiral end poking out from the shelf, so he shoved it deeper and placed the shoebox on top. The letters had consoled him, but the notebook unnerved him again. However, he understood that poison was a central part of her book. This must have been research. And that's what she was good at. She always did her homework before a case.

He sighed and looked down at the loose page lying on the floor. He picked it up and walked toward the bed. He turned it over and began to read.

This is the hardest letter I've ever written. You mean so much to me. We've grown so much together. But I can't let it go on this way. I know you will understand. And you know how much I love you.

—

David's stomach turned. His face flushed as he thought of who this letter was for. Him? Was she planning on leaving him? Was it for Jefferey? He examined the paper. The paper was bright. It was recently written. Had she carried on an affair with him until recently?

David took a deep breath. The book. It must have been for the book. He scratched his temple, trying to remember if he had read anything like this in "A Kiss During Mourning." He didn't, but he also hadn't finished it yet. He had to do that. It was going to be published within a few months and it wouldn't look good if the supposed author of the novel had not even read it yet. He walked back to the closet and set the piece of paper under the shoebox with the notebook. He didn't feel any better after reading the letters, the notebook, and the love note. If anything, it raised more questions.

"It's probably nothing," David said.

"*Probably.*"

David covered his ears and peered back at his bed. Even though Haddie had been gone for three months, her pillows were still there on her side of the bed, her jewelry on her bedside table, her workout clothes stacked on a chair in the corner. It was time. Time to put her things away. Or throw them away. He grabbed a few plastic bags from the kitchen and placed her things in a bag selected for either storage, recycling, or garbage. He tried not to look too long at an item. He quickly decided which bag it would go into and never looked back. He found the owl pin in a bedside drawer and placed it in his pocket. When he finished he had several bags in separate piles.

Her corner of the room was now empty. Her half of the closet was empty. The shoebox and notebook were tossed in the garbage bag. As he surveyed the bedroom, he felt like he was starting anew. He was erasing Haddie from his life and it made him feel sad and guilty. And a new life did not necessarily mean a good life.

He fingered the owl pin in his pocket and thought of calling Cat. It was late afternoon. He had just seen her this morning. He said he would stop by tomorrow after work. If he went by today, would she think he was acting too needy? David rubbed his chin and gazed out his window. The sun was shining through, the warmth of the rays inviting him to go on a walk. There had been so few sunny days this spring. It wouldn't hurt to go for a walk, and if he ended up at her apartment, so much the better. He strode out the door and into the exhaust.

David wandered in what he believed to be randomly selected directions. However, soon he stood at her threshold, and realized that he had made a beeline to Cat's residence. He fingered the pin in his pocket and looked up at the Victorian brownstone building. It was a quiet neighborhood, quite unlike his own, which were cluttered with aged, barely converted meatpacking warehouses. If he had been teleported here, he wouldn't have known if he was still in Manhattan or some quiet upstate suburb. The light was starting to fade as he took a deep breath and walked up the stairs, opened the door and stepped into a foyer. On the right wall, opposite the mailboxes, there was a line of buzzers with names taped next to them.

David surveyed the list. At first he didn't recognize her name. And then he saw C. Pilleur. He realized that he never knew her last name. But, that was the only name with a C as the first initial.

He pressed the buzzer and suddenly hoped she wouldn't answer.

"Yes? Who is it?"

It was definitely her.

"Hi, Cat. I have your owl pin, and I happened to be in the neighborhood ..." He grimaced. That was a stupid thing to say. The silence was deafening.

"Oh. David." She emphasized David, as if she just recognized his voice. "I'll buzz you in."

David climbed the well-lit stairs to the second-floor apartment. The door was mahogany with stained glass windows. It was completely opposite of the industrial-grade metal doors in his neighborhood. He watched her blurry form approach through the glass.

"Hi, come on in. Don't mind the mess."

David smelled her fresh scent as he walked into the darkened room. It was quite a contrast to the bright foyer and stairwell. As his eyes adjusted to the dimmed light, he noticed the Victorian style of the building stopped at her apartment. The furniture was leather, heavy drawn curtains, and mahogany shelves lined with books.

"Have a seat."

He obediently sat down on a sofa. There was a low, curved wooden table in front of it, with brochures strewn across it. Cat knelt on the other side of the table and began gathering the brochures, at the same time, watching him. David shifted in his seat, looked at the brochures, and caught a glimpse of palm trees, ocean, and sand.

"Planning a trip?"

Cat cleared her throat. "Yes," she said, no longer looking at him.

David sat quietly, watching her putting the brochures away. Her apartment smelled fresh, but felt cluttered, as if you could hide almost in plain sight. She must have eaten dinner in here, because a plate remained on the table, with fish bones poking out from beneath the napkin lying across it.

Cat sat on the table and crossed her legs. "I love New York. But, I feel a need to escape on a vacation for a little while."

She watched him intently and David had a sudden urge to flee. Instead, he gazed around the room. He had no idea what he saw because his thoughts were on her looking at him. He felt a bead of sweat form on his bald head, and when he looked back at her, he felt that she was enjoying his discomfort.

"So," he said, "where are you going?"

"Indonesia." Her look softened.

"Indonesia?" David's voice cracked. "That's quite a trip."

"Yes it is." She stood directly in front of him. She wore tapered tight black pants and an untucked cotton shirt. "Would you like a drink?"

"Sure."

She turned and walked into her small kitchen. "I have some red wine. Is that OK?"

"Yeah, sure."

David looked at his watch and realized he had left his apartment over two hours ago. He heard Cat in the kitchen pouring wine into two glasses. He suddenly had the urge to pee.

"Can I use your restroom?"

"Sure," she called from the kitchen. "It's off the bedroom to the right."

David stood and walked through the living room along the short hallway, through the bedroom, and then to the bathroom, passing detailed bronze sculptures, exotic ivory carvings, and tasteful impressionistic water colors. And it all blended with the apartment. She had great taste in art, and much of it looked like it cost some real cash. He closed the door behind him and flicked the light switch. He jumped and shuddered at a large carved wooden mask hanging above the toilet. The face was drawn into a savage scream. He approached and stared at it as he relieved himself. It was carved in obvious agony. His thoughts turned to Haddie. He missed her so. And as he finished, he felt like the mask. He felt like he was in a permanent state of agony. He suddenly yearned to be alone. Away from everyone. Even Cat.

He finished, washed his hands, and pulled the owl pin from his pocket. He rolled it in his hands, feeling the tiny ridges that made up the feathers. He examined it more closely. It looked to be made of bone, with the pin made of stainless steel. He opened the door and walked out to see Cat on the couch holding a glass of wine, and one resting on the table.

He walked up to her. "Here's the pin. I'm sorry, but I have to go."

Cat remained seated and took the pin from his hand. Her face was expressionless. "You haven't had your wine."

"Yeah," David scratched his forehead. "I'm sorry. How about a rain check?"

Cat's face broke into a thin smile. She leaned back, accentuating her feminine curves. "OK. I'm leaving the day after tomorrow. How about when I get back?"

David stood with his hands in his pockets, taking in the final sight of her. "I'd like that."

He turned, walked out the door and into the chilly night.

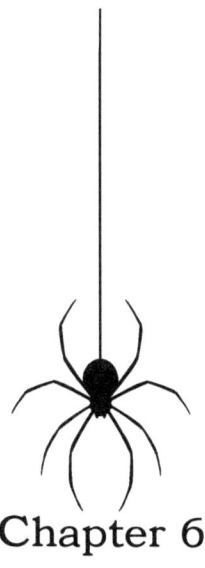

Chapter 6

"I KNOW WHO YOU ARE," HE SAID, ALMOST IN A WHISPER.

Hannah watched him like a spider watches a fly caught in its web. "Do you really? Who am I then, Mr. Private Detective?" She slowly pushed herself away from the counter and moved toward him. Moments ago, she was completely alone in her seaside room in Rio de Janeiro. He had surprised her with his entrance, but she did not let it show.

"You are the woman I've been chasing since Romania. Remember Nicolae Tomsa? Murdered with cyanide. He left behind a wife and four children. And a large life insurance policy. I was sent to investigate."

Hannah slowly walked toward him, her long legs slightly crossing with each step. She thought, Nicolae was a family man? He didn't act like a family man with her. He was all over her. And he slobbered. She couldn't wait to poison him. She almost shoved the cyanide down his throat.

She placed a finger to her lips and pouted. "I have no idea what you're talking about, Mr. Private Detective."

She stopped a few paces in front of him. He was thirty something. Maybe. Maybe forty. Well tanned and fit. Ruggedly handsome with a full head of jet black hair. He could be a catch.

Or just another disappointment. She planned to find out.

He continued. "I've been following the bodies ever since. I've found six, but I bet there's more. You're hard to trace. Don't you like credit cards?"

He stood inside the doorway. She could tell he was a man used to getting his way. And she could tell he was attracted to her. So much, that the purpose of this visit could become muddied.

"Do you have a name, Mr. Private Detective?"

He ignored the question. "It appears your vehicle of choice is red wine. The authorities are getting tired of cleaning up your messes."

Hannah held out her hands, palms down and let her wrists go limp. "Are you going to arrest me?"

She watched him closely. He gazed at her hands, and then ran up her arms, over her shoulders and to her breasts, which were barely covered in a negligee. He was a confident man. Perhaps overconfident.

When he spoke next, he was now staring at her long legs. "There have been eyewitnesses. And, unfortunately for you, there are very few beautiful redheaded women who have traveled six of the continents over the past eight months. We have fingerprints from several scenes. I am willing to bet they match yours perfectly, Ms. Hannah Roule."

Hannah smiled coyly and dropped her hands. "You are so smart, Mr. Private Detective. Do you want to play a game?"

"Your games are over, Ms. Roule. It's time for you to come with me."

She pulled at her negligee. "In this? I am a lady, Mr. Private Detective. It would be a scandal. And I might catch my death from cold."

"Then change. But don't take long. And don't try to escape."

He almost half-smiled when he said that. There was no breeze coming off the Atlantic. It was warm in the room and beads of sweat had appeared at his temples. She would make her move now.

"You are a gentleman." She reached up to her shoulders and let the negligee slip off and slide down her body, leaving her naked save for a locket around her neck, revealing everything a man could wish for.

The private detective had seen many things in his life. But nothing he had experienced could brace him for the beauty in front of him. And she knew it. His jaw slacked in amazement. She took the final *steps toward him and pressed her body against his. She raised her chin and kissed him, and his hands immediately fell to her waist ...*

"Oh God, this is gross."

David looked up from the manuscript. He had put off reading it, but with the publication date looming, it could wait no more. And how did his agent talk him into doing a book reading? And tonight? It wasn't even published yet. However, he felt obligated (legally and morally) so he was left with no choice.

He fingered the page in his hands. The edge had dulled a little bit since Haddie's death. It had been almost six months now. His overactive imagination had quieted. At least there were none of her belongings left to call out to him. But he felt alone. Gil had taken up a girlfriend and now was out of commission. He went out with them once, but felt like a third wheel.

He felt a void without Haddie. He still could not get his mind off the things he found in the closet, especially the letter. He searched out Jefferey the attorney and found out he lived in Buffalo. He started to call him several times, to confront him, but always hung up before anyone answered. He had to let it go. The logical portion of his brain convinced him, at least for the time being, that he read too much into her private letters.

And Cat. He had called her several times since that last night he saw her, but all he got the first month was her answering machine, and after that, just a message that her voice mail was full. Although he missed Haddie almost as much as he ever did, he missed Cat, too.

So, he had become a bit of a recluse. It would be good to get out tonight, even if he had to read in front of a bunch of people he didn't know. Who would want to go to a book reading by an author who hasn't even published a book?

The private reading was for several literary critics and VIPs that his agent Mary Lamb had convinced to show by calling in some favors. Each had received advanced copies of "A Kiss During Mourning." Of course, David had never done a book reading. He was going to look like an amateur to these people. He certainly had nothing to lose. But he had to finish *reading* the book in case they asked questions. He was on the second to last chapter now. It was mildly entertaining. The poisoning scenes were pretty good, but her "spiritual" growth and the romance scenes he could have done without. It could have used some car chases, maybe a few explosions.

"Wait," she gasped, pushing and turning away from him. He slipped his arms around her. She heard his heavy breathing and felt his chest heaving against her back. With her hands, she felt he was ready for anything.

He was impressive. But would he come to his senses and take her to jail, or would he follow his heart and run away with her? Was she destined for the bedroom, or death row? She spied the open, yet full wine bottle on the counter. There were two glasses nearby. She sighed. She could take no chances.

She pried herself from his grip and walked naked over to the counter. "Would you like a glass of wine?"

With her back to him, she could not see him, but heard his breathing slow. He hesitated to answer. She poured each glass half full, and then picked them up, swirling the red elixir in the glasses.

"Do you take me for a fool, Hannah?"

She turned and saw the anger in his face. She smiled, and as she walked toward him, the anger melted. He was mesmerized by her walk, the flow of her hips, her bright green eyes.

"Mr. Private Detective. I am naked with nothing to hide and I am drinking from the same bottle as you." She took a sip from her glass. "How could I poison you?"

"My name is Andrei." He took the glass from her hand and held it in the light.

"That's a good name for a man."

Hannah reached out to him. Andrei stared at her naked body and took a drink. She stroked his body.

His eyes widened and he dropped the glass. He reached for his throat and collapsed to the floor. He looked at her, pleading, as if saying, how could you? How?

She fingered the locket around her neck. The secret compartment held enough for a single dose. It had come in handy before. Was it Tasmania? She shook her head. No matter. With authorities now on the trail, it was time to go home and lie low. She believed Andrei stopped breathing long before she walked out with her night bag.

David flipped through the final thirty pages. One chapter to go. He glanced at his watch. Mary would arrive to pick him up in four hours. He tapped a pencil on the manuscript and turned the page.

It was late spring in Kansas and the roses were in full bloom. Hannah deplaned among fields covered in a carpet of young corn. She was alone and well tanned (she was one of the few redheads who was not sun adverse), her hair a slightly lighter shade of red than when she left. She came to realize the destructive path she was on, and that it could only lead to a "Thelma and Louise" like death. It was time to come home ...

David scratched his head. What kind of romance was this? She travels the world, poisoning dozens of men, looking for perfection, only to come back to her small Midwestern town? Why? What was this, a morbid *Wizard of Oz*? There's no place like home? He stared at the manuscript and stroked his chin. He stood, a glint in his eye, and smiled.

The limousine was long, black, and slick with rain. David stepped in and sat across from Mary. He felt like he was going to prom. Except in high school he didn't go to prom. He never dated until he met Haddie. He met her in college.

"Are you ready David? This is your big night."

Mary was dressed for business. David looked at her, and around the inside of the limo. All black leather and chrome.

"You went all out tonight, Mary." David smiled.

"Yes, you deserve it. A couple of the reviewers called me. They enjoyed the novel very much. It's very important we wow these people. They will be providing the buzz for your work. These people will be writing the snippets that will show up on the novel's front and back covers, and the reviews in the *New York Times* and strategic blogs. I think we're off to a good start." Mary stared at the papers cradled in David's arms. "Where's your advanced copy? You can't do a book reading without the book."

David flashed the manuscript. He left his book at home. He preferred to read from the copy he printed months ago. "Don't worry, I've got it covered."

Mary reached into an ice bucket and pulled out a bottle of champagne, and to David's surprise deftly popped the cork. Her hands shook as she tilted the bottle toward a glass and poured until it was nearly full. She handed it to him.

"Here, this will calm your nerves."

David took the glass and said nothing. He felt relaxed and not too nervous, except that he was never crazy about speaking in public. But Mary looked almost beside herself. It surprised him, because she was a veteran of this business. Why was she so nervous? Was it that big a night? That important? Was she nervous about him? Was there something she sensed in him that made her feel uncomfortable?

"I feel pretty good, Mary," he said, and patted her knee. "Don't worry, everything will be all right."

Mary stared out the car window. "I hope so. Things have been a bit slow in the publishing world. I could use a home run."

David was just hoping he wouldn't strike out. Mary took a sip from her glass. There was no ring on her finger. David knew that publishing was her life. But she had a stable of good writers that made money. A little money, anyway. She must be nervous like this at all these launches. It was clear to him that the people at the reading tonight were important. They were the heavyweights that could steer readers to his book (Haddie's book), write rave reviews for the papers, get them placed on a conspicuous shelf in the biggest bookstores—if they wanted to.

The limousine pulled into an alley and stopped at a simple wooden door. David felt his tie tighten around his throat. His skin felt moist as he began to sweat. He grunted. If Mary hadn't gotten so nervous ...

"Behind that door is the backroom of Dinozio's. A nice restaurant. And lots of room for us to have the reading. They should be well fed and watered by now. Are you ready?"

"Yes," David said. It didn't quite come out as he expected. His voice felt tight. He loosened the tie around his neck, though he did not expect that to help.

The wooden door was blackened with age. This restaurant and a few others were all that were left of Little Italy. He remembered it as a child when they'd visit from upstate, a bustling area of noise and music. And great food. He missed it. Chinatown and various other Asian groups had taken its place. They were interesting too, but he still felt nostalgic about the way it had been. And this restaurant was a hold out, complete with red and white checkered table cloths, Sinatra crooning through the speakers, the smell of garlic and tomatoes whetting the appetite.

Mary moved quickly for being so plump. She practically burst through the door, with David trailing behind her, the manuscript under one arm. They walked through a narrow hallway of tile and concrete that opened out to a large room. At the far end were tables in a semi-circle. The people were talking noisily and a large quantity of opened wine bottles sat before them on the tables. Mary turned and touched his arm.

"Come with me and we'll work the room a little bit before you speak."

David nodded. Nearby there was a single wooden chair and a microphone. A bottle of water sat on the floor next to the chair.

"Mary, how are you?"

A short, slight, thickly accented Italian man with gray hair hugged her.

"Antonio, good to see you." Mary looked out over his shoulder at the crowd. "How is it going?"

"Wonderful, wonderful. Even Ms. Parker is happy. I think she has had two bottles of Chianti all by herself."

Mary leaned toward David and pressed a glass of wine into his hand. Mary waved to someone in the crowd. There were about twenty people present. As David shook their hands, he could tell the critics from the spouses and friends. The men had soft hands and beards with a touch of gray. The women were all points, and David walked carefully, lest he fall and be pierced to the bone. Many appeared to be present with their spouses, or partners. The spouses and partners were typically the ones drinking a bit too much and laughing a bit too loudly.

Ms. Parker was seated at the center table with her husband. She wore a severe look on her face, dressed sharply, and exuded an air of tyranny, calm, and ruthlessness. She was the Queen Bee and could decapitate an aspiring writer with her pen. Mary whispered she was the chief editor for *Romance Review*. A positive review from her was better than (or at least as good as) an endorsement from Oprah. David stood a bit straighter when he shook her hand.

"Hello, Ms. Parker," Mary said, "how have you been?"

David could tell she was asking Ms. Parker whether she had read his book, without actually asking if she had read his book. It appeared asking Ms. Parker a direct question such as that would lead to bloodshed.

"I am fine, Mary," she said stiffly. "And I have not yet finished Mr. East's book. I have been terribly busy." She kept her eyes on Mary.

Mr. Parker sat in silence, his hands folded on the table. His eyes were wide and large, as if half expecting that his wife would beat him if she realized he was present. David took pity on Mr. Parker and almost felt obligated to provide a diversion so he could flee, perhaps upstate to White Plains, where he could live a normal life with an equally mousy wife.

"Mr. East?"

David shook his head and looked at Ms. Parker. She was now regarding him down her long sharp nose. "What are you going to read for us tonight?"

He glanced at Mary before responding. "The last chapter, Ms. Parker."

Mary stiffened. A smile briefly appeared on Ms. Parker's lips before she squashed it with a frown that accentuated her facial wrinkles. "Ah, very efficient. It better be good. Otherwise I'll have no reason to continue reading it."

"I hope you like it, Ms. Parker."

Mary and David turned toward the single chair and microphone. He felt the cold touch of her hand through his clothes when she gripped his shoulder. "Are you sure you want to read that? The end? Nobody does that at a book reading. Probably half the audience hasn't finished it."

"It'll be OK," David said, though he wasn't sure it would be. But he had only brought the last chapter with him.

He stood to Mary's right as she spoke into the microphone.

"Thank you all for coming. Although I know the only reason you came was because of Dinozio's calzones." Mary smiled and the audience responded with polite laughter. Mr. Dinozio beamed in a corner. "I know this has all been on short notice. With a void in our romance section due to the lawsuit, Mr. East's novel was added at the last minute to fill it. I hope you all have had a chance to at least start it, and I know I have talked to a few of you that actually finished it. And finally, I hope you love it as much as I do. It's the best romance novel I have read in a long time."

Mary straightened her jacket and continued. "Tonight Mr. East has joined us to read a chapter from the novel. I am grateful that all of you have come to listen. So, without further adieu, I present to you, Mr. David East."

Mary stepped away from the microphone as David approached. David fingered the final chapter as he bent to the microphone. "Thank you, Mary."

He sat in the chair. The microphone was too high now, so he set the manuscript on the floor and adjusted the microphone to the correct height. He cleared his throat and picked up the pages from the floor. The audience sat quietly. The room was lit well enough for him to see them, and to read, but just so. As he looked out at the critics and their spouses, he felt light-headed. It took him back to high school and the presentations required in many of his classes. He heard once that the number one fear of people is public speaking. A distant second is death.

"I'd like to thank everyone for coming tonight. As you know, I am a new writer." He cringed. He was a salesman. Haddie was a writer.

"Mary asked me to read a chapter to you. I decided on Chapter 33, the last chapter—"

There were a few mumblings from the audience. And then one man called out, "But I haven't finished it yet."

David smiled, because he hadn't read the chapter yet either. "Then we'll see how it ends together, shall we?"

The audience laughed, and there was a small but perceptible collective sigh. It is the feeling that every speaker wants. When the audience becomes comfortable with the scene. David crossed his legs and put the chapter on his lap. He briefly thought about explaining the book leading up to this point, but decided it was best to leave it to each person's devices. Besides, he was completely lost as to its meaning, if there was one. Instead, he first laid the chapter flat on his lap, and then tilted it slightly to catch the light. He glanced up one final time at the audience, and then began to read.

It was late spring in Kansas and the roses were in full bloom. Hannah deplaned among fields covered in a carpet of young corn. She was alone ...

David read his wife's words, immersing himself into her story. Soon, although he read the words aloud, he felt alone. Just him and Haddie's creation. Occasionally he would pause to turn a page, or to clear his throat of phlegm. At those times he would look up and see the trimmed goatees and soft hands, the pointy women, and feel disgusted. What did they do to earn hearing her story? To decide whether it would be a big success or just end up on the bottom row of a back shelf at Walmart? And each time he would bow his head again and read, knowing that Haddie would want it this way. She would want it to be a best seller. So each time he continued for her.

The story took a soft turn. Hannah returned to Kansas and married her one-time beau Daniel. David paused at the name and paused a second time when she described him as "ugly as a conch shell on the outside, but beautiful as nacrea on the inside." Haddie grew up on the beaches of eastern Long Island. One night when they were up in their Adirondack cabin, drunk on screwdrivers, he had asked her what she saw in him. She told him that he was "unique, and had a soul, and looked like a conch shell on the outside, but was beautiful as nacrea on the inside." He took it as a compliment, poured another screwdriver, and promised himself he would look up the meaning of "nacrea" in the morning.

Nacrea is the inner shell of crustaceans, and in some species can be quite stunning. The nacrea of abalone is a rainbow of colors and is used in jewelry.

David glanced up at the audience and caught the reflection of the overhead lights off the wine glasses and the glasses on several critics' noses. He was in the story now. As he paused, just a few pages from the end, he realized this really was a *Wizard of Oz* story. There's no place like home, Toto. Was this a message that Haddie actually believed? That Haddie could have roamed the world, been with exotic men in postcard settings, and yet knew she was happier here in New York with a conch shell? It warmed him to think so.

And then he read the last few pages.

But soon, after a few short months, Hannah became restless. As she did when she was on her world conquest, she rode horses much of the day, jumping rail fences, racing down old wagon trails, and often not returning until dark. One day she stopped her horse on a small ridge overlooking a creek. She looked off into the distance, realizing she still hadn't found what she was looking for. Her life was comfortable, but stagnant and constricting. She had no want for money, but she had many other wants. Of what she did not know. But it was time. Time to move on. But what of her husband? Fortunately, there were no children.

Where to go? What to do?

She dismounted, and on foot, led her bridled horse the three miles back to the homestead. It gave her time to think. To think about her needs. The evening was cool and smoke rose from the chimney of their stone house. It had once been on many acres, but the land had been divided, and subdivided, until the charm of the house they now called home was dissolved among a sea of other houses with vinyl siding and shingled roofs. The new homes were one of four types, repeated and repeated onto what seemed like infinity, choking the life out of the stone house and making the smoke coming out of the chimney seem comical instead of inviting.

She took her horse down the road to the community stables and walked the final quarter mile to her house, smelling the beef and potato stew resting on the stove. Hannah was now thirty-two and she still did not know what she was searching for to make her happy. But she knew her future happiness did not include who or what was behind the front door of the stone house.

David paused. Another curveball. Another piece of information in the Haddie odyssey to mess with his sanity. It's just a story, he said to himself. It's just a story, for chrissakes. He cleared his throat and continued.

"Where have you been?" Daniel asked. "You've been gone all day."

Hannah put her arms around him, knowing her touch melted his iciest mood. "I was out riding. You know how I lose track of the time when I ride." She kissed him.

Daniel smiled in spite of himself. "Well, let's eat. It's going to get cold."

They began their meal in silence. Hannah fantasized of Pacific tropical islands, the breeze through her hair, the sun kissing her beautiful body. She had never been there. It was full of secrets, and there was never winter. Winter was closing in on Kansas. She thought of the tropical islands, the pina coladas, sandy beaches, and endless rushing waves.

"Hannah," Daniel said, "you seem preoccupied."

Hannah quickened a gentle smile. "Oh, you know how I get about riding." She took a spoonful of the beef and potato stew. It tasted like trailer park trash from a can. "The stew is very good," she cooed.

"Thanks. I wish we had some Merlot to go with it."

"Yes." Hannah fingered her empty locket hanging around her neck. She would have to fill it soon. "Yes. Pity, isn't it?"

David raised his head and swallowed hard. *It's just a story.* The audience applauded. Ms. Parker stood shakily and applauded enthusiastically. Mary's jaw dropped. She peered at David and raised her fingers to her mouth. He realized that she had gambled on doing this reading, not knowing how it would turn out. It could have been disastrous. But now, all was right in her world. He saw the dollar signs in her eyes.

He looked back down at the story. The questions about Haddie kept rising, like bubbles to the surface of boiling water. She wrote these words and yet climbed into bed and slept next to him each evening? But, it's just a story. If it was so negative about him, why would she beg him on her deathbed to publish it? He was being crazy. He was ruining this moment for Haddie, even though she was gone. This was her moment. He had to let it go. Was he jealous? Is that why he could not let the book breathe? *It was just a story.* He relaxed his shoulders as the applause died. Mary stood and went to the microphone.

"Does anyone have any questions? I'm sure David would be happy to answer them for you." She glanced at him and he forced a smile. He'd rather just go home, but he had no choice in the matter.

A woman's hand shot up. It was the wife of an online critic. "What made you write this book, sir?"

Mary would tell David later this was an easy question to get him started. For David, however, it was more difficult because, of course, he had not written the book. He made the most honest reply possible without divulging that his wife had written it.

"To fulfill a promise I made to my dying wife."

Gasps came from the audience. Even Mary gave him a sharp glance. David said nothing more. All was quiet for several seconds.

"A well-worded ending, Mr. East," a goateed man said. "Obviously, there will be sequels?"

David smiled and brought a finger to his lips. "Sshhh. That's a secret."

A man with thick glasses who critiqued books for one of the local magazines crossed his arms. "So, why couldn't Hannah get the wild hair out of her ass? Didn't she know what she wanted?"

David cleared his throat to buy time for an answer. As he started to speak, Ms. Parker interrupted him.

"Sir," she said to the critic, "all women know what they want. Sometimes, it just takes a lifetime or more to find it."

The man looked away and said nothing. David eyed the man and then Ms. Parker. The room was as quiet as a tomb. Apparently, Ms. Parker was a force to be reckoned with.

"It never ceases to amaze me how men think they are the most amazing creatures on the planet. That they hold a power over women. It's simply not true. Obviously you agree, Mr. East?"

"Y-y-yes, I do." David felt himself begin to sweat, though he was unsure why.

"It just doesn't seem the kind of book a man would write. Does it, Mr. East?" Her eyes were looking down her sharp nose at him. It was not a question, it was more of a frontal assault.

"I guess I just don't believe I'm an amazing creature with a power over women, Ms. Parker."

Nervous laughter emanated from the audience. All eyes were now on Ms. Parker.

Ms. Parker smiled. "You have wisdom beyond your gender, Mr. East. My review will be out in a few weeks. I hope you read it."

—

It's just a story.

He climbed out of the limousine and up to his apartment. His mood became gloomier by the minute. *He* was Daniel. Was she bored with him in real life? Why did she hide the book? Was what she wrote her true feelings? If she had let him read it while she was alive he probably would have understood. Writers write what they know. Usually anyway. Having a character similar to him in her book would not have been that odd. But why hide it unless deep inside, at least, it was how she was feeling?

It's just a story.

"You're so critical," she said in his dream. Was that it? No, those were his feelings about why she didn't let him in on the secret. He wasn't critical of her. At least, he didn't think he was.

His negative thoughts rose to the surface. And it was becoming a deep pool. What about the love note in the spiral-bound notebook? That wasn't in her book. Was it destined for her second book? Or was it a draft note to someone real? He just knew Jefferey had something to do with all this. A fancy lawyer with an expensive practice. He was probably a hotshot lawyer in Buffalo. Big home, fancy cars, seducing Haddie with his power and gifts of glittering jewels. Why else would he be at the funeral, and not even come up and pay his respects? Unless he had a good reason not to. Haddie was susceptible to power. Though in his opinion, it was more like she wanted the power, and not just be associated with a man who has the power.

He would call Jefferey tonight. David glanced out his window into the dark. Well, first thing tomorrow morning. And he would set up a meeting. He would drive to Buffalo and talk to him. He would put an end to all this, one way or another, once and for all.

Route 17 hugs New York State's southern boundary for most of its length, traveling through the Appalachian foothills, small- and medium-sized towns, and crossing famous rivers such as the Delaware and Susquehanna. It was a rare, bright, sunny summer day with hardly a cloud in the sky.

David drove almost straight through, stopping only three times; once for lunch at the Park Diner, behind which was the Susquehanna River, where he had once fished for walleye pike; once to fuel up and buy a Pepsi; and once to pee the Pepsi out of his body.

Jefferey had been pleasant enough on the phone, though guarded, and reluctantly agreed to meet him in a small pub down the street from his house. David made it sound like he would be "in the neighborhood," and just wanted to meet up for old time's sake.

Not that you had any good times with the dork, but was he going to call you on it?

David told him he saw him at the funeral. Jefferey admitted he was there, and gave a lame excuse about not being "comfortable" approaching him after Haddie was laid to rest. David liked meeting him at a neutral place outside his home. He was going to confront the shithead, and didn't want his family around in case there was a fight. Snide Jefferey. He acted concerned and shocked about Haddie's passing when they talked on the phone. He probably knew within days, if not hours of her death. Probably because she hadn't called him, or he called her, however they worked it out, and she didn't call him back. Maybe he called someone at her office and they told him what happened? All those damn lawyers stick together.

By the time he reached Buffalo in the late afternoon, David's muscles were tense from head to toe. He got lost around the University, so he was a little late reaching Morrison's Pub. He pulled into the nearly empty parking lot. There was an older dark sedan parked next to the rear exit, and a small two-door Honda parked in a middle space. David pulled up and parked next to the Honda, feeling the BMW was out of place here.

He turned off the engine. The large sedan was probably the owner's/ bartender's. The Honda? Who knows. He thought he must have beaten Jefferey here. Where was the Jaguar? BMW? Lexus? Or maybe a Hummer? That would be Jefferey's speed, the snide piece of shit.

David's hands shook as he hoisted himself out of the car. A drink would calm his nerves while he waited. Confrontation was not his strong suit. But if he didn't find out today if Jefferey had had an affair with Haddie, the big "if" would gnaw at him the rest of his life.

The pub bar was aged dark wood, with a large mirror behind the bar with "Guinness" etched on it. The bartender was a large Irishman, his nose smushed like an ex-fighter. A trim man sat at the bar. David sat a few stools down and ordered a Genesee. The barman pulled a draft and set it in front of him. David drank half in one gulp. It tasted good after a long drive on a summer's day.

"David?"

David looked up from his glass and stared at the man. The man was dressed in denim and a T-shirt, with sneakers and white socks. His receding hair was short and brown. This was Jefferey? "Yes. Jefferey?"

"Yeah." Jefferey walked over and shook his hand. He was not much taller than David. "You wanna grab a table?"

David glanced at the barman, who was now busy changing out a keg. "Sure."

They walked over to a table with cushioned chairs near the front window. David suddenly felt his "overactive imagination" had shifted once again into overdrive. Haddie bedded this? What was she thinking?

Hold on, David. Don't count old Jefferey out yet. You were pissed off enough to drive all the way out here, weren't you? Finish it.

They sat down and there was an awkward moment of silence.

"New York is a long way from Buffalo. What brings you to the hinterlands?" Jeff asked.

David looked into Jefferey's eyes. He suddenly felt very stupid. He had imagined Jefferey as some kind of powerbroker. But, here he was, dressed like some hick fresh from Target, and he drove a Honda. He wasn't Haddie's type.

Wait a minute. You're a victim of an hourglass head and middle-aged spread. You can even make a $1,000 suit look bad. You're Haddie's type?

David took a deep breath. "Were you having an affair with my wife?"

Jefferey acted like he'd just had cold water thrown into his face. "Me? Are you kidding? She dumped me twenty years ago."

"I'm serious," David said, and he tried to keep his voice low and as calm as possible.

"David, no way. Honest." Jefferey sat back and wiped his lips. "Shit, I haven't seen her in years. It was before you two were married, that's for certain."

David remained silent. What could he add? That he found a letter Jefferey had written to Haddie back in the 1980s? That she wrote a novel that suggested she was no longer happy in her marriage? That Haddie wrote an apparent anonymous love letter that David had concluded must have been for him? This was a very dysfunctional meeting.

Jefferey tapped his fingers on the table. "Listen," he said, "Haddie was beautiful, God rest her soul." He sat straight, his face turned a shade of red. He leaned onto his left butt cheek and pulled out his wallet from the right back pocket. He opened it and showed David a portrait of his wife and three children. All smiles. "I've got a family."

Now David's face began to turn red. A wild goose chase. David's imagination running wild on him, overreacting to a book and some letters? Jefferey was not what he expected. Ten minutes ago he wished Jefferey was dead. Now he felt stupid for having such a thought. He let out a deep breath.

"Look," David said. "I'm sorry. I haven't quite been myself since Haddie passed away."

Jefferey's normal pale Buffalo color began to come back to his face. "I understand. It took me a long time to get over Haddie." He shifted in his seat, gazed at David's almost empty beer and turned to the bar. "Can we get two more here?" He turned back before the barman replied.

Jefferey leaned into the table as if expecting to hear a deep dark secret. "I bet it's been pretty tough."

David certainly didn't want to rehash everything, but he felt he owed Jefferey some explanation. "Well, as I told you over the phone, I was going through her things and I found her writings."

"About me?" Jefferey's voice sounded almost hopeful, as if Haddie was a memory he could never quite throw away, but kept it in a dark corner of his brain to pull out occasionally during the quiet of night.

"No."

Jefferey deflated a bit and David now was sure that Haddie and he had not had an affair. David almost felt that Jefferey might have wished for it, maybe fantasized about it; he did love her greatly at one time, after all, but David was convinced now an affair had never happened.

David continued. "I found out that she loved to write. But she never told me. I found her … writings and some of them were a bit, well, unusual."

Two more beers were placed in front of them.

Jefferey's eyes were gripped on David's. He wanted to hear more. As if hearing about her intimate thoughts would bring him closer to her. Or satisfy some morbid curiosity. Or help him understand her better. He sat there like a drug addict waiting for his next fix. David realized now that Haddie once had a tremendous grip on him. And her memory still did. But only her memory. It was clear to David that Jefferey had been away from the big city, in this backwater, living his life.

"I don't know. I guess I'm going crazy, that's all. I thought I knew her, and then I find out she wrote a"—he stops before saying novel—"bunch of stuff, and she never told me. I thought she told me everything."

Jefferey laughed. "Dave, let me tell you. I knew Haddie for several years before you. And although I'm sure I didn't know her as well as you, one thing I can tell you, she didn't tell you everything."

David clenched his beer glass.

Jefferey continued. "I don't mean she was cheating on you. I'd be surprised if she was. But Haddie was, well, a control freak. She had to control everything. And she was a hot girl who always got her way. I remember I'd hate to go to a bar, or even a party with her. Because the guys would stare. I mean, all of them."

David knew what he meant. Even after they married, if they went to get a drink, he made sure it was a small neighborhood pub. "She was beautiful."

Jefferey picked up his glass and pointed it at David before taking a large slug. "She was something. I think most guys were afraid of her, but the ones with big enough balls would come up to her, with me sitting right there, and try to hit on her. She always knew what to say. To some, she'd just wave her hand and they'd melt back into the crowd. With others, some of the big, fighter types that wanted to knock my teeth out and drag her back to their apartment, she would soothe until they were big smiling dummies with glazed eyes, wandering off." Jefferey finished his beer and waved to the barman for another. "Goddamn, she was a pain in the ass. But I loved her. And I knew all along I couldn't keep her. She had me wrapped around her little finger, glazed eyes and all, just like those big guys in the bar. Haddie knew how to get her way. And make you thankful she got it."

David suddenly saw himself in Jefferey. Jefferey couldn't let go. Not completely, not after twenty years, a pretty wife, three kids, and a million non-Haddie memories later. Is this David's future? Twenty years from now, would he still be trying to decode their relationship? Chasing windmills? He looked at the time. It was six o'clock. If he hurried he could be back at his apartment by two. He breathed a sigh of relief. He had been overreacting. His wife liked to write, for

Chrissakes. Did he have to know everything? Could she not keep anything to herself?

The barman put the beer in front of Jefferey. He looked at David. "Would you like another?"

"No thanks."

Jefferey looked down at his beer guiltily. "I don't remember the last time I had three beers in one sitting."

David smiled. "Thanks for talking with me. I feel better." He took a drink. "One thing I've gotta know. I've never seen a lawyer drive a Honda Civic. What's with that?"

Jefferey laughed. "I defend those that can't pay much. I don't collect the big paychecks, but it's morally satisfying."

David shook his head. "Haddie would have never bought into that."

Jefferey sighed. "Fuckin' Haddie. She could drive any man crazy."

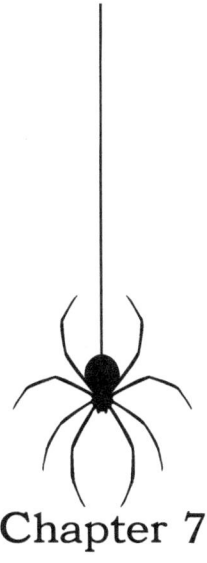

Chapter 7

WHEN DAVID PULLED OUT OF THE BAR PARKING LOT AND ONTO THE highway heading east, the sun was in the western part of the sky, but still well above the horizon. The day had turned hot and sticky. David turned the air conditioner on and found a classic rock and roll station blasting Thin Lizzy. He turned it up and settled in for the long ride.

Haddie knew how to get her way. And make you thankful she got it.

Even after twenty years, Jefferey still thought of Haddie. But Jefferey's mild obsession could not compare with his own. Of course, David shared a bed with her for twenty years. But David's fixation on Haddie was not constructive. It was expected that she would stay close to his heart and in his memory for the rest of his life. But to try to reconstruct her intentions on actions performed when she was alive, and to attribute them to some kind of disloyalty, was obsession bordering on paranoia. He didn't have these negative thoughts about her when she was alive. Why have them now?

He was wrong about Jefferey; that's another thing. His imagination went off the deep end on that one. That is settled.

So, why didn't he feel any better?

The look on Jefferey's face when they talked about Haddie. She sure had him by the short hairs. Jefferey could not let go. Was this his own fate? He just drove three hundred miles to Buffalo, and was now driving back to New York, because of her. Did she write the book to spring this upon him at the time of her death? To keep him beholden to her? As a cold pit formed in his stomach, he realized he was being crazy. Why would she do that? That was crazy thinking. Overactive imagination thinking. So, what was bothering him now?

Haddie knew how to get her way. And make you thankful she got it.

David put the car in cruise control and stretched his legs. Did she get her way most of the time? He thought about the important decisions in their lives. When they first got married, David was leaning toward a job he really wanted upstate. Haddie talked him out of it, saying the city was the place to be, to build a career. And the cabin. David had inherited that from his father, and he wanted to hand it down to his kids. When it became apparent they were not going to have any, and the opportunity came to sell for a nice profit, it was Haddie that pushed the deal. He loved that cabin. And what about kids? David wanted to adopt, but Haddie talked him out of it, saying that lower Manhattan was no place to raise a child.

And what was he doing now? Devoting his time selling *her* book. Yet he had to tell everyone that he wrote it. Even now she was controlling his life. Mary was planning a big book tour around the launch date. If it sold well, the tour would be expanded. He could be on the road for months.

David thought hard all the way to Owego, trying to recall any important decision *he* had made while they were together. He racked his brain and came up empty on every spin. There were none. A part of him thought he was being incredibly self-centered, considering that Haddie's novel had already earned him a comfortable living, and maybe much more. Yet it was always about money. Haddie's decisions always boiled down to the bottom line.

By the time he parked his BMW in the Manhattan parking garage, he felt like a used snot rag. And about as worthless. Had he spent the last twenty years playing mamby pamby to his wife's wishes? David took a deep breath. It was not important. She was gone. He had to let it all go. All the suspicions, the apparent clues, the criticisms. Everything. All it did was spoil the wonderful life they'd had together.

And most important, no more dreams of her. This is what sent him to Tippingdale the first time. His father died not long after he met Haddie. And then the dreams started. They always took place at the kitchen table. And he and his father talked. They talked about his mom. They talked about his grandparents and great-grandparents. Stories that he had mostly never heard before. Stories that he obviously made up. Stories that were part of his "overactive imagination." For several weeks he had these dreams nightly. Although he now knew they were delusions, at the time he really enjoyed spending the time with his father. Talking away about anything and everything. And all those stories about his deceased relatives.

He enjoyed the stories so much that he stopped eating. He stopped going to his job with the city. He stayed in his apartment and wrote all those stories down. Finally, Haddie escorted him to Tippingdale. Tippingdale wasn't a bad place, but there were tight rules and strong medications. And the counselor penetrated his mind, told him that he had to control his imagination; that he had to rejoin the living. The dreams stopped abruptly, and never returned. He was cured. At least he thought he was cured. Until his dream of Haddie. But it was only one, and it was several months ago. Maybe it was an aberration, a beyond extremely unlikely event that would never repeat.

He remembered what Jefferey said. *Fuckin' Haddie. She could drive any man crazy.*

"You said it, brother," David said, as he took off his clothes and slipped under the covers.

"Hello, David." She sat on the edge of the bed, her slim legs stretched out, heels resting on the floor.

David lifted his head from his pillow and blinked. Her scent filled his nostrils. Although it was dark and she was revealed only in varying shades of gray, he knew immediately it was Haddie.

"Jesus," he moaned. "I can't even escape you in my dreams."

Haddie sat quietly at the edge of the bed, watching him. David propped himself on his elbows, looking at her from between his feet. She looked so real. He felt that he could reach out and touch her, just like when she was alive. She was haunting him. She was dead and she was haunting him through his dreams. No, it was his imagination. It was *he* who had the problem. But he couldn't take his eyes off her. She was dressed in denim and a silk sleeveless top and was as beautiful as the day he met her in college. She smelled so good. The bedroom was full again. It opened a flood of memories. Simple pictures of them in this very room.

"Thank you." Haddie smiled, apparently not hearing what he'd said.

"For what?" he replied, staring at her form in the dark.

"For publishing my book. Just as you promised."

"I had to use my name as the author. There was no other way."

"I know," she said.

David was mesmerized by her presence. He wondered for a moment how she knew that he had published her book, but had to list himself as the author. Then he remembered, this was a dream. But it all seemed real. Like he could reach out and touch her. He wanted her to vanish. To leave him alone so he could get on with living and not end up back in Tippingdale. But he couldn't help but ask.

"Why didn't you tell me about the book, Haddie?"

"You asked me that already." She playfully slapped his foot that lay beneath the covers.

"I'm asking again." He watched her, almost frozen by her beauty, as if seeing her again for the first time.

"I didn't know if it would be any good. And you're so critical of me."

David felt the hairs on his neck rise. It was exactly the same thing she said before. It sounded … rehearsed. His face turned warm and red. "There's more to it. Hannah looks just like you, and she kills all these guys, and then she goes back to Iowa—"

"Kansas," Haddie corrected.

"What?"

"She goes back to Kansas."

"Oh yeah. Kansas, Iowa, they're all the same. And then at the end she's going to kill her husband, who looks a lot like me!" David was breathing hard now.

"David, it's just a story."

"And that's what you said before, too. And I found that love note. What was that about?"

Haddie raised an eyebrow. "A love note?"

"Yes!" David was riled now. He lost focus that this was just a dream. "That love note. About a soul mate and all!" He sat up and folded his arms across his chest.

Haddie hesitated, studying David carefully, as if measuring up an opponent. "Is that why you went to see Jefferey today? Did you think I was seeing someone?"

"Yeah!" David stopped and squinted. "Wait a minute. How'd you know I went to see Jefferey?"

"I'm still in the waiting room." Haddie brushed the hair out of her eyes. "The jury is still out. I get bored and sometimes look to see what you're up to. It's easy to get out now, once you know the system. Nobody knows I'm gone, or nobody cares."

David rubbed his eyes. He felt light-headed, as if he would float up to the ceiling if he threw the blankets off him. She was here and he was absorbed in their conversation. Just like with his father.

Was this a dream? It had to be. He couldn't be awake. That's impossible. You die and you're gone, period. If he was awake, he was hallucinating. And that was a one-way ticket to Looneyville. He had taken that train before, and it made him shiver to think he might be on the platform, with a ticket in his hand, ready to go again. He thought of Tippingdale's white walls, custodians with broad shoulders and massive forearms who made sure you swallowed those little capsules filled with "make you feel better" medicine. A prison with drugs.

"David," Haddie said quietly. "You're the only man I ever loved. I never saw another man when we were married. Don't you believe me?"

"I believe you," David said, simply because it was the easiest thing to say.

He looked down at his hands and clenched and unclenched his fists. This felt awake. This *was* awake. Which meant he was hallucinating, or, maybe she wasn't really dead. Maybe she was trying to drive him crazy.

He threw the covers off and advanced. Haddie flinched as he grabbed her by the arm and then touched her face, her body. She felt real. She was real.

"What's going on, Haddie! You can't be dead!" He shook her. "What are you trying to do to me?" David jumped to a crouch, staring at her intently, his face within a foot of hers.

Haddie placed her hands on his chest. "I don't know. I'm dead. But in a way, I'm in between, like purgatory. The jury's still out. That's the only way I can explain—"

David retreated to the head of the bed. He now sat with his knees into his chest, his arms wrapped around his legs. He saw her in the hospital. He knew how bad it was under that sheet. The doctor told him she was dead. She had an open casket funeral; everyone saw her. And now he was talking to his dead wife. He was insane. Next stop, Tippingdale. Unless he could make it all go away. Make all the crazy brain cells retreat to a cold dark corner. Or seal them off for good, so he could not retrieve anything out of them, and they couldn't leak and infect the part of his brain that was still normal.

"No! No! This isn't happening!" He covered his ears with his hands, lay down, and shut his eyes.

"David. Calm down." Haddie stood and walked toward him.

"Leave me alone! I don't ever want to see you again! I'm not crazy!"

He squeezed his eyes so tight he saw fireworks; purple light, orange and yellow flashes, red streamers, and dark spots swimming through his vision. His hands were pressed to his ears and shut out the world except for his own breathing and heartbeat. He pressed his knees into his chest and rocked back and forth. Nothing would penetrate these walls. Nothing crazy could slip through, or slip out. He found himself breathing very hard and suddenly felt very tired. He relaxed his breathing, let his legs fall to the side, and opened his eyes.

She was gone.

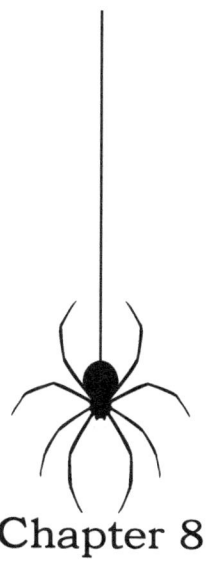

Chapter 8

"THANKS. I WISH WE HAD SOME MERLOT TO GO WITH IT."

"Wine?" Hannah fingered her empty locket hanging around her neck. She would have to fill it soon. "Yes. Pity, isn't it?"

David closed the book. He looked up from his book at the crowd. Mary was right. Midwest women loved their romance. The women mostly varied from their thirties to early sixties, all of them clutching copies of "A Kiss During Mourning" to their breast. Tissues dabbed tearful eyes, some nodding. Hannah could not settle for anyone less than her ideal man! What a tragedy. In her voyage around the world, the one man she could have been happy with was her pursuer. But he was a man of principal. He would have turned her in to the authorities. How ironic! In her depression she settled for less. Until she came to her senses. She was going to try again. As soon as she refilled her locket. The man in Kansas was disposable. Hannah's happiness was paramount.

It was early October in Madison, Wisconsin. The hardwoods were a mix of colors, perhaps slightly past their prime. David had no more dreams of Haddie. He kept her out of his thoughts. He could not afford to summon her, to risk her appearing once again in his dreams. His sanity depended on it.

The book was selling briskly. The readings kept him busy, and the crowds from August to October had swelled. Although Ms. Parker gave the book a favorable review, sales had started tepidly. Mary said it was because "A Kiss During Mourning" was a tragic romance. These often started slow out of the gate. She reassured him sales would pick up once word of mouth and blogs chimed in. Sure enough, it hit the *New York Times* best seller list in late September, and David was on the cusp of making big money.

Mary Lamb stood next to David, applauding with the audience. The smile on her face told David everything he needed to know. Big money was imminent. "Mr. East will be glad to answer questions now."

Arms shot up, hands flapping back and forth. David called on a fortyish-looking lady that appeared to spend half her day at the gym, and the rest of it in plastic surgery.

"Are you single?" she asked slyly, giving him a wink.

David laughed politely.

"Hands off, girls," Mary said. "I have plans for him in that department."

David laughed politely again. Mary had been overly friendly to him, and he was careful to avoid situations where they would be alone. She could be aggressive in her manner, but never directly came on to him. Deep down, she probably knew he was not interested. He liked her, but in an agent-writer sort of way.

"Yes," David said, smiling at the woman, "I'm single."

Giggles from the audience were quickly followed by arms shooting skyward. David sat in his chair, legs crossed, and pointed to a lady who was particularly enthusiastic in getting attention.

The lady clutched the book in both hands and pressed it to her breast. "You understand women so well. You understand our 'condition.' What do you attribute that to?"

David folded his hands over his crossed leg. He had heard this question in multiple variations throughout the reading tour. At first the question unnerved him. After all, he was just a salesman for Haddie's craft. A poor mouthpiece that put a face to the work. A human voice behind the story. But now, Haddie was becoming more and more distant. David, in order to preserve his sanity, stopped thinking about

Haddie. He stopped reminiscing about their good times. He removed all physical traces of her from the apartment. In fact, he was moving soon to a larger place uptown. It was sad, but necessary. He could not afford to have her penetrating his psyche, dominating his dreams, and tipping the scales to another breakdown. So, he developed and rehearsed an answer. An answer that made him wince at first. It made him wince to use the first person in interpreting Haddie's story. But he was getting used to it now.

"Well," David said, "we all know the sacrifices women make for their families." He paused and watched the smiles and heads nod in the audience. "I guess I've always been insightful when it comes to women. I started with the premise that Hannah would not settle for less than the ideal. That she would not sacrifice her happiness. The men she met were not merely less than ideal, but fatally flawed. She dispatched them as a matter of course. I had her kill them as a metaphor for loss, and to set up the irony between her and her pursuer. The one man she met on her travels that she might have loved, who was worthy of her mind and body, she could not risk having. But where there is tragedy, there is hope. And the ending is hopeful, that she will go in search again, and meet a man she can love."

David took a sip of water. The hands shot up again.

"Will there be a sequel?"

David had no intention of trying to write a romance novel, but he certainly couldn't say *that*.

"Would you like to see one?" he asked.

The audience applauded and shouted so loud that David covered his ears in feigned defense. That drew more laughter. He smiled. The audience was in the palm of his hand. Whose novel was this? He may not have written it, but he sure as hell sold it. The accolades had grown larger with every reading. He felt himself sucked into this new world of celebrity.

As the applause died down the hands shot up again, waving more frantically than ever.

"Where are you staying?"

The audience erupted in laughter. David waited for things to quiet down. "The Hyatt downtown."

Mary gave him a sharp look and David covered his mouth with both hands.

"Oops," he said.

The hotel room was spacious and looked out over the city lights. David stood at the window with a cold beer in his hand. A bucket of ice with four more bottles sat on a cart in the middle of the room. It was quiet, and at times David would think of Haddie and just as swiftly sweep her from his mind. It was difficult at first, because she starred in so many of his memories. But with time, thoughts of her diminished, and when they did occur, were easily erased. It made him sad, but it forced him to look forward and get on with life.

Cat partially filled the void. Memories of Haddie were replaced with fantasies of Cat. Her voice mail filled quickly after she left for the Pacific Islands. And over the last several months David continued to call, sometimes daily, sometimes weekly, and heard the same error message. He wondered why she did not return his early calls, and why she let her message center fill up. He hoped she was all right. He knew he should move on, there were plenty of women around, but he still felt a pull toward her.

He walked across the room and picked up his cell phone. His fingers automatically punched in the numbers.

"Hello. You've reached Cat. I'm not home. Please leave a message."

David's pulse quickened. Her message box was not full anymore. Which meant she either was back home, or at least had cleared her messages.

"Cat. This is David. Just wondering how your trip went. Give me a call."

David lowered his phone. He would be back in New York in a couple of days. Hopefully he would get to see her soon. He sat down on the couch. She would want to see him. Who wouldn't want to see a best-selling author? He finished his beer, strode over to the ice bucket and pulled out a fresh cold one. He glanced around the room; a king-sized bed and armoire with a flat-screened television took up most of the space. Next time he would insist on a suite.

These last few weeks had filled David with confidence. There were smiles all around from his readers. Every reading was a success. His newfound popularity hit home with him early in the tour in Terre Haute. He had taken a short nap prior to the reading and woke up groggy. Mary was late picking him up and they arrived at the bookstore to a crowd. They pushed their way through the crowd, 95 percent women, eyeing him and patting him on the back (and a few on his butt). When he reached the signing table and turned around, he saw the look of adoration. He couldn't shake his fatigue, so he looked to the nearest employee and asked for a cup of coffee. He didn't mean it to, but it came out a bit rough. The poor girl ran off, *ran*, and he wasn't sure if she was fleeing from him or rushing to get his coffee. She came back quickly, having had to purchase it down the street at the corner café. He didn't know how she did it so fast. And then he found out she wasn't just a kid working there part time. She was the owner. He realized he had made it. As ZZ Top once said, "I'm Nationwide."

David surveyed the plush but sterile hotel room. He suddenly thought of the Adirondack cabin he once had, and the look on Haddie's face with a large brook trout next to her on the grass (she would not hold it). He pushed thoughts of Haddie out of his mind and thought of Cat again. She was safer to think about. She never led to bad dreams, and would not take him back on the road to Tippingdale.

There was a knock on the door.

David rose and rolled his eyes. He knew it was going to be Mary. She wouldn't leave him alone. She was a great agent, but had a butt the size of a Buick. He opened the door. A brunette about his age stood in the doorway in a very tight dress. It was the woman from the reading who asked him if he was single. His heart jumped into his throat.

The woman's gaze met his eyes and then surveyed the room behind him. She held a bottle of wine loosely in one hand. "Are you alone?"

She smiled. The old David would have said, "Yes, how can I help you, ma'am?" But the new David knew better. He had seen that look from many women the last few weeks. And he, balding, with a slight paunch and hourglass head, was getting attention. Lots of attention.

David looked at her and smiled. "Not anymore." He stepped aside and let her in.

"These crackers suck," David said, a bit loudly.

Mary glanced at him out of the corner of her eye. They were in the air toward Tulsa, their last stop on the reading tour. David's knees ached. The seating was cramped. And people constantly brushed past him on their way to the bathroom. He stared at the curtain that divided the first-class passengers from the masses. Why wasn't he up there? His book was selling better than ever. He knew the numbers. In August, 52,000; 113,000 in September; and nearly 200,000 the first two weeks of October. At $20 a pop, that was a good chunk of change for the publisher. They could foot the bill for a first-class ticket. If Mary wanted to sit back here, fine.

At least Mary took the middle seat. There was no way he was going to sit next to the cowboy with a Bible on his lap.

Jesus.

"Are you ready to go home?" she asked.

David rubbed his head. He was ready. He would sleep better. He would eat better. All this restaurant food had put several pounds on him. And he was drinking too much. He wanted to sleep in his own bed and walk the island. And see Cat if she had returned.

"Yeah, I suppose so." He stared at the curtain again. "Next time, let's fly first class." He looked across the aisle. A mother rocked back and forth in her aisle seat, consoling a baby crying in her arms. Next to her sat a little boy, probably not even in school yet, the tray down and filled with plastic toy army men, blasting phantom airplanes and helicopters out of the sky. The noise did not help his head. At least he wasn't the father huddled in the window seat with red, swollen eyes and looking out the window at the clear blue sky wishing for freedom like a prisoner suffering a long sentence.

The children briefly made him think of Haddie, but he swept her from his mind quickly. He thought of the woman last night. Dolores. Very pretty. The first lady he had been with since Haddie passed. It was fun, but he drank too much and now he had a headache. She left soon after they finished rolling around in the bedroom. He felt a bit like a notch on her belt. But he was lonely, and she made him feel better for a short while. She flattered him and pleased him.

His mind drifted to Cat.

"First class? Aren't we getting uppity." Mary smiled at him.

David stretched. "I know the numbers. Our publisher can start taking better care of us. From now on, it's the Four Seasons. And a personal chef. I'm getting fat on all this restaurant food." He smiled, to show he wasn't too serious.

"I'll see what I can do," Mary said. "But I can't change tonight. It's the last reading, and we're staying at a Sheraton."

"A Sheraton?" David rolled his eyes.

"What's wrong with Sheraton? It's a nice hotel chain."

David shook his head. "Their breakfasts are lousy, their fitness room is non-existent or has no working equipment, the beds are—"

"OK, OK," Mary said. "We'll find a nice, healthy restaurant tonight. I'll take care of it. But let's gut out the hotel, all right?"

"Fair enough," he said.

David looked out the window. Mary was good to him. In fact, everyone had been good to him on this tour. He couldn't remember one time in his life that he received so much attention. He had a best seller. At least, he was out hawking a best seller. Haddie wrote it, but it was his now. It was his to make blossom, to sell to the public. A copy of "A Kiss During Mourning" in every pot! He was becoming a celebrity, and he would use that to sell more copies. Did he not deserve the attention? His dad once told him, "If you want to make money, David, go into sales." And that's what he was doing. He smiled and told the readers what they wanted to hear. And they *listened*. They stood there quietly, some with their books clutched to their chest, some with mischief in their eyes, some with middle-aged spread covered by tight dresses. But they all came to listen and hang on every word.

He thought back to high school when he tried out for the track team. The coach took him into his office and had told him he wasn't fast enough and wasn't strong enough. There was no place he could put him. David walked home that day, his gym bag hanging off a shoulder. He had tried football (not aggressive enough), tennis (not coordinated enough), music (tone deaf!). He never felt so much as a failure as during that long walk home. He later joined the bowling team and learned how to drink beer. But his high school days passed with anonymity.

It was downhill from there. Until he met Haddie. She paid attention to him. Why? Because he always did what she wanted? He danced to the beat of her drum. He lived in her shadow. Well, now he was in the light. This was his time. This was *his* novel, to make or break. And he was going to make a lot of money. He might just be a pimp for Haddie's novel, but now he was in control. And he was going to go first class from now on.

End of story.

He leaned back in his seat and his mind drifted to his last dream while at Tippingdale. He was seated at the kitchen table with his recently deceased father, and they were discussing everyday things, with tidbits of family history thrown in by his dad for good measure.

"Your mother and I always worried about you when you were in high school."

David took a sip of his iced tea. "Why, Dad?"

At that time, David thought his high school days were fairly normal. His grades weren't bad. He wasn't teased or beat up by any of the bullies or smart asses. He thought it went pretty well, actually, except hardly anybody ever noticed him.

He sighed. "You just never seemed happy. You never had a spark. I wanted you to be passionate about something. I wanted you to be hungry, to have fire in your eyes, about something, anything. But, I never saw that. At least, not until you met Haddie."

"She has a way of getting me fired up."

His dad smiled. "I see what you mean."

David stared at his father. He never noticed so many wrinkles on his face, or the jowls, and loose flesh around his throat. He was beginning to look like a bloodhound.

"Well, let's just say I don't worry about you as much anymore."

David took a sip of his coffee and his father lit a cigar.

"When I was kid, probably fifteen or so, I went to visit my grandfather, your great-grandfather Jim, up in the Adirondacks. I stayed up there for nearly the whole summer working on his small farm, feeding the chickens and pigs, baling hay, cleaning out pens, tramping through the woods, jumping off the dock into the lake …"

He sat back in his seat. "There were hardly any neighbors around, much less kids my age. Yet it was the best summer I ever had. By August, I was as strong as an ox, or at least thought I was. And I had a great farmer's tan."

They laughed.

"Well, one night my grandma went to bed early, and Jim starting drinking whiskey. He would often have a drink after dinner, but the only time I saw him drunk was after Grandma went to bed. Anyway, he told me that I had worked like a man that summer, so I deserved to have a drink like a man."

"You never told me that before." I watched the cigar smoke swirl around his face.

"Yes. I know. Your great-granddad got sauced that night, and told me an interesting story. He said that when he was young, his father had died and he inherited the farm. He was working it hard, but still had a lot to learn. Well, he said his father came to him in dreams and explained to him the things he needed to know. He said the dreams lasted about three weeks. He even said one night he dreamt he was out at the barn with his dad teaching him how to fix the tractor. When he woke up, he was lying right next to the damned thing."

"That's very odd."

"My granddad believed it was a gift. I thought he was a goddamned nut, until very recently." He gave David a knowing nod. "You have a gift, David. Just like your great-grandfather. I'm not sure how this gift will help you. I certainly don't have anything I can really teach. Not that would be of any use to you. I've been selfish, and keeping time by telling you stories around the kitchen table."

"I've enjoyed the stories, Dad."

"It's not everyone that can talk to the dead, son. But it's not healthy for you. I need to move on, and you need to get on with living. It doesn't do any good for you to sit around and talk to the dead. So do me a favor."

"Sure." David felt removed from what his dad was saying, as if he was reading a story about someone else.

"Get the hell out of this junk joint and get on living with Haddie. She's quite a prize. And she makes you want to thrive. You've got that spark in you now."

David realized his psyche had created that story about his granddad to make him feel more … sane. Or, at least not alone in his insanity. He stared out the window at the undulating grays and whites of the clouds. He checked out of Tippingdale the next day. And he had no more dreams of his dad. And he was happy with Haddie. She completed him. Maybe that's why he had that spark once he met her. He was empty before her and she provided the fuel to get him going.

He often wondered why the dreams stopped. He thought it was because after that last dream he stopped obsessing about his father. And so he faded from his memory where dreams are manufactured. He was sure of that now because it worked with Haddie. He had pushed her from his memory where dreams are made, and so now he slept in peace.

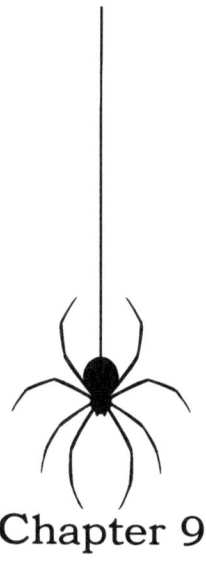

Chapter 9

"Mother fuckin' sonuvabitch!"

David was leaning against the stairwell with the oak rolltop desk pressing against him. The desk did not want to make that tight turn. It was stuck on a landing one flight below his apartment. Those damn union movers. Laziest workers he ever met. The elevator was out in his new apartment building and they wouldn't haul it up the stairs.

"How about an extra hundred?"

The two guys had stared at each other like it would result in a heart attack. He probably shouldn't have told him they were a bunch of wimps. He was lucky a policeman happened along or they would have splattered him on the pavement. Those guys were each pushing 250 pounds if they weighed an ounce. Instead of beating him black and blue, they unceremoniously dumped his new desk onto the sidewalk and drove away. It was a cold morning, and the movers had steam coming out of their mouths like freight trains as they dumped it and sped off. David glanced at the policeman and he retreated and sped off almost as fast, as if he thought David might ask *him* to help haul the desk up to his fourth-floor apartment.

David stood there, a hand on his new desk in the middle of uptown near the park. The apartment had a clerk, but no other help. She was skinny, barely a hundred pounds, not more than twenty years old, and was reading the latest Nora Roberts novel. She offered to call a friend to see if he could help lug the desk up the stairs. David thanked her but said everything was taken care of. That's when he called Gil. Gil was a trooper. He was there in less than thirty minutes, dressed in gray sweats with the hood up and wool gloves on his long, bony hands.

"Can you move your end a little more to the right?" David was still smushed against the wall.

"I'll try. This thing is a behemoth." Gil was dripping through his heavy sweats, and cursed himself for removing his gloves and stuffing them in his pockets. His fingers were aching and cramped.

"If I'd known oak was going to be this heavy, I would've had it made out of pine," David grunted.

"Or Styrofoam," Gil added.

Gil heaved the desk to the right, until there was barely an inch between his hand and the wall. David squeezed out and scurried backwards, taking small steps like a Japanese woman with bound feet, to the final flight of stairs. David's arms screamed at him as he held them waist high, the edge of the desk digging into his hands, his legs shaking with each step up the stairs. Near the top, he felt his body tip forward and his right leg shake uncontrollably. He hunched over and caught himself by dropping his left foot to a lower stair. Gil looked up at him as the desk shook from side to side.

"I've got it," David reassured him.

"I hope so. This monster will crush me into a pancake."

"Not all of you. You're too tall," David grunted. "Your feet will stick out like the wicked witch of the east when Dorothy's house fell on her."

"That's a pleasant thought."

They lowered the desk to the floor at the top of the landing. David shook his hands and they slowly turned from pearly white back to bright red. He rubbed his arms and glanced down the hall. His apartment was less than fifty feet away.

"We're almost there," David said.

Gil jeered. "You said that back on the second floor."

"Yeah, well, I mean it this time."

"Let's get it over with. I want one of those beers you promised me."

They picked up the desk and hauled it down the hall. David thought it was funny that his arm muscles always knew when he was almost finished carrying something heavy. They always gave out right at the end. The desk dropped with a small thud. David pulled out his keys, and his hands shaking from the effort, found the right one and slipped it into the lock. They dragged the desk through to the main room.

"This is good."

David saw the gleam in Gil's eyes as he surveyed the apartment. It was approximately one thousand square feet, "large for the price," the saleslady had said. The main room had wood flooring, and at the far end were floor to ceiling windows. Off to the left was a kitchen large enough for both a small dining table and a butcher block island. The appliances were all stainless steel, the cabinets maple, and the floor granite tile. To the right was a bedroom with a king-sized bed and a walk-in closet covered with floor to ceiling mirrors. David wasn't crazy about the mirrors, but he could have those removed eventually. The room smelled of fresh leather from the new couch and matching chairs.

Gil let out a soft whistle and walked over to the windows. The direct view was of a taller apartment building across the street, but if he pressed the side of his face to the glass, Central Park was only two short blocks away.

"This is sweet."

David surveyed the apartment and possible locations for the monstrosity they just dragged up the stairs. Even if he wasn't a writer, he'd sure look like one sitting at this desk. It was sturdy oak, and he made sure the designers placed real wood in the bottom and back of the drawers, not cheap plywood or veneered particleboard. The rolltop portion easily opened and closed, yet he could stop it at any point along the way and it never slipped. The legs were straight and clawed at the bottom. As he stared at it, he realized he needed a good chair to place in front of it.

"Where's my beer?"

David looked up from the desk. "Hey, I'm in deep thought over here."

"Well, I'm in deep thirst over here." Gil strode over to the refrigerator and pulled out a 12 Horse Ale. "You want one?"

"Sure."

David pried his eyes from the desk and grabbed the beer. Gil dropped to the couch and David sat across from him in the leather chair. He gazed beyond Gil at the desk and smiled. His arms and legs ached and would probably be sore tomorrow, but right now his body buzzed with energy. He took a sip of his beer and thought how good his life was. Sales were over 1,000,000 copies and accelerating at over 100,000 per week. *Hardcover* copies. He was thinking of doing a few select readings. His alma mater called him to see if he would guest lecture. The *New York Times* interviewed him. And the young girl clerk downstairs kept eyeing him and giggling when he walked by.

Mary Lamb was possessed. She attended to every detail for his readings, scored interviews, and generally kept the buzz going on the novel. "A Kiss During Mourning" will never die! That was her mantra. Their relationship had evolved too. She had stopped flirting with him, especially after seeing a young lady, disheveled and still a bit tipsy, come out of his room in Tulsa the morning of their flight home. Their relationship evolved into a mutual respect for their individual talents, a symbiotic relationship that added up to a lot of money. And David would need that money for this new apartment, plus all the things he suddenly felt he needed, like the handmade desk and the Guzman pencil drawing on the living room wall. He would have to point it out and mention the price he paid, because Gil would have no idea of its value.

Gil looked around the apartment again and then held out his bottle. "A toast."

David stood up and clanked bottles.

"To Haddie," Gil said.

He had just meant it to be a friendly toast, but it dug into David like claws. David did not want to think about Haddie. For his sanity, and now also his pocketbook. For obvious reasons, he did not want anyone to know she had written "A Kiss During Mourning." And Gil knew.

"You look a little pale, Dave. Are you OK?"

David nodded and focused on Gil. "Yeah, I'm fine. Just a lot has been going on, you know?"

"I bet." Gil sat forward.

David thought about the double entendre in his dedication at the front of "A Kiss During Mourning." He wrote, *"To my beloved Haddie, the true creator of this novel."* Although everyone took it to be a metaphor, one lady asked him about it during his readings. She wanted to know who Haddie was and what he meant by "the true creator." David had carefully crafted his response. "Haddie was my wife," he said, "and she showed me the way." He left it at that, and no one pressed him further.

"Have you decided on a charity in dedication to her?" Gil asked.

David hadn't, though he remembered telling Gil it was in the plans if the novel was published. He never thought it would sell like hotcakes, and then once sales took off, he had been so busy marketing the novel, and buying things, that he had barely considered a charity. His face turned red.

"Oh, there are so many. But, I'll decide soon." David took a swig and wiped his mouth. He stood and walked over to the window, gazing at the balconies across the street. "You know, I never thought the book would create such a sensation. It's grown into a monster. A monster that could eat me if it got out that I didn't write it."

"No one knows, though, right?"

David turned. "You're one of the few."

"Shit, Dave, I'm not telling anyone." Gil regarded his friend. "And don't overreact. I think the whole story is ... well ... heartwarming."

"The lawyers won't see it that way. I could be accused of fraud, plagiarism, whatever." David began pacing the floor. He had told Gil too much. He should have kept quiet about it.

"You were going to tell everyone the truth, eventually, right? Get a publicist. Spin it right, and nobody can touch you."

David stopped and stared back out the window. *Would* Haddie begrudge him this? Probably. She'd probably roll over in her grave if she knew his intentions of riding the celebrity wave and enjoying the money for himself. But he couldn't think about Haddie. That was Tippingdale territory.

"You believe me, don't you?" Gil asked.

David wiped the sweat from his forehead. What was he thinking? Gil had just helped him lug a three-hundred-pound desk up four floors and now he's grilling him. His overactive imagination was clocking overtime. David stretched his neck and dropped his shoulders. Gil was smart and a good friend. He didn't need to worry about him.

David turned, sighed, and smiled at Gil. "Of course I do." He looked at the bottle in his hands. "You look empty."

"Yeah." Gil watched David cross the room, downing his beer.

"Then let's have another."

David opened the refrigerator. There was only one beer left. He pulled out the bottle and poured part of the beer in a glass and gave the bottle, still more than half full, to Gil.

"We'll have to get some more."

Gil expressed an ironic smile. "You're not going to get me drunk and pull an Edgar Allan Poe and seal me up in the wall, are you?"

"Ah, no," David said, with a wave of his hand. "I'll poison you. Much cleaner. How about some dinner?"

"Sounds good to me. Stephanie is out of town this weekend."

"How are things going for you two?" David sat back down in the leather chair.

"Pretty good. She keeps me amused."

David laughed. "That doesn't sound serious."

Gil shrugged and sipped his beer. "She doesn't think it is."

David shrugged it off. Obviously, Gil's relationship wasn't going well. But David wouldn't ask about it. When Gil was ready to talk, he would, and David would listen. He reached for the phone.

"I have an idea. Let's go out to dinner to Merle's. I'm buying."

"Shit, Dave, it takes weeks to get into that place. I tried to take Stephanie there a month ago."

"Let's see." David picked up the phone and connected to the restaurant. "Good afternoon. I'd like to make a reservation for two at six thirty, please."

"We have nothing available, sir," the man sniffed.

Oh, not one of those snooty reservationists. The last time David came here Mary had made the arrangements. Everyone was polite and attentive. He even met the owner, who stopped by to ask how the food was and complimented David on his novel. His wife was a big fan. He even autographed a napkin for him.

"Oh," David answered. "This is David East. Is the manager there?"

"I am the manager, sir. Did you say you were David East?" The man had an annoying nasal accent.

"Yes," David said.

"The writer?"

"Yes."

David heard a shuffling of papers, and the nasal man cleared his throat. David wished he would clear his nasal passages. He pictured the nasal man as a little twerp in a penguin suit. Perhaps he was bowlegged, too, and waddled when he walked.

"Mr. East, it looks like we just had a cancellation. We'll see you at six thirty, sir."

"Thank you." David closed his phone.

Gil looked at him, his head cocked to one side, like Pudgie did when he was expecting a treat but it had yet to materialize.

"We're set." David eyed Gil in his sweats. "But you're going to have to change."

David had reasons to select Merle's besides the good food. Mary told him it was the place to be seen, and with "A Kiss During Mourning" approaching #1 on the *New York Times* best seller list, now was the time to be seen. Photographers hung out at this restaurant in droves, and getting his picture in one of the tabloids would be publicity. "No publicity is bad publicity," she said, "especially if you're a writer." David was a bit surprised that the maitre d' had recognized his name. They probably kept a list of notables and up-and-comers at their podium when potential guests name-dropped. And having the owner's wife as a fan didn't hurt either.

I must be on the list, David thought. Gil had left to change clothes and would meet him at the restaurant. David was now looking the part, wearing carefully choreographed clothes that Mary had picked out for him for the readings. His shirt and pants were ironed. Mary had insisted that he do that before going any place special. And his shoes were so highly polished he could see his reflection in them. Polishing his shoes came naturally. Ironing his clothes took a little work, and a few lessons from Mary. He slipped a sport coat on. That would be sufficient, he surmised. He was a *writer* after all.

As he stepped out of his bedroom, he felt the desk's presence. It seemed to fill up the living area, its deeply grained wood and classic lines proclaiming its territory. This was one of David's tools, a significant one to practice his craft. At least it would be if he was a writer. It loomed against the wall, daring him to come over, have a seat, and produce. *Produce.* David felt sweat on his neck. He bought it for effect. To impress anyone who might walk into his home that this is where he practiced his craft. Yet, for him it wasn't a tool. It was a trophy. He won the lottery. He had married into greatness. And now he reaped the benefits, and with his winnings, he bought this trophy to impress all who entered.

David glanced at his watch, shook his head, and walked out the door.

The restaurant was busy for a Sunday evening. The décor was overstated in gargoyles and red velvet. David still saw spots from the camera flashes when he stepped out of the taxi. Perhaps he should have taken a limo? Too ostentatious. Maybe if David had a lady with him. If he stepped out of a limo with Gil, that would have been too weird. Gil would've gotten a kick out of it, but the tabloids would probably assume he was some sort of boy toy. David chuckled to himself. In this town, that might actually *help* his career. They walked inside where the maitre d', much taller than David had expected, was dressed in a dark silk suit, and all the wait staff wore bow ties with white shirts and black slacks. They were promptly seated, and David tried not to stare, glancing out of the corner of his eyes this way and that at who might be dining. He recognized a local politician sitting with someone who was probably not his wife, and at the far end, a young actor that he had seen in a movie recently.

Gil looked around the restaurant and quietly whistled. "You did say you were paying, right?"

David laughed. "I'm gonna have to sell a million more books to pay for this."

The waiter came over and discussed the specials and they both ordered beers. As he walked away, David noticed an older lady walking toward him. She walked with an air of arrogance, her legs cutting a large swath of dominance around her. Her head was up, emphasizing her hawkish nose, and her penetrating eyes made him shift in his seat.

David stood. "Ms. Parker. Lovely to see you." He shook her hand, careful to make it with a firm grip. Gil stood up as well.

Ms. Parker ignored Gil. David glanced briefly at the tortured Mr. Parker seated at a corner table.

"Mr. East, I see your book is selling well."

"Yes." He felt himself turn red. "I have been very fortunate."

"Indeed," Ms. Parker said. "Did you read my review?"

How could David not? Pieces of it adorned the second printing. It was extremely complimentary.

"Yes, I did, and I am very grateful for your opinion." David smiled. And why not? He was happy. And Ms. Parker's review was instrumental in getting romance readers to pick it up.

"Are you?" A thin smile spread across Ms. Parker's face. For a moment, David was reminded of the Grinch. One of the songs sung by Boris Karloff briefly meandered through his brain.

Ms. Parker continued. "You must read it more carefully, David. It really is one of my favorites."

David scratched his chest and glanced at Gil, who was trying to be invisible. "Um … OK."

"I really can't wait until your next one. Are you busy writing a sequel?" Ms. Parker was smiling ever so broadly.

"I … I don't know. I've been so busy with readings …"

"I imagine Mary is being very patient with you. Being a new writer and all. I happened upon her the other day, and she briefly mentioned that you had signed a *three*-book deal. That's why I wondered. They say many writers have a sophomore jinx, or that they have only one book in them. I call it 'Harper Lee syndrome.' But I'm sure you have another great book in you. Any author that could write a romantic masterpiece such as "A Kiss During Mourning" should have plenty of ideas for an encore." Ms. Parker licked her lips, as if savoring every word.

David felt his stomach turn and rise into his chest cavity, pushing his lungs into his ribs and cutting off his air supply. A *three*-book deal? Is that what he had signed? He and Mary had chatted about another book. But, he honestly couldn't remember actually being on the hook for another one. He felt his skin turn clammy.

"Mr. East, are you OK? You suddenly look a bit ... peaked?" Ms. Parker stood there, her nostrils expanding, taking in his scent.

David rested a hand on the back of his chair. "Yes, I'm fine, Ms. Parker. Thank you."

"You are so welcome, Mr. East. Enjoy your dinner." She slowly turned, cutting her way back to her table. Mr. Parker looked up with wide eyes, as if he was about to roll onto his back and pee his pants.

David and Gil sat back down.

"One of your adoring fans?" Gil asked.

"I'm not sure," he said honestly.

Gil picked up his menu. "Well, now that the drama is over, what's for dinner? I'm starving."

David picked up his menu, and although he was sure he had been hungry when they walked in, he no longer had any appetite.

David tried to be pleasant and stay relaxed during dinner. The six beers helped with that. He tried to fend off the sickening feeling about having to produce another book, thinking he would just discuss it with Mary in the morning, or even tonight if it wasn't too late. Was he on the hook for another book? And if so, what if he couldn't *produce?* Would that be a breach of contract? Or, would he be laughed out of the exclusive club he had just joined? A world of apartments near Central Park, good tables at the hottest restaurants, and hangers-on. He liked this world. It was comfortable. Everyone was *nice*.

He was making great money, but that would dry up quickly if he screwed this up. And what if it was found out he stole his wife's work? He could lose everything. A scandal. He'd be anathema. If that happened, he might as well join O.J. down in Florida.

David saw Ms. Parker as she was walking out of the restaurant, her husband in tow. He suddenly felt like he had been filled with ice cubes.

Did she know he didn't write the book? She seemed to enjoy telling him he needed to write two more books. Was it just his overactive imagination kicking in again? How could she know? Gil knew. But Parker didn't know him. What about that other lady? Beasley. Could Parker have possibly spoken to her?

That was possible. Beasley was a writer's agent, after all. And they were both, probably not the same age, but from the same generation, the Victorian Era, or Cretaceous, or whatever.

As he looked out at the sea of manicured hair and haute cuisine, his mind drifted to Haddie. This time he let it flow. To a simpler time before Manhattan. When they were still upstate, and took vacations in the Adirondacks. He could see her on the front wooden porch, her long legs reaching out, her feet on the railing. He could almost feel her touch as she reached out to him, her smile, inviting, almost daring, at a time before they had a care in the world. Or so it seemed.

David returned to his apartment a little after nine and soon wished he had stayed at the restaurant. Alone, there was no escaping his thoughts. No escaping his overactive imagination digging deeper and deeper pits of despair and woe. He paced his apartment, calling Mary Lamb several times but only getting voice mail. Each time he hung up and cursed. If he could talk to her, maybe she could put him at ease. She was quite good at that. After the initial reading, she helped calm him and organize the endless details of travel and lodging. The beer high had long disappeared, leaving only a dry sour taste in his mouth. He started to punch in Cat's number, but stopped. She must have been back by now. In any event, she had definitely received his many messages and was not returning his calls. That road was a dead end.

He finally gave up, brushed his teeth and went to bed, though certain that rest would not come easy. It didn't. He cycled through his side to back to other side many times while lying there before falling into a dreamless sleep.

Mary answered on the sixth ring. "Hello?"

"Mary, it's David." He tried to speak casually, but felt the tension in his voice.

"What time is it?"

A shuffling of items came through the receiver, as if she was trying to get a better view of her bedside clock. He had woken her.

"It's early," David said, trying to act cheerful, as if he called her every morning at this time.

"Oh, my God," she said. "Writers!"

"I was just curious," David said. "I saw Ms. Parker last night, and she said she had talked with you."

Mary sniffled. "Yes. Anytime she wants. You always talk to Parker when she wants."

"She mentioned I had a three-book deal with Entropy Home." David tried to act casual and hung the last word as if he had more to say, thinking if it was wrong she would have time to speak, and if it was right, he could make it sound like he hadn't finished his thought, instead of just being a complete dummy not knowing what his contract said. He really wished he could have found a copy of it before he called. He looked for an hour after he woke but with no luck.

She was silent.

"So," David said slowly, "if I'm on the hook for a second book ..." He hesitated.

She was silent.

"When would the publisher want to have it completed?" he finished.

"Actually, David," she started, "I was going to call you about that. At a more reasonable hour, of course."

David laughed nervously, and Mary chuckled, too.

"The contract states you will produce books two and three ready for publication within two years of the previous novel publishing date. That's typical for romance novelist contracts. Since we published your first book last summer we have about a year and a half to publish the second book."

David took a deep breath and let it out. A year and a half was practically a lifetime away. Anything could happen in that amount of time. He could die. Or, be stricken with some kind of dementia. Or, maybe even become a romance novelist.

Mary continued. "Which means I need a clean draft by summer. It's December now, so ... in about six months."

"Six months?" He said the words before he could stop them. David clutched the phone. He sounded a bit desperate. Six months was not a lifetime away.

"Don't worry. I know you've been busy with the readings and marketing "A Kiss During Mourning." Because you're a new writer, I didn't want to pressure you. But, now that the readings are over, it's time to get to work. I've done a lot of editing. If you like, send me a rough draft in the spring, and I'll help you edit, and we'll have a clean draft for the publisher by summer. How does that sound?"

In spring? David brought his free hand up to his ample forehead. "Uh, I dunno ..."

"Please. David. Don't worry. It *has* been six months since your first novel was published, after all. I'm sure by now, that you've been writing and have some great ideas for your next project."

David remained quiet.

"David? You have been writing, haven't you? I mean, you are a writer, that's what you do."

David glanced at his rolltop desk. The top was slightly open in a thin grin. "Of course. I've been thinking about it a lot ... I mean, I have a lot of ideas I've jotted down." *Jotted down?* David grimaced.

Mary hesitated before she spoke. "Ah, well, good then. I think it would be a great idea if you sent along a rough draft in the spring, OK? Now, chop chop, off to work you go."

David closed his eyes. "OK. If you need to talk to me, you know where I'll be."

Shit.

A short twelve hours ago he was on top of the world. Now he had major stress. He sat down in his plush leather couch and gazed around his expensive apartment. He couldn't lose this. He would have to write a romance novel. He would have to try. David sat forward and rubbed his face with both hands. He lifted his head, sat back, and folded his hands on his lap. How hard could it be?

David stepped out of the shower and spent extra time towel-drying his hair. It was only eighteen degrees outside. He had decided to run down to the bookstore and buy a few romance novels to get ideas for his next book. He had briefly toyed with the idea of not drying his hair so he could catch pneumonia and maybe not have to write again ... er ... at all. Finally, he decided that the last thing he needed on top of all this stress was pneumonia. With his luck he'd survive it.

He stepped out into the cold with a scarf wrapped around his face. His breath warmed the scarf before escaping into the dry air. He kept his hands rolled up into fists inside his pockets. Rush hour was over, and he had the sidewalks to himself. No one recognized him with the scarf wrapped around him, and considering his goal for the day, he was glad. He felt a bit like a spy walking down the streets, making his way to the bookstore to retrieve romance novels that he could steal ... gain inspiration from. He found himself furtively glancing from side to side, and continuously telling himself to stop and just get on with it. He was a writer, for chrissakes, and writers had to read. Grabbing several romance novels shouldn't raise an eyebrow. It was his genre, after all. He stopped at the corner for a red light. He looked both ways and the streets were so empty he walked against the light. It was something he never did.

I'm becoming a deviant.

David laughed at himself and soon turned the corner to the bookstore. He looked at the table where he and Haddie used to sit. As he walked through the door, the warm air rushed around him, bringing welcome relief from the frigid outside air. He thought of Cat as he unwrapped his scarf, feeling like a mummy removing his bandages. He couldn't help but look for her as he stood inside the door. She had fallen off the face of the earth. She left for her Polynesian vacation and never came back, or came back and simply forgot all about him or didn't want to see him. It felt odd to him, like a dumped lover, and he preferred to think that she enjoyed the islands so much she never came back, but checked her voice mail once in a while for kicks.

He walked down an aisle to his normal table to hang his coat over a chair, but when he emerged from the books, a young couple was sitting in his place. They were cream skinned with large soft eyes, and didn't even notice him, even when he stood there for several seconds with his mouth open in disbelief. In the many years that he had come with

Haddie, and then alone or met Cat, he couldn't remember a single instance of not having that table. David turned and skulked off and dropped his coat onto a table near the self-help section.

David bypassed the cheap romance serials in paperback on a metal turn stand and instead walked down the aisle that contained hardbacks. He perused the aisle, surveying the rows, looking for a book that might catch his eye. He smelled the estrogen. A lady halfway down the aisle stared at him.

Oh shit.

She walked toward him, staring at him as if the closer she got, the more in focus he became. "Are you David East?"

He smiled. "Yes. I am."

"It's such a pleasure. I loved your book."

"Thank you very much. I appreciate it." *Please leave. I need some privacy for this.*

She looked around at the books and back at him. Her eyes seemed to be full of questions. David stood patiently, his hands folded in front of him. She bit her lip, and then suddenly grabbed a book off the shelf. "Would you sign this for me?"

He looked down at "A Kiss During Mourning." For some reason, it surprised him that it was in this aisle.

"I mean, I'll buy it," she added quickly.

"Sure," David replied. He patted his clothes and realized he did not have a pen, but the lady was already rummaging through her purse.

"Ah," she said, "here you are." She handed him the pen, her hand shaking slightly.

He took it, and after several false attempts that left indentations in the paper, the ink flowed, and David wrote his signature on the page.

"Thank you so much," she said, clutching the book to her breast. She bit her lip again. "I imagine you're a big romance fan. Do you have a recommendation?"

David first thought about grabbing any book off the shelf and placing it in her hands, saying it was the best romance novel written since *Romeo and Juliet.* But, he shrugged it off, not wanting to be mean to a fan. Anyway, he wasn't sure if *Romeo and Juliet* had ever been a novel.

"Hmm," he murmured, a hand resting on his chin, a finger tapping his cheek. "There are so many. What do you think?"

He had just blurted that out without really thinking. The lady's eyes widened like she had just been asked a challenging question on a doctoral oral exam, and took her free hand and waved it in front of her face. "Me? You want my opinion?"

David nodded. Accidental pure brilliance. She obviously was a romance novel fan. She could actually point *him* to a good book. He'd get at least one good example. And then he could work on some variety with uneducated guesses.

"Oh my gosh. Well ..." she wrung her hands. "I love Jordan Dane, Catherine Jones, Stephenie Meyer, Mary Stewart ...oh, and who could forget the grandmother of all romance writers. Jane Austen!"

Jane Austen was a romance writer? David cocked his head. Wasn't she from like, the medieval times? They were too busy working their land and being filthy and starving to write romance. A book was shoved into his hands. *Passionate Nights and Sweaty Days.*

"Try this one. The girl, the heroine, is very feisty. You'll love it."

David looked down the aisle. There was another woman, with jowls, staring at him. This could get out of control. "Thank you," he said hastily, and quickly walked the other way and slipped into science fiction. No one would notice him there.

He sat on a foot stool, his butt seeping over the sides, and leaned back against a shelf. A thin boy with acne and a vintage Star Wars T-shirt walked by, perusing the titles. David thought back to when he was a teenager. He never read, and wouldn't have been caught dead in a bookstore. He did enjoy building models; cars, bridges, planes, just about anything. Why didn't he become an engineer? He loved to build things, and once had an honorable mention at the State Fair. He almost earned a place at Nationals. But, it didn't matter. That was the year he caught mono. Why not an engineer? Chemistry. He hated chemistry. Those symbols and equilibrium equations made him cringe. Now, math was OK. Math was great. And that was his ticket to accounting.

"There you are!"

David stirred from his daydream. Four women came rushing into the science fiction section, trapping him in the covey. The youngest was younger than him, the oldest could have been his mother. Each of them had two or three books in their hands. One was the woman who gave him *Passionate Nights and Sweaty Days.* Jowl lady was there, clutching three books. The younger lady had two, looking at him through her thick spectacles. The oldest one had a thick slab of skin hanging from her neck, like a turkey. They wrestled for position, pushing books into his hands, shouting recommendations to be heard over the others.

David couldn't take his eyes off the turkey neck.

It reminded him of a day he spent with Haddie at their Adirondack cabin. It was late spring and they took a hike down a trail to a small clearing dotted with apple trees. They were halfway through a picnic lunch when a flock of turkeys entered the clearing. A big tom with a long beard strutted around, showing off his plumage to the hens. There were nine or ten, and they were clucking and calling, maneuvering closer to David and Haddie, who froze mid-bite and watched them. The turkeys circled around the clearing and huddled maybe ten yards away. The turkeys were full of spring fever, oblivious to the hungry pair at their picnic. David and Haddie watched them for fifteen minutes before they finally flew off.

"Excuse me," a man said, rather loudly.

The women turned from David and looked at the man. He wore an official bookstore shirt. He must have heard the noise and came by to see what was going on. David looked at him and shrugged.

"Could you please quiet down?" he said quietly. "And let's give Mr. East some peace. We'd hate to have him shopping at another bookstore, wouldn't we?"

There was a gasp from the women, a final, fleeting glance at David, and then a mass migration from the science fiction section. David stood there, grasping eight books, watching them disperse.

"Would you like me to reshelf those for you, Mr. East?"

David stared down at his bundle.

Those ladies just saved me several hours of mundane research.

"I'll take all of them," David said.

The man's eyebrows shortened his forehead. "Really? Well, uh …

let me take them from you. When you're ready I'll ring you out and you can pick them up."

David handed the books to the employee and walked over to get his coat from the chair on the other side of the store. He turned the corner of an aisle and came face to face with Cat.

"Oh, Cat. Hello."

Her face hardened. David was so close he saw her pupils shrink. Cat's mouth opened and closed quickly into a grimace. David's heart pumped in his chest. Whatever friendship, or anything else they might have had, was gone. Those were hateful eyes staring at him.

"Hello, David," she said coldly. "I can't talk now."

David knew that if he was going to find out what went wrong, now was the time, no mater how much it hurt. He touched her shoulder, and she slipped it off with a shrug.

"What's the matter, Cat? I thought you were going to call me when you got back? What'd I do?"

Cat looked past him and took a step sideways. David stepped with her. When she looked up at him, her eyes were on fire. "How *could* you? How could you, David?"

"What?" David spread his arms. But he had a cold feeling inside.

"That was *her* novel," she growled. "She wrote it, you scumbag. I read the interviews, the articles. You took credit for everything *she* did."

David dropped his hands to his side. She knew. So, Haddie had told her, but not him. She was mad, and it hurt to hear what she was saying. But even more than that. There was something bitter, real hatred in her voice. At that moment, he felt that if they were alone and she had a gun, she would have shot him in the head. He quickly looked around. Although a few people were looking in their direction, he didn't think anyone had overheard their conversation.

"Don't ever talk to me again. Don't call … don't … anything!"

Cat stormed out of the store, her black woolen coat billowing behind her.

It was a long walk in the cold. David could feel the frigid air through his gloves, stinging like pins and needles, as he carried the books down the sidewalk. Twenty-four hours ago he was walking on air, the world was his oyster, sowing his oats and all that. Now he actually had to write a novel, and a girl he cared about thought he was a scumbag. He felt awful about Cat, the way she looked at him when she said those things. Hatred. There was no overcoming that. That was a closed door. Now that he knew she knew that Haddie had written the novel, it was even more important that he write a sequel, and do it well. Although Cat knew, it didn't appear she had told anyone, yet. At least she hadn't gone public with it. But she could at anytime. She certainly seemed angry enough to expose him for what he really was, a fraud. And there was still Ms. Beasley and possibly Parker who knew as well. And Gil! He'd forever wonder when the ax was going to fall. When it would hit the papers that he stole his wife's work. He could lose it all. Lawsuits. He shivered. God, maybe the cops would even think he murdered Haddie, just to steal her work.

Jesus Christ, David. Settle down.

He breathed in and out deeply, the dry cold air making him cough. His only hope now was to write a good book. If he did that, he could counteract his detractors. It was time to act. And the sooner the better. Before all hell broke loose.

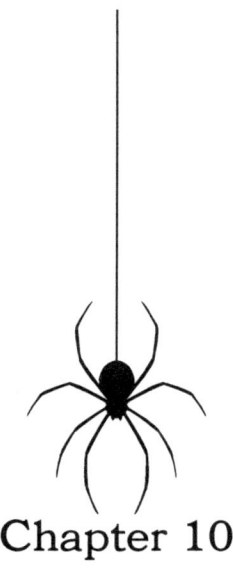

Chapter 10

"WHERE DO I START?" DAVID MUMBLED, SITTING IN A CHAIR NOT WORTHY OF his oak rolltop desk. The books were splayed out before him. He picked up each one and turned it over in his hands. Illustrations of shapely legs, buffed men, and windswept hair; cleavage, roses, a stormy sea. It was enough to make David lose his breakfast, if he had eaten one. One had a drawing of prim and proper English types. Jane Austen's "Pride and Prejudice". He had at least heard of that. He contemplated reading that one first, but then concluded it was too old fashioned to be of any use. The other seven varied from thirty to a few years old. He placed Austen's novel to the side and decided to read each of the remaining seven novels, from oldest to newest. He would take notes of the plot and themes of each one. He was hoping that based on his notes, he could construct a novel to rival "A Kiss During Mourning."

As he stared at the books, he realized that besides his wife's novel, he had not read more than a magazine in over a decade. What was the last book he read? Maybe something by Stephen Hawking?

Yes, that was following the movie Dr. Hawking had made. David and Haddie had gone to a matinee. They came out of there and bought his book and David read it in three days. It was physics for dummies; black holes, time warps, and all that space junk. He even went out and bought a cheap telescope and took it to their Adirondack cabin. They would go up almost every weekend, but it was such a wet, gloomy summer that it wasn't until late fall that the skies were clear enough to see anything. He stood out in the yard tracking down planets, adjusting the scope, his hands burning from the cold. When he successfully spotted an interesting object he would run inside and drag Haddie out; she wearing purple woolen mittens and holding hot chocolate, and he praying that the wind hadn't knocked the telescope out of alignment. He smiled when he remembered finding the Orion nebula. He ran inside, exclaiming he had found the object in the celestial archer's crotch. Haddie rose from her warm comfortable seat out into the cold night, took one look through the eyepiece, and remarked, "It's a fuzzy white blob."

He used that telescope all winter, even in the bitter cold, looking at the stars. However, as summer returned, it was like watching reruns. The same planets and objects came into view as the year before. He lamented he hadn't bought a high-end telescope, which would have made the objects more interesting. Sometimes a meteor shower would liven up the night sky, though most of them turned out to be duds. It wasn't long before astronomy fell by the wayside in the East home.

David let Haddie float into his memory, her heavy woolen coat and mittens, the high collar that bunched her red hair so it framed her beautiful face. How warm she felt in the bitter Adirondack winter when he held her, how he felt her warmth through all her thick garments. It was a radiant heat he could almost feel now, alone in his apartment just a few short blocks from Central Park.

He shook his head, stood and stretched. It wasn't healthy to think of her. He gazed down at the books, selected one, sat down on the leather couch, and started reading.

David was amazed how much one could read when it was a full-time job. Within two weeks, the crisp white pages of the seven books were dog-eared and coffee-stained. Days were constant. Breakfast while reading, then more reading until lunch. After lunch more reading, and then dinner. The evenings were filled with poring over notes taken while reading that day, finding common threads or themes, changing trends over the decades, and plot.

David did make time every day to go to the gym and lift weights to boost his testosterone. Reading the estrogen-charged books day after day, he worried that without the daily workouts, he would develop man boobs and a penchant for Broadway musicals.

The two weeks went by quickly. He took one evening off to have dinner with Gil at a Chinese restaurant down the street. The rest of the time was devoted to learning the inner workings of romance novels. He hardly had time to think of anything else during that time, but now, in the early morning, he sat at his window, and watched a couple bundled in wool and leather stroll down the street toward the park. He thought how different his life had been a year ago.

A wave of loneliness poured over him, filling every pore in his skin. Since Haddie died life was empty. He had one friend, Gil. He had met no woman of consequence. At least none that was still talking to him. And to keep his sanity he couldn't even think of Haddie. He couldn't relish her in his memories. At least not for more than a few moments. He didn't dare. It had been many months since he dreamt of her. Was it safe now? Could he enjoy some time with her memories, visit her grave, toast a drink to her? He had acted crazy in the few months after her death. Accusing her of all sorts of trespasses. Was that normal behavior for a spouse of the deceased? He didn't think so. But he had never been normal.

No matter. He had a task at hand. He sat on his leather couch, gazing at the large sheets of construction paper, taped together and propped against the wall. The paper was covered with volatile marker ink that wafted through the air, making him light-headed. The analysis outlined the salient features of each novel in a table: columns headed with characters, plot, theme, and anecdotes. The rows were filled in with observations from each book. As he waded through the romance morass, he began to see trends in the genre, or at least among his collection of stories. This is what he was looking for. Trends that he himself could follow as guidelines. A safe story. One that would sell, and he wouldn't make a fool of himself.

The plots were the most obvious. Each story typically started with a beautiful heroine, who had no idea she was beautiful, getting into a real bind. To her rescue arrived a flawed hero, who on the outside was a rascal, but on the inside had a heart of gold, or at least formed one because of the beautiful heroine. Of course, they don't like each other at first, but they slowly find common ground, and usually end up in the sack halfway through the story. The final half is their struggle to destroy evil, though there might be some misunderstanding near the end, and the hero has to chase the heroine down at an airport or bus stop to convey his undying love. They all ended optimistically; he guessed one could say emotionally satisfying.

The characters had shared traits across the novels. The heroine is a good woman who must be true to herself to find unconditional love. Her name reflects that trait. Simple and honest. The rascal hero is different. He moves easily, and if he's especially virile, will have a last name like "Straddler" or "King." True villains were usually all bad. There aren't a lot of grays in the evil characters.

What about themes? Blooming flowers, representing blossoming love, were referred to constantly in two of the novels. Others commented on the inward struggle of the characters, representing a tug of war between the lovers. A few others really had no theme, just a lot of sex. David figured that sex might be the theme, though a bit obvious in a romance novel.

In the anecdotes section he wrote comments and summarized the story. Again, all the stories had a happy ending. The literary devices used to describe the love scenes were meant to titillate, but were not graphic, or at least not pornographic. One thing he noticed was that there were subtle changes in the heroine character from the earlier novels to ones published recently. The heroine was more empowered in the recent releases, and the hero perhaps a little more realistic, while in the older novels the heroine was weak, and saved from disaster by a dominant hero.

David folded his arms across his chest and shook his head to clear the solvent vapors from his brain. "A Kiss During Mourning" seemed to buck the trend in a few areas. Hannah was certainly empowered, leaving a trail of corpses in her wake, but was that romance? And is murder ever OK for a "good" person to commit? True, the men left for dead were all scoundrels, or at least most of them. But the ending certainly wasn't happy. What was it? What was positive about it? He bit his upper lip. All he could think of was hope. At the end there was hope. That was optimistic.

So what to do for an encore? David had settled on a sequel. He stared at his rolltop desk and the cheap chair in front of it. The desk was partially opened in that evil grin that dared him to sit at it.

Come on, Davey boy. You can talk the talk, now walk the walk. Produce!

He grabbed his laptop and sat at the desk, the rolltop looming over him. David opened his laptop, and with thousands of pages of romance streaming through his brain and the desk hanging over him like a large dead creaking tree, as if it might collapse and crush him at any moment, he began to write.

For the next three months David immersed himself in prose. There were long periods of time when he sat staring at a blank page, willing the words to appear on the monitor. To him, words did not follow a logical sequence like an equation. He could not add several words together to equal a good sentence. What were the damn rules? Why did you usually use the past tense, and then suddenly something in the present? Why did a novel have to have so many words? His head often hurt, after so many times of slapping his forehead in frustration. In fact, he had done that so many times that it was perpetually pink. But the words did come. Very slowly at first. And then over time, faster and with slightly more ease. His shoulders relaxed as the story unfolded.

He had actually finished what he considered to be a rough first draft in six weeks. For a moment or two he sat there, beaming, his pink forehead atop a goofy grin. He quickly realized it was not enough. It was only seventy pages, or about 20,000 words. That wasn't even a novella! He set it down for a few days, and got out of the apartment, took walks in the snow, visited the bookstore, and went out to dinner. When he opened the file and read his novel, he couldn't believe how ... unformed it was. Hannah was a cardboard cut out. She had no life to her. She was a skeleton. In fact, the whole story seemed like a skeleton. Twenty thousand words just wouldn't do. A novel needed at least 80,000 words; "A Kiss During Mourning" was nearly 120,000 words. He could not fathom increasing the word count to 80,000, much less 120,000. But he had to try. And that's when he came up with the plan to use "prose ideas" from the romance novels stacked on his desk to create texture to his work.

Ah, yes. This looks like a great beginning.

And then he would type.

This antagonist is pretty cool. I bet I can fit him in … somewhere.

Oooh, a chess game. That could be good. And it could have a double meaning. The critics would like that—

I like how this scene evolves. Let's see where it might go.

David lived on coffee, sleeping pills, and very loud alarm clocks. He wrote at least fourteen hours a day. His hair stuck out on the sides, and with his shirt collar up, typing violently on the keyboard, he looked like a mad pianist.

The story plot: redemption and love. Hannah learns that the detective pursuing her wasn't dead at all, but had been poisoned to a zombie state and was wandering aimlessly in a fog. Hannah finds out he's still alive and searches for him, finding that each time she atones for a murder, she comes one step closer to her true love. Being true to herself, she plunges on, tackling her demons and the wicked world. In the end, she finds happiness with her true love, and they have multiple children, a home, et cetera, et cetera.

Often when he thought of Hannah's motives, his thoughts slid to Haddie. Was he wishing he was the detective and Haddie was Hannah, and instead of going childless, they had so many kids they were outnumbered? Perhaps they would have kept the Adirondack cabin, a place to take the kids to swim and fish. He could have taken them down to the dump near Old Forge to see the bears. There were four thousand in the Adirondacks, and some of the biggest showed up at that dump. Some people even said a grizzly showed up at times, scaring off the other bears while he gorged himself on leftover twice-baked potatoes and pork chop bones. David had seen that massive boar, and knew it was just a cinnamon-colored black bear, but a rogue grizzly made a great story for the tourists. That bear was ornery. Once, when he was a kid, he waited for the bears at the dump with a group of other locals and a few tourists in lawn chairs. At dusk, a rusted out green station wagon pulled into the parking area and slammed on the brakes, lurching forward before it finally stopped. A bearded hunter, still in his orange vest, stumbled out. It was a warm evening for November and the hunter's vest was unzipped, his prominent belly hanging over his belt. Holding an almost empty whiskey bottle, and obviously drunk, he staggered toward the beast, screaming at the top of his lungs. The bear was chewing on a large hambone, cracking it easily in its mammoth jaws. David remembered those teeth. They were huge and yellowed by age. As the sun set behind the pines, the man staggered closer and closer, while the bear grinded the hambone to bite-size chunks, apparently oblivious to the intruder. It was then David learned what was meant by the term "wild animal." As the man was about to reach out and smack it a good one "to show him who's boss," the bear pivoted, slapped the drunkard to the ground, and stood over him. It happened so quickly that if David had blinked he would have missed the whole thing.

The man lay there frozen. It was severely quiet. The audience sat there transfixed. It was so quiet he could hear the bear breathing as it straddled the drunk. Its massive head was inches from the man's face, regarding him with what David swore was disgust. After a few seconds, which seemed like hours to David, and probably an eternity to the man beneath that six-hundred-pound ball of teeth and claws, the bear moved off him, brushing his face again with his front paw, and trotted off into the darkening woods. The crowd was still quiet, and when the man sat up, dazed and confused, David saw there was not a scratch on his face. Not a drop of blood. The bear had struck him softly enough and without using claws that it left no physical mark, though David knew the man would forever remember the event. As the man staggered to his feet, the smell of fresh shit filled the air.

Of course, David would have warned his kids not to provoke the bears. He lamented the loss of the bear, who was already old when David was a boy and was surely long dead. But he also lamented the loss of risk. As stupid as that drunk was, he was allowed to be stupid, to take his chances with that bear and get his brains knocked out. David was sure that now the dump was fenced to prevent bear intrusions and reduce potential encounters with humans. Save us from ourselves, and our own stupidity. No wonder earth's population was exploding. There was no longer a way to weed out the idiots.

It was March 2nd. He had expanded his novel to almost 80,000 words. He printed the 260-page manuscript, sat on the plush leather chair, and set it down on the coffee table. As he settled into the plush leather chair, a heavy weight seemed to lift off his shoulders. He had done it. It might be a bit short, he was sure it could use some editing, but at least he had a first draft. The desk sat on the other side of the room, its narrow grin sneering at his sense of accomplishment.

He sat forward. Who could he give the manuscript to before he sent it to Mary? She was a professional editor as well as an agent. But he wanted someone to look at it before he sent it on to her. There was really only one person that he could trust and was still talking to him. Gil. Although it was the obvious decision, David wrestled with it nonetheless. Gil was a numbers guy, like him. His reading was limited to *Discover* magazine and the required novels in high school. But Gil was a good friend, and David knew he'd try. Plus, he was detail oriented. Maybe he would find inconsistencies and bad grammar. Maybe.

After he gave the manuscript to Gil, David found himself anxious, as if waiting for his final grades for the school year. For the next several days he found himself wandering about Manhattan as winter let go of its grip on the city. One windy drizzly day, as he stood in a quiet part of Central Park listening to the cold rain tapping on the bare tree branches, his thoughts drifted to Haddie. As hard as he tried to push her out, he kept seeing those pleading eyes as they wheeled her through the gray metal swinging doors, where she died minutes later. When he succeeded in pushing her out of his thoughts, for moments at a time, he saw Cat's cold eyes full of hatred. The images both unnerved and depressed him. The images kept repeating themselves in a do-loop until David retreated back to the streets, full of taxis, limousines, and buses.

David invited Gil over for dinner (takeout of course), jokingly stating, "on the condition you have finished the novel." Gil, ever the trooper, said he had ploughed through the manuscript, and showed up promptly at five. David set a couple of beers, dim sum, chow mein, and fried rice on the table. When Gil walked in, David noticed that his rumpled clothes and unruly hair contrasted sharply with the neat, unwrinkled manuscript he held under his arm, with the same rubber band around it that David had placed before giving it to him. He eyed the novel as Gil placed it on the table, freeing his hands to shovel the food into a heaping pile onto his plate. David filled his own plate, sat down, and tapped the table with his fingers while Gil settled in.

David's hand shook as he lifted the chopsticks to his mouth. He was surprised how nervous he felt about Gil's take on the book. "So, how'd you like it?"

"It was good," Gil replied. He stuffed his mouth with chow mein.

David blinked twice and began tapping his fingers on the table again. "And?"

"Well," Gil started, trying to swallow the chow mein. "I'm not really an expert on romance novels. But it read all right to me."

David sat with his chopsticks halfway to his mouth, waiting for Gil to finish his thought.

Gil cleared his throat. "I never read a romance novel before, Dave. I didn't even read the signed copy of "A Kiss During Mourning" you gave me. But I'm sure your book is better than all the other crap being published out there." He quickly added, "And I like the title. "Hannah's Last Ride". That's very good."

All the other crap out there?

"Gil, did you even read it?"

Gil sat up straight and raised his hands. "Of course. I read it through the week. And, I read a lot last night because you wanted to meet today."

David watched him, his chopsticks poised in the same position.

"And I skimmed some of the parts. You know, the romance stuff—"

David dropped his food back to his plate. "It was all romance. It's a *romance* novel. Did you read any of it?"

"Yes. Honest." Gil's eyes opened wide. "I read every evening until I fell asleep."

David looked up at the ceiling. "That's a glowing endorsement."

Gil pointed his chopsticks at David. "You know what I mean."

"No, I don't," David said. He was beginning to feel he should have had dinner by himself. He took a deep breath. "Perhaps you could tell me what you liked, and what you didn't like."

Gil sat chewing his chow mein, apparently in deep thought. David stared at him and chewed on his tongue, realizing he could not get blood from a stone. His three months were up almost a week ago. He would have a few days to do any final edits, and then he would have to send it to Mary Lamb. He was surprised she hadn't called him yet. He took a deep breath. It *was* only the first draft. It wasn't going to be perfect. Of course, Haddie's work had almost been perfect. The editing was minimal on her manuscript. He had a feeling that wouldn't be the case for "Hannah's Last Ride". Well, what was Mary getting paid for, anyway? She could do some work and help edit the damn thing.

Gil continued to sit there, chewing on a new bite of chow mein.

What the hell is he thinking about? Does he think if he sits there long enough, I'll forget that I asked him a question?

"There were some funny parts," Gil said at last. "You know, the part with Hannah and the border guards."

"Good," David said. He thought that part was funny, too. "What else?"

"Um ... well," Gil said. "Some of the parts, well ..."

"Yes. What?"

"You know, the romantic parts," Gil lifted his hands and bent the forefinger and middle finger on each hand as if to put quotes around "romantic." "They were strange."

David straightened up. "What do you mean?"

"Well, I knew you wrote it. It was freaky," Gil said, shrugging.

David sighed. "Who else is going to write it? Of course I wrote it."

David examined the manuscript after Gil left. Gil had marked up grammatical corrections, though David didn't agree with many of them. He was up until after midnight sifting through the comments. He felt like he was all alone now to do battle with Mary. Although she had taken excellent care of him during the previous reading tour, pampering him and putting up with increasingly greater demands, he had the feeling she would not tolerate a lame writing effort. Although it was a first draft, it had to be semi-presentable. At least it was the right length. Sitting in a pile on his table, it at least *looked* like a novel.

In the morning, he began reading the entire manuscript in earnest. He was surprised at how well it did read. Hannah was wild and unpredictable, just like in the first novel. The action was nonstop, and David could visualize the characters clashing, escaping, and creating general havoc. However, he wasn't sure if it was because he had written it and knew what the action should look like, or that he was visualizing the action because of the writing. At any rate, he spent a couple of days reading it, marking up a few corrections, and then e-mailing it to Mary Lamb as she had instructed during their phone call. Then he called her, and she was happy to hear from him, and had asked how *he* thought the writing went. He was cheerful, feeling like he was unloading a large primate off his back and loading it onto hers. He talked of plot, themes, and metaphors. He tried to stop before he made a complete fool of himself, but was not sure if he succeeded. By the end of the conversation, Mary was very quiet. Meanwhile, the rolltop desk grinned in the corner. He remained optimistic while he waited for Mary's inevitable return call. However, when fans came up to him for an autograph, or to have their picture taken with him, his manner was tepid at best.

Mary's return call came quicker than David expected. She was noncommittal during their brief conversation, but he felt the tension in her voice. And she asked to meet at her downtown office, not at a nice restaurant or bar. Whatever she had to tell him, she wanted it to be private. Nevertheless, she might have wanted to meet in her office because of his celebrity and she didn't want them to be constantly interrupted by adoring fans. Maybe. But, as David dressed in his khakis and silk shirt, covered by a cashmere sweater, he felt like he was going to the hospital to visit a very sick friend.

Mary greeted him in the lobby dressed in severe business attire and a forced smile. David followed her, and staring at the back of her head, she suddenly reminded him of one of his stern elementary school teachers. Mrs. Smith. She didn't take any crap and had slapped every child in class at one point or another during the school year. He got his in line to the bathroom when he kept poking Phillip Jones, the boy standing in front of him. David wasn't sure why he kept poking him, but when Phillip complained, old Mrs. Smith was over there like a shot. The slap wasn't painful, just a bit unsettling for a seven-year-old boy.

Mary's office was well lit, clean, and sparsely furnished. There was a pot of coffee in the corner and the aroma of freshly steamed coffee beans filled the room.

"Would you like some coffee?" she asked, already pouring him a cup.

"Um, sure." David saw a pigeon fly to the window and land on the ledge. It gazed at him, cocking its head back and forth. At that moment, he wished he could change places, at least for the next hour or so.

Mary set her cup on the desk and settled into her high-back leather chair. David saw a pile of paper next to her cup. The pages had pink post-it notes jutting out of the sides, and the title page was covered in red ink. It was his manuscript, and it looked like it had been through a war.

"David, David. Where do I start?" She rested her chin on her hands.

"Um, did you like it?"

"No," she said.

David flinched at how quickly she said that. She didn't have to think about it. She didn't even think of a way to soften the answer to spare his feelings. "Well, what didn't you like, the grammar, the story?"

"Yes."

"What, the grammar?" David scratched his head.

"Let's start with that, shall we?" Mary gave him a quick smile and continued before he could answer. "I know you wrote this rather quickly, what, three months? How long did it take you to write "A Kiss During Mourning"?"

David shifted in his seat and looked up at the ceiling. "Oh. A while."

"I thought so." Mary sounded like maybe they had found a piece of common ground. "Because your first novel was so polished. So complete. This is the complete opposite. As if two different people wrote these works."

David continued to look away from Mary. Now he was staring at a photo of her on her desk. It was at an oblique angle, but appeared to be her in a church staring up at Christ on the cross.

"So, I figured this is probably a very rough draft. The grammar isn't good. It's full of errors, passive voice sequences, alliterations and metaphors that I could have constructed in junior high. And I'm a terrible writer, David."

"Well, like you said, I felt rushed."

"All that being said, I can help you with the grammar. Somewhat. But before we can look at the grammar, you have to fix the story." Mary was now leaning on her desk, her arms folded before her.

"What's wrong with the story?" David wiped the sweat off his forehead. This was going to get worse before it got better. At least she hadn't thrown him out of her office yet.

Mary's smile was ugly. "Let's start at the beginning, shall we?" She leafed through the first pages of the novel. "A complete stranger shows up in Hannah's bedroom, waking her from a deep sleep. By your description of him he's obviously up to no good—"

"Well, how do you know that?" David interjected.

Mary glanced at him and shuffled a couple of pages. "Because right here, it says he was wearing a black ski mask."

"Oh yeah, right."

"And she ... wait, let me get this right, 'falls into his massive biceps'?"

"Yeah." David was staring at his shoes. He swore he modified that scene from one of the classic romance novels he read. Of course, he wasn't going to tell *her* that.

"David, if a man in a black ski mask suddenly showed up in my apartment, I wouldn't fall," she glanced down at the page in front of her, "into his massive biceps. I would scream, and throw a lamp at him, or shoot him, or something."

She shook her head. "Women want to escape into a fantasy, David. Not into a felony act." She straightened the manuscript between her hands. "OK. So Hannah now starts looking for the Romanian detective, who is a zombie, and is not dead. That's not actually that bad."

"Oh," David inflated a bit in his seat, his chest rising.

"But you never explain how Hannah found out. Is she psychic? Because if she is, we never knew that about her. Oh," she said, like she had swallowed something bitter, or smelling a piece of food that had been left in the refrigerator for a month too long, "these sex scenes have gotta go."

"What's wrong with them?"

"Oh my God, David." She shuffled through to the middle of the book. "Here we go." She cleared her throat. "Their bodies crashed together, their thundering thighs thrashing and thrusting ..." She looked up at him. "That's just gross. I don't feel like I'm escaping anywhere I want to be when I read that passage. I just feel like throwing up."

David felt his face turn red. He bowed his head and counted to ten.

Mary let out a sigh and tapped her fingers on the desk. "You have to start from scratch, and rework this story. It's got to be crisp. I can help you with some of the grammar. The Entropy Home editor can even help you with some of the plot sequences. But you have to bring us a proper manuscript first."

"I did," he said through gritted teeth.

Mary's face hardened. "No, you didn't. You brought me something I see in my in-basket every day. Unsolicited manuscripts from writers who can't even spell their own name. I toss them into the garbage after the first paragraph. Sometimes even before I finish their query letter."

David felt his face boil and sweat form under his arms beneath his sweater. "I am a successful writer! I'll take my business elsewhere! To someone who appreciates my work! I'll make another agent rich!" He glared at her.

Mary tossed the manuscript across the desk. "Suit yourself. But, if you take that piece of garbage to another agent, they'll toss it in the trash, too."

David stared at the manuscript, but made no move to pick it up.

"You wrote a beautiful first novel, David. You can write another. But this isn't it. And listen. I have sacrificed a lot for you. I've been paid well. But, I deserved every penny of it. I scheduled everything for you.

I worked twelve hours plus a day for months, answered my phone late at night to listen to your spontaneous requests, made sure everything was just right at your readings. You think limousines, lemon water, and dark chocolate on your bed pillows, just appear by themselves? I did everything I could to make you happy. That thing you wrote is supposed to be a sequel? You can do better. I deserve better. Hannah deserves better."

Mary wiped her brow and lowered her voice. "This is a business, David. First and foremost. Second novels are usually not as good as a writer's first. Publishers often are disappointed with a writer's sophomore effort. But, it has to have some value. Otherwise, we could end up with a big embarrassment, even a breach of contract. You ever hear of the musician who got sued by his record company because he made an album that "didn't sound like him?"

Breach of contract? He had briefly thought of that. He could be ruined. He could lose his apartment, his lifestyle ... he'd have to go back to *accounting*. David rubbed his face and imagined himself staggering down Spring Street, a bottle in one hand, the new gentry looking down their noses at him. Forget the apartment near Central Park. He'd be sleeping in Central Park, hiding in the Brambles—

"David? Are you all right?"

David looked up at her. His eyes felt moist, his face pink. "Yes." He sat up and slapped his thighs. "What do we do now?"

Mary nodded at the novel. "Fix it. This reads like a textbook. Bring in passion. Real passion. Fall in love with Hannah. Make her real. Keep the storyline about the zombie Romanian detective. Women love a good mystery. Bring me a rich mystery romance full of passion and life. I know you can do it."

David walked out of her office, stunned. He walked all the way back to his apartment, occasionally glancing down at the manuscript he held in his hand. He felt like he had just gone ten rounds with a heavyweight boxer. Mary pulled no punches. She was upset. What the hell was he gonna do now? Take a writing class? Hire a personal editor? God, what if that got out to the press? He should have seen this coming long ago. He should have known a second book was required. For chrissakes, he did know, he signed the damn contract. Why didn't he *read* the contract? Why did he waste so much time? He spent six months doing nothing useful. And now he had three months to produce a proper manuscript. Full of "passion and life." He was in deep shit now.

David staggered into his apartment, exhausted, and collapsed onto his bed. He always felt at his loneliest when he lay here. But once he lay down, he felt he didn't have the strength to get back up again. As he lay there, he thought of Haddie. Why did she have to write that damn book? Why did he tell Mary he wrote it? It would have been better if it had never been published. There was no way he could write a good manuscript. Not in three months, not in three years.

He needed Haddie. For the last ten years of their marriage, it seemed they hadn't needed each other. They simply passed by each other as they chased the gold ring. He visualized them wandering like zombies at their work all day, talking about work over dinner, going to sleep, and waking up to do it all over again, like automatons. Once she died, he knew he needed her. He knew he wasted so many years of not telling her he loved her. And he needed her now. But she was gone. Gone forever.

As he started to drift off to sleep, he heard himself softly say, "Haddie."

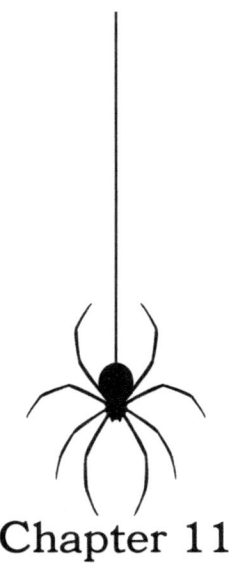

Chapter 11

"Hello, David."

David looked between his feet. Haddie sat at the foot of the bed, turned toward him, dressed in a tank top and skirt. Her red hair flowed over her shoulders. She was beautiful.

"Oh no," he grumbled as he sat up. She was there. He couldn't believe it. He wanted to yell at her to go away. He opened his mouth several times, but the words would not come out. Instead, he stared at her.

"Honey, you called *me*." She eyed him, as if unsure of his mental state.

Yes, he remembered now. He had called her name just before he dozed off. And here she was. And if she stayed, he was on a one-way trip to Tippingdale. On the other hand, she could give him some tips on writing "Hannah's Last Ride". No, that was really crazy. If he actually believed she was there, he should check himself into Tippingdale. And yet, if this was his overactive imagination working, maybe he could harness this mirage so that he could write a really good manuscript. Crazy? Perhaps. But, she was sitting there, wasn't she? He could see her, couldn't he? Perhaps he could use her for a while to finish the novel, and then go back to being sane. Maybe he could just be crazy for a little while. That way he could avoid Tippingdale, but maybe write a good book. He could keep his apartment. His adoring fans. All of it. Maybe.

Haddie gazed at his bare chest. The covers had fallen to his waist. "You've lost some weight." She smiled.

"Yeah. You look beautiful," he replied. Her eyes were set wide on her slim face. Her body looked soft, yet so firm it seemed to defy gravity. She was a woman of contradictions, and at that moment, David realized he probably knew only half of them, at best.

"Thanks." She slowly moved her hand and placed it on his blanket-covered foot. He felt her pressure, ever so lightly. He swallowed and closed his eyes for a second. He opened them. She was still there, and so was the pressure. "You said mean things to me last time I saw you."

"I was going crazy, Haddie. Remember my dad and Tippingdale? I thought I was on my way back."

Haddie looked off, and partly opened her mouth, like she had not considered this. Like she had been so self-absorbed in her own predicament that she had been incapable of understanding his. David watched her as her face blushed pink. It made him uncomfortable that she was uncomfortable. After all, she was dead. At least he was alive. He rooted around his brain to say something to break the awkward silence.

"Your book has sold over two million copies."

Oh my God, I'm reasoning with a mirage.

Haddie's eyes widened, and she clasped her hands together like a little girl who has been handed a piece of chocolate. "Wow! I was just hoping that it would sell a few thousand! Really? It sold how many?"

"Over two million."

Haddie stood up and walked around the room. "I can't believe it!" She twirled and let her head fall back, her red hair whipping around her back. She suddenly stopped. She walked over to David's dresser. She lifted a package with two fingers on her left hand, as if lifting a dead mouse for the garbage can. "What is this? Condoms?"

David's face froze.

Haddie's face hardened. "Well, explain this."

David grimaced. He was being accused of adultery by his dead wife in his dream. "Haddie. I mean ... you're *dead*."

Haddie's face contorted and tears welled in her eyes. David jumped from the bed.

"Don't you come near me, you … you … auugh!"

"Haddie, understand the circumstances—"

"Jesus Christ, David." Haddie's jaw dropped. "I remember now. You took credit for my book, and it's really popular." She shook the condoms at him. "Are these for groupies? You are screwing groupies because of *my* book?"

"Haddie—"

"You're nothing but a pimp! You're pimping my book and taking all the credit, and getting a little on the side—"

"A pimp? Now, wait a minute."

"Do you know what I've gone through the past year? Waiting in that … that … horrible place? And I'm not alone, you know. There are plenty of dead people there. And there's this one gladiator who's been stuck there for like, two thousand years, and he's been very nice to me. How would you like it if I started seeing him? He's got hair!"

David visualized a metal clad warrior wooing his Haddie. He shook his head. It seemed the whole world had turned against him. Now he was arguing with his dead wife, clearly a figment of his imagination, about whether he should be celibate now that she was dead, while she was threatening to bonk a dead Roman soldier.

"This is insanity. Haddie, calm down."

Haddie's cheeks were puffed out and her fists were clenched. He had always thought she was cute when she got mad. A little scary, but cute. However, at the moment, there were bigger concerns, like his lavish lifestyle. "Haddie, I need your help."

She put her hands on her hips and raised an eyebrow. "Oh, yeah? Well, I'm not feeling very *helpful* right now. I think I'll go back to my waiting room and screw a gladiator!"

David rubbed his face. *My mirage is arguing with me.* "Listen. My contract … I mean, the contract I have with the publisher requires a second book—"

"And you want my help? Ha!" She narrowed her eyes and looked around the bedroom. "This isn't our apartment." She strode out of the room. David could hear her gasp. "Holy shit! That's Central Park!

You moved uptown? With my sweat?" She strode back into the room. "With the royalties of my book? My God!" She ran to the closet. "Look at these suits. Armani? David, you're not a pimp. You're a whore!"

David buried his head into his hands. *I don't deserve this. I must have massive guilt. It must have been the charity I promised to start.* He looked up. His dead wife, wild-eyed, red-faced, and red hair made her look like she was on fire. David sat on the bed. This dream had to calm down. It had to become civil.

"Listen, Haddie. I need your help."

Haddie paced the room, her arms crossed, glaring at him. For the first time he felt like he knew what it was like being cross-examined by the shark lady. He readied himself for the grilling.

"You want help? Find someone else!" She shoved him onto his back.

David bolted awake. He wiped the sweat from his forehead with his right hand. He looked out the window. It was still spring bright outside. He hadn't slept long. What a nightmare. *What did I expect? Cat hates me, Mary's pissed off and will probably sue my ass, and my dead wife refuses to help me.*

David wasn't sure why he would dream that Haddie wouldn't assist in his new novel endeavor. Perhaps he did need to get that charity going. His dreams might become more pleasant, he would be helping someone, or something, and it would be good publicity. Yes, as soon as he finished the manuscript, he would look into that.

David walked out of his bedroom and past the rolltop desk with the evil grin to the kitchen. She was so vivid. And livid. And beautiful. And she still had him under her control. He thought as long as he believed that, he would never be free of her. Why was he feeling guilty about seeing other women now that she was gone? Didn't he have a right to be happy? And now, with a second book on the line, it was as if he was under her control again. He couldn't write the second book on his own. He was just a salesman. A pimp. He must believe it if he dreamt it. But instead of hawking Haddie's body, he was hawking her book. He certainly wasn't a whore. He'd had some fun. What was wrong with that? He'd like to find a good woman to spend his time with. He thought of Cat, and immediately thought of that hateful look she gave him.

He made a sandwich and sat at the table. He had to use his overactive imagination as an inspiration to kick-start "Hannah's Last Ride". He was desperate. It couldn't hurt to try. He had to bring Haddie back into his dream and somehow transfer that energy into writing the manuscript. To do that, he had to outthink his psyche. What did he know of Haddie, and how could he use her traits to get *her help*? He stared at his sandwich. She wasn't sensitive. She was the shark lady. She was manipulative. And pragmatic. How could he make it a win-win for her and himself? He had to figure that out by the time he fell asleep tonight. It was his only chance. Otherwise, he was back to accounting. He shivered at the thought and wolfed down his meal.

David spent the day studying his novel. As evening fell, he sat in bed, the manuscript scattered around him. He needed the novel fresh in his mind so that when Haddie offered suggestions he would remember where to put them.

Jesus. I need to have the novel fresh in my mind so that when I dream about my dead wife my brain will know exactly how to configure the novel so that Mary and the editors will like it. I really am crazy. Why do I think this will work? Why do I think my subconscious will be able to pull Haddie out of the hat, and that the prose I develop under that spell will be any better than the crap I already wrote?

The fact was, he didn't believe it. But he was desperate. Desperate times lead to desperate measures. When darkness took over the room, save for a small reading lamp by his bed, David gathered the manuscript, placed it in a neat pile next to him, and lay down.

"Haddie, I need you," he said, and closed his eyes.

David woke to laughter, and when there was a quiet snort at the end of it, he knew exactly who it was.

"Haddie?"

"I'm sorry, David. I didn't mean to wake you. It's just that this is so ... *horrible*." She giggled and snorted again. Half the manuscript was spread around her. David had been worried he might wake to her wrath again. He didn't anticipate she would be *entertained*, albeit in a bad way. She looked at him like he had a real hourglass head. One she could see through perfectly.

"I'm sorry I got mad at you." She patted him on the leg. "I should be the last person to judge you. If you want to be a whore, be a whore. I won't stop you."

David adjusted the covers as he sat up. "Well, thanks, honey." He thought about her ability to manipulate. Why was she so nice all of a sudden? Was it guilt? "Did you find that Roman gladiator?"

"No," she answered, sounding disappointed. "I think he was out racing his chariot." She glanced at him. "Oh, you're jealous. Jealous that your dead wife might be sleeping with a Roman soldier. How crazy is that?"

David had to admit that was crazy. But, Haddie was here and perhaps ready to help. He looked at the manuscript strewn about the bed. "Horrible? What's horrible about it?"

Haddie rolled her eyes and dropped her hands to her lap. "Honey, don't you see? Now, your general plot isn't bad. The detective walking around an amnesiac wanderer, a zombie from being poisoned, is morbidly romantic. Your execution is what's horrible. What did you do? It's like you took scenes from other stories and pasted it into this manuscript, like force fitting square pegs into round holes."

David turned red. "Haddie, I'm not a writer, I'm an accountant. I had to do something. I signed a contract for three books. You only wrote one."

She held a few sheets of the novel in each hand. "How long do you have to finish it?"

"A few months on the outside."

"We have a lot of work to do." She gathered the manuscript, organized the pages and placed it neatly beside David. "You need to understand, first and foremost, what the first book is about."

That's a good start. "OK," David said. "Shoot."

"I am a beautiful woman."

"You sure are." He performed eyebrow push-ups like Groucho Marx and then reached for her leg.

"Yes, I know. All men think I'm beautiful. I've known that since I was fourteen."

"Actually, mesmerizing is a better word."

"Oh, that's very sweet." She stopped a second. "Let's remember that word. We can use it in the book."

David watched her and thought, just for a fleeting instant, how vulnerable she was. As if being beautiful was more of a curse, than a benefit. To be constantly harassed, thought of only for your looks instead of any of your other strengths. Perhaps that's why she was so driven at her job. To show she wasn't just a pretty face. She was cunning and vicious, like a shark.

"Hannah is the same way. She is very beautiful and all men want is to be with her. They see nothing else. The story isn't about Hannah killing all these men. It's really about Hannah rejecting these men because they only wanted her for her looks. Then she meets a man in Kansas who loves her for something besides her looks. So she falls in love with his reason for loving her. But, she doesn't love him. And that's why at the end of the story she pines to get away."

"Hope," he whispers.

"Exactly."

"You know, I couldn't help but notice that the Kansas guy had some similarities to me." David watched her. Had she only loved the reason he loved her? He must have fooled her pretty good, because he always thought she was damn hot. Maybe he just hid it better than the other guys.

"You liked me for more than my looks." She looked at him. "Yes, you did. I could tell. You're one of the few people I met in my life that loved me for more than my looks. And I loved you for your kindness, and your good heart."

"Not my wonderful good looks?"

"Heavens no. But, your looks did grow on me over time. You carved a new standard for handsomeness."

David grumbled. "You certainly are full of compliments tonight."

Haddie wasn't listening. She was staring off at the far wall, biting her lower lip. David began to feel warm and felt a tingling that would do him no good with a mirage.

"This will work out. The detective didn't want Hannah for her looks. He succumbed to her looks and that was his downfall, but that's different. He wanted her because she was a criminal. It fits the story. It fits Hannah's journey, her motivation to find someone. He searched her out for her crimes. And she wants to right the wrong for poisoning him and making him an amnesiac wanderer."

"Wait," David said. "What about the others? She murdered them, too. Are they going to come back, like zombies? It'll be like *Dawn of the Dead*."

"No, you pathetic idiot." Haddie grunted and shook her head, slapping his leg with her hand. "Those others were vapid airheads, or unfaithful scumbags. The detective was chasing her out of justice. The rule of law."

"Ah, now I get it. This is right up your alley."

Haddie's eyes widened. "Isn't it?" She looked off again. "Yes. This will work out nicely."

David watched his dead wife staring off, dressed in a tank top and shorts, her body radiating enthusiasm. Now he was looking at her not as his wife of nearly twenty years, but as a woman who just walked into his bedroom, fresh from a day in the sun. There were no tired, day to day familiarities to blur her beauty. It was all new, and her mesmerizing beauty stunned David for several seconds before he looked away and blinked several times to break the spell. When he looked back at her, she was now staring at him.

"What's wrong? Don't you like the plot?"

He thought the plot was good. And he couldn't believe that he was sitting here with her thoughts, the two of them. And yet for five years she had had these thoughts in silence. She must have had them in his presence, even epiphanies, that excited her, perhaps when they were eating dinner, or getting ready for bed, yet he saw none of it. He felt cheated. Yet, Cat had known. She had confided in Cat. And in the last half of the ten years she worked for Haddie, they had probably spent more time together than Haddie did with him.

"Why did you tell Cat about your novel, and not me?"

Haddie did not speak for some time. She turned away and straightened. Her posture made him think of how she must have presented herself in court, which seemed odd since she was the one being questioned. "How do you know that?"

"She told me, just before she called me a scumbag and didn't want to see me again. She thought I stabbed you in the back when I took credit for your book. She wouldn't even let me explain."

Haddie shrugged. "Cat was very faithful. She was just defending me."

David cocked his head. "You didn't answer my question."

"Do you really want to go over old ground when I was alive? I was working crazy hours. When I had a few minutes I would write. She was always with me, doing the things I needed done. There was no way she *couldn't* know, David. And as I said, she was faithful. She kept our secrets, and I didn't want anyone knowing about it." She looked closely at David. "I was going to let you know when it got published. I wanted to surprise you."

David felt himself turn red from jealousy. "She kept your secrets. You were married to me. We shouldn't have had secrets from each other."

Haddie rose and paced the room. The only thing missing at this point was the witness stand and jury box. "Why are we rehashing this? I'm dead, David. Doesn't that mean anything to you? You asked for my help because you got yourself in a bind for taking credit for my book? I'm the one who should be asking questions. Do you want my help or not?" She stood there, practically on fire.

David couldn't help but think her anger was primarily for show. When you're on the defensive, go on the offensive. He thought back on their last several years of marriage. They never had lively conversations such as this. Perhaps they should have. But that was all water under the bridge at this point. And he wasn't going to push his luck. He needed her help.

David folded his arms across his chest and fixed his gaze. "OK. How do we fix the novel?"

Haddie's face softened, as if the weight of a thousand cases had been lifted off her back. She stepped over to the bed and shuffled the papers. David realized that this second story was really her baby. He just hoped he was up to task to write it.

"Do you want me to be frank?" she asked.

David smiled. "I like you better as Haddie, but if you really want to be—"

Haddie lifted her chin and groaned. "Oh ... one of the advantages of being dead is not having to hear your horrible jokes."

"Sorry."

"Now I will be frank—" She stared at David as if daring him to make another bad joke. David kept his mouth shut. "The writing sucks. The sentence structure is elementary, the characters have no life, and the sexual parts are disgusting, even laughable." She gave him a thin-lipped smile.

"You are cruel," David said, and placed his hands on his throat and fell back in mock death.

Haddie ignored him. "On the other hand, your general plot is imaginative and fits something I might have done." She pointed a long index finger at her breast.

Haddie began an in-depth analysis of the poor sentence structure and suggested some fixes. She explained the challenges of each page, what could work, how it might be told, and its purpose. If a paragraph did not move the story along it was stricken. As David sat and watched her become increasingly animated in her explanations, he felt an uncontrollable pull that reminded him of their second date. After they had gone out to lunch and were walking around the university, they stopped beside a small grove of maples. She was talking about her sociology class, which she considered as useless as politicians. She was convinced that sociologists existed because they had no idea how to communicate and function in their society. They were not trying to explain our behavior to our society as a whole, or even to their colleagues. They were trying to explain it to themselves. And they were trying to do it on the taxpayer's dime. Haddie's demeanor became more and more animated as she explained her hypothesis and used her sociology professor as a fitting example that proved it. David couldn't have cared less about her sociology professor's shortcomings as a human being, but she sure was hot.

"What are you doing?" Haddie's face was scrunched up and looked like a Halloween pumpkin.

David had apparently crawled across the bed because now his face was only a few inches from hers. He looked to each side, wondering how he apparently had appeared there.

"However," she continued, "some of the fixes can't be done with the pen. There must be an underlying emotion. Passion. This is a romance novel, you know." She was staring at his lips, which he thought was one of his better features. She smiled and this time it was not a thin smile, but a mischievous one. The kind of smile that resulted in long lazy mornings, chaotic bedcovers, and capsized end tables. A smile he hadn't seen since they were first married.

And then she pounced.

David woke with a start and sat upright, the sun streaming through the bedroom window. He tilted his head to the left and rotated his shoulders. His neck and shoulders ached, his back was stiff, and his legs were sore to the touch. In fact, his whole body felt sore. He looked down at the covers. They were in complete disarray. He peeked under the covers. He was completely naked, though he thought he had gone to sleep with his underwear and T-shirt on. His clothes were strewn about the floor. He slipped out of bed and stretched, his back and shoulders cracking so loud someone across the room could have heard it.

I must have really thrashed around in bed last night.

Pictures of Haddie filled his thoughts as he walked into the shower. She had never looked so good. The images came in split-second shots, flashing before his eyes, causing him to pause and stand motionless with the bar of soap in his hand. What a dream. If he had dreams like that every night, he'd sit and wile away his days, just waiting for bedtime to come around again. It felt so real. His body ached as he tried to soap down; so stiff he could hardly reach his shoulder blades. Most of his back went untouched. His lower back strained as he bent to soap his feet. He stood and let the hot water pour down his body. He felt like he'd had a real workout for the first time in years.

His overactive imagination ran wild last night, like a renegade through the wilderness, the hounds baying on his heels. Would it translate to the written page? He toweled off, got dressed, made a cup of coffee and sat at the grinning desk, now with a gaping hole, the rolltop retracted all the way to accommodate his computer. He opened the file and began to write.

His hands could barely type fast enough to record the prose that poured from his brain. His fingers played the keys like a master pianist, and he found himself closing his eyes, the words shooting past like the dashed dividers on the two-lane roads that he watched as a child on Sunday drives. Sentences flowed, and were peppered with words he believed he had never heard before, yet he knew they were perfect. The paragraphs overflowed, so full of life that he read and reread each one two or three times in amazement before starting the next. The pages fell in a flurry like autumn leaves, one by one, so that by midday he had completed thirty pages. By evening he had written thirty more, and he was so stunned by his accomplishment that he stopped to read it all in one sitting. He expected that reading it now would reveal all the errors, the amateur that he was. But as he read the pages he came to realize that the story really was good. How could he have written sixty pages, or approximately 18,000 words, of wonderful prose in one day, when he spent three months writing about a thousand shitty words a day that had combined to make a pile of drivel he couldn't have paid someone to read?

He heard his stomach growl and realized he had not eaten all day. But he was on a roll, and he wasn't going to stop now. Somehow, the dream of Haddie last night had inspired him. It actually worked. He was going to continue writing until he could write no more, to wring every last piece of prose from his simple mind while his writing was hot. He worked through the night and all the next day, stubble appearing on his chin, subsisting on coffee and story, until at last he came to Hannah and the detective's first meeting. David pounded the keys as their conversation turned to a quiet interlude. He thought of his dream of Haddie as he painted a picture with words. A picture that conjured the imagination, lust, a feast of activities that titillated either when taken wholly as a quick read, or carved up into smaller pieces to savor slowly. David read it over and knew he had it right. He got an erection.

As the night passed and dawn arrived, David worked harder, as if racing along the road before a barrier could cause him to crash. His clothes were wrinkled, a foul odor seeped from his armpits, his eyes blurred and came back to focus only reluctantly through his sheer will. It was sometime during the third day that his head began to buzz. His concentration vanished. The roadblock had fallen into his path and he crashed into it head on, at speed, without a seatbelt. Partially due to his hunger, and partially due to the lack of sleep, his imagination began to go wild and haywire. Although they weren't hallucinations, he began to visualize crazy scenes, some nonsensical, some nonsensically violent, until he shook with fear that he had finally lost it completely. He stood and shook his head, and the room began to spin, the windows, the walls, the ceiling, and floor all becoming one big blur until he collapsed on the floor.

It was dark when David finally woke. He immediately went to the computer and sat down. He restarted the computer and opened the file, but even before his fingers touched the keyboard he knew the spell was past. His fingers ached from use. His eyes burned, his back and shoulders stiff from hunching over the keyboard for three days. The computer screen gave off a glow that caused no reaction inside himself. The desk seemed to yawn.

You had a good run. Now hang it up and go back to accounting.

His stomach ached. Perhaps some food would help. It would certainly prevent him from dying of starvation. David prepared some food, and the more he ate, the hungrier he got. He continued eating until he became so bloated he thought he might burst. He thumped his distended belly and it sounded like a tight drum. He burped and crawled over to bed. The only comfortable position was on his left side, his knees brought up to his waist, his arm folded beneath his head, where he spent a dreamless night asleep.

David avoided the computer all the next day. The computer sat open on the rolltop desk, a blank screen eye that seemed to follow him when he walked by. The gaping hole of the desk lurked behind the computer, ready to swallow it whole. David eventually sat by the window looking out over the street and through the apartment windows on the other side. His mind felt fuzzy from the lack of sleep and he mostly stared at the activities in the neighborhood. A vendor serving hot dogs, couples walking their pets, women cleaning and walking through apartments across the way. The whole time he felt like he was being watched. His eyes would dart back to the computer and then back outside. By noon his imagination was going into overdrive again.

Poor David is too tired to write. No, you just aren't up to it, are you David? Give it up, boy.

David took a final glance at the computer and desk. "I've gotta get out of here."

David walked briskly along the sidewalk, a chill in the air, but the sun out and bright. After a little goading, Gil agreed to meet him for a late lunch at a nearby deli. Gil had a report due, but when David agreed to buy, Gil decided he could carve out an hour of his busy day. The deli was bright and narrow, with a counter at the end, various cuts and sausages displayed on metal grate shelving. Sodas and juices were in a case off to the side. There was barely room for three tables along the other side, and although the deli was crowded, no one sat at the tables. Behind the counter was a stooped man, stiff with age. David knew he had once been a butcher (his forearms gave away his former profession), but now his business was limited to cold cuts and specialty sausages. They ordered their sandwiches and sat at the table nearest the door, which had a little more leg room than the other two.

David lifted his ham and provolone on rye, while Gil wrapped his fingers around a monster sub, chock full of various meats, onions, lettuce, and dressing. He took a bite and the sub oozed dressing around the sides, forcing Gil to grab a napkin to contain the mess.

Gil grunted.

"What?" David asked.

Gil chewed, holding up a finger. David took a bite of his sandwich while Gil cleared the decks.

"How's your novel?"

"Ah," David said. "Great. I've been on a tear. I have about a third of a second draft. And it's pretty good, if I say so myself."

"That's great. I guess my comments *did* help."

David chuckled. "Well, maybe. It's funny. Haddie's book was so good, at least for a romance novel. And I got this idea to, like, channel her. So, I thought of her before I went to bed, and she came to me in my dream. When I woke up, I wrote for three days straight. It was awesome."

Gil stopped his sandwich short of his mouth. "Wait. She helped you with your novel? Haddie? Are you freaking out on me?"

"No, no, no," David said quickly, raising both hands in protest. "I think I always had it inside me, obviously. The dream just let my subconscious bring it out. Of course, it wasn't real. I'm not crazy."

Gil had just finished swallowing another bite, his tongue exploring his back molars to free a chunk of bread. "Hmm." He smiled smugly.

I swear I've seen that smile before.

After lunch, David was walking back to his apartment, preoccupied with that smug expression. It reminded him of something, but he just couldn't quite place it. He knew what it meant, though. Gil thought his comments were what got David back on track, as if a few editorial changes could have fixed what was wrong with the manuscript!

He stopped at the local bakery to get his weekly fix of chocolate éclairs. He suddenly remembered where he had seen that smile before. It was in the fifth grade and he was working with some foreign second graders. A Chinese kid kept boasting how good he was at chess, challenging him to a game. Finally, David relented and played him. The kid wasn't bad, but David eventually took all his pieces except his king and then checkmated him. The Chinese kid sat there, lips pursed, his head barely breaching the table top. He looked at David, stuck his finger up his nose, pulled out a huge green booger, and wiped it on David's king. And then he smiled. Just like Gil. David had given Gil a hard time about reviewing his novel and Gil had marked it just like that Chinese kid did his king. And Gil thought his comments were what made "Hannah's Last Ride" better. Gil had left his mark, just like that kid did.

But David knew better. He knew what he had to do to bring out his inner writer. It was the memory of the only woman he ever loved. The woman who was capable of anything. A formidable lawyer, extreme competitor, wonderful writer. Smart and beautiful. Why didn't he spend more time with her? Take advantage of the time he had?

Familiarity breeds contempt.

David smirked when he walked by the writer's desk and computer.

I'll see you two tomorrow.

And he lay down on his bed and said the magic word. "Haddie."

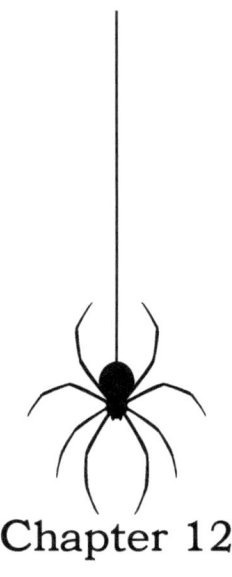

Chapter 12

THE NEXT SEVERAL DAYS WERE A BLUR. HADDIE BEGAN MAKING NIGHTLY appearances at David's call. He no longer stayed up for days, because he could conjure up his mirage wife each night as he slept. On the other hand, he felt as though he never got a good night's sleep. Each morning David would wake to find his bed a mess, and increasingly, the rest of his apartment. When Haddie appeared in the dead of night, they would spend several hours discussing the merits and fixes for a section of the novel, and end up in conjugal forays across the apartment. These forays fueled his romance writing. He was glad they were only dreams, because if it had been real, he most certainly would have woken the neighbors. He certainly felt under control; that is, he knew his time with Haddie was only a dream, and knew that he let it happen only to meet his goal to finish the novel. He was controlling the action, and admittedly, having fun to boot. He could finally enjoy Haddie's memory, and enjoy it in ways he hadn't ever thought possible.

What, deep in his psyche, allowed him to enjoy her sexually in ways they had never experienced when she was alive? It was so intense that David came to enjoy his dreams more than his waking hours. And he made incredible progress on the book. By the end of the week he had only two chapters left to write. The first, the exciting climax where the Romanian detective vanquishes the archenemy hired to avenge the death of one of Hannah's suitors, followed by, well, an exciting climax. The last, Hannah's commitment to unfettered, undying love, and all that crap. David's midnight visits had culminated in a novel being written in record time. Nothing could stop him now. It was almost done. And his progress just seemed to get quicker and the writing easier and easier.

Until last night.

Haddie sat on the edge of the bed, her tank top strap threatening to fall off her shoulder. She gripped several pages of the manuscript in her long fingers. "Oh, I don't know. This part needs ... something. It needs ... real passion."

David slid his hand up her thigh. "I think we can manage that."

She looked at him in a way that made him shrivel. "I mean *real* passion."

David cocked his head. "What do you mean by that?"

"Now, don't get mad. I don't mean we don't have passion. But this is a special chapter. This is where Andrei slays the killer in a big duel for Hannah. The emotions are running at a peak. No matter how hard we try, we can't reach that level just hanging out here. It would be forced. It wouldn't be real."

David sighed. "What, you want me to go out and kill a homeless guy or something?"

"Now you're just being silly." She stroked his face. "We just need to ... amp it up a little."

There's that diabolical smile. I've seen it so many times.

Flashbacks streamed through his mind. That smile preceded each of them. Just before he took the job in New York City. Just before he sold his Adirondack cabin. How many times had witnesses seen it before cross-examination? How many times had old boyfriends seen it before she left them, or talked them into doing something totally against their better judgment?

"I was thinking more along the lines of role play." She moved closer to him.

A man in love is a man lost. Stranded in the ocean on a boat without oars. Floating helplessly on the current, the waves lulling him into a stupor of indecision. Waiting. Waiting for the next moment when he could take action, the natural reaction of men. But that action would be preceded by a look to his love, like a dog to his master. David sat still, his head bobbing softly from left to right, waiting …

"I was thinking of something heroic. Something that would stir our creative juices into a frenzy. Something that, when transferred to the written page, would make women explode."

"What do you have in mind?" David asked. He felt that at this moment, he would jump out the window if she asked him to.

"Well, we'll need a gladiator outfit for you, and I can be the damsel in distress."

David frowned. "Wait a minute. A gladiator outfit? Is this about that Roman guy you know up there? What's going on?"

Haddie brought a hand to her breast. "I'm hurt. It's not about him." She eyed him for a moment. "Well, maybe a little. Seeing him in that armor helped me think of this idea."

"Just *seeing* him?"

Haddie stood and looked down at him. "I am dead, David. What do you care? Were you thinking of me when all those little girls were hanging on you? Huh?"

Uh oh. I'm arguing with my dead wife.

"OK, forget it, forget it." David held up his hands. "I'm sorry I said it. But it does make me jealous."

"It should. He was hot." She stuck out her chin in defiance.

The shark lady was coming to life. Time to ratchet down the tension a bit. Although she was acting as if this gladiator idea just came to her, he was sure it was planned. Everything Haddie did was planned. He realized that now. It's how she had controlled him over their twenty years of marriage. She out organized him. But, if she wanted to act like this idea just sprang from her breast, he wasn't going to challenge her. The book was almost done. He needed her.

"You know, role play. We'll create a heroic scenario where you save a vulnerable, but not helpless, lady in distress."

David rolled his eyes. "Can't we just imagine this? Acting it out seems ridiculous. Next you'll say you want to fly to Rome …"

Haddie's jaw dropped and her eyes bugged out. "What a great idea!"

"No, no, no … that's not a great idea—"

"What do you mean? We can't do it here in this apartment. I'll never get in the mood to write my climax for "Hannah's Last Ride", here in this apartment. It smells. Italy would be wonderful. It's romantic, scenic—"

David ignored the "it smells" comment. He had to hire a maid. "It's six thousand miles away. Look, let's be reasonable."

Haddie gave him a look that David knew too well. It was that "OK, smartass, you come up with an idea." She preached on many an occasion that you're either part of the solution, or part of the problem.

Produce.

David contemplated a solution. If Haddie insisted on this hero and vulnerable but not helpless heroine bit, he certainly wasn't going to act it out where anybody could see him. Imagine the tabloids! If not the apartment, then where? Central Park? Unless they were inside surrounded by four walls and heavy curtains, they would get no privacy in Manhattan. No, they had to get out of the city. A place in the country. The Poconos? Yuck. Then it hit him. Of course. The perfect place, with great memories. At least for him.

"How about the Adirondacks?"

Haddie's face broke into a wide devious smile. "It's a date."

"I'd like to rent a gladiator suit, please."

The man sniffed. "Leather or metal?"

The party store was located on a small side street and was highly recommended during his Internet search. It had a museum feel, or maybe a Madame Tussaud's Wax Museum feel, with costumes draped over mannequins filling the floor space. Animal costumes, medieval costumes, and lots of leather. David felt he was at a crowded Halloween party even though he and the clerk were the only ones in the store.

I must be crazy to be doing this.

"Metal, I guess."

The clerk clicked his tongue and shook his head, causing his orange hair to quiver around his slim face. "Metal is so passé." The clerk focused on David's face. "Oh my God! You're David East! I'm such a fan!" He inhaled sharply between sentences.

"Thank you. That's very kind." David surveyed the store, hoping a gladiator suit would suddenly appear that he could grab and get the hell out.

"I read "A Kiss During Mourning" three times! That Hannah is such a scoundrel! I—"

"Yes, she certainly is. Do you have any gladiator suits in stock?" David tapped his fingers on the counter.

"Yes, I believe so." The clerk disappeared behind the counter and reappeared with a cloth tape measure in hand. He walked around to David's side and stared at him, a long index finger tapping his cheek. "I'm not sure we have your size. I better measure you."

David did not like the smile that appeared on the clerk's face. "Um, I think I'm a large."

"Oh, don't be silly. This isn't Sears! We want to make sure it fits." The clerk began measuring his waist, arm length, and neck, humming a tune that David did not recognize. David grabbed one end of the tape before the clerk measured his leg length. He moved swiftly, and just as swiftly out of sight saying he would be right back, the scent of lavender hanging in the air.

David sighed. He was completely packed and his car was parked out front. Several days in the Adirondacks at the cabin he once owned. At the old cabin where he spent summers in his youth, and that now he was paying $120 a night to enjoy. He was surprised that he was able to get the same cabin. There had been several cabins on the lake back then. There were probably more now to increase rental revenue for the resort that appeared after everyone, including him, had sold out. *Bear Lake Resort.*

"Don't you think the leather is better?" The clerk stood with the metal suit hanging from a rolling hook on one side, the leather one draped across his shoulder. He glanced at the thin leather suit, and thought it would be perfect if he was going to some kind of perverted sadomasochistic pagan party. The metal one was bronze and looked like it might have been pried off a dead Roman soldier's body. He walked over and lifted the suit off the hook.

"This must weigh sixty pounds," David said.

"See? You can't have fun in that. Now, this leather one fits snug—"

David pointed to the metal suit. "Perfect. I'll take it."

—

The late April sun gave way to clouds as he drove through the Delaware River Valley. Even so, the clouds offset the still bare trees, and the heavy fog in the valley bottom obscured the river, blanketing it, reassuring him of warmer days to come. The Appalachians gave way to rolling hills and then the flatlands around Utica. It was still cloudy. The air chilled, and he adjusted the car's ventilation to add warm air. He passed towns, and outside the towns, barns and old stone farmhouses. He passed a baseball field, the grass green, the dirt wet from the constant dew and rain of April. Baseball. A game of nervous habits. Spitting, grabbing the crotch, knocking mud from your shoes.

The state roads narrowed as he entered the Adirondack area. Snow covered the ground in shaded spots within the dense pine forests. The smell of pine brought back a flood of memories. Fishing off the dock, hiking on the trails, weasels in the henhouse. The pictures came on and on. He rolled down his window. Although it was late afternoon, the temperature was in the 30s. He had only brought a light jacket. And the gladiator suit. He was going to be cold if he ventured out in the evening. Ten years ago he would have brought a heavy coat without thinking twice. He just didn't think of it this morning. As he followed the old roads through the small Adirondack towns, the scenery around each bend was familiar. Driving through Old Forge felt like coming home. The carved wooden figures outside the mercantile, wood-framed houses with steep slate roofs, gravel driveways, rusted cars. It was beautiful. He breathed in the cold air, filling his lungs, seeping into his bloodstream and pushing out the big city toxins through every pore.

He stopped for some groceries at a small corner store. He recognized a few people shopping, and thought that maybe the lady behind the counter was a daughter of one of his old cabin neighbors. But she didn't seem to recognize him so he stayed silent. He got back in his shiny, rustless, silver BMW, out of place in this section of New York, and took a turn onto a dirt road at the far side of town.

The dirt road was bounded by fir and spruce, seemingly overfilling their space and threatening to fall across the road. This area had been logged sixty years ago and the new trees competed in the resulting void, causing them to be stunted and gnarled. David maneuvered his car around several sharp bends to a clearing overlooking Bear Lake. This lake had escaped much of the acid rain damage in much of these mountains, mostly due to the limestone geology that cradled the depression, neutralizing the acid effects with calcium carbonate. As he came around another bend there was a steep slope, the lake before him, the cabins nestled around the shore.

The cabins had multiplied since he sold his cabin and parcel to the real estate developers, but not overly so. The lake was free of ice, but in the cleared areas around the lake the grass was still mostly brown. At the bottom of the hill was a lodge made of thick cedar logs. There were steps sprinkled with rock salt leading to a long, covered wooden porch with *Bear Lake Resort* burnt into a cedar sign hanging by a double chain. David walked across the barren ground, the cold nipping at his hands, opened the outer storm door and then the wooden door.

It was warm inside, a long, narrow room with shelves covered with grocery items and toiletries. A man sporting a torn ball cap and a graying beard sat behind a low counter with a cash register.

"David! I saw your name on the register. We haven't seen you up here in a long time." The man rose and shook his hand.

"Mel. It's been too long. How are you?" David remembered him as one of the loggers in Old Forge that frequented P2s, a local bar where David constantly lost at pool. That had cost him many beers to his opponents. He was very popular in that bar.

The smile melted from Mel's face. "We heard about Haddie. Kate and I are very sorry."

"Thanks, Mel. It was quite a shock."

"They ever catch that sonuvabitch?"

David heard the anger in his tone. Mel had gone to seed, somewhat stooped and with a pot belly, but he still looked strong enough to take on most men. "No. Police said it was probably a taxi, or some drunk."

"Damn foreigners, I'll bet."

"Most likely." David did not feel like arguing. It had been a long day and he wanted to settle into his cabin.

"We're sure glad you came to visit us. We even got you your old cabin for your stay."

"Thanks, Mel." When he made the reservations he had talked

to a young lady, and she wasn't sure if that one was open. Mel was obviously the caretaker. It was a quieter, safer occupation than his last one.

"Kate told me you're quite the celebrity now. She read your book and I can't get her to stop jabbering about it. She had to go out to see her sister in Plattsburgh, but she'll be back tomorrow. You have to see her before you go."

"Sure." David told Mel it had been a long drive and he wanted to settle in. He bought a few groceries, including a six-pack of Genesee, walked back to his car, and drove slowly down the rutted dirt road toward the lake. The cabin was off to the right, a loft with a wraparound porch. A short pier jutted out into the lake. David smiled and then shivered as he thought about how many times he had jumped off it in the summer. He parked and, ignoring the cabin, zipped up his light jacket against the cold wind coming off the water and walked out onto the pier. About halfway out he glanced at a notched pylon where he used to rest his fishing pole while waiting for a brook trout to strike. The wood was gray with age and creaked more than he remembered from ten years ago. Although he didn't keep the place up as well as his dad, David had been able to keep the elements at bay for the most part. The pier now looked neglected. In another ten years it would sag and bend as the wood rotted away. He took a last look across the water at the forested far bank and turned back to the cabin.

The steps up to the cabin creaked almost as much as the pier. The painted window panes were cracked and ill fitted with cloth drapes. He opened the door and stepped inside. A large stone fireplace sat to the right. The handmade leather and heavy wooden furniture had been replaced with a mass produced sofa and several chairs covered with stain-resistant upholstery. The floor was painted cement and a picnic table served as the dining area. David looked up at the loft and could almost see Haddie poking her head over the bannister, her red hair hanging down around her face.

He walked to the back door and looked for a garbage can. The porch was bare, so he tossed the plastic bag containing empty cans and dregs of food from his drive onto the gray wood. Then he walked back inside.

The cabin brought back memories. It made him feel more lonely than at almost any time since Haddie passed. The feeling sunk deep into his loins, and circulated through his body like writhing snakes. He grabbed the six-pack out of the bag, sat down, and cracked one open. Its taste numbed his mouth, throat, and stomach. It wound its way through his body and as the feeling ebbed, he followed it with another large drink, and then another, until he sat in a stupor, watching the ghosts that he knew and loved pass through scenes from a distant past. Memories entertained his wounded soul for the next several hours. Memories that ended up making him feel that his best days were behind him. That what was left in front of him was a shell of his past, a shell full of people who only cared about his money and what they may be able to extract from him, as if pulling his arm like a lever, snatching up the coins, and letting him entertain them until his pockets were empty.

It was now dark. He was tired. He had this place for a week. There was no rush. Haddie could wait until tomorrow night. David grabbed a few sleeping pills and swallowed them down with the last of his beer. And as he started to close his eyes, lying on a couch made in China, his belly full of beer, lulled by a distant growl, he let go of his past to a world of dreamless sleep.

In the morning, David made a cup of coffee, placed three heavy blankets under his arm, grabbed a fold-out chair in his free hand, and walked out the front door toward the dock. Garbage was strewn about the barren yard. Food packages, a can of peanuts, the torn plastic bag hanging on a downed tree branch, flapping in the breeze. He quickly recognized it as *his* garbage, the remnants of the sustenance from his drive that he had placed out here and forgot. He cursed, knowing he should have placed it in the common area metal receptacle that would keep the critters out.

"Goddamn raccoons."

He set his coffee, blankets, and chair on the porch and went inside. He returned with a plastic bag and began picking up the litter. A wind must have kicked up last night, because the lighter pieces had been

carried up to fifty yards from the porch. The breeze and cold nipped at
him, and his hands went numb by the time he picked up the last piece
of garbage and dropped the bag into the common bin. As he returned
to his cabin, he walked through a muddy section of yard and noticed
a large oblong track. He bent over and recognized it immediately as a
bear track. A large bear track.

"It wasn't a raccoon after all," David whispered. His hand fit
neatly inside the track and he thought of the Inlet dump. He hadn't
seen a bear in years and wished he could have spotted it last night
as it made its nightly rounds. He'd have to mention it to Mel. He
stood and stared at the other cabins around the lake. The place was
almost empty except for a few cars. It was early in the season. He was
sure by June these cabins would be packed with couples and families.
He picked up the blankets, chair, and coffee, now growing cold, and
walked out to the pier. He wrapped himself up with the blankets and
sipped his lukewarm coffee.

During summer mornings the loons would make their characteristic
calls. That is, if all these cabins and their noise didn't run them off.
Although there were more cabins around the lake, the trees were still
thick on the opposite shore. Maybe the loons still came back. And in
the morning the tourists still wake to their lonely calls, and their dives
for breakfast. Maybe.

The lake was a little choppy in the breeze, but not too bad. He
would have to talk to Mel about where to find fishing gear. He could
not remember what happened to it after he sold the cabin. The small
waves sparkled, even on this foggy morning. Everything above the first
few rows of treetops on the opposite side of the lake was obscured by
the fog.

The blankets kept him warm in the cold breeze. It comforted
him. A trout jumped from the water. David watched, finishing his cold
coffee. He watched for another trout to jump, and then for anything
familiar to jog an old memory. But, whatever it was he was looking for
was long gone. After a few minutes waiting in vain, David packed his
things and went back inside.

—

The fog lifted before noon and David worked up an appetite collecting firewood from a nearby grove. They sold wood at the lodge, but he'd be damned if he'd waste his money when there was a forest full of downed logs. It was wet but with any luck would dry well enough by evening to have a roaring fire. Sure enough, the sun came out in the afternoon and after David had lunch and unpacked, he walked back to the lodge for a six-pack of beer.

Mel was behind the counter, an apparent fixture at the place. David nodded to him as he walked in. There was a family of four milling through the store. David grabbed a six-pack of Utica Club and placed it on the counter.

"Hot out there?" Mel asked.

"It's warm." David pulled out his wallet and placed a five on the counter. "I saw a big bear track near my cabin. It … was big." He started to say that it had torn up the garbage bag he had stupidly left out and not placed in the bear-proof dumpster, but decided against it.

Mel glanced at the family. They were over in the corner picking out ice cream from the freezer. "Yeah, we've been seeing him around. A big boar," he said quietly.

David looked over his shoulder at the family, then back at Mel. "Is that right?"

"Yep. Kate saw it the other evening when she was taking her walk. It didn't back off. In fact, it started toward her. Slow like. I usually go with her, but my gout was acting up. I go with her every evening now, and carry my rifle too. I think it's a problem bear. I called the County, and then the State Conservation office, but with all the job cuts up here, it didn't seem like a big enough problem for them to send manpower. Me and a couple guys went out looking for it the other night. Tried to bait it. It didn't work. It's a smart bear. But we haven't seen any sign of it in several days."

"Kind of like the big cinnamon-colored bear at the dump thirty years ago?"

"Ol' griz?" Mel smiled. "Kate said the same thing. I didn't know you were old enough to remember that monster. Yep, Kate said that bear could have been his great-grandson. He's cinnamon colored too."

The family moved toward the counter, the kids squealing for their ice cream.

"I'll see ya later, Mel."

"Enjoy that beer. And watch yourself after dusk."

David laid the gladiator suit out on the bed. He took a sip of beer, and glanced at the windows to make sure he had drawn the blinds. *God, I must be crazy. Driving all the way up here. Putting on this suit. And going to bed. If anyone sees me in this thing, I'll be committed for sure.* He felt the metal shoulder shield between his fingers. It was thick and stiff. It felt like the real thing. It could probably take a direct sword hit without cracking or breaking.

He sat down on his bed and took off his shoes. In an hour or two he would be asleep, dressed for war, and Haddie would appear in his dreams. And the dreams always felt … real. While he was dreaming he realized that he was talking to his dead wife, but the interactions did not feel like a dream. He never thought that it was a dream he was having. He was only absolutely sure when he woke in the morning.

He stripped to his underwear and then put on a cloth shirt and fur loincloth. He picked up the chest armor and slipped it around his torso, clasping it in front. He then placed an arm and shoulder guard on his right arm, and then the leg armor on his left leg. He placed the helmet over his head and adjusted the fit so he could see through the slits. He hefted the sword and shield and turned to face himself in the mirror.

Jesus. I look like one of the Village People.

The point of the steel sword touched the floor and the hilt reached his waist. His arm shook when he tried to hold it out in front of him. The shield was large, rectangular, and adorned with concentric ridges. He swung the sword. Its momentum carried him in a half circle, and he had to lunge to keep his balance. His helmet went askew, and he dropped the sword and shield onto the bed, then adjusted and tightened his helmet.

I better lie down before I hurt myself.

—

David opened his eyes.

Haddie sat at the end of the bed, wearing jeans and a pink turtleneck sweater. She always looked good in sweaters.

David clanked as he sat up, his helmet askew such that he could only see out of his right eye. It was dark outside, but the full moon illuminated Haddie. "I thought you'd be dressed as a wench."

Haddie looked down her slim nose. "I'll change in a minute." She leaned over, her fingers exploring David's uniform. "It feels authentic."

He looked down at his loincloth. "Yeah, I got it at a place on the upper West Side." He jumped from the bed, brandishing the sword and shield in mock warfare.

Haddie giggled and quickly placed her hand over her mouth.

David looked down at himself defensively. His arms didn't exactly fill out the protective armor, and the sword and shield were unwieldy and cumbersome. He looked at Haddie. "Hey! This was your idea. And I still don't see *you* in the wench costume."

She sat on the bed leaning back on her hands, eyeing him coyly. "Yes, I'm going. And I'm going to look *good*." She slapped his thigh and stood.

David stared at a bag under her arm. She *will* look good. He was sure of that. He felt ridiculous in his armor. It was all for the book. All for his craft. Or, her craft. Inspiration. What would they do when she came out? Role play some hero-femme fatale actions, leading to a thrilling primal climax that would then pour onto the written page and be talked about for generations of romance readers to come?

I certainly hope so.

Haddie disappeared into the bathroom, closing the door behind her. She had to make an entrance. He lay on the bed. The armor and weaponry were weighing on him. His arms ached, and his legs felt like he had taken a long hike. Haddie would be a while. He also knew it would be worth the wait.

A woman screamed.

David startled, sat up, and looked out the window. He turned an ear, wondering if he had actually heard what he thought he heard.

She screamed again.

He rose and strode out the cabin back door. Fog had settled around the lake and cabin like a white blanket. He saw nothing, but heard footsteps crossing gravel to his right. He circled around the cabin. A woman ran into him, crashing into his armor. She shrieked, pulling her hands back, her eyes transfixed on his armor and helmet. David looked past her and saw a large brown hump with legs running away, fading to gray in the fog and disappearing into the trees. The woman stood there, her eyes wide. He patted her on the shoulder and then walked past. Slowly at first.

Turn around idiot. It'll rip you to pieces.

He walked faster, the thick pine woods drawing him in. He jogged, the metal weighing on him. This was destiny. This was the confrontation necessary to complete his night with Haddie. To complete the book. If he survived it. He reached the edge of the clearing. In front of him the trees stuck up like fuzzy gray posts, thick and close.

Stop. Be smart. The woman is safe. There must be other ways to finish the book.

But his legs only moved faster. He reached the trees, and the lower dead branches of the pines stopped him, seemingly pushing him back, as if trying to protect him from the monster that lurked nearby. He swung his sword through the dead obstructions, the branches scraping and screaming against the metal armor. He lowered his head, now swinging both his shield and his sword, debris raining down on his head. All he saw was the needle-covered earth as he slashed his way through the thicket of trees. Step by step he advanced, having no idea where he was going, thinking that the bear would be long gone by now. He slashed with his weaponry, now yelling at the top of his lungs with a voice he never would have believed to be his own. A guttural cry of war. David had announced his calling with sword and shield and scream, crashing through the wilderness and scaring even the most dominant of beasts into submission and flight. Juices flowed through muscles that he had not used in eons, perhaps never, fueling them into a frenzy, his limbs moving faster than ever in his life, intent on taming this thicket and all its harbored life. He took another swing and his sword sailed through only fog and air. He twirled in a complete circle and collapsed on the ground. Grunting and breathing heavily, he felt the warmth of the steel helmet around his mouth, warmed by his breath, and raised his head.

He had reached a small clearing inside a grove of ancient spruce, their lowest limbs well above his head. The monster bear sat facing him, its ears forward.

The bear was less than ten yards away. David, still on his knees, adjusted his helmet, breathing so heavily he thought he might pass out. He took a deep breath to slow his breathing, but it only made his lungs hurt. The beast was massive, and rose onto its hind legs. David watched the bear rise and tower over him. The air smelled of rotting meat. Bear breath. Its body rippled with muscle; pure wild animal muscle. He knew that at this moment he was relatively safe. A bear rises on its hind legs when it's curious. It probably wondered what was whacking through the impenetrable pines.

David glanced at his metal armor. *I hope he doesn't think I'm a garbage can.*

He checked the surrounding woods for an escape. The trees rose like columns, quickly fading in the darkness and fog. If he ran, the bear's predator instinct would take over and it would tear him apart. He grunted and stood, his whole body shaking, brandishing the sword and shield in self-defense.

This is the stupidest thing I've ever done. Maybe it will go away?

The bear dropped to all fours. It turned sideways and began to circle counterclockwise around the edge of the clearing. The moonlight glistened off its fur. It moved easily. And it was moving toward him.

Oh shit.

The grove of spruce made a natural enclosure. David circled counterclockwise as well, trying to keep pace with the bear. The irony was not lost on him. The Romans used to feed gladiators to starving bears. And here he was, all dressed for the occasion, hoping the bear had made a trip to the dump and eaten well prior to their meeting. All that was needed now to make the scene complete was an audience. Perhaps the squirrels, in place of the Roman audience, were sitting on the spruce branches rooting for their favorite.

The bear charged.

It was a blur of fur and teeth. David screamed, and closed his eyes, waiting for the quarter-ton impact at thirty miles per hour to roil him into a pool of mush. Nothing happened. David peeked out of one eye to see that the bear stopped a few feet in front of him. Its breath crystallized in massive bursts. It all happened so fast, he hadn't moved his sword or shield. He now lifted the sword and pointed it at the beast. His hand shook with fear. He did not hate this bear. In fact, it was a beautiful, though disgustingly smelly, animal. The charge was only a bluff. At least this time.

David circled the bear slowly, his heart beating double time. Beating a natural rhythm. A rhythm perfectly set for an encounter of predator and prey. The rhythm of battle. The bear growled and turned to face him. The moon shone directly off the bear's muzzle, casting a depth into its eyes. A depth that spoke of the ages. Predator and prey. David took a deep breath to calm his shaking body. Had the bear falsely charged him because there was doubt in its mind that he was prey? Was the charge meant to flush out his cowardice? To have him turn and run? He would have been easy prey if he had turned his back on that killing machine. Yes, David was convinced that the bear had doubts as to whether he was prey. It was time to press his advantage.

David screamed and swung his sword. The sword clashed against his shield, steel on steel that made David's temperature rise. It was suddenly very hot in the armor. He swung again, and the bear retreated a few steps, an incredulous look on its face. If it could have spoken, David swore it would say, *Look at that soft little human in the heavy hard suit.*

He rested his sword. All this warring made him exhausted. Suddenly, the bear cocked its head and trotted past him, passing so closely that David could have reached out and touched him. It moved so fast that David had no time to react. If it had decided to attack him, he would have been in that same pose, right hand resting on the sword hilt, his shield resting against his thigh. The bear could have swung freely, decapitating him before David could have shrieked in protest.

He watched the bear pass him and just before it reached the thicket of young trees, turn, and look at him. If it could have spoken, it might have said, *That was entertaining. I'll let it live.*

David knew one thing. He wasn't going to stand there in case the bear changed its mind. He thrashed back through the thicket. Near the edge of the trees where he had entered the first time, voices echoed from a distance. He stopped and listened. The voices were too far away to tell what they were saying, but one thing was for sure. He wasn't going to be caught dead in this gladiator suit. He could see the headlines now. He circled away from the voices and entered his cabin through the back door. As he was closing the door, he swore he heard a woman's voice.

"I'm not crazy. There was a knight in armor that stopped me and then entered the woods after that bear! Why do you keep looking at me like that?"

David sat down on the bed, still clothed in the heavy armor. His head buzzed. He could still smell the bear, the metal, muscle and blade, and the very unlikely outcome, at least in his opinion, that he came out of it not only alive, but in generally good condition. Or at least "as is" condition. His body weighed into the mattress and he closed his eyes.

"Ready or not, here I come!" Haddie stepped out of the bathroom, dressed in a soft leather dress, one side trailing off her shoulder. Her hair was tousled and she slinked toward him. She stopped and squinted. "What happened to you? Where have you been? You look like you've been rolling around in the dirt."

David looked up, only able to see her with one eye through the helmet slits. "I fought a bear."

Haddie walked around the side of the bed. "No, really. You're filthy."

David explained what happened. As he told his story, he became more animated, and soon was on his feet, swinging his sword and lifting his shield in battle. In his retelling, the bear nearly had him by the throat, but he was able to roll out of its grasp. Brandishing his weaponry, he showed how he thrashed the bear and nearly laid him six feet under. But, in the end, he took pity on the beast. A beast that was trying to survive in an ever shrinking ecosystem, a relic from aboriginal times. Alas, he could not smite the beast, and let it escape with its life and dignity intact.

"Wow!" Haddie exclaimed. She moved closer to David, their hips dangerously close. "You fought that bear for me? You fought it for inspiration?"

"Um …" David thought. *Don't screw this up, big guy.* "Yes, m'lady." David smiled and bowed.

She placed the back of her hand on her forehead. "And me, just a lowly wench!"

"Yes, but you are *my* lowly wench." David suddenly felt very hot in his armor.

Haddie reached up and pulled his helmet off. What was left of David's hair was plastered to his head. She put her face close to his. "Oooh, I can smell the beast right now."

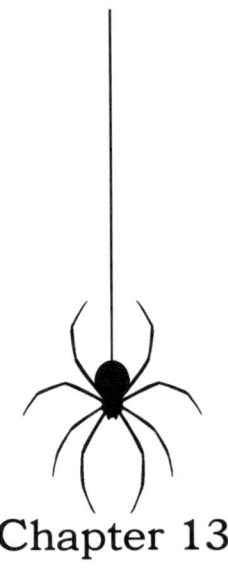

Chapter 13

HE WAS ON FIRE FOR TWO DAYS. HE WROTE IN HIS OLD CABIN, SUBSISTING on beer, potato chips, and locally raised eggs. Sleep was non-existent. Waking hours were not controlled by the sun, but by the muse. His brain rattled off word after sentence after paragraph through his fingers. All senses were heightened and focused on the computer monitor. Day turned to night and back to day and he hardly noticed the changes. Often the only light in the entire cabin came from the monitor, the dark night going unnoticed. The novel's climax flowed onto the electronic page. David never looked back on a word. He was sure it was perfect as written.

Once done, he drove down to the Old Forge library and e-mailed the completed manuscript to Mary (his cabin did not have Internet service). He stayed at the cabin for another two days, hiking along paths that had worn out a pair of shoes every summer when he was a kid; caught a few trout from the lake through cold drizzling rain; drank hot chocolate by roaring fires fueled by wood collected from the nearby woods. The pressure of writing a novel was now off his shoulders. He didn't mind the mud caked on his shoes, the cold rain freezing his exposed hands holding a line, or patiently gathering enough kindling so the fire would be hot enough to catch a big wet log when placed in the fireplace. Every deep breath, every physical effort, peeled away another layer of stress from the pressure of the last several months. The threat of failure—breach of contract, financial ruin, fraud.

He also found himself peeking out the window at dawn, listening intently for rustling noises about his porch in the late evenings. The bear never returned. And Mel hadn't seen it again either, though he told him a story about a crazy lady who thought she saw the beast, followed by a knight in shining armor. "But after all," Mel said, "she was from Vermont."

"David, I absolutely love the book."

"Thanks, Mary." David breathed a large sigh of relief. He was certain that it was good. Well, as certain as he could be. And now it was validated by Mary Lamb. He was back in Manhattan, the land of gas fireplaces and concrete.

"I knew you could do it."

David smiled. He had no idea *he* could. His methods were unorthodox, that's for sure. But effective. He knew how to call the muse.

"OK. We have a lot to do. The publisher is chomping at the bit to get this out. Let's plan a book tour, maybe the morning shows ..."

David sat quietly on the leather couch in his apartment, his cell phone held to his right ear. Mary was in a zone. He would let it ride. It would take a few months to finish the edits, but they couldn't dawdle. They were already behind schedule. She wanted a final manuscript to production by June. This meant a late summer tour, nationwide. Hit mostly the big cities, with a few smaller venues thrown in. That's good publicity. She would take care of all that, of course, while David worked with the editor, cleaning up loose ends on the novel.

"And we can't forget the VIP reading. Just like last time. They were so nice to listen to you when you were a nobody. Now, they get the first reading."

"That's fine, Mary. Just fine."

Mary breathed out heavily, as if releasing a pressure valve. "I knew you could do it, David."

—

The lights from streetlamps flashed across David's face in the back of the limousine. It was a hot August night. Novel proofs had been generated and distributed to VIPs. The edits had been few and far between, mostly minor grammatical corrections. He managed to revise them himself, with no midnight "visits" from Haddie. He frankly missed those visits, but felt they overfed his imagination, something best left to simmer, always below a rolling boil. No more tickets to Tippingdale. Yes, it was best not to think of her too often. But, God, it had been fun writing that novel. To live his life within his imagination, at night, while others slept. He felt more alive then than during his daytime waking hours. The last few months had been full of edits, movies downloaded from his computer, and eating out, mostly with Gil, and occasionally Mary. He had to limit the outings with Mary. He didn't want her to get the wrong idea. But when the loneliness struck him hard, and Gil was busy, he would dial her number. It's not that he couldn't find someone to spend time with. There were plenty of groupies and other hangers-on that would love to hang out with him. But all they wanted was a piece of his fame, a pot of his money, or sometimes, he thought, a slice of his soul.

Mary sat across the limousine, a glass of wine in her hand. She leaned back, legs crossed, looking much more relaxed than the first time they did a reading to these VIPs. He knew what she was thinking. She was riding the elevator with a rising star celebrity. This was *it*. She had marginally successful, competent authors; maybe a minor celebrity author; and *him*. He was the one that allowed her to buy that second house out in the Hamptons, to fly first class, and to stay at high-end resorts without a thought to the cost. This was her moment, too. And she worked hard for it. Perhaps, harder than he had. She had kept him busy and happy during the first tour, stroking his ego and leaving chocolates on his pillow. But unlike the first novel, which was entirely written by Haddie, *he* wrote "Hannah's Last Ride". Sure, it was inspired by Haddie, but it was his hand that scrawled out the story on electronic paper.

The limousine pulled to the front of Dinozio's. This time, he would be dining amongst the VIPs. The reading was secondary. This was his time to give thanks for all the great reviews on "A Kiss During

Mourning." Certainly it was *their reviews* that launched his career. David smirked. He will be humble and thankful, shaking the critics' soft hands. Hands that have never known real work. People who never accomplished a thing in their own lives. Parasites that sucked off the energy of others who created, who entertained. He will let them deceive themselves into thinking that they were part of his success; that they were part of the big show.

There was a loud round of applause when David and Mary walked into the restaurant. Mr. Antonio Dinozio, his bald head shining brighter than ever, escorted them into the crowd. David walked from table to table and then to the bar, shaking hands, a smile plastered on his face. Mary brought him a glass of Merlot. David liked Merlot, and sipped it to numb his emotions.

"Mr. East."

David turned and saw the piercing eyes looking down her hawk nose at him. "Good evening, Ms. Parker. How is Mr. Parker?"

"Drunk somewhere, I'm sure." Ms. Parker tapped his forearm. "I have to say that I am very surprised to see you. I have arranged to sit at your table for dinner. There is so much I want to ask you."

"Of course, Ms. Parker. I am honored." David's smile was beginning to feel like it was set in concrete. She melted back into the crowd, and David couldn't help but shiver, even though it was steaming in the restaurant.

Slowly, the wine began to take effect, and David started to enjoy himself. The atmosphere was jovial and everyone was glad to see him. He had not been out at a public gathering in quite some time. Mary kept his wine glass full as he worked the crowd. When they finally sat down to dinner, Ms. Parker was waiting there, Mr. Parker beside her, sullen and quiet. Mary was digging into her lasagna, stabbing the noodles, strings of mozzarella hanging from her fork, clinging to the pasta in sinewy bands. Mary looked like she had put on a few pounds. Although Ms. Parker joined them in small talk, David knew she had a purpose for seating them together. Was it merely because of his book? Had he finally made it in the literature world to such a status that even Ms. Parker was reduced to a common groupie? In fact, she gushed on and on throughout dinner how good the book was. That it achieved new heights for a romance novel. That it set a new standard. She gushed so, that by the time Mary excused herself to go to the restroom, David was relaxed and loose.

Ms. Parker watched Mary leave the table, and then glanced around the room, making brief eye contact with anyone who might have had the audacity to interrupt them to speak to Mr. East.

"I am surprised, rather pleasantly so, that you were able to pull off the second book so well." Ms. Parker raised her glass of red wine to her lips.

"It was a chore," David said. "But I really enjoyed it."

"Did you? As much as you did writing the first one?"

Ms. Parker smiled when she said that, but David began to feel a trap. He looked into those cold blue eyes. Did she know that Haddie wrote the first book? He kept seesawing back and forth on whether she did or not, but he insisted on responding in a noncommittal way to everything she said tonight.

"I really enjoyed writing the second one." David smiled.

Ms. Parker raised her eyebrows and glanced down at her wine glass. She swirled the liquid clockwise until it threatened to overflow the rim. "I had lunch with Margot Beasley not long before your first book came out. Pleasant woman. But she has never taken care of herself. She has terminal cancer now. Do you know her?"

David gulped a little wine. The dinner crowd seemed very distant now. The voices appeared to call from miles away. "Yes, I met her once. Would you like some more wine, Ms. Parker? I was thinking of getting myself another one." He pushed back his chair.

"Don't leave, my dear boy." Ms. Parker smiled. She was all teeth. She lowered her voice. "I know your secret. And I think, I could be wrong, but I never am, that very few others know. At least," she played with the edge of her napkin, "no one interested in profiting from it."

David remained silent. He would not give her the satisfaction of a confession. Ms. Parker stared at her napkin for a long time while David felt his heart drumming in his chest. *What did she want? Money? A piece of his soul?* She opened her mouth a few times, her lips twitching. She was calculating her next move. And David knew her decision of what she said would be based on what she could gain most from his answer.

"Dear David. You don't have to confide in me. We both know what you've done. I promise I won't say a word. On one condition. Tell me, how did you write the second book? I saw Mary Lamb a few months ago and I could tell when I asked her about you that things were going terribly." She took a sip of wine. David looked around the room, wishing Mary would hurry back.

"Then, out of thin air, you write "Hannah's Last Ride". I know it was you, because Margot told me that Hadraniel had written only one book. How did you do it? Tell me, and I'll never speak a word of this again. To anyone." She peered at him over her wine glass as she took another drink.

David's lips froze. What could he say? What was the truth? Could he speak it? She would think him mad. Should he lie? Jesus, he couldn't even think of a good lie.

"Come on, dear boy. Enlighten me."

David cleared his throat and set his gaze on Ms. Parker's eyes. "I was at the end of my rope trying to write a sequel. As I lay in bed one night, I asked Haddie to help me. For several weeks after, she came to me in my dreams. We wrote it together. That's the truth." David fumbled with his glass on the table.

Ms. Parker sat back in her chair and looked down her hawk nose at him. Then she let out a laugh. A huge, very un-Ms. Parker like, guffaw. People turned in their seats. Mary was walking back to the table.

"What a perfect answer! I love it. I think you have the plot for your next romance, Mr. East." And when Ms. Parker smiled at him, David swore he saw just a hint of respect in her look.

The novel was huge. "Hannah's Last Ride" flew off the shelves and was downloaded onto e-books around the country. The money poured in. Through it all, David watched it like last summer's reruns. The morning television shows, publisher meetings, and endless social dinners came and went, passing by in increasingly mundane succession.

Going out in public was the worst. The attention never stopped. Shallow, pointless, attention. Goofy smiles, squeaky voices questioning his identity on street corners. Why did he hate the attention? When did he get sick of celebrity? He thought it over and over each night alone in another hotel room, a drink in his hand. It all seemed so empty. There were times he wished, even if Haddie could not be with him, that he could at least have his old accountant faceless life back. He dropped that fantasy quickly, though. He enjoyed the money. He enjoyed the freedom it had given him, to be his own boss. But in ways, there was no freedom. The paparazzi even followed him. It was a circus, and he was just a clown being chased by the elephants.

At first, the book readings had been fun. He enjoyed reading the novel that had apparently sprung from his imagination. When he read, it was like walking through a cool lush garden, sampling fruit here, picking a vegetable there. And always thinking of Haddie. Thus, the actual reading was enjoyable. He still enjoyed sharing the book with a quiet attentive audience. But the circus before and after drained his soul to the point that each night when he came back to his hotel room and looked into the mirror he only saw a drab pale shell of a man. He was no longer full of life. And no longer in control of it.

That changed in Seattle.

It was a night like many of the others. He hid in his room until showtime. When he stepped out with Mary and another escort, the crowd thickened the closer he got to the show. That night he was doing both a signing and a brief reading. The throngs closed in as he reached the bookstore. He waved and smiled but always looked over the heads of the crowd. Making eye contact was dangerous, it caused the crowd to become unpredictable. One time the crowd rushed in, collapsing the space and his entry to the store. Wild eyes, groping hands, and the heated excitement of women that had not known love for years wanting to cling to him, to touch his robes. Why the hell don't they get a life?

He remembered looking behind him. There was no escape. And escape is what he wanted. He'd had enough. No more crowds. No more fans. He wanted peace and quiet. His thoughts drifted to his old Adirondack cabin and anonymity. But presently he had no choice but to push on, through the crowd. Ahead there was a small open area with a podium and three young people standing awkwardly nearby, two girls and a boy, looking barely out of college, wide-eyed and wringing hands, clearly out of their element. They were going to control this mob?

David walked up to the podium and gave the young workers a reassuring smile. He turned and looked out at the audience. It looked like the dozen previous readings. Women with middle-aged spread disease clutching their books like a lifeline, their eyes set intently upon him. Their looks were hopeful, lustful yet innocent, if one could believe the contradiction. They lusted for the words on the page, and the fantasy promise of romance by the author who penned it. But, it was just fantasy. These women's love lives were all fantasy at this point, and virtually all of them would be too frightened to allow it to cross the boundary into reality, to a place full of trappings, disappointment, and eventual loss. He was simply the creator of their fantasies, or perhaps not even that. Maybe just a facilitator. A salesman. A pimp to middle-aged women's fantasies that remained anchored deep within their imaginations. Where their lustful thoughts were safe. They all seemed happy. Safe and happy.

He needed to be rid of them. He wished he could just write the book, throw it out his cabin window, and collect the checks. He could hike and fish all day alone, and sometimes, not too often, of course, but sometimes, hail Haddie in the dark of night, and enjoy his own middle-aged fantasies. How could it hurt once in a while to dream of her? It was harmless, as long as he kept the reins on his imagination. It was his life after all.

"Are you ready, Mr. East?"

He looked at the young lady who spoke to him. Her eyes were wide and anxious. The crowd was silent. He got the feeling that he might have been operating in his own little world. He patted her shoulder. "Of course."

He glanced over at Mary, who was standing near the Erotica section. When he looked back at the crowd his frustration grew, turning his face red and making him dizzy. What right did all these fans have to control his life? Why couldn't he do what he wanted? Didn't he deserve to be happy? He wasn't happy here … where the hell was he … Seattle?

He knew no one here. He grimaced. He knew no one anywhere. His life had evolved around Haddie and their careers. He had nurtured no other friendships. His family was gone. His former career was gone. He was now a lone writer. A lone scribe. Was he going to stand here and read another passage from his book and listen to sighs and applause from an audience living inside their own imaginations? That's what *he* wanted to do. That was *his* gig. He produced. He delivered. Now he wanted to be left to his own devices. He wanted to pursue the fantasies within his imagination. He wanted to be with Haddie, the only way he knew how.

"Excuse me, please."

And David walked out of the room. He remembers the silence. He felt Mary's eyes boring into him, trying to figure out what he was doing. He could hear her trying to get through the crowd to him. But, while the seas parted for David, Mary had no free corridor to pass through. David was on the street and into a taxi before the crowd knew what was happening. He heard a few whispers on his way out.

He must have forgotten something.

Maybe he has to pee?

David closed the door of the taxi and glanced at his watch. It was seven.

"Where are you going, sir?"

"To the airport, please."

David caught a red-eye to New York. The plane was empty in first class, and he ordered a martini, sat back, and closed his eyes. He talked to no one. He simply sat, sipped his drink, and emptied his mind. He was back in his apartment by the wee morning hours. He had left all his luggage back in Seattle, but he didn't care. All that mattered now was that he was alone. He was left to his own devices. He stripped and slipped into bed. He spoke his last conscious thought.

"Haddie."

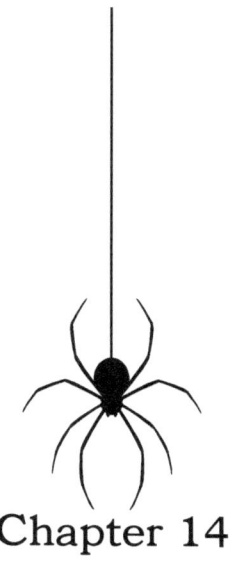

Chapter 14

"HELLO DAVID."

She sat still at the foot of the bed, her long flowing red hair wrapping her face like a blanket. David could not see her legs stretched out beneath her, but sensed they reached almost to the closet door. Her face was calm but alert.

"I missed you, Haddie."

Her face broke into a smile. "I missed you, too. Where have you been? I've been here waiting."

David sat up and the blanket slipped down his torso. Haddie's eyes drifted down from his face, making him wish he had been watching his diet more and working out harder. He thought of the readings and the rabid fans. "It's been chaos. I haven't had a private moment in months."

"You poor ... *live* thing, you. Having to deal with attention. How miserable!"

"Oh come on, Haddie. Yeah, this is something you'd definitely enjoy, you attention monger." David grinned.

Haddie raised the back of her hand to her forehead in mock indignation. "Me? I never enjoyed being the center of attention. God, David, you're pathetic. You can't even imagine what I'm going through."

"I can understand that decay would be disturbing ..."

"Oooh, that was a low blow. I'm still stuck in this waiting room. It's been forever."

"Yeah, but you have that Roman soldier to keep you company."

Haddie rolled her eyes. "Him? I haven't seen him in months. I don't know where he went off to." She looked at him. "And don't look so glib." She ran her hands through her thick red hair. "So, how's our book doing?"

"Wonderful. Sales out of sight. I think over six million at last count."

"And you're lying here all alone? Where are your cheap slutty groupies?"

"I'd rather be with you."

Haddie raised her eyebrows. "Oh, thank you. I'm *honored.*"

David pointed a finger at her. "Why are you being so ornery?

"Why did you wait so long to call me?"

"I've been busy." David cringed. Even though it was the truth. He had been busy on the tour and trying to keep his sanity reined in. But, it sounded like a cheap copout.

"Oh, please. That's what I used to say to my ex-boyfriends when I got bored and stopped returning their calls."

"We're here now. Isn't that all that matters?" He formed the most sincere face he could muster.

She pinched his cheek. "You're so full of shit. But I love you, anyway. And I don't have to, you know. Our contract said, 'until death do us part.'"

"You're so sweet and vulnerable," David said.

They talked for hours. David was completely relaxed. It was the best he felt since the Adirondacks last spring. Talking about the editing, touring, and loneliness with Haddie seemed to release the tension from his mind and body. Plus, he wasn't on the road. He was in his own apartment. And with Haddie to talk to he felt like he was home. The warmth of flannel sheets and soft skin. The rhythmic breathing, the pressure of her chest rising and falling against his. It was sweetness and grace.

"You really need to get a life," Haddie said, brushing her hand along his cheek.

"I've got one, thank you." David kept his eyes closed, and felt the soft strokes against his skin.

He woke to a cold room, alone. The bed was a mess. He shivered and rubbed his arms as he walked to the window in the predawn hour. Naked, he blended in with the gray concrete of the surrounding buildings and sidewalks. It was the quiet hour before the daily rush and hustle of Manhattan. He used to enjoy this time. But now, it only made him feel lonelier than ever. Several pigeons dove from the roof of an old meatpacking plant recently converted to apartments toward the street, diving deeper and deeper into the concrete jungle, snatching at a bagel dropped by an early commuter. He dove right along with the pigeons, his mind sinking deeper into a vacuum, into something that felt like depression. And it scared him.

He was happy when he slept. Peaceful and happy. Why couldn't he feel that way when he was awake? It was Haddie, of course. Why was his imagination so strong when he slept? These were not normal dreams. He knew that. But, they made him happy. What was so wrong with that? Why couldn't he build his own cocoon, wrap himself completely, and wait for the depression to pass? How long could it take? A week? A month?

A movement out of the corner of his eye caught his attention. Two girls in an apartment across the street were snapping his picture and giggling.

Oh great. Now I'll have naked pictures of me splashed across the Internet and the tabloids.

He stepped away from the window and closed the blinds, wishing again that he had kept up his diet and workout schedule.

Mary called his cell phone in the afternoon. David did not rise from his chair to pick it up. But he knew it was her. Fifteen minutes later the phone rang again. He checked the number. It was Gil. Mary must have called him and asked him to see what he was up to. Obviously, she was worried. Her sugar daddy had skipped out on the tour and was no longer answering his phone. Well, he was a writer, after all. A moody, eccentric artist. It was the muse that caused this antisocial behavior. At least that was the public version. Inside, he knew that his mood ran deeper and darker, down black passages beneath the streets, like the Paris catacombs.

He called takeout twice a day. Otherwise he sat in his chair most of the day, staring at the far wall, waiting for dark. Each night he summoned Haddie. She filled the blackness. They would often talk until dawn, their conversation running the gamut of old times, lamenting their childless marriage, laughing over the trials and minor embarrassments that sprinkle everyone's lives. He was alive and she was dead. But they had one thing in common. Waiting. And neither knew what they were waiting for.

On the fourth day there was a knock on the door. He felt himself coming out of a fog, and wondered how long the knocking had gone on before he heard it.

"David! It's me, Gil. Are you in there?"

David was in his chair. He was not thinking of anything in particular, and certainly not doing anything of consequence or otherwise. Yet, Gil's visit felt like an extreme intrusion on his privacy. He considered not answering, but there was a trace, maybe more than a trace, of worry in Gil's voice. If he did not answer the door, he risked police coming and tearing it down. Or worse, the white uniformed men from Tippingdale.

David opened the door. Gil's eyes were large.

"Are you OK?"

David tried to appear casual, as if his four-day beard and wrinkled clothes was the norm for him. "Sure." David waited and wondered how he could get rid of Gil quickly, but he could see in his face that he wasn't going to leave before he saw what Dave was really up to. Mary definitely had a hand in this. "Come on in. You wanna beer?"

"All right." Gil walked in, peering at leftover pizza boxes, cardboard take-out containers, and bottles of soda littered about the condo. It smelled of sour food, soon to turn much worse; that of decaying garbage. "Jesus, Dave. This place is a mess."

David had his head inside the refrigerator. There was no beer, only a jar of mayonnaise and a stick of butter. He closed the refrigerator and pulled out a glass and filled it with tap water. "Here you go." He handed Gil the water. "I've got to get to the store."

Gil took the water and gazed around the room. Food containers covered most of the furniture except the chair David had been sitting in. Gil pushed a pizza box to the side and sat on the couch. David glanced around the room, too, and realized how messy it was. He sat back in his chair.

"Mary called me. She said you skipped the end of the tour. She's worried about you, and asked me to stop by."

David rubbed the back of his neck. "Yeah, I've been meaning to call her." He looked around at the mess. "I've been a bit ... busy."

"Is everything all right?" Gil asked. He added quickly, "I've got to ask. Mary made me promise."

David stared out the window for a moment. Was he all right? He certainly felt better now than he did on the tour, especially those last few days, when the fans' piercing shrieks and repetitive questions made him want to put a gun to his head. He looked around. His place was a mess. He had not cleaned up after himself for four days. His days were spent staring from his chair and his nights were spent with Haddie. Was that normal? Probably not. But Gil had not asked that. He asked if he was all right. He felt all right. Almost happy. He'd *be* happy if Gil would just get the hell out and leave him alone.

"Yeah, I'm all right. Thanks for asking."

David started to stand but could tell Gil was reluctant to leave just yet.

"So how are things at the old office?" Not that David cared. But, it would put Gil on familiar ground and perhaps settle his suspicions. Gil talked and David smiled. But his mind was on something else. He wanted to be left alone, and once Gil was gone, David was going to make sure he was not interrupted again until he was ready. There was unfinished business to attend to. He had made inroads with Haddie. They had talked about so much. He knew more about her now than before she died. Yes, the conversations were all in his head. It was his capacity for insightful, deductive reasoning that allowed him to get closer to her now than he had ever been. But, it felt good. And Gil was in the way.

"David?"

David stood. "Good to see you again, Gil."

Gil stood. "Were you even listening to me?"

"Oh, of course I was." David slapped Gil on the back and pushed him toward the door. "Now, don't be a stranger."

Gil reluctantly walked into the hall and David shut the door behind him. He clapped and rubbed his hands. "That went well."

But he knew better. Gil was not one to pry into another man's business, but Mary was. She will find out how it went, and Gil will be less than enthusiastic. Mary will advance to Plan B. What would she do? Up to and including anything. David was her house in the Hamptons, her first-class seat, her $1,000 a night spa treatments. If he stayed here, he would get no peace. He looked around at the mess he had made over the last four days. He hated to leave; he had no energy for travel. But it was necessary to finish what he started. To finish his time with Haddie. Wherever it would lead, and whenever it would end he had no idea. But he was going to stay on it until it was time to get off. Perhaps this was his way of mourning. Yes, that was it. He was finally getting a chance to mourn.

So, he couldn't stay here. Then, where to go? In a flash, it was as obvious as the stubble on his face. David smiled, and packed his things for the Adirondacks.

It was a beautiful early autumn day, the kind that lifts the spirits and eases the usual aches and pains of life. The sky was western blue, and the leaves still summer green. The BMW trunk was full of canned spaghetti, chili, and beef stew from a supermarket in Utica. David was listening to his sixth CD when he crossed the Blue River Gorge Bridge. He always had mixed feelings crossing that bridge. On the one hand, the scenery really changed to Adirondack mountain vistas on the north side of that bridge. However, it also creeped him out. Several teenagers jumped off the bridge in the 1970s, the end result of a death pact. By the time the bodies were found, the coyotes and wild pigs had torn them up so badly they had to be identified through dental records.

David shook off the thought and continued deeper into the forest, past the dump, and around the ever tighter turns to Bear Lake. He saw his old cabin sitting off by itself, and noticed how different it looked from the newer structures. It was then he realized that he had forgotten to call the lodge and make reservations. What if it was booked? His stomach did a somersault as he pulled in front of check-in. Another place wouldn't do. No. He had to have his old cabin. That's where the memories were. That's where the ghosts of the ones he loved thrived, the cracked wood crevices filled with olfactory remnants of Sunday fried chicken and the summer lake.

David took a deep breath as he walked into the lodge. "Good afternoon, Mel!"

Mel looked up from his paper and squinted. "Well, holy bear shit. You growing a beard, Dave?" Mel stood and peered at the growth.

David rubbed his chin. "Oh yeah. Yeah, I guess I am. I was wondering about my old cabin—"

"You've gotta good start. Yep." Mel pulled his face away. "What can I do you for?"

"David!"

It was Kate. She moved fast for an old lady, her hips lowered as she streaked over. She placed a hand on each side of his face and then gave him a big hug. She had always been affectionate with him, but hadn't given him a hug like that since he was nine years old. David hugged her back and looked over at Mel.

He rolled his eyes. "She's been reading your books. Stayed up until four in the morning reading the last one." He shook his head.

"I didn't know you were such a good writer! I couldn't put it down. Mel kept telling me to turn the damn light off, and I kept telling him to go to hell." She sighed. "I didn't get to see you last time you were here. My sister wasn't feeling well. I remember picking up your book down at the market. It had your name on it! Then Betty told me how you were becoming famous." She let go of him, cocked her head to the side and whispered like she was letting him in on a big secret. "Sometimes news is a bit slow getting up here."

"I'm glad you like my stories, Kate."

"And I'm glad you're here. Are you staying for dinner?"

David looked out the window toward his cabin.

"Oh, you've got to. I'll prepare roast venison. You loved it when you were a boy."

Mel bit his lower lip. "No, Kate, Dave's a busy man. He probably doesn't have time—"

"Oh, of course I do. But I was wondering. Is my old cabin open for rent?"

"Shit. That place? Hell, no one's stayed in there since you last spring. Well, we had one family, but they switched cabins. They complained about mice."

David smiled. "That will suit me just fine."

Supper was long and tortuous. David smiled and nodded and listened to Kate's accolades, while he gripped his thighs, squeezing the pants fabric in his fists. Mel ate over half the venison and burped his contentment, the salad still resting on his plate. David stared at the wall that made a beeline to his cabin. Kate stated over and over that she had to clean the old cabin before he stayed there. It hadn't been rented all summer, guests preferring the new cabins instead. David insisted that was not a problem, the rustic quality is what he liked about it. That, and the memories. Mel and Kate smiled in agreement; the old places had a lot more character than the new. But, it was hard enough to rent any cabins, even the new ones, in this economy. The supper was great, but the thin carpet, unrepaired cracked windows, and small black and white television told a different story. One of struggle to make ends meet. A struggle he guessed they were losing.

After enduring more hugs, he excused himself to the cabin. He drove down, parked, pulled the several bags of groceries and his duffel bag from the trunk, and opened the cabin door. He fumbled for the light. Its dim glow cast an eerie shine off the damp log walls. Cobwebs stuck to the corners, mouse droppings littered the floor, and one little rodent scurried to make an exit behind the refrigerator. But it smelled of aged wood and family history. He lit a fire in the fireplace and grabbed a beer. He sat in front of the fire. There was no television, no land line, no e-mail, and his cell got sparse reception. It was perfect.

"You are *so* pathetic." Haddie lay naked on the bed, tossing a pillow into the air.

David turned to his side. "I think it is a legitimate question. Jefferey said, 'Haddie always got her way.' And it was true. I never would have sold this place without you harping on me. I love this cabin."

"I haven't thought about Jefferey for years. How's he doing?" She turned to face him, her emerald eyes searching.

"Well, he's still enamored with you, if that's what you're wondering."

"No, not at all."

But to David it sounded like it was. Typical Haddie. She had to be the center of attention, even with men she had ditched years ago. He imagined her fantasies of these ex-Haddie men gathering around watering holes, drinking themselves into oblivion, unable to keep a job, whispering her name in reverence. "You ignored what I was saying about the cabin. I loved this place. Why did you want to sell it?"

Haddie put the pillow under her head and turned to David, her breasts defying gravity. "Someone had to make a decision. And you wouldn't make it. We hardly used it, and you wouldn't spend the time to keep it up. The wood was old, the balcony sagging, that oil heater sounded like a poltergeist. There were rats everywhere—"

"Wait a minute. It wasn't that bad."

"David, look at it. It is bad and was bad. You wanted to keep a place that was falling apart. You wanted to hang onto it because it was part of your childhood. That's great if you want to commit the time to it. Otherwise, let it go."

"And what do you mean I couldn't make a decision?"

Haddie squeezed his bicep flexed beneath him. "Honey, I love you, but you have never made a decision. You could never even pick out a restaurant. I had to make the decisions, or we would probably have starved to death and they would have found our bones when we were so behind on our taxes the IRS kicked our door down."

David raised his eyebrows. "You're exaggerating."

Haddie stroked his face. "Maybe a little. But not much. You probably aren't aware of all the decisions I made for us. I paid the bills, took care of investments, hired all the help to keep our place clean, Cat helped me on some of those personal duties."

David gave his dead wife a second glance. "Cat won't even speak to me now. She thinks I stole your book."

"Cat was very loyal to me," Haddie sighed. There was silence. Haddie eyed her living husband. "So, why do you care if Cat speaks to you?"

"Uh, I dunno," David felt the flannel sheets between his fingers. "I just don't want her to think me a traitor."

"Well, I wouldn't worry about it," Haddie rolled onto her back. "I do have to say, after having this time away from the law firm, that I don't miss it or the stress. It makes me wish I had worked in a different field. I would have been happier."

"And probably even happier if I hadn't spent all my time with my nose buried in ledgers and financial statements."

Haddie rolled over and reached out to him. "Then we would have *both* been happier."

David sat in a wooden rocker in front of the fireplace. The sun shone brightly through the threadbare curtains. A half-eaten bowl of noodles was next to him. He was slept out. The beard had made steady progress the past several days. Haddie had liked it. He lamented that it was only early afternoon. It would be eight or nine hours before he would be able to sleep again and see his Haddie.

They talked about so many things now. He wished they had talked like that when she was alive. He first believed the conversations were his subconscious merely reconciling their past, making him realize that they were both human, with all the faults and idiosyncrasies to bear, and that they truly were deep in love. But, he began to think it was much more than overcoming grief and realizing that what he had was true love. How could he know her deepest thoughts? They seemed so real. Her questions, answers, and overall discussion seemed so *Haddie*.

Although he never spoke it out loud, not since going to Tippingdale for thinking the same thing about his conversations with his father, but maybe it *was* real. He looked about the cabin, as if the thought police had heard him utter it deep inside his brain, and would usher in the men in white coats. But maybe their conversations were real. Maybe Haddie was in a netherworld where she could communicate with him when he was in deepest slumber. Perhaps the world of sleep and dreams intersected with the world of the dead, like some cheap horror movie.

A shadow crossed his chair followed by a sharp rap on the door. David flinched. He stole a glance at the door and then quickly looked forward again. He stayed still. He became keenly aware of his rumpled clothing. Although he bathed daily for Haddie, he did not change his clothes during the day because he did not do much more than sit in this chair, and he never wore them to bed. There were many wooden bowls strewn about the floor that once contained cereal, chili, stew, or something else out of a can and heated in the microwave. He didn't want to answer that door. Whoever it was might perceive he wasn't ... *quite right*. Maybe they were checking up on him. Maybe Mary had called the lodge, speaking her concerns, and asked them to check up on him.

Several sharp raps followed.

David sat quietly. If he didn't move, the intruder would go away. He wanted to talk to no one. He simply wanted the day to pass to night. He came up here for some peace, goddammit! Can't they just leave him alone? A large shadow passed across the window. Although David did not look, he envisioned Mel's large veined nose pressed against the window. After a few moments the sunshine returned and David relaxed.

"Forever? That's a long time." Haddie lay next to him, a smile across her lips.

"I really do want to spend forever with you. Just like the vows we made."

"I already told you. Our marriage vows were until death do us part. I'm dead. Game over."

Haddie rolled onto her back, the full moon silhouetting her flat belly and plump breasts. David placed his hand on her thigh.

"Yeah, but someday I'll be dead. And then we'll have forever." David lightly rubbed her thigh with long circular strokes.

"Maybe being dead doesn't last forever. Maybe there's something else beyond that. Like … poofdom." Haddie snickered.

"Poofdom? Jesus, what the hell is that?"

David laughed and moved his hand to her lower abdomen, using slow circular strokes. He felt the flat firm skin. Haddie softly moaned.

"Hmmm, maybe forever isn't so long."

David watched her. Each passing night tightened the bond between them, to the point where he did not want it to end. He wanted to stay wrapped in this night cocoon with her. Where food and water did not matter. Where it seemed timeless, just the two of them lying quietly on the bed. What happened outside their cocoon was of no concern. He wanted this to last forever. And he was convinced, at least now he was convinced, that the only thing standing in their way was his current state of being alive. Once he was dead, they would have forever.

At least until poofdom claimed them.

The shadow crossed the window again as David ate his morning cereal, followed by a knock on the door. It was Mel all right. David weighed his options. If he didn't let Mel in, he was going to become suspicious, or more suspicious than he already was. David didn't want that. He wanted everyone calm and happy. He had a big day today, and didn't want anyone to ruin it.

David walked over, shifted the bowl to his left hand, and opened the door.

"Good morning, Dave!" Mel said.

There was a big smile on his face. That was very unlike Mel, who was usually stoic.

"Haven't seen you for a while; just wondering what you're up to."

David smiled. "Keeping busy, Mel. Doing a lot of writing. You know how it is when the muse hits."

Mel kept a smile on his face as he observed David's appearance.

Then he nonchalantly craned his neck to see past him into the cabin. "Kate's finishing breakfast. She wanted to clean your place up a bit for you."

"Oh, no, no." David said it a bit too quickly. He cleared his throat. "I mean, don't bother. I was going to do some cleaning myself this morning."

"It's no bother, Dave."

David felt Mel's eyes boring into him. Mel knew of his past. He knew about Tippingdale. He knew that story. All of it. David looked down at the ground and then met Mel's eyes again.

"It's just that right now I'm writing. I have to put pencil to paper while the iron is hot, if you know what I mean." David felt beads of sweat form on his forehead.

"OK. Just offering. Why don't you come by for dinner tonight? Kate will fix up something special."

"Sounds good, Mel."

Mel turned but not before giving David a last, long look.

David shut the door. He let out a deep breath and gazed around the cabin. He couldn't do it here. The cabin meant too much to him, and frankly, Mel and Kate as well, to do it here. He searched his garment bag and pulled out his jacket. He slipped on his shoes and walked out to the car. He drove up the dirt road and turned left toward the Blue River Gorge Bridge. He still remembered the faces of the kids in the local paper. Drugs had to be involved. What else could drive a group of people to commit suicide together? He shrugged it off. What he was doing was completely different. He had a plan. He believed a logical plan.

He had a gift. It was true when his father died, and it was true with Haddie. He could talk to the dead. And the people he loved most were dead. There was nothing left for him in this world now. He grew warm in the car. It was a beautiful sunny day, the leaves of the deciduous trees still bright green. But he saw it as a dying day. In a few short weeks the leaves would turn a brilliant color and then brown and fall to the ground. The leaves were dying, the annuals were dying, and he was dying.

The car stopped at a pullout near the bridge. He got out, took off his coat, tossed it into the front seat, and walked briskly to the center of the bridge. He could not hesitate. It had to be done quickly. He placed his hands on the three-tier steel railing and leaned forward, the railing pressing against his navel. He looked over the edge, five hundred feet to the rushing water below. Boulders stood in defiance of the current, water splashing over and around, creating small eddies on the leeside. He thought of trout for a moment. Every small eddy on the leeside of the boulder would contain a trout, waiting for food to drift by. Well, weren't they in for a big surprise.

He stared into the swirling waters, his hands gripping the railing so hard they shook. The logical portion of his brain told him to jump. It would solve his problems and let him be happy with his loved ones again. He had a gift! This jump was his for the taking, to dive headfirst into the great unknown. But not unknown to him. He had been visiting the dead for decades now. Then why were his feet seemingly cemented to the narrow sidewalk?

"Hello, Dave."

David flinched, his eyes big and glassy, focusing on the greeter. It was Mel.

"Oh." David looked briefly over the railing again, the sound of the current rushing in his ears. "Hi, Mel."

Mel walked over to him and rested his forearms on the railing. He stared into the waters below. "I've known you a long time, Dave. I remember when you were in diapers. You were always an inquisitive kid. Very imaginative. It doesn't surprise me at all that you've become a famous author. And I know you've had your share of shit thrown at you. And that you've had your difficulties dealing with the shit, like we've all had." Mel spit into the waters.

David said nothing, but continued staring into the waters below, the violent thunder of the current now ringing in his ears.

"Fifteen years ago, I stood exactly where you are now. I had lost my job. There was no income, no prospects. Just a life insurance policy. How selfish I would have been if I had done what I was thinking to do." He chuckled. "My wife would have killed me."

David smiled and loosened his grip on the railing.

"I found a new job, enough to feed my family, and stay in the place

I love. Yep, you're pretty lucky, if you ask me. A lot to live for. And a lot of people who care about you." Mel straightened his arms and looked out at the mountains. "Kate's making antelope stew. I shot it in Wyoming on a trip early this year. We expect you there."

David gulped. He knew he should not have hesitated. Now he had doubts. He knew that today was not the day he would jump into the gorge. "I'll be there, Mel."

Mel sighed. "Ah, good."

And he turned and walked back to his truck, limping stiffly from forty plus years of cutting down trees, working their course down the rivers, and planing lumber.

"You idiot! You were going to kill yourself?" Haddie glared at David so hard it made him almost throw up the antelope dinner.

"Well, I didn't actually *do* it. I just want to be with you," David said sheepishly.

"And end up in purgatory, wandering around forever? Do you think I want to wander around purgatory forever?"

David frowned. "Purgatory? Is there such a thing?"

"How the hell would I know?" Haddie shook her head.

"Well, you're *dead*. If anyone would know—"

"Oh, please. Stop reminding me." Haddie sniffed and wiped at her eyes. "Promise me you'll never think of killing yourself again."

"OK, OK. I thought you'd be supportive." David crossed his arms across his chest.

"You are crazy. I want you to promise me you'll get help." Haddie sat up, her breasts defying gravity again. David was really glad he waited until *after* they had sex before he mentioned his little suicide issue with her.

"OK, I will. Just don't be mad." David saw that her eyes had welled with water. If he didn't know her any better he would have sworn they were tears.

"And we need to take a break from each other."

David shot up and grabbed her shoulders. "Now don't get hasty, Haddie. I can control this."

"I don't want to see you before your time. This isn't worth it. Don't ask for me again until you've gotten help." Haddie sighed. "Maybe we should not see each other again until you die. Naturally, in your sleep. When you're ninety."

David's jaw dropped. "Are you kidding? I'll look horrible. I'll be old and wrinkly, and … more bald. I'll be ugly, while you're all beautiful."

Haddie glanced at his paunch and his hourglass head. "Believe me, it'll barely change how good looking you are."

David woke. It was gray dawn outside. A lone loon called, its sound penetrating the cabin, and making him feel like he was the only person in the world. He sat up and threw the covers off. It was time to go home.

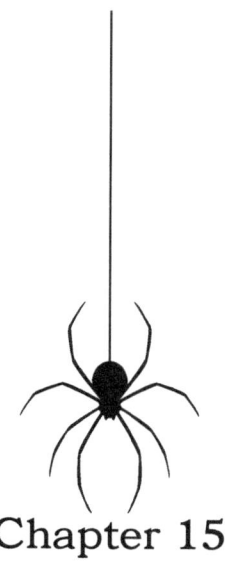

Chapter 15

"Yes, well, I guess we were worried about you. Just a little." Mary smiled and took a bite of her salad.

Sure, we were worried about you. David leaned back in his seat. He had gotten the story out of Mel after the antelope dinner and Kate had gone to bed. It was Mary who had called and asked Mel to check up on him. And he said that she was very happy that David was there because she had been looking all over for him. Her gravy train had left the station and disappeared into the night. Mel had calmed her fears. Perhaps it was because he knew about David's overactive imagination issues and could reason with him.

Mel had watched him all right. That's how he showed up on the bridge. Fortunately, when he talked to Mary, he didn't mention the "bridge thing." Actually, after thinking about it on the ride home, David thought he probably wouldn't have jumped, even if Mel had not arrived and chatted with him. It was enticing to think of eternity with Haddie, but staring down at those boulders far below seemed like a violent end. He was irritated at being followed by Mel like he wasn't right in the head, but at the same time, it was nice to know that people cared enough about him to go searching for him. And prevent him from splashing his brains on boulders hiding trout in the Blue River.

"I'm fine, but thank you for thinking of me." David's pastrami sandwich tasted really good after eating canned food exclusively for a week. He didn't tell Mary, but he also started seeing a psychiatrist. Three sessions for $250. What a deal. When he arrived for his first appointment, he realized why. The psychiatrist was barely out of college. She was fresh from the Midwest and a diet of milk and honey. It didn't seem like the sessions would solve anything, but they were amusing. So, he sat there for forty-five minutes, twice, and probably learned more about her than she did about him. Her father was overbearing, her mother worked at the racetrack, and she had an abortion while she was still in high school. After the second session, he began to wonder who was the patient, and who was the doctor.

David looked around the restaurant. They sat in a quiet corner at the front where they could look out at the street and watch the people stroll by. It wasn't really cold, not for a stroll, but too cold to sit outside, except for a few hearty souls in leather jackets and Scottish sweaters. The restaurant windows were spotless, and the interior looked like a 1955 Buick Special, all shining chrome and steel. The restaurant owners recognized him. He was a regular. They seated him anywhere he wished. He could tell that they especially liked it when he asked to sit by the front window, or out on the front walk. He was one of the celebrities. He attracted other customers. People were always giving him a second glance as they walked by, and if they asked for an autograph, Mary made sure to tell them that she was his agent. She basked in the attention. But he really didn't care. The only reason he was here today was to ease Mary's mind, for he was much better and wanted to make sure Mary thought so, too. And The Canal made a helluva pastrami sandwich.

"I've gotta get going, Mary. I have an appointment." He was going to his psychiatrist for his last session. He didn't expect much, but he paid his ticket, so he'd finish the ride. Mary looked genuinely disappointed when he said he had to leave. She had a pout on her lips and a furrow in her brow. She pried a bit to find out where he had to go, but he stayed coy on the subject. He didn't want the tabloids to get wind of his visits to a shrink. The last thing he wanted his fans to think was that he was just another neurotic writer from New York. An agnostic Woody Allen.

Dr. Stein's uptown office was cheerful and open. It was not in a converted warehouse, which was a plus. The carpet was soft, plush, and blue. There were cushy chairs with large pillows. David realized that part of the reason why he wanted to come back was to relax in the soft ambience and smell the fresh womanly scent. He really needed to find a girlfriend. The rustic cabin was all wood, stone, and nails, and his apartment was austere hard leather. And his apartment also smelled like dog urine, which was funny, because he didn't own a dog.

"Have you noticed a trend during our conversations, Mr. East?" Dr. Stein sat in her chair, dressed in a skirt suit.

David stared at her, wondering if her glasses were prescription, or just filled with glass to make her look more professional and smart. "What do you mean?"

Dr. Stein lowered her notepad. "I ask you questions, trying to find out why you're here, so I can help you. Instead of answering me, or talking freely, you probe my private life. I have amused you thus far, because it has opened you up a little, but if we really want to get to *you*, Mr. East, then you need to cooperate."

David suddenly felt that Dr. Stein looked much more serious than he ever thought before. As he sat there, he realized that he wasn't really seeking answers to any of his supposed issues. He was merely playing out what all celebrities did when they reached the brink of the abyss. Rehab. In his case, he wasn't addicted to booze or drugs. He was addicted to his dead wife. And, yes, happened to see her so vividly in his dreams that he preferred sleep to his waking hours. But he was over that. He spent time in Tippingdale because his kitchen table discussions with his dead father led him to withdraw from normal social ties. What did the doctors say to him there?

Overactive imagination, young man. Now get over it, go forth, and multiply.

Dr. Stein knew that much about him. She knew he had those dreams, that he yearned for his wife. She knew about Tippingdale. She knew about his obsession, though he left "the bridge thing" out.

Dr. Stein's eyes were soft but unyielding. Her black hair was fairly short and straight, barely brushing her collar.

"Now, is there anything of substance you would like to tell me?" She glanced at her watch. "We have fifteen minutes."

David was surprised by her directness. He was a celebrity, after all. "Do you think I'm crazy, or do you think I have an overactive imagination?"

"Neither," she said flatly. She recrossed her legs.

David was surprised again. "Oh, could you expand on that answer?"

Dr. Stein smiled. "You should have been a psychiatrist, Dr. East. Now, I haven't heard much of your story, because you have shown so much interest in mine. But, talking to past loved ones is actually very common, and in some societies, both past and present, accepted. The Tibetans, ancient pagans ..."

"How about normal societies?" David asked.

"You mean Western society? Well, in Western society you would be diagnosed with *acute prolonged grief syndrome*. Does that make you feel better?"

"Not really," David said, shifting in his seat. "It sounds like big words for not getting over it."

Dr. Stein smiled. "Yes. It does. It's not unusual for you to hear Haddie's voice. It's rather common after a death of a loved one. It is unusual to experience the kind of dreams you've been having. Not unheard of, but unusual. I know this is another example from a non-Western society, but the medical literature discusses certain Indonesian cultures that experience something similar to what you are going through. It's sparse, however, and I'm not very familiar with it."

"Yes, yes," David waved his hand. "But those are jungle societies. I'm talking about American society, or maybe Western Europe ..."

"You're a writer. Perhaps this is your curse for having such an active imagination."

Dr. Stein tilted her head to the side and raised her pencil to her lips. "Would you like to know what I recommend, Mr. East?"

"Yes, I would." And he actually did.

"Find a nice lady and get into a relationship. The literature is clear that men that remarry do best long term."

"We'll see," David said. She was fifteen years his junior, a bit too young for him, but he couldn't resist teasing her. "What are you doing tonight?" He smiled.

"Taking a long hot bath," Dr. Stein said, "alone. But I do have to say that I really enjoyed your two books. And if my mother ever decides to date again, I'll have her get in touch with you."

David left feeling a bit older than his years. He walked to the street corner and realized he was at the bookstore café there. He had not been in there since he was accosted by the romance reader cult. He walked down the side street and entered, intent on a good espresso and a few new books to read in the evening.

The smell of paper, ink, and coffee filled the air. It relaxed him. He wondered how he could have gone so long without coming here. How long had it been? Six months? A year?

"Hello, David."

He knew that voice. It was Cat.

He felt ice in his blood. Her face had such hatred last time he saw her, he was hesitant to look at her again. But, when he finally turned, he saw none of the anger of their last meeting. Her face was calm, her blonde shoulder length hair pulled back from her beautiful face. Her green eyes were bright and vulnerable. As usual, she wore black. She held a coffee cup in her hand.

"Hi, Cat." He was still waiting for her to explode at him. To accuse him of being a thief of his wife's artistic creation.

She glanced at the empty table where they had sat during their visits together here. "Are you going to get a coffee?"

David felt his face turn red. This was confusing. "Ah, yes. Do you want to sit down?"

She smiled and looked at the table again. "I'll meet you over there."

David wandered toward the coffee counter. His head hummed as he absentmindedly ordered an espresso. How could he get his head around this situation? Why her sudden change in attitude? She absolutely hated him last time they met. He picked up his drink and turned back to the table. What should he say to her? Should he explain the whole thing about Haddie? She would think he was really nuts. No, a soft approach is better. Take your time. Do something you never do. Listen.

She bit her lower lip.

"I'm sorry I was so mean to you. I was angry when I found out you published Haddie's book. You had all that money, those expensive clothes … it made me sick. And then the second book came out, and was so good, it was almost like Haddie had written that one, too. But I knew she hadn't. She would have told me. The only way you could have written the second novel was if you truly loved Haddie and were so close to her, so in tune with her feelings, that you could have written a book like her. And if you published the first novel under your own name, you must have had a good reason."

David remained silent. He felt so sorry for her he wanted to give her a big hug and just keep repeating that it was all right.

"It's just all so romantic." She blinked the tears out of her eyes, and dabbed at them with a tissue.

David watched her in amazement. An hour ago his romantic future was limited to trophy-hunting women. And now he was sitting with the one woman he had not been able to get off his mind since their coffee together two and a half years ago. What was it about her? What caused this obsession?

"Let's have dinner tonight," he said.

She sniffed. "You don't have to leave right now, do you?"

"Oh no, I don't have to go anywhere."

"Good." She smiled.

David felt like a school kid again. He felt his heart pounding, and his hand began to sweat, which was too bad because he didn't want to take his hand back. He didn't want to gross her out on their first date. The hours melted away. The subject turned to Haddie a little too often for him, but he realized they were the two that knew her best. And while David mourned through his nighttime fantasies, Cat probably needed to talk to someone (and who better than him?). The discussions about her weren't mournful, but more how she made them laugh, or comforted in some way. Cat's spirits brightened over the course of the afternoon, and he thought she was flirting with him too, coyly eyeing him and touching him with her hand or foot when admonishing him, or laughing at his jokes. Even the bad ones, and they were mostly bad. She had a new job, held herself confidently, and all around seemed to be content. There was no sense that she carried any baggage as when he saw her before her big excursion to the Pacific Islands. Her demeanor clashed with her black attire.

"So, how was your vacation to the Pacific?" he asked.

Cat set down her third cup of coffee. "It was disappointing compared to the brochures. But, I coped." She glanced down at her watch. "I have to go see the lady I'm caring for. Would you like to come along? And then we can have dinner?"

"Sounds great."

They walked out into the chilly air and down the sidewalk. Mid-afternoon traffic was thick and their course took them past several active building façade repairs. In most places there was scaffolding and plywood to walk under to avoid walking out into the street, but in a few areas they had to walk out in traffic, hugging the curb. David walked on the outside, somewhat protecting Cat from the traffic. David kept glancing over his left shoulder. Every other car was a taxicab in Manhattan. Ever since he lost Haddie, he was paranoid about cabs. He looked both ways twice before crossing and always assumed taxis wouldn't stop at a red light. And now, walking down the right side of the street with his back to the traffic, he felt more vulnerable than ever. Cat seemed oblivious to the speeding cars and commented on a department store across the street that was having a big sale the next day.

Cat steered him toward a substantial building. "I've been with her for a year. She's been in hospice for the last month. Lung cancer. It's horrible."

The building atrium was high-ceilinged. A beautiful crystal chandelier hung above a small fountain. They walked toward the back to the elevators.

"She is lucky that she'll be able to pass her final days in her own home. We have nurses around the clock to tend to her, morphine for her pain, and such. Up until September I took care of all her appointments, scheduling, errands. Now it seems like I spend all my time with estate lawyers and watching her slowly waste away."

They stepped into the elevator. Cat popped a piece of mint gum into her mouth.

"Would you like a piece?" she asked.

"Sure," David said. He didn't really feel like having one, but he suddenly felt self-conscious about his breath.

The elevator stopped at their floor. She handed him a piece and smiled. Seemingly reading his mind, she said, "Your breath smells fine. I just *hate* the stench of impending death."

The door opened and they walked down the hallway strewn with Oriental rugs and antique mahogany tables. The air smelled of money. David thought that this woman must be rich to be able to live (and die) in a place like this. Cat maintained a brisk pace, taking out her keys and opening a dark paneled door. The first whiff of antiseptic stung David's nostrils and brought back strong memories of Haddie's last moments in the hospital. Machines whirred, the sucking of air from a respirator filled the room, a dying body behind a plastic curtain. Haddie's vision came back to him, her reaching hands, her pleading eyes.

The nurse greeted them. "Ms. Beasley is stable and coming in and out of consciousness. It seems to coincide with her morphine levels."

"Thank you, nurse."

David took a double take. Ms. Beasley? He walked to the head of the bed. The nurse pulled back the plastic screen to reveal an emaciated ancient woman. She was still, her skin apparently too large for her. Her face was layered in wrinkles. Her veined, translucent hands stuck out of her blouse. Her hair looked like a wig. David didn't recognize her, but wanted to be sure.

"Who is she, Cat?"

Cat stared down at Margot Beasley. "She used to be an agent. A writer's agent. She's only sixty-three. And tough. She won't die. The doctor said she should have been dead weeks ago." She looked up at David. "We'll just be here a minute while I check a few things out and then be on our way."

David looked at her again. Margot Beasley, the agent. She was the agent David had talked to. The one who had given David the idea to put the book in his own name. When she was relatively healthy and still puffing like a chimney he thought she must have been seventy or more. Now she looked like an Egyptian mummy with the bandages off. David stared at her in amazement that someone who looked this bad could still be alive.

Her hand flickered and she opened her eyes. Cat glanced down at the old woman's hand. The old woman shifted her gaze from Cat to David. She blinked twice, and then her lips parted.

"She's trying to speak," Cat said.

David instinctively placed his hand on hers. He could feel the bones. It was like touching a skeleton.

Cat spoke to the nurse. "No change, then?"

"No. Although this is the first time she has tried to speak in over a week."

The nurse studied David for a moment and then looked away, busying herself with the whirring machines. David expected she was going to ask him whether Ms. Beasley knew him. He was glad the nurse stayed silent. Cat did not seem to notice anything, and right now things were going so well with her that he didn't want to have to explain how he met Ms. Beasley. His stomach churned. Of all the rich people in New York, why did Cat have to be working for her?

The old woman closed her eyes. David breathed a sigh of relief.

"Let's go," Cat said, and squeezed his hand.

Cat cheered considerably when they left and stopped for dinner at a small bistro nearby. David thought it was too ostentatious, with the French accents and snobby waiters, but Cat enjoyed it, especially after a few drinks. He thought to himself that she had seen a lot of loss in her employment. Haddie, and now Margot Beasley, though Cat did not seem to have the affection for Ms. Beasley as she had for Haddie. As she relaxed during her third glass of wine, Cat confided in him about the loss of her first and only husband. He had never heard the story, and wondered how much Haddie had known.

"It was a cold night. It had been raining all day, and we had way too much to drink to be driving," Cat started. They had come to this dip in the road once before when it was flooded. They were sober that time and turned around, spending a night in a nearby hotel until the waters receded. But, this time Donald was confident they could cross. That was the booze talking. He insisted that their Subaru had clearance, and the water wasn't as deep as it looked. The car was swept downstream before the back tires hit the water. The car jostled from side to side and gained speed as it crashed along the current, their heads knocking against the headliner. It was then that Cat saw her husband's head break the windshield. They hadn't been wearing their seat belts. The car quickly filled with muddy water and soon Cat couldn't see anything. The force of the streaming water knocked her into the backseat. She blindly searched for her husband as she held her breath. She found a window handle and rolled it down, still reaching for Donald with her free hand. With the oxygen in her lungs consumed, the need for fresh air forced her out of the car and to the surface. Gasping, her body turning numb from cold, she swam and waded to shore. Donald's body was found the next day three miles downstream. He had apparently been ejected from the car, unconscious, and drowned.

David ordered another drink.

"He always took good care of me. Donald was a whiz in real estate. He owned several properties here in Manhattan. I sold all but my apartment."

Cat told her story as a matter of fact. She had come to grips with that loss, but David couldn't help but feel that it had put a severe damper on the evening. So, he was surprised when Cat suggested they go back to her place. Perhaps her situation with Margot Beasley, and remembering her dead husband, left Cat feeling lonely and in need of company. She hid it well. She was cheerful on the walk home. He had his hand in his pocket, and she slipped her hand through the space between his arm and body. She squeezed his arm as they walked, and he could barely keep his eyes off her beautiful face, her cheeks pink from the cold.

Her apartment jogged his memory from the first brief time he was there. It contained a mishmash of art from exotic places, from Mayan ceremonial war masks to carved African savannah predators and prey. The knickknacks contrasted with the soft lighting and Victorian furniture.

Cat drank several glasses of wine at the restaurant and now brought out a fresh bottle from the cupboard. David watched her, recognizing the transition from wanting her to having her. There was no doubt inside him that they would be together now. He felt uneasy in a way, having a relationship with a woman who was so close to Haddie. It had been overwhelming last time he was here. But now, he felt a certain calm, as if knowing Haddie would have wanted him to be happy with her. It had been nearly three years since her death. Perhaps it was time to be happy with someone else.

Cat joined David on the couch. She handed him a glass of red wine. "Do you like Merlot?"

"It's my favorite," David said. He took a sip, and it tasted overly tannic.

"I'm so embarrassed. I've been talking about myself all evening." Cat looked a bit glassy eyed.

David smiled. "Oh, that's fine."

"How've you been? Are you enjoying your new career?"

"Yeah. I'm my own boss. At least when my agent is not harassing me about deadlines."

"And financially rewarding?" she asked, smiling behind her glass.

David laughed and moved closer. "Yes, my dear. I'm filthy rich."

"Oooh. Keep talking dirty to me." She pawed at his arm like a cat playing with a wounded mouse.

David really was rich. And one needed money to enjoy New York. He had over $10 million in the bank, a condo off Central Park, a brand new BMW, a significant stock portfolio, and was swimming in residuals. He now had a beautiful woman. He felt lucky to be with her. She was intelligent, purposeful, efficient. He watched her lips as she moved closer, smelling her perfume, wine fresh on her breath.

David woke to the smell of bacon. It was bright and sunny. He rolled over and stretched, staring at the Africa savannah predators carved in ebony resting on the mantle. He put on a shirt and wandered out into the kitchen, where Cat was cooking breakfast.

"Good morning," she said, stirring the pork around the frying pan.

Her hair was wet. She was dressed in a black bathrobe, and David thought her bare feet must be cold on the kitchen floor. He scratched his bald head.

"Go get cleaned up for breakfast." She smiled at him.

David wandered into the shower. The hot water stung his back as he washed himself. He remembered the pain Cat had inflicted with her nails in the midst of their passion. As he rubbed himself down with soap, his muscles were sore and stiff. He slipped out of the shower and looked into the mirror. There was a purple bruise on his neck, and several on his chest. She was downright savage. He turned and looked at his back in the mirror. The cuts on his back formed dark red raised welts.

Jesus. She's an animal.

David settled into as normal a life as he ever had since he lost Haddie. Although Cat and he kept their separate apartments, they saw each other almost every day. They would have their morning coffee in the café, talking and he signing the occasional autograph, take walks in the afternoon if David wasn't busy on some kind of public relations stunt devised by Mary, and meet up at dinner and for the night. David learned that Cat was a complex woman. Her interests and desires ran a spectrum of diverse, and sometimes, at least in David's mind, conflicting interests. Why was she interested in an author discussing voodoo rituals at the Strand when she was (previously unknown to David) a devout Presbyterian? David never even knew there were any devout Presbyterians. She often chided him for not attending services with her, but as he always said, Sunday football, baseball, or any other show on television, took precedence over church.

They had other differences. She exercised intensely almost every day to work off the dark chocolate she craved. She was a surprisingly heavy drinker, too, but tolerated it well. David liked his beer and chocolate éclairs in moderation, and his exercise in even lesser moderation. All in all, though, David felt like they fit well together. He was infatuated with her and her lithe body, and as winter turned to spring, his feelings only grew stronger. He was, for the first time in a long time, happy.

And then David became convinced she planned to kill him.

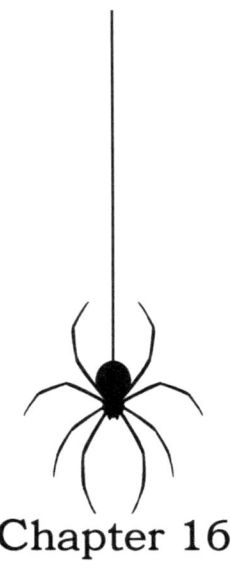

Chapter 16

"LET'S MOVE IN TOGETHER," DAVID SAID, GRINNING, HIS CHIN RESTING ON his hand.

"Yeah, and then what?" Cat responded, taking a sip of Spanish wine. She sat with her legs crossed, her toe circling clockwise in a steady motion.

"What do you mean?" he said.

"I'm old fashioned." She ran her hand through her blonde hair. "My mother told me that a man will never marry if he can just live with a girl instead." She raised her cup to her lips.

David cleared his throat. It was a warm evening. A summer evening in May. They sat in front of a sushi bar on the sidewalk. He scratched his back against his chair. His welts were healing and he wasn't sure if it was because she was more controlled in her lovemaking, or his skin had toughened. He stared at her. Her emerald green eyes, blonde hair with bangs that always seemed poised to stab her eyes, her sharp eyebrows, and subtle smile. Could he wake up to that every morning? They had only been dating five months. But, he had known her much longer.

She stared back at him. She always seemed to have a look of wanton lust on her face when she stared at him. He loved that about her. Maybe if he set a date down the road, way down the road. He wasn't keen on marriage, but frankly, the evening commutes to her apartment were getting old.

"OK. Let's get married," he said.

David rubbed his chin. How far off could he set a date? He was crazy about her, but … was money an issue? Maybe so. He had a lot of it now. What if it didn't work out? Should he ask for a prenuptial? *That* wouldn't go over well. Sayonara, Cat. His chin suddenly felt raw. How long had he been rubbing it? He used his chopsticks and swallowed the saba. He loved mackerel. A lot of people didn't like it because it was too fishy, but to him, it tasted like the sea. That was another thing he loved about Cat. She was the only Caucasian woman he knew who loved raw fish.

"You look deep in thought, David." Cat leaned over, her cleavage clear through her low cut blouse.

"Christmas is romantic," David blurted. Her damned cleavage could get him to say anything.

"I like Independence Day. It's ironic." She looked at him with those emerald eyes, slicing away his defenses.

"I feel like I'm in negotiations," David said.

Cat sat back in her chair and crossed her arms. "You are, and you're losing badly. And once you say yes, you're mine." She looked away, off into the far distance, past the skyscrapers, seemingly past the horizon.

David smiled. He couldn't imagine spending his days with anyone else. She was beautiful, and he had a lot of money. All he had to do was write a blockbuster novel once in a while to keep it all going. He briefly pictured them as bride and groom, and could think of only one place for a wedding. "OK. Independence Day. In the Adirondacks." He pointed a finger at her. "No more negotiating."

Cat laughed. "I love it when a man takes charge."

David's smile faded. He had put off telling her about his bouts with *an overactive imagination*. But if he was planning to spend the rest of his life with her, he had to get it out in the open. He would never be able to hide it from her forever. There had been minor stories in magazines and the newspapers that touched on it. He was "unstable," but after all, an artist! One magazine had stated, *Weren't they all screwed up?* Nothing that rehab couldn't cure.

"Cat, I need to tell you something." David's hand shook. He feared losing her.

"What?" Cat looked at him without expression, as if she was ready for anything.

"Well," David started, searching for the right words so he wouldn't sound too crazy. "There was a time, during my college days, when I wasn't quite myself ..."

"We all went a little wild in college, David." She winked at him.

"No, this was a little different." David took a deep breath, ready to plunge into a monologue on his overactive imagination period.

Cat took his hand and leaned toward him. She spoke in almost a whisper. "You mean when you went a little crazy, dreaming about your father? Don't worry, Haddie told me all about that."

Sure enough, Cat knew about Tippingdale. Haddie had told her. David sat there with his mouth open. Did Haddie and Cat have no secrets between them? Certainly, Cat knew nothing of his dreams about Haddie. After all, besides the obvious fact that Haddie had passed, David had dealt with it on his own. He was master of his domain. King of his mind. At least at the moment.

"I also had dreams about Haddie," he confessed.

Cat's hand froze on his. Her face turned from a mild, knowing smile to a frown. She bit her lip. "Really ..."

She did not expect this. This was clutter penetrating an organized mind.

David sat forward. Cat leaned forward also. "Yes."

"Did you go to counseling, or talk to anyone about it?" Cat watched him. "I mean, to get over it?"

"I went to a psychiatrist for a short time. She said my case was unusual, but not unheard of."

"What did she say?" Cat asked.

"She said I need to find a good woman and settle down." David squeezed Cat's hand and smiled.

Cat sat still. "No, I mean Haddie. What did you talk about? I mean, did she talk about me?"

"You? Cat, it was my imagination running wild. It wasn't real."

Cat ran her hand though her blonde hair. "Of course. It's only natural to be upset about Haddie's death. I had to deal with my husband's death many years ago. I understand." She squeezed his hand. "And any dreams you have in the future will be about me," she purred confidently.

She sat back in her low-cut blouse and crossed her shapely legs, giving him that look again. David swallowed his last piece of tuna. She was probably right.

David stood in the middle of his apartment enjoying the last moments of his bachelor pad. It was mostly void of *things* and that's the way he liked it. However, Cat was moving in this weekend, and if there was one thing he knew about women, maybe the only sure thing he knew about women, is that they claim their territory. Soon, he will not recognize the place. It will have throw pillows on the leather couch and trinkets on shelves. There will be wooden spatulas he will be forbidden to use, and flowered bedspreads. It will be feminized. A home. At least it won't smell like dog piss anymore. That was one of the things he liked about women. They knew how to make an enclosed space smell good. It is something that no heterosexual bachelor knows how to do.

Cat did have eclectic tastes. Her apartment was full of contradiction. But, it did smell good. He was curious what she would do to his place. She had wanted to keep her old place for now. The market was down and she didn't want to sell it for a loss, or at most, a small gain. So, there was a question of how much of her stuff she would bring into his world. She decided to buy all new things for *his* place. All her things, all the stuff she collected from around the world, stayed at *her* place.

Ms. Beasley treated Cat well in her will. She left her a sum in the low six figures. Cat said Ms. Beasley's relatives and friends gave her dirty looks during the will reading, but she didn't care. Cat had spent much more time with Ms. Beasley in the last year than anyone else. Ms. Beasley was just showing her appreciation. David said it didn't matter what Ms. Beasley gave her, because now that they were getting married, Cat would never have to worry about finances again. David knew she had acquired some money from the salaries she had earned, her former husband's will, and other willed gifts. But, this was Manhattan. If you wanted to live well in Manhattan, you needed millions, and he knew, or at least suspected, that Cat didn't have that kind of money, if one didn't count the condo she owned.

There was something else that surprised him this morning. Cat had left early to start her shopping spree, and David felt a sudden urge to write. It was the first time since he finished "Hannah's Last Ride" that he felt like exercising the muse. He sat at his desk for an hour, thinking of a storyline. He thought of a third installment of Hannah, but it seemed like her story had been told. "Hannah's Last Ride" had finished with her happy and married to the detective. He briefly thought about an adventure with them as a duo, fighting crime or what not. But, Hannah was a loner. And the sexual tension between her and the detective was over. They *were married* after all. The one thing he was sure of, the one thing he knew, was that it was going to be a mystery. And of course, a romance. He was, like it or not, a romance author.

He sat down at his rolltop desk. Maybe a short story. That would allow him to at least exercise his writing muscles. He had to be rusty. It had been a year since he had written anything. He hadn't even thought about writing. Or reading, for that matter. Yes, writing is what he needed, and if Mary asked him if he was writing, which she would surely do soon, he could tell her, yes. That would make her happy.

But, could he actually write something his readers would want? Haddie had inspired the last novel, after all. He now knew his overactive imagination was key to stirring the muse. He tried not to think about Haddie for too long. She was bad for his sanity. And he now had Cat. It wouldn't be fair to Cat to bring Haddie back into the mix. Sure, she didn't cuddle as well as Haddie, and sex was more of a battle call than an intimate experience. There was still a wall between them, a translucent one, perhaps, but a certain distance. Intimacy. He did not feel the intimacy with Cat that he had felt with Haddie. Certainly that would come with time.

Why did he expect that it would come with time? Was it because they would settle into their lives together, growing closer with increased familiarity and trust? Was this a gamble? David thought about it for a moment. Was intimacy important in an otherwise healthy relationship? David felt sympathy for Cat. She has experienced substantial loss. If he ever wrote a story about her, she would be a tragic hero. A woman who tasted happiness only to have it wrested from her grip. The loss of her husband, the loss of her favorite employer. He was now hoping the intimacy would come. He wanted her to be happy. He wanted that badly for her. And he realized now, that he would do anything for her. Absolutely anything.

He looked at his rolltop desk. The oak cover was slightly open in a smirk. It knew better than to try to intimidate him. He had conquered its dare to *produce* with "Hannah's Last Ride". But, it still did not seem to take him seriously.

You just got lucky. I bet you can't do it again.

"Oh, fuck you." David rose from the desk to make breakfast.

The next few weeks were a whirlwind. As expected, Cat was leaving her imprint on his place, though not nearly as heavy-handed as it could have been. David had his own concerns. Who should be his best man? He thought of Mel, who graciously offered the lodge to him and his guests. The wedding would be held in a nearby historic barn built in 1899, the same year and in the general area where the last wolf in the state of New York was killed. In the end he selected Gil, who was closer to his age, as best man. With all the events of late he had not recently talked with him, but when he did Gil was enthusiastic in accepting David's request. Gil had been busy too, recently becoming engaged to Melissa, an artist from Montreal. She spoke French and was a bit too "European" for David, but very sweet and seemed crazy about Gil. They met when he took Gil, Cat, and Melissa to Dinozio's, where the wine and conversation flowed so freely that David woke with a hangover.

Gil had suggested the boys' night out. They were going to be married men soon, after all. This was their last chance to go out as bachelors. However, in the end, with Melissa out of town, they ended up with a twelve-pack of beer at Gil's place watching the Yankee game. The Yanks were slaughtering the Red Sox. David surveyed the apartment. Gil's place had been taken over by Melissa, who was definitely a throw-away gal. That meant she threw away everything that wasn't tied down, especially if it belonged to Gil. But the chairs were comfy and the place smelled good. And the beer was cold. He wasn't sure who set the refrigerator thermostat.

Gil had settled into what would soon be married life. His flat stomach sagged a little and his hair was shorter. The day was hot, and the windows were open to let in what little breeze seeped through. The cold beer sweated large drops that soaked David's pants when he rested the bottle on them. And they drank them fast before they got warm. The beer was gone by the seventh inning stretch.

"How about some tequila?" Gil asked.

David needed little coaxing. It was his bachelor party, after all. The tequila went down smooth with lime and salt. By the ninth inning, they were both slurring their words and staring glassy-eyed at the game.

"So how does an ugly guy like you end up with hot babes like Haddie and Cat?" Gil asked.

David burped. "It's my tremendous pecker." He actually wondered the same thing as Gil. He, with the hourglass head and less than athletic build, scoring not one, but two beautiful wives in his lifetime. What did Haddie say? He was beautiful on the *inside*.

"Well, that explains it, then." Gil picked up the bottle and held it up to the light to see the liquid level through the amber bottle. There were about two fingers remaining.

"Melissa is pretty, too," David said. It felt forced. Although Melissa wasn't ugly, her face had no character, and her body was thin but dumpy.

"She's all right," Gil replied. "I always liked Haddie. I only met her a few times, but she was pretty cool. And Cat, well, she's kinda dangerous."

David was slouched in his chair. He was very comfortable. "Dangerous?"

"I guess," Gil slurred. "I'm not sure why I said that. She just is."

She just is? David always avoided comparing Cat to Haddie. Haddie was special. His wife of twenty years. His first love. The woman he thought of when he woke every morning, and his final thought at night. Even with Cat in his life. Cat was special, too. But, she could probably never have the effect on him that Haddie had. He was infatuated with

Cat now, no doubt about it, and he thought he could spend the rest of his life with her. He *wanted* to spend the rest of his life with her. But Haddie would always have a place in his heart. A large place that he would dip into often. A place that Cat would never enter, and could only suspect existed.

And they were different. Haddie was intense, competitive, and flirty. She enjoyed attention. But, David was convinced, at least now, fiercely loyal to him. And, she did like to cuddle when she wasn't stressed out by a big case, or making partner. Cat was different. She was intense, maybe not dangerous, but almost animalistic, primal, when they were alone. And there was a distance between them. Did he cause that? Maybe. Or maybe it was just her nature. Or maybe she felt his still strong attraction to Haddie. Maybe she was jealous. Maybe she still had strong feelings for her dead husband. It didn't seem like that to David, but how could he know what lurked deep inside her heart? Would he ever know? Would she ever know what residual feelings he would forever hold for Haddie? She could only guess. He would never tell her.

"Dangerous," Gil repeated, and then quickly added, "not that there's anything wrong with that."

David and Cat lay naked on the bed on a warm summer evening. She was on her stomach, her head cradled by her arms and a pillow. David was on his side, stroking the small of her back. It felt firm and smooth under his fingers. He listened to their breathing and suddenly wondered why they had never talked about children. Sure, she was forty, or would be next year, and he was forty-three. But they weren't too old, and he certainly had the income to support a family. She would have plenty of time. He had told her to not work again. She didn't need to. He wanted to pamper her. He had briefly thought about a prenuptial agreement, but he felt if he couldn't trust her now to stay with him for life, he should just not marry her, period.

Why not children? It seemed like a perfect time. Then he thought of Haddie, and all those years they tried to conceive. He felt a moment of betrayal to her, thinking of having kids with another woman. But, she was dead after all, and he was very much alive. Cat was good about taking care of people, planning, all that stuff. She'd be a great mom.

"What do you think about kids?" David asked.

Cat had her face turned toward him. She opened her eyes, gave him a quick glance, and then faced forward, her chin buried in the pillow. David waited on her. He was in no hurry, and it seemed Cat was taking her time crafting a response.

"I thought about it when I was younger." She looked back at him. "But, I can't have children. Sorry."

It was apparent from the way she said it that she was physically unable to give birth. And with his low sperm count, and their age, maybe it was best left alone. He stared at the curve in her back, her firm butt, and stroked the back of her leg. He was in deep, he thought. Cat was in his thoughts, now. She was mesmerizing, just like Haddie had been. And each day, he feared himself thinking less and less of Haddie, as Cat filled the void of his needs and desires. He hadn't been this happy in a long time. Not counting his crazy periods when he thought he was frolicking with Haddie across the chasm that separates the dead and the living, he was happier now than at any time except for his years with Haddie.

He feared his thoughts of Haddie were fading, and when they arose, would not be crisp and sharp, but dulled. He shouldn't be sad about it. His mourning was over. It was his time to live the rest of his life.

"That's OK." He moved closer to her and brought his lips to her ear. "I like things just the way they are."

Mel and Kate were ecstatic when David called them to ask if they could have the wedding ceremony and reception at the lodge. Kate went on and on about how the lake overlook just a few hundred yards from the lodge would make a great place to hold the ceremony, if the weather cooperated. If not, they converted an old barn for dances and other local events. David and Cat could even have a live band if they wanted to.

"What are we going to do with all that hay?" David teased.

"That's all been hauled out, silly," Kate gushed.

David knew the lake overlook. He agreed it was the perfect spot. He insisted on the old cabin. Cat would just have to put up with it. Kate sounded exasperated about his insistence on that "old run-down shack," but gave in, saying she would somehow make the place sparkle. For the reception, they agreed on the old barn and live music, and catering through a local company that bought local organic produce and livestock. David left it all up to Kate to make it happen, and said to add 15 percent to the bill for their "management services." He knew that this would provide much needed revenue for both them and an area hit hard by the recession. Manhattan didn't need his money. But for this area of upstate New York, it would be significant for the local economy.

Cat was mostly silent about the whole thing. She said she was just happy getting married. She didn't want to plan the event. Almost all of the invited guests were David's, too. When he asked her to make a list of who she wanted to attend, she provided only a few names, and then said they may or may not come. She did not plan on anyone giving her away, or a bridesmaid. This was curious to David, since she was such an engaging woman. Yet, when he thought of it, she never did have friends she hung out with. She insisted that everyone she was close to had died or left the country. She was "starting anew" with him. Even though she said it convincingly, he couldn't help but feel a pang of sympathy for her.

It's not that David was loaded with friends. He only had a few he really wanted present—Gil, Mary, and Mel and Kate. He invited some other people in the publishing industry, mostly from New York. He was hoping that the long drive to the Adirondacks would dissuade most of them from taking the trip. And Mel and Kate wanted to invite a few locals. Mel said it would be a "blast from the past" for David. David gave free rein to Mel and Kate to invite anyone they wanted.

Mary said the bride and groom should not see each other before the wedding. So, Mary drove Cat and Melissa in her Mercedes while David and Gil drove separately in the BMW. Mary had been very helpful to Cat, helping her pick out a dress (David hoped it wouldn't be black!), and chatting with Kate about the flowers. Cat insisted on a minister. There were loads of them up there, and Mel and Kate selected their church minister.

"Preside over the wedding of David East! Of course!" the minister had exclaimed.

Cat seemed indifferent to the details. David once mentioned it to her, and she had replied that she just wanted to get the ceremony over so they could get to the wedding night. That answer certainly satisfied David.

So, David and Gil drove north through the Delaware Gap, the hills dressed in full summer green. They stayed on lesser known roads, Utica being the only city of consequence. As they left the Appalachians and crossed the flatter areas before reaching Plattsburgh, the skies darkened and a steady drizzle welcomed them all the way to the mountains. It washed the day in gray, replacing the summer colors, and the humidity seemed to bring out the smell of wet dog in David's car. He was glad only Gil was in the car, since he didn't seem to notice, and if he had, would certainly have understood.

Gil pulled out several peanut butter and jelly sandwiches from a paper bag. He handed one to David. David bit into it, the crunchy peanut butter attaching itself to the roof of his mouth, and his tongue had to wrestle it away and down his throat.

"So, d'you ever think you'd marry again?" Gil was wrestling with his own peanut butter.

"Never thought about it." David took another bite. It was better. It had more jelly.

"You're lucky. She's a babe." Gil stuck a finger in his mouth to dislodge some peanut butter.

David shrugged, but pride swelled inside him.

"And she's gotta be what, ten years younger than you?"

"Not even five," David corrected. He looked over and saw Gil smiling, starting his second sandwich.

"Cradle robber."

"You're just jealous. Gimme another sandwich."

Gil laughed. "At least Melissa's not after my money."

"Hell, Gil," David replied. "You don't have any money. That's why we're eating peanut butter and jelly sandwiches."

"When we go to my wedding, you're bringing lunch."

Large farms gave way to pine forests. The clouds grew thicker and the drizzle fell steadily, until it was hard to tell where the clouds ended and the rain started. The kind of day when it's hard to believe it will ever be sunny again. David was reminded of the months after Haddie died, when the spring was cold, wet, and dreary. And he remembered sitting with Cat in the café, drinking coffee and watching the white-collar workers walking by under their umbrellas.

He suddenly thought how odd it was he was marrying the woman who served Haddie so long. And though he was thinking about Haddie less and less, Cat still talked about her regularly. He didn't speak much of Haddie to Cat because he didn't want to make her jealous. But, he felt pangs of jealousy the way Cat would talk about Haddie. How odd was that?

"David, did you hear me?"

"What?" David looked over at Gil.

"Are you dreaming up your next book?" Gil crushed the paper bag and placed it under the seat. David glanced at him but didn't say anything. "How much longer? I gotta use a restroom."

Mel and Kate were excited to see him. David found himself glancing around during check-in, but Cat had been whisked away into hiding, lest she burst into flames if their eyes met. At least David got his favorite cabin. And Kate had cleaned it well. The cobwebs and mouse pellets were gone, the bathroom chrome sparkled, and Mel had breathed life back into the wood. He must have used gallons of oil to make the wood look like it did. It was nice, and Cat would like it. But, David preferred the way it looked before. Minus the mouse droppings.

David settled into bed, the flannel sheets snug against his skin. Even in summer they felt good out here. A light blanket kept in the heat. He felt if it was any colder, he would have needed one more layer. The steady drizzle was relentless. It landed softly on the roof, barely making a sound. He liked falling asleep to the sound of a hard rain beating the roof, but this he could only hear if he strained, and even then he wasn't sure if he just imagined hearing it.

—

David woke to sobbing, the dark in the cabin so complete he could not see his hand when he waved it in front of his face.

"Haddie?"

"How could you?" she asked.

He froze. Why was *she* here? He had not thought about her, or wished she would appear. What tricks was his mind playing on him? He stayed silent. Maybe she would go away. Or maybe he would really wake up.

"How could you marry her, David?" She sniffed and moved restlessly on the bed.

"I love her, Haddie. That's why. Why are you here?" He suddenly felt defensive. And worried. Was his sanity going on vacation again the night before his wedding? Why *was* Haddie here? Would she show up again tomorrow on his wedding night? This could screw up everything. Or, he could, if he let himself slip into his past habits of communing with the dead.

She started to cry again. He could not see her, but he felt the bed shake as she sobbed. "Haddie, you're dead."

"You don't have to keep rubbing it in! I know I'm dead. You don't want to see me?"

"Haddie, you told me you didn't want to see me again before I died, like when I'm ninety." God, why was he arguing with his imagination?

"I changed my mind. I can do that. And her. Why her?"

"I thought you'd be especially happy if I married Cat. You two were so close. You left her money, for crying out loud."

Haddie sighed. "Cat was my assistant. She was efficient and indispensable. As an assistant. I left her money because she deserved it. Frankly, I don't know what I would have done without her. But, I never really liked her. And I like her even less now."

That was it, David thought. They were both beautiful. She was jealous. She didn't want to be upstaged by Cat. He would never state this to her, though. Not if someday he was going to be spending eternity with her. She would never let him forget it.

"But you spent so much time with her. She knew things about you I didn't. She knew you wrote a book. Why didn't you like her?"

"David, I had to spend time with her. Again, she made herself indispensable. And it was hard to hide the book from her. Anyways, I did like her until I finished my book. It was in those last months that things soured."

"Haddie, there's not much I can do now even if I wanted to. I'm marrying her tomorrow." David thought of what Haddie just said. "What do you mean, soured?"

David's eyes had adjusted to the darkness enough to barely make out her silhouette. She sighed. She said nothing for quite some time. And when she did, David could tell she was holding back her anger. "Because ... she's a manipulative shit, David, who always had to have her way. There, I said it."

Now, that was Haddie all over, David thought. But, he held his tongue. That whole eternity thing again.

She tapped her leg several times. "It's just a feeling I get. I sometimes felt she was ... well ... ruthless."

David sighed. One hundred percent Haddie.

"David, I can tell this is going in one ear and out the other. Why aren't you talking?"

Because men learn early in a marriage when to keep their mouths shut. At least the smart ones do.

"I was always so busy, David. All I ever thought about was my career. Cat would say things. I never paid attention as long as everything got done and my business ran smoothly. Her comments went in one ear and out the other. But then, when I finished my book, I started listening. My goal was to write something beautiful so I would never have to work in a stuffy office again. You don't know how much I despised my work at the end. Anyway, when I started listening to her, when I took my blinders off, I realized she was really mean. She said mean things."

"Haddie—"

"Don't say anything, David. I'm just going to finish saying what I need to say and then I'll leave."

First she asks me why I don't say anything, and now she tells me to shut up. Jesus. Women.

"I love you very much. And I am jealous, but I do want the best for you. It's just that when I started listening to her, I realized what cruel things she said. That woman is capable of anything."

Haddie stared off, avoiding eye contact, and David got the feeling she wasn't telling him everything.

"I just wanted to let you know. If she's marrying you, it's not because she loves you. She wants something. Maybe it's your money, maybe ... something else."

"Haddie, are you holding something back? What is it?"

There I go, trying to reason with my imagination again.

Haddie continued to stare off across the room. David shrugged at the silence.

"Haddie. I don't know what to say."

"Don't say anything." Haddie leaned over and kissed him.

Jesus. I must be crazy. He sat up and looked out the window. It was the gray part of dawn. Why would he have a dream like that? Why would he dream that Cat is just out for his money? That she's ruthless? Is that what he really thought in his subconscious? Is that what he really thought, and it manifested itself through Haddie? Or was it guilt toward Haddie? He loved Cat. He thought she was wonderful. He must be nuts. There was no reason to think this way. It was his overactive imagination taking over again. And he felt, if he didn't control it, it was going to take over for good.

He rose and took a shower. He scrubbed himself down, as if trying to wash away the guilt of his dream, the mistrust that seemed to come out of nowhere into his psyche. Forget it. Today was going to be a good day. And it was going to be only one of many, for years to come. He stepped out of the cascading water and toweled off. He walked back into his bedroom, and smelled the unmistakable scent of Haddie's lotion. His imagination was running wild.

I've gotta get hold of myself.

It was a gray morning. The drizzle soaked everything. Dirt was mud; shale walkways, wooden platforms and railings were dark and slick. David stood out on the covered porch in his robe. A breeze brought the cold and wet into his sheltered area, raising goose bumps on his skin. He stared out over the lake's dappled surface. A bald eagle swooped down from the sky, slammed into the water, and lifted back into the air. Its talons clutched a fish, wriggling for its life. The eagle flapped its wings several times and was gone. It all happened so fast. Although it was a dreary morning, it was peaceful, until an eagle murdered another life. The fish was now suffering a horrible death being eaten alive. Yet, to David, it was pretty cool. You don't see that every day.

It's all a matter of perspective, isn't it?

He was cold. He thought of Cat, her many smiles, intelligent discussions, primal interludes. He was sure he wanted to marry her. Or was he? Was he rushing into marriage? Why a dream like that? Was it just the remnants of his overactive imagination, returning for one final act of chaos, trying to screw up his life when he finally could be happy with someone special? He wasn't going to let that happen, not as long as he had a sane cell in his mind.

"You wearing that to the wedding?" Gil stood at the porch side, his arms folded over the railing.

David looked down at his gray robe, loose threads hanging off the bottom. Gil walked around the railing holding a pressed black suit covered in cellophane. Mary had told him she was taking care of his wedding clothes to make sure he didn't show up in khakis and a red bowtie.

David took the suit. "Have you had breakfast?"

"Nope. I was hoping you'd feed me."

David turned and walked through the door, Gil right behind. "On *my* wedding day? Where's the service here?" He laughed and closed the door, keeping the cold outside. "I would have thought Mary would have planned our breakfast, right down to the number of eggs."

"As a matter of fact," Gil said, "Kate's gonna cook us breakfast as soon as Cat and Melissa are finished." Gil walked over and gazed at an old musket hanging above the fireplace. "It's that whole, you can't see each other before the ceremony, thing."

"Ah, good. Because the only thing I've got in the refrigerator is beer." David regarded the suit. "I'll put this on after breakfast."

The rain did not stop for the wedding so it was held in the big barn.

There was a faint smell of hay in the air, rich and organic, as David stood in front of the minister waiting for Cat to enter. Everyone was inside, close to a hundred guests in all. David warily watched a stray pigeon above him on the rafters, cooing and bobbing back and forth. His suit fit him perfectly. Leave it to Mary. She could have organized the Normandy invasion. The sea of people sat quietly, except for the sobs coming from a few of the emotionally high-strung women from Greenwich Village. Mel and Kate sat up front, Mel with his hair combed over to cover his bald spot (one of the few times David had ever seen him without his cap), and Kate looking comfortably round in her matronly clothes. Melissa sat near Mel and Kate, with a smile on her face that foreshadowed Gil's future. Gil stood next to him, sweating more than the temperature called for.

Gil had the rings. David had them made special in 22K gold. Cat said she wanted the Manhattan skyline etched in them and that each of them would get half, to show their union. Is that a statement a woman would make to her fiancé if all she wanted was his money? David shuddered. He had briefly thought, stupidly he knew, about just using his and Haddie's old rings. Cat was loyal to her; he thought she might have liked the gesture. He never discussed it with her, and after his dream last night, he was glad he hadn't. Haddie would have rolled over in her grave. At least that's what he thought she would have done. That was his dream last night, after all.

The music started. Two violin players, locals from the looks of them, played a vaguely familiar tune. One was a portly old man, the other a skinny young protégé. The music radiated through the barn, relaxing David's muscles. He unclenched his jaw, dropped his shoulders, and listened to the men play. It sounded beautiful. He could see now why dances were held in barns out in the country like this. The acoustics were amazing. He found himself swaying to the music, so relaxed he felt like closing his eyes.

Cat entered through the open doors. She walked alone, gracefully past the congregation toward him. She wore a knee length off-white dress, a bright smile showing off her perfectly white teeth. Her green eyes were intensely radiant. He smelled her rich perfume. David stood mesmerized by her beauty wondering how he could have ever doubted her, or her intentions, even in his dreams. She was perfect.

Cat reached David and they held hands. Gil stood silently by. There was no bridesmaid. David felt a twinge of pity for her, but realized as he looked into her startling eyes that he would fill her social life. He would be her best friend. David never remembered what the minister said, or how he mumbled in agreement. He vaguely remembered placing the ring on her finger, his hand trembling slightly. She was now his. Until death.

The reception was held in the barn, with overflow into the big lodge. The chairs were folded and pushed to the side, guitars and drums were added to the band, and things got really loud. David drank and danced. All the men wanted to dance with Cat. She entertained the men, dancing with one after another, but David could tell it was strictly toleration on her part. Haddie would have soaked in the attention and teased everyone, but Cat was aloof, her body moving gracefully, but to its own beat. The men were drunk and did not seem to notice how they were being cheated out of a harmless flirtation, and David couldn't help but smile. Cat was no flirt, and that suited him just fine. As the afternoon wore into evening, David made his way to the main lodge to find a bathroom. Guests hung around outside, taking a break from the noise, some playing horseshoes or lawn darts, their suits and dresses getting wet in the light drizzle. A small group stood around the empty fire pit, smoking cigarettes. The lodge was well lit, and David saw people milling about through the windows. David walked through the kitchen on his way to the bathroom, passing Kate, Melissa, and Mary, who pinched his butt as he walked by. All three giggled.

David turned the corner. The bathroom was occupied. He waited a moment, and then remembered there was another one upstairs. He climbed the creaking stairs, polished from a century of footsteps, past photographs of people long forgotten. He turned right into the bathroom and shut the door. The bathroom was added in the 1930s. A heating vent was added at that time that indirectly plumbed into the same vent as the kitchen. When David washed his hands and turned off the water, voices from the kitchen drifted upstairs and through the vent.

"He loves her, Mary, that's all that counts," Kate said.

"You've had too much wine," Melissa teased.

"Oh, Melissa, you said it, too," Mary slurred.

"As long as David's happy, I'm happy," Kate said.

David stood still, his hands dripping on the floor. The voices echoed through the bathroom. *What are they talking about? You know who they're talking about. Stay quiet and you'll hear more.*

"Melissa, admit it. You said she was a wench," Mary said.

"Stop it, Mary," Melissa said. "Someone will hear us."

"The wench just wants his money. You both know that."

"Mary, dear. That's enough. It's David's day."

"Hmmphh."

David gripped the sink with his wet hands. Why would they talk about Cat like that? She was ... amazing. She was wonderful. He loved her.

"David's blind. Love's blind. But we know better, don't we?" Mary said. "I told you about her first husband. It was suspicious, if you ask me."

"Stop it, Mary," Kate said. "It's not our business. David loves her. Let him be happy."

"I don't care," Mary slurred. "She's a bitch. You said it too, Melissa."

David turned from the sink and walked out the door. He stood at the top of the stairs. He couldn't walk through that kitchen. They would see the anger in his face. He did not want to make a scene. Not tonight. He clenched his fists. How dare they talk like that? Cat was his wife, for chrissakes. He closed his eyes, the beer coursing through his body. Why did this bother him so much? Why did he have that dream last night? He took a deep breath and opened his eyes.

"Hey, handsome," Cat purred.

"Shit!" David felt his whole body come off the ground. He gasped and clutched his heart. "You scared me." He forced a laugh.

Cat's eyes never left him. She did not seem to startle at all. "Are you OK?"

"Ah ... yeah," David took a deep breath.

"Wedding night frights?" Cat poked him in the stomach.

He felt the finger through his paunch. He really needed to start working out again. Her eyes were locked on his, and other thoughts melted away.

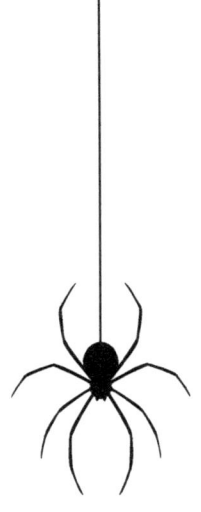

Chapter 17

THEY HONEYMOONED IN THE CARIBBEAN. CAT LOVED THE ISLANDS. TO watch her smile, swim, and jiggle on the beach was enough to make David sell his apartment in New York and live down here full time. Hell, he could write anywhere. And with the cost of living down here, even if he couldn't write another blockbuster novel, his money would last the rest of his life. He sighed. He was on contract to produce one more book.

Produce.

He was still writing short stories, trying to keep nimble for when the big novel storyline hit him on the head. However, Mary was going to start asking about his next novel soon. What concerned him more was that his short stories weren't very good. It's not that they were poorly written, it's that they were uninspired. Drivel that only a hard-core David East fan would sit through.

He watched Cat cavort in the waves, the bright sun obscuring her through his shades. She was splashing in the water, as if in her own world. He had never seen her just play before. She was always so serious. Everything was a competition with her, just like it was with Haddie. Or, maybe not like Haddie. Haddie was competitive, uber-competitive, but she had her boundaries.

Take sex for example. Haddie could be very sexual, and a very willing partner. But she was demure. Her enthusiasm did not overshadow her submissiveness. It was a wonderful combination to a man, and he expected she honed it because she desired all men to desire her. She played men like a finely tuned instrument, and right up until the day she died she was pretty enough to turn even the young studs' heads.

Cat was a wild animal in the bedroom. When he joined her, he always felt the need for body armor. It was a battle of wills; a test for dominance. It was work. The most fun work ever, but it was still like going into the heat of battle. And he had the sore muscles and bruises to prove it. It was not an intimate interlude. She got rough. Although it was fun, a little variety, of the *softer* variety, would be a good thing once in a while. He would have to talk to her at some point. He couldn't imagine, ten years from now, trying to explain yet another bite mark on his forearm, or throat, during a celebrity interview.

Maybe that's how she got rid of her first husband.

Mary had said, "I told you about her first husband. It was suspicious, if you ask me."

David grinned. He had to admit that he searched for the story on the Internet one day when she was out on the beach. During their honeymoon, she stayed out most of the day. He didn't find any details, but what he did find corroborated her story. Her husband drowned in the car. He didn't spend too much time searching, but found enough to satisfy himself. He now enjoyed watching her bounce around in her bikini. The other men on the beach did, too. But, unlike with Haddie, David felt no jealousy with Cat. He believed it was because she never flirted with any of them, or even acknowledged them for that matter. She only had eyes for him, and that made him feel good. Really good.

Mary felt snubbed that David did not find her attractive. That had to be why she disliked Cat. David loved Cat and she loved him. His imagination was just going to have to take a break. It's amazing what things one could believe hid under their bed when their imagination ran rampant. David knew that firsthand. And he was not going to let his overactive imagination control him on this. It would ruin a perfectly good marriage.

David took out a pair of binoculars and glassed several dolphins rising over the water beyond the breaks. They jumped clear of the water, their acrobatics a sea dance that had run across the millennia. They eventually disappeared beneath the water for good, so he glassed his wife jumping about the shore, the ocean water rushing around and between her legs and then retreating back. She pointed her face to the sky. Her eyes were closed. A group of young children appeared into David's field of view. Cat's eyes quickly opened and glared off to her right, where the three children were splashing each other and giggling. Although none of their water splashing reached Cat, she looked at them with pure hatred for several seconds.

She has a helluva temper.

He knew that.

Don't piss her off.

He knew that, too. And maybe he would put off any more conversations about children as well. Cat jogged across the beach, watching him and beaming as she reached her towel. She only had eyes for him.

David rubbed his throbbing temple. He vaguely remembered Cat rising early to go for a run along the beach. She had laughed at him last night when he said he might join her in the morning. That was the margaritas talking. The throbbing head was the margaritas talking, too. The thing was, she probably had more margaritas than he did.

She's an animal.

Last night was their last on the island. They were flying back to New York this afternoon. He rose from bed and looked out the bay window towards the rising sun. He poured himself a cup of coffee and began to pack some things into his suitcase. He walked around the cabana, looking for odds and ends, like a stray sock under the bed, and his personal shampoo in the shower. He tossed the items into his luggage and walked into the kitchen.

Cat's computer sat on the breakfast table in a nook facing the water. David was already packed but wanted to check his e-mails and catch up on the news, if he could log on. Cat hardly ever left her computer out, and never left it on. David hit the return key and surprisingly, it was still connected. She must have been in a hurry to go jogging before breakfast. He sat down and logged onto his e-mails. He shifted in his seat and found himself glancing out the window for her return. For some reason, he felt he was invading her privacy. She had never told him he couldn't use her computer. She just never told him the password so he could use it if necessary. And this was the first time he needed to use it. The e-mails he opened now were of no urgency; mostly just congratulatory on his marriage. He checked the news sites and found little had changed from any other week. War in the Middle East, unions striking in France, starvation in Africa, and so on. He decided to turn off the computer and make breakfast, so he closed the various windows, but stopped at the last one.

It was a table of monetary figures that caught his eye. There were royalty deposits and check outlays. It harked back to a former time when he slaved as an accountant. He scrolled to the top of the file and saw it was a bank statement. *His* bank statement.

What the hell is going on?

He searched and found summaries of his investments, real estate, stocks, bonds, Treasuries. Cat had organized his entire portfolio. His face flushed, anger welling up inside him. How dare she take his personal financial information like this without telling him? What was she doing? David glanced up from the computer and looked out over the beach. It was empty. He eyed the other files within the same folder.

What else had she stored?

He opened the first file. It was a retirement schedule at age forty, fifty, and sixty, using his personal fortune as a starting point.

He sat back in his chair, his mouth open, shaking his head. Yes, he had insisted that there would be no prenuptial. Yes, all accounts were now joint accounts, and she had the right to access all accounts. But they had only been married a week. Why rush in and examine and manipulate all his financial statistics?

"The wench just wants his money. You both know that."

There was a noise outside the cabana. Instinctively, David quickly closed the windows and shut down the computer. He stood, feeling angry about what he saw, yet also feeling guilty about using her computer and invading her privacy. The door opened and Cat came in, smiling, greeting him lightly to avoid covering him with sweat, and sauntered off to take a shower. David froze, apparently mute, still feeling her warm lips on his cheek. What was he going to say to her?

"My dear, you have been rooting about my financials. Are you planning my untimely demise?"

David dropped to a chair. There had to be a reason for her organizing his fortune and planning her retirement. Maybe that's all it was. Maybe she wanted to help him with his finances, to optimize his return on his money. He admitted that as good an accountant as he was, he was no whiz with investment instruments. Maybe she was. Or maybe she thought she was. That must be it. There was nothing unusual about that. At least, not too unusual. Cat was his wife. He had to trust her.

Was he going crazy again? Was he on his way back to Tippingdale? Did he need to go see a psychiatrist again, to get grounded?

In the end, he decided he would not speak to her about her computer. Not yet. If she wanted to help him financially, she would probably bring it up soon. Or, maybe not. Maybe she felt uncomfortable broaching how to invest his fortune for their collective retirement. The funny thing was, her retirement calculator was only for one person. Her.

The door opened and Cat came out naked, her skin pink and glowing from exercise, gliding toward him.

"Screw the money," he whispered.

David sat in first class staring out the jet window while Cat read a magazine. He heard the crisp shuffle as she flipped through the pages. He wanted to discuss what he found on her computer, but now it seemed awkward. Why didn't he say anything when she first walked in? What was he scared of? Jesus, and why so paranoid? She probably just wanted to manage the finances. That was fine with him. He didn't want to work with numbers ever again.

"This poor woman," Cat said.

David looked away from the window. "What's that?"

"This couple worked their whole life saving their money. And then he died, and right after, she found out he had invested their entire nest egg with Madoff."

"Wow," David said. "The guy who went to prison?"

"One and the same." Cat shook her head. "That woman got hosed."

David chuckled, and suddenly got an idea. "Yeah, I'm no good at managing money. Do you want to invest it for us?"

"Oh God no," she replied. "All that investing stuff is over my head."

David raised an eyebrow. "Then how are we going to plan for our retirement?" He nudged her in the side.

Cat winked back at him. "Just keep making lots of money, Mr. Bestseller."

David smiled, but felt his torso get carved out like a pumpkin. "I'll do that, black widow."

"Oooh, I like that."

A stewardess appeared behind Cat. "Would you like another scotch, Mr. East?"

David tore his eyes from Cat and looked up at the lady. "Yes, please." He cleared his throat. "A double."

David and Cat worked out a daily schedule that would allow David to write in peace. After breakfast, Cat would leave David to his writing. She would often go to her old apartment, or shop around town. They would meet up again at his apartment in the mid-afternoon. Meanwhile, he would write, creating drivel when he could create at all. Every time he sat at his desk was a new adventure in frustration. Where could he take Hannah? How about a new, unique story with new characters and a fresh plot? Instead of buckling into his chair and pushing his imagination to the brink, God knows it had certainly pushed *him* to the brink on a few occasions, he would settle for a short story about his youth, or even worse, a love poem. His imagination was a wasteland of ideas, at least novel ideas.

He also spent a lot of time searching the web for information on Cat. Mary's words of her husband's "suspicious death" kept ringing through his head. But the more he looked, the more he realized that any information on that event would be limited to small town newspapers, and no searches thus far had revealed anything significant that had been transferred from hard copy to the web. Since web information on the event was sparse, he would have to look the old-fashioned way.

The New York Public Library was a wealth of information. It was cavernous and overwhelming. Various librarians and assistants asked if he needed help (many recognized him), but he politely turned them down. He didn't want to advertise his purpose for being there. This kind of thing could be leaked to the press. Through his book readings he had come to appreciate libraries and bookstores, and he loved libraries even more than bookstores. While bookstores had the "new book smell," libraries had something else. Maybe it was just the musty odor of the older works, but he thought it was something more. Unlike the "new books," these books had been held by human hands. Studied by human brains. These books had a history. And some of them were older than the library itself. He felt, each time he walked into a library, that he was walking back into history.

He felt an especially strong attraction in Indiana at a library rumored to have Kurt Vonnegut as a frequent guest. David was reading a middle chapter of "Hannah's Last Ride" when he felt a pair of eyes boring into him, causing shivers down his spine. He could almost see Mr. Vonnegut's bulging eyes and wild hair, muttering "More satire! More irony!"

David was never a good researcher. The last time he did research was in college. It was the days of card catalogs and microfiche. So now, after several days of computer searches, he bit his tongue and called Mary. He invited her to lunch at a quiet place where he knew they could talk privately. He had to find out what she knew. He didn't tell her the reason for the lunch, and was sure she'd assume that he had made significant progress on his third novel. He had to tackle this lightly. He didn't want her to know he had overheard the kitchen conversation on his wedding day.

They had not seen each other since the wedding. Mary lost a little weight, perhaps about the same amount David had recently gained.

Funny how that works. Conservation of mass. It was a beautiful sunny day, the restaurant was fairly busy, and most people were sitting out on the sidewalk. They sat inside in a corner away from the crowd. David ordered a pastrami sandwich, and Mary a salad. David surveyed the scene. He wanted privacy so that he could talk to Mary about Cat without well-meaning fans coming up and asking for autographs and photo snaps. People around them were in conversation, apparently oblivious to his presence. He also had to be mindful of eavesdroppers with his celebrity. Especially when trying to broach a sensitive subject with Mary. At least it was sensitive to *him*.

"I received a call from the publisher yesterday asking how your latest novel was coming along." Mary crunched on her Romaine lettuce.

David doubted if that were true. However, he was sure *Mary* wondered how his latest novel was coming along. "Some ideas are gelling. It will be a while yet. I've been busy."

She smiled. "So, how is Cat, anyway?"

"Good," David said. He detected sarcasm in her question. It irritated him. After coming to dead end after dead end along various media he pursued, he had become impatient with running down this issue with Cat and her first husband. And the only reason he had worried about it was because of something Mary said in the kitchen while drunk at his wedding reception. Everything after that, including the financial spreadsheets, would not have garnered that much attention if he hadn't overheard her at the reception. Although he had told himself countless times on the way over to broach the subject tactfully, he had to get to the bottom of this once and for all.

"Mary, why do you think the death of Cat's first husband is suspicious?"

Mary's hand froze, the fork full of avocado, slightly shaking. "What do you mean?"

"Mary, I need to know what you know." He leaned forward and touched her hand. "I'm not mad. I just need to know what you know."

Mary glanced to the side at a woman who seemed to be walking extra slowly by their table. The woman looked back, picked up speed and headed toward the bathroom. Mary turned to David.

"I checked her out when you two got serious. A lot of women go after a celebrity because of his money. You never talked about her, so I did a background check."

David didn't know what to say. His first thought was that it was none of her business. However, she was his agent, and he, her livelihood. And the reason he never talked about Cat in front of her was because he knew she'd be jealous.

"And?" He suddenly felt very protective of his wife.

Mary set down her fork and sighed. "I found an article on her first husband. How he died in a car crash. The article was a bit odd. It had names of two of the police officers involved at the scene. So, I looked them up. One was dead, but the other was alive and we talked."

"What did he say?"

"He remembered the case. He thought it was suspicious. Like," she looked up at the ceiling, "he had recommended an autopsy but the body was cremated before one could be done."

"Mary, a lot of people opt for cremation. That's no reason to call my wife a murderer."

Mary gasped. "I never called her that." She stopped and looked away. "It's not my business, David. I'll never speak of it again."

"Let's stop speaking about it after I know everything you know. There's gotta be something else."

Mary fidgeted in her seat. She diverted her eyes, and placed her hands on the table. She looked at him. "The officer's name is Haskins. Sergeant Haskins. He was first on the scene and had helped pull Donnie from the water. He said Cat tricked the other officers to believe her story that they drove into a flooded road during a storm, thinking they could make it to the other side. He said the captain let her go, and even gave her a ride home. When Haskins later went to the captain and said her story didn't add up, he told him to shut up if he ever wanted to make lieutenant."

"Why didn't her story add up?"

"I don't know. He got really quiet and wouldn't answer any more questions. The only thing he said after that was that she batted her pretty green eyes at the captain and got away with murder."

—

He told Cat he was driving north to do some research for his new book. He didn't tell her he was going to Vestal to speak to Sergeant Haskins. Haskins was hesitant to talk to him until he said he married her and had suspicions. Fortunately, David did not have to reveal his whole name, and Haskins didn't seem to recognize his voice (who recognizes an author's voice?). Because it was such a sensitive issue, David preferred a face to face meeting, and Haskins agreed to meet. Strictly off the record, of course. David got the feeling as he hung up the phone that Haskins was on the fence as to how much to divulge. He would have to be patient.

About his second hour into the drive, David began to question his sanity again. Didn't he drive all day to Buffalo to talk to some old boyfriend of Haddie's? Why was he doing this again? Why couldn't he just enjoy his life and his marriage to Cat? Which, by the way, he thoroughly enjoyed. Why did he have to make his life so complicated? He assured himself, this was it. It's hard to fathom what the old cop could say that would convince David that Cat was a killer, and was out to kill him.

Maybe you just like the drama, Davey boy.

The day was hot and muggy, the trees dressed in deep, late summer green. The retired officer lived on a macadam road off the parkway. His BMW climbed the hills easily, and David gave it a little extra gas when he crested peaks, feeling his stomach jump on the downside. Sergeant Haskin's house was dark brick, low and wide. As David walked up the concrete walk from the driveway, a dog growled and barked. Sergeant Haskins opened the front door before David had a chance to knock.

He was a lean man, tall, gray, in a white T-shirt and khaki pants. He shook David's hand firmly. "How was your trip?"

"Fine, thank you." He followed Haskins inside.

The house smelled like leather and dog piss, just like his place before Cat feminized it. The house wasn't dirty, but was disorganized, with magazines lying about and photos on just about every horizontal surface but the floor. David knew that Haskins must be a bachelor. Or more appropriately, based on the photos, a widower. He looked down at the dog.

"That's Prince. He's a good dog, and keeps me company since Sally died."

"I'm sorry," David said.

"Oh, that's all right. We had a lot of good years together." He scratched behind Prince's ear. David smelled alcohol, and it was only 10:00 a.m.

Haskins glanced about. "I forgot my manners. Would you like something to drink?"

David smiled. "A beer would be good."

Haskins broke into a smile and David knew that had been the perfect thing to say. "OK. I think I'll join you."

Haskins returned with two cans of beer. He moved stiffly, but not overly so for a man his age. They chatted a bit. David liked Haskins. He was a likeable guy. However, drinking early in the day is never a good sign. He had lost his wife and was elderly. Was he just waiting to check out? And how much could he believe what this guy said? Maybe he'd been drinking like this all his life.

"So, David," Haskins said abruptly. "What do you want to know about Catherine Pilleur?"

David shifted in his seat. He had rehearsed what he was going to say all the way up here, and now words escaped him. A clock ticked. The dog licked himself at Haskins's feet. Haskins began to speak so David blurted his words out.

"You thought Cat's husband's death was suspicious? I was wondering why."

"Well, you would, wouldn't you, since you married her." Haskins stiffened his back and shifted his neck from side to side, his vertebrae cracking loud enough for David to hear. "I got my badge when I was nineteen years old. One thing you learn in my profession is how to read people. Some cops do it better than others, but as a whole, we're much better than your regular Joe.

"I was there when they brought her into the station, wrapped in a blanket. She was cold and shivering. The captain took good care of her. Brought her coffee, even. That was funny for two reasons. He hardly ever questioned any witnesses, or suspects. And I had never seen him bring coffee to anyone. She put a spell on him, and I could see why."

Cat? He never saw her flirt with anyone.

"I thought it looked funny, anyway. When I got out to the scene, the car was hung up in some logs. The passenger side window was down and the windshield was smashed. But when they pulled the car out, it had very little damage. Seeing that smashed windshield compared to the condition of the rest of the vehicle seemed out of place. We didn't find the body until the next day. It wasn't in the car. I found it downriver in a small eddy, sunk to the bottom. I would have missed it if I hadn't seen the sun's reflection off his gold watch." He sat back waiting for David's face to change, to register why that was all wrong. David sat stone-faced.

"Why wasn't he floating? He wasn't stuck under a log or beneath a dam, I found him in a quiet eddy. He should have been floating." He stared at David, as if that was a huge revelation. After a few moments, he continued.

"He was dead when he entered that river. Otherwise, he would've had air in his lungs. I most likely would have found him *floating*."

David saw Haskin's point, but though he was no forensic scientist, he imagined there could have been other reasons for him not floating when found. It doesn't spell murder. As Haddie would have said, "this is merely conjecture."

"I examined the body myself. It looked like it had tumbled around that river awhile, but there was no significant trauma. I think she covered her tracks too well. The body was in too good a condition for the river to have caused his death.

"Vestal's a small town, David. People police their own. She wasn't popular before her husband died, and certainly wasn't after. She always kept to herself. Her husband was known about town. But once he was gone, the mudslinging began. Unfortunately, she had the body cremated before an autopsy could be performed. The captain didn't listen to me or Jim, my partner. She had her hooks into him."

"Mr. Haskins, I don't see the evidence for murder."

Haskins shook his head. "She bought a Mercedes right after the cremation. And left town not long after that. Went to New York, I heard. Did you know she collected over a million dollars?"

"Yes."

"What more motivation do you need? She's guilty as hell, all right, sure as shit." Haskins looked out the window, and then stood. "I'd bet he was dead when the river rushed in through the broken windshield. She must have drugged him. Or poisoned him. I bet she broke the windshield herself, and tossed him separately into the swift current to make sure there would be some damage to his body." He looked at David. "Well, that's my opinion. If she kills you, I'll make sure to call the coroner to have him do an autopsy on your body before she turns you to ashes."

David stood. "Thank you for your time, Mr. Haskins." He glanced at his watch. He would get back to New York by rush hour.

"Listen, I know this is hard on you. And hard to listen to an old guy like me spout off about your wife. But, I've been wanting to tell this story for a long time. Good luck." He slurred his words slightly.

David nodded and walked to his BMW.

"Where have you been, honey?" Cat wrapped her arms around him.

David forced the image of her flirting with the captain out of his head. He pushed back fleeting scenes of water gushing through the windshield, a dead man racing along the current, Cat watching from the bank, and then easing herself into the cold muddy water, hanging onto an overhanging bush, briefly immersing herself, ensuring she was completely drenched.

"Research, honey." Why was he even considering the statements from a jealous woman and a crazy old man? Why couldn't he just let it go? There was no real evidence of anything. Only, what would Haddie say, circumstantial evidence?

She pulled back from him. "What kind of research, David?"

David looked into her green eyes, which could change expressions like a chameleon changes colors. Was she hiding thinly veiled anger or was it just his overactive imagination? She had never questioned him before, but her gaze made it seem that she was not going to let him off the hook without an explanation. Should he just tell her the truth and they could both have a hearty laugh and forget the whole thing? Hell no.

You're gonna have to lie to her. You tell her the truth, she'll skewer you in your sleep.

"I can't tell you, Cat. It's a secret. You'll just have to wait until I finish my book." David broke into the biggest smile he could muster. Her eyes seemed to bore into him, and then she suddenly turned away.

"Any revelations on your journey? Any questions answered?" she asked.

"Answered some, created more," he said honestly.

She stood looking out the window, her back to him. He realized he could not let this continue. The bottom line was, she was his life, and he promised to stay loyal to her and she promised to stay loyal to him, for the rest of their lives. His investigations had to end. He had to put it all behind him. And he would, as soon as he did one more thing.

"Pity," she said, looking over her shoulder. "But, then again, I've found men to be too self-absorbed to see answers even if they're staring them in the face."

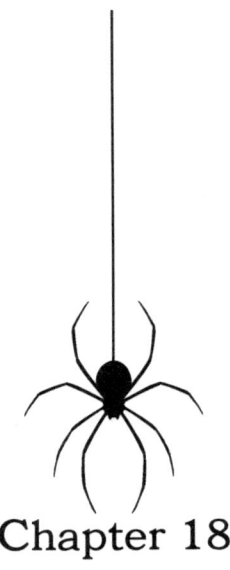

Chapter 18

DAVID HAD NOW EXHAUSTED MOST EVERY LEAD AND STILL THERE WAS nothing that convinced him that Cat had ever done anything wrong. His obsession with Cat's true intentions had achieved a fever pitch. What evidence did he have that her intentions with him were less than true love? That she was only out for his money, or worse, would expedite his exit so she could enjoy *his* money? Her apparent financial planning of his fortune on her computer? As he thought before, the statements of a jealous woman and a drunken old cop? Cat's financial planning could simply be part of her organized mind. Haddie had always said she was "so efficient and organized." Mary was clearly jealous, and the cop, well, his story sounded like he had read too many Agatha Christie novels.

There was something else. The apparently coincidental deaths of people who bequeathed her money; her husband Donnie, Haddie, and Margot Beasley? Her husband, maybe, but the evidence wasn't strong. And Haddie only left her $50,000, and was tragically run over by a cab. And David couldn't imagine a reason for Cat killing Haddie. They were so close, and frankly, Haddie was worth more alive to Cat than dead. And then there was Ms. Beasley. Ms. Beasley left her six figures, but she clearly died of natural causes, unless Cat had some gift of inflicting cancer on her victims.

So, why was he so obsessed with this?

There was something else. It was his gut instinct.

She's ruthless ... That's what Haddie had said in his dream, clearly a projection of his own subconscious thoughts. He loved Cat, and everything about her. But she was cold at times. Never to him, but to others. Cat really had no friends. And his friends did not harbor the same warm feelings for her as they had about Haddie. Especially his women friends. Did they know something he didn't? Is love blind?

He decided to investigate what he believed was his last remaining lead, and if nothing concrete surfaced, he would let it go. He felt he really could let it go. And if Cat had any secrets, wouldn't she harbor them at her own apartment? He never went there. But he often wondered why she kept it after they married. So she could go there and leave him at his apartment with a quiet place to write? There were plenty of other options besides maintaining an expensive Manhattan condo. No, he felt that if she had any sinister thoughts, they would be hidden out of sight, away from his prying eyes, at her apartment.

The toughest part was making a copy of her keys. He had joked with her about maybe doing some writing at her place, just for something different. She laughed, but did not offer her keys to him. He thought that was odd. Why shouldn't he have keys to her place? They were married, after all. But, he didn't want to push it because it would make her suspicious. He didn't want that. He wanted to get in there, look around, and get on with his life, which he was mostly confident would be a normal long life with the woman he loved.

Mostly confident, Davey boy?

He got his chance at a picnic in Central Park. They loaded up on sandwiches from Kramer's deli, Dutch cheese, and a few bottles of beer and spread a blanket on an open meadow near the ball fields. The weather was cool but the air still. David was warm in his light jacket, perhaps too warm. They watched some teenage boys tossing a Frisbee across the meadow, people jogging on a nearby trail, and many other couples and families dispersed on the field, as if knowing that autumn and its cold weather was just around the corner.

David watched a couple jogging past them. They looked like they stepped right out of a fashion magazine. He was young, tanned, and smiling. The woman filled out her matching jogging bra and tight shorts perfectly.

"See something interesting, David?"

He laughed. "They look like models. I'm sure they'll have beautiful children together."

"Mmm, I don't think so. He's just her boy toy."

David glanced at her. She sat back and raised a beer to her lips. "Now, how do you know that? Maybe he's the one who's rich."

Cat gasped. "You don't notice anything, do you? She has to be ten years older than him. Rich men don't date older women, believe me. And kids? They didn't even have rings on. He's just a hanger-on."

"Yeah, but you probably thought he was handsome, right?"

"No. I didn't."

Her words came out so harsh that David thought she was mad at him for noticing the woman. "Hey—"

"But, the woman had an air about her," Cat interrupted. "And I agree with you. She was beautiful." She winked and smiled at him.

When they finished the beer and food, they gathered their things and that's when David saw her keys on the grass.

They must have slipped out of her jacket pocket.

He calmly placed them into his pocket and made sure he was the first to their apartment door, bringing out his keys before she reached for hers and noticed them missing. He had a copy made and had her keys back in their rightful place before the next morning, Cat apparently completely unaware that they were ever out of her clutches.

As luck would have it, on Tuesday there was a sale at a boutique downtown. Cat loved that store. She was always tastefully dressed, if perhaps a little dark. But black fit Cat. She was reserved, private, a bit mysterious. It was one of many things he loved about her.

"So, what are your plans today?"

"Lots of shopping," Cat said. "It's your birthday tomorrow. I'm going to give you something special."

"You don't need to go to a store to give me something special." David smiled. At forty-four, he didn't think about birthdays much.

They were more of an annoyance, a deadly reminder. But he was intrigued by what gift he would receive. It sounded like she was putting some thought into it.

He felt guilty as he watched her leave the building, turning right, away from her apartment. He sat and quietly drank a second cup of coffee. His thoughts shifted from anger at himself for not trusting the woman he loved, to guilt for sneaking around behind her back, to cold logic. Wouldn't anyone in his shoes do what he was about to do, based on the cold hard facts? He was rich with a lot to lose, much more than the average man. He had thought briefly of hiring a private investigator, but at this stage his efforts were almost complete. And in a morbid way, he found the whole thing fascinating.

He got dressed. As he buttoned his shirt he wondered how much time he had. Two hours? Three hours? No, two hours tops. Get in, get out, and move on. He fingered her apartment key in his pocket as he took the elevator down to the street.

The neighborhood in which she had lived had gentrified over the past fifteen years. It was probably a bit rough when her husband Donnie first bought in. But, he was shrewd. The area was now very desirable, and the flood of taxis, boutiques, and women walking their poodles proved it. When he arrived in the taxi, he took a deep breath as he climbed out. He looked up and down the street, watching for her graceful walk and blonde ponytail. He walked into the building and headed straight for the stairs. He cast his eyes downward and walked quickly to minimize the chance of anyone recognizing him. The lobby was large and the stone floor made the sound of his footsteps reverberate like a horse pounding its hooves against the hard floor. He glanced at his watch. It had been nearly an hour since Cat left their apartment.

"Mr. East?"

David flinched at the sound of his name. It was a young woman in a hotel uniform. Her nameplate read "Claire." When he looked at her she raised a hand to her breast. "Sorry, I didn't mean to surprise you. You are David East, the writer?"

"Yes." David folded his hands in front of his body and tried to stay calm.

She giggled and produced a notepad and pencil. "Can I have your autograph? It's for my mom. Her name is Bridgette."

"Sure," David resorted to his patient, pleasant smile. *You wouldn't have the money if they didn't buy the books.* He signed the paper and handed it back to her and then cast glances around him. The lobby was quiet.

He gave her a final smile and then walked into the elevator. When the doors closed, his windpipe seemed to close with it. His peripheral vision disappeared. He quickly became light-headed, and grasped the side railing for support. He knelt down and lowered his head, trying to will oxygen to his brain. The elevator creeped upward, and he took slow, deep breaths to calm down. The doors opened and a young couple walked into the elevator. David stood, and his surroundings began to spin. He pushed off from the railing and stepped off the elevator just as the doors were closing. He heard the couple snicker and then fade. He gripped the wall for balance. The hallway tilted left and right, left and right, and then became still. He wiped the sweat off his face and stared at the door across the hall. At least he got off on the right floor.

It's the stress. You suspect your wife is out to kill you. It's a wonder you haven't collapsed into a coma by now. Better take the stairs down when you're finished. Can't have you collapsing in the elevator. That would make all the papers.

The key fit perfectly and David stepped inside. The heavy curtains blocked any natural sunlight through the windows. David flicked the switch and yellow light filled the space. Her apartment looked much like it did last time he was inside it, just a week before the wedding. Dark, austere, and exotic. He surveyed the living room. It was neat and clean. A sofa and love seat upholstered in black leather surrounded a small coffee table. An end table sat next to the sofa. The tables were made of mahogany. On the end table was a lamp. Upon closer inspection, it appeared to be made of elephant tusk. He gravitated toward the built-in wall shelf covered with carved figurines. There were a variety of animals, including many owls. He quickly identified the owl that Cat had given Haddie. The top shelf was covered in feral cats: leopards, jaguars, lions, tigers, each with prey in their mouths. David smiled. It reminded him of their nighttime wrestling matches.

What was he looking for? David wandered into the bedroom, in and out of the bathroom, and back out into the short hall. He walked into the kitchen and found a hand-written note lying on the table.

Dear David,

I love you so much. I want your birthday to be the most wonderful ever. You complete me and I want you to be with me forever and ever.

David stared at the prose. It certainly didn't read like it was from someone who wanted to "off" him. The handwriting seemed vaguely familiar, somehow.

A key clicked in the door. David spun around.

Shit.

He dropped the letter and slipped into the bedroom as the door opened. He stopped and listened as keys jingled in the other room. He glanced around, his heart racing, opened a closet door and pulled it shut behind him.

This is crazy. Why am I hiding from my own wife?

It was dark in the closet. He heard footsteps in the kitchen, and pictured her in her black pumps, her hips swaying inside her tight black skirt. The footsteps stopped. She was at the table looking at the note. Had he dropped it so fast that she would notice it was in disarray? Why wasn't she still shopping? It had only been a little over an hour and a half. Didn't women shop longer than that? Not that he knew many women ...

Cat cleared her throat and the sound carried right into the closet. Where was she? Why didn't this closet have slats in the door so he could peer out like in all the movies? He pressed his ear against the hardwood door. He could almost feel her breath. She seemed just on the other side of the door, poised to spring it open at any time. His back was flat against a metal object, a handle digging into his lower back. He peered to his left and right. It was so dark he could see nothing but a sliver of light at the base of the door. He sensed there was no place to hide in here, and if he tried to move, he would make too much noise, giving the game away.

This is stupid. I should just step out and explain myself. We'll both have a good laugh.

But he didn't move.

Shopping bags rustled on the bed. She was definitely in the bedroom now. David tried to calm his breath so he could hear her movements. A drawer slid open, a rustle, and then slid closed again. Would she have a reason to open the closet door? She began to hum. The song sounded foreign and unfamiliar. The humming faded and a metallic squeaking followed. Did she just open the medicine cabinet in the master bathroom? It squeaked closed.

The humming stopped. David listened to his breathing. Had she detected something amiss? This was ridiculous! Why was he hiding from his wife in a closet! What kind of man was he? Why didn't he jump out, demanding a reason for her apparent treachery, and force her to submit to him?

Because he didn't want to lose her. He wanted to believe that this was all a mistake. That she was eccentric, but was devoted to him for life. He wanted to believe that.

And, she scared him some, too.

Something scraped against the door. He caught his breath, standing deathly still, while her soft footsteps shifted just outside the door. David moved his arm and it brushed against some hanging clothes. Could she hear that? If she opened the door, what would he say?

Just thought I'd drop in, my dear.

Her footsteps retreated from the door, fading away. The next sound was the apartment door opening and closing shut. He let out a deep breath. He opened the closet door a crack. All was quiet.

How much time did he have? Probably none. She must be back on her way to their apartment. As he turned to close the door he saw what had been digging into his back. It was a metal filing cabinet. It seemed odd to him that a filing cabinet was sitting in the back of her closet. It had four file drawers, and a key was in the lock at the top. He reached out, turned the key and opened the top drawer.

The drawer had green folders divided by metal slings. Within each green folder were thinner manila folders. The smell that rose from the drawer reminded him of the New York Library. He read the title of the first folder. *Donald Cardigan*. Who was that? The rest of the titles contained the same name, plus subdivisions: childhood, publicity, wedding, financials.

David frowned and pulled the wedding folder. Inside was a photo of a younger Cat in a wedding dress with her groom.

Donald Cardigan. Donnie.

Cat was smiling large in the photo. Donnie was beaming. He looked at his watch. He looked back at the folders sitting in the drawer. She organized her time with Donnie with precision. The folders contained notes on his childhood; stories he must have told her and she, for some reason, typed up and archived. The financials were very detailed. They contained all assets at the time of his death, how much she expected, and where she planned to place them to optimize both risk and return. She was certainly concerned about her future. There was so much of Donnie in these files that he suspected if he read everything in the drawer, he'd know as much about Donnie as his own family had.

He looked at his watch again. Twenty minutes had passed since he checked it last. Cat was going to beat him home. He glanced down at the remaining three drawers, and pulled the second one. There were various names on multiple folders, but one caught his eye. *Margot Beasley*. David felt a shiver go up his spine. He didn't pull the titles, but pulled back on the top of each manila folder. Childhood, News Items, Family, Financials. The file on Ms. Beasley was much smaller than that for Donald. The family folder was razor thin. He pulled that file. It consisted of a single sheet of paper that read:

Margot Beasley

*Margot Beasley - born July 21, 1943, to Gerald and
Edith Beasley in Philadelphia, PA.
One sister, Mary Jane, born September 18, 1941,
deceased, no children.
Parents, both deceased.*

Margot Beasley has no children and no apparent contact with extended family. Discusses one longtime friend, Emma Watson, who died in 2003 (cancer). Has casual friends, mostly literary types, including writers she represents. Well respected by people in the business.

Conclusion - Good potential contact. Strong woman, but must have emotional needs that are not being met.

Margot Beasley - deceased, February 8, 2012.

David's pulse quickened. He had to get out and back to his apartment, but he couldn't pry his eyes from the file cabinet. There were two more drawers. He squatted and grunted as his knees tightened. He opened the next drawer. David East - Childhood; David East - News Items; David East - Family; David East - Financials.

She kept a dossier on him? Why? Could she just be obsessive compulsive, a sort of information pack rat? Did this satisfy some type of fetish? No, this was her financial file. It was her financial plan.

He leaned his body against the closet door and felt it shift against his weight. He backed off, the door's hinges squeaking as it relaxed back into place. Is this what he was? A statistic for her files? Did she just want him for his money? Was she mad? He had heard of "packrats" who could never throw anything away. Eventually, authorities would find them dead, half-eaten by their starving cats, piles of junk rising to the ceiling in all the rooms, forming narrow corridors that led to kitchens filled with dirty dishes, bedrooms with mattresses on the floor, and backrooms filled with vomit and excrement. Was she an information packrat? Did she have to document every spoken word, every formal paper, every experience, with those she loved or cared for?

No. She's out to kill you and take your money, you shit for brains.

David held his breath.

It's time to confront her and find out what the hell is going on.

His heart raced. He looked down at the last drawer.

I know what's in there.

He reached out, his hand shaking, his fingers slipping around the handle.

I know what's in there.

He didn't have to look. He no longer wanted to look. He let go of the handle and slipped out of the apartment, passing the shopping bags full of merchandise that probably set him back thousands of dollars.

It was cloudy and muggy, and the traffic was loud and continuous. He settled his thoughts on what logic there might be to all this. The sidewalk was crowded, and though he tried to concentrate, he felt himself jostling for position just to make progress along the human stream. After a few blocks, he hailed a taxi, and although the air conditioner was off, there was at least a breeze through the window when it accelerated between cars.

She batted her pretty green eyes at the captain and got away with murder.

She's guilty as hell, all right ....

She's ruthless.

David rubbed his forehead. At the very least, there was something unstable about Cat. People just don't have dossiers on people. These weren't photo albums, for chrissake. These were ... documentaries. Research. So, what did the pieces really mean?

She met Donnie, perhaps they fell in love. Eventually, they had a falling out, and instead of divorcing him and sharing the loot with the lawyers, she poisoned and drowned him. She enjoyed the high life alone for a while, but Manhattan is an expensive place. So, she worked for Haddie. For *ten* years.

David looked out the taxi window. He suddenly felt revolted. He was riding in the same type of vehicle that had run over his wife. His *first* wife. What went through Cat's mind when that happened? She got $50,000. Did that get the wheels turning in her pretty, ruthless mind? Did she think, "hey, this is easy. I'll ingratiate myself with the affluent, and collect a portion of their estates"? That didn't make sense. Why wait ten years? What did Cat gain by waiting that long if all she wanted was Haddie's money?

Why did Cat go to work for Ms. Beasley? Did she sense her ill health? Was Ms. Beasley like a wounded animal, sick and slow, that needed to be culled from the herd? He imagined Cat, sitting in a chair in her tight black skirt, her shapely legs crossed, wearing black-framed glasses, taking copious notes as Ms. Beasley barked out her orders. And quietly, inside her predator mind, she watched her, slowing to a limp, unable to keep up with the rigors of life. But, all the while, on the outside, Cat maintained her toothy smile, her apparent commitment to her boss.

I hate the smell of death.

David thought Cat rather liked it. Or at least, knew how to gain from it. And she had gained. She received a sizeable inheritance from Ms. Beasley. A hard, but nice woman, who had no immediate family, and few good friends. Cat could have taken advantage of that. And she did, just like the folder note read. *Strong woman, but must have emotional needs that are not being met.*

And now she had her sights on him. Mary saw it. The old cop saw it. People at the wedding saw that she was probably only out for his money. Was it only her and the aura she projected? Or was it as much him? Who could love a middle-aged man with a soft middle and an hourglass head? Once he became a famous writer, he had plenty of attention from women. They may have been enticed by his money, but he thought it was more. He thought it was his talent. His art. His muse. At least, as much as it was him. Haddie wrote the first novel, of course. But he had written the second novel, hadn't he? It wasn't logical to think Haddie had anything to do with it, aside from inspiring him, a phantom he created of her from his many years of living together. A product of his overactive imagination. In that sense, his imagination had served him well.

So, women were attracted to him for more than the money. Why not? Didn't he deserve to be happy? That didn't matter at the present. What mattered were the facts. And the facts point to a beautiful, but unstable, and possibly dangerous woman. What was he? An ugly, definitely unstable, mild-mannered man. Don't opposites attract?

Maybe. But he didn't think so. When he thought of it in a strictly logical manner, it pointed to his early demise by a beautiful black widow.

He paid the taxi driver, bought two double chocolate éclairs at the corner bakery and gorged himself as he walked up to his apartment. When he walked in, he was surprised Cat wasn't there, and his familiar surroundings seemed to envelop him like a cocoon. A wave of fatigue spread over him, like a heavy blanket, drawing him into the bedroom. The bed was soft and inviting. He lay down, and the bed cushioned his body, floating, soft and warm ...

As he drifted off, he heard the distance sound of keys fumbling in a door. They rang like bells. Not Christmas bells, but like a church bell, each ring distinct and deep, its bass reverberating through his body, causing it to tingle, the sense of falling.

He opened his eyes to silk. Everywhere. Covering his body, wrapping his arms, smothering his nose and mouth. Tangled in a web strewn across the bedroom, his arms pinned to his side, he struggled breathlessly at the silk threads anchored from the corners at the ceiling like a giant hammock. The tension was suffocating. He forced air in and out of his mouth in short, sharp breaths, his arms struggling, the silk strong and secure. His mind fought to stay oxygenated, his arms slowly breaking through the tangled web that enveloped him, and believing that at any moment a giant spider would spring from sight unseen, and drive its dagger-like fangs into his neck.

"David!"

David felt the adrenaline course through his body as he struggled to rise, pulling at the silk cords that bound him. He knew that voice. He strained his neck and saw Haddie. She was sprinting across the room to him, her arms outstretched, hands reaching, eyes bulging, her face contorted into fear and rage.

"David! Get out!"

David felt his body tossing from side to side like in a wild amusement park ride. Haddie faded from view, her voice turning to squeaks, unintelligible, and then falling silent as she disappeared. He felt his body tingling again, his head shaking, a weight on him, as if strapped into his seat on this wild ride. He opened his eyes and looked into Cat's green eyes, her body straddling his torso.

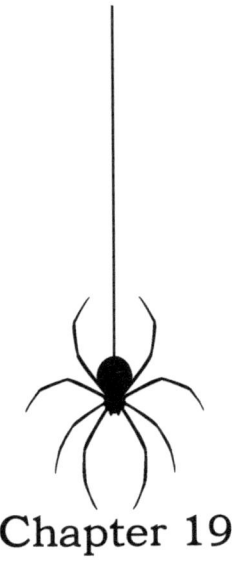

Chapter 19

"DAVID? ARE YOU OK?"

He woke panting. He writhed beneath her, and she quickly hopped off him, softly landing on her feet next to the bed. He shook his head, rubbed his temples, and struggled to sit, shaking, as if a weight still held him prone to the bed.

"That must have been some nightmare. You were screaming. I ran in here as quickly as I could."

Her eyes looked soft and caring. David had never seen that before. "I'm fine. It was just a nightmare." Expecting the inevitable question, he quickly added, "I don't even remember what it was about." He touched her hand and she squeezed it. "I'm fine, thanks."

He wasn't fine, but at that moment, it seemed to the best thing to say. As he shook off the nightmare, the events of the day rose to the surface. How would he handle her ... idiosyncrasy of documenting certain people in her life? How about the rumors, opinions, and circumstantial evidence associated with it? How about him? What are her intentions?

"OK," Cat said. "I thought we'd celebrate your birthday a day early. How's that?"

"Fine," he murmured.

"Come into the other room when you're ready," Cat winked.

David swung his legs off the bed and stood. Cat walked out of the room, her swaying hips inside her black dress catching his eye. He watched her. He'd follow her to hell if she wanted. He shrugged off the dream and cursed his imagination. He was bordering on paranoia. Watched too many movies. It was as if he had become a character in one of his books. The most beautiful woman, after Haddie, that he'd ever known was in the next room, ready to celebrate his birthday alone with him, and he was thinking her a murderer. And even though he could rationalize his suspicions by connecting all the dots from the little things he had found (and maybe the files were a bigger problem), picturing her as a murderer just seemed too "out there." It was the creation of an unsound mind. She was odd, just like him. And he wasn't a murderer, was he? He had his idiosyncrasies, didn't he? Hadn't he recently dressed up in a Roman period gladiator uniform to fight bears, scare the local women, and commiserate with his dead wife? What would Cat think of *him* if she knew that?

The living room windows were covered with a heavy fabric. He walked in to the scent of incense. Numerous candles illuminated the space, giving it almost a religious atmosphere. Cat's back was turned from him as she stood at the kitchen counter.

"Isn't it romantic?" she asked. "Summer is just so bright! I wanted something special for today."

David felt a bit groggy. "It's kind of early to start the celebrations, don't you think?"

Cat turned, holding two glasses filled with red wine. "But we have so much to do." She gave him her lustful look.

He nodded. It was romantic. A little dark, perhaps, but ...

"Have a glass of wine." Cat placed a glass full of red wine into his hand. She turned back to the counter. There was a large box on the dining table.

"That looks like quite a present." David walked over to the table and placed a hand on the package.

Cat moved quickly and took his hand. "Not now. We'll open it later."

David smiled. He placed the glass to his lips and suddenly thought of "A Kiss During Mourning." His hand froze. Cat watched him quietly, her face calm. She brought her glass to her lips and drank deeply, the red liquid disappearing into her mouth. She took a step toward him, looked up and pressed her lips against his throat.

"It's Merlot. Your favorite," she whispered.

David stared down into the blood red liquid. Was this a test? Was she testing him, or mocking him? *She knows what I'm thinking. She knows I mistrust her. She's toying with me.* He glanced at her and she calmly stared back, a thin smile on her lips. She raised her glass to her mouth and drained the final ounce, snapping her head back, and still smiling, watching him, a drop of wine dripping down her chin.

"I've never known you to reject a good Merlot. Is anything wrong?"

You're trying to kill me. You killed your first husband for the money, liked it, and clamped onto others, collecting inheritances along the way. You kept files on them, studied them, and now it's me. I am rich, and you know I would do anything for you. Except die soon enough. So, you planned your investment strategy with my assets, planned my murder, ironically imitating Haddie's novel, and once I drink this, you will be finished with me.

David tried to speak but his lips remain closed. He forced a smile.

Anything wrong? A minute ago you loved her. You just said you would follow her to hell. If you don't drink it, you'll never know. You'll be paranoid until ... next time. If you drink it and the wine is not poisoned, it's over. She's yours. If the wine is poisoned, you'll get your wish, except she'll be following you to hell. What's it going to be?

David had enough of that annoying voice in his head. He closed his eyes and drained the glass in one gulp. He waited for the instant asphyxiation to make him collapse to the floor, glass shattering, dead on arrival. But, there was no gagging, no pain, no sense of drowning. He suddenly realized that his eyes were shut so tightly it drew his face into a grimace.

"Don't you like it?" Cat purred.

He opened his eyes. She was looking up into his face. She had *that* look. The birthday lunch was going to have to wait. David smiled. He felt absolutely giddy. She was looking into his eyes with love, or at least, lust. Who cares if she knew his financials? She could have it all if he could enjoy this for ... well, at least a few years.

She kissed and leaned into him, pushing toward the bedroom. David, as always, was surprised by her strength. He grabbed her arms to turn her but she slipped his grip, keeping him off balance. He was stronger but she was quicker. He picked her up and soon felt her nails in his back, her teeth inches from his jugular. They turned and turned, each vying for dominance while not making their efforts seem too obvious. David knew the game's rules. It had to seem effortless. Pure strength or quickness would spoil the game. As they entered the bedroom it was biceps and hips, teeth and nails, and David wondered if they were going to make love or if he was just the next prey in a lioness's kill. He miscalculated the distance to the bed and lost his footing. Cat leapt onto him, wrapping her legs around his torso. David grunted as he fell back on the bed. By the time he recovered Cat had torn off his belt and mounted him, her lithe hips drawing him in, her arms around his neck.

The battle was over almost as quickly as it started. David's physical release left him breathless and relaxed. His body tingled. He looked at Cat, her hips still in control. He reached for her and found his arms would not move. He frowned and tried to raise his arms again. They were frozen. As were his legs and the rest of his body below his neck.

"Are you OK?" Cat asked.

"I can't move. I can't move my arms. Or my legs." He immediately thought that it was their lovemaking. It had finally paralyzed him.

She withdrew her hips from his now limp member. She examined his eyes. "Great. Thank God I don't have to fuck you ever again. You're gross and—" she looked down at herself, "and messy." Her voice was cruelly matter of fact.

David couldn't believe his ears. This must be some kind of joke. "Cat?" he asked, waiting for an explanation.

"Do you think I was going let you fuck me for free? That hasn't happened in a long time." She leaned forward, her hands on his chest, and looked off into space, searching for a time when she was innocent. However, she found nothing. She was evil. She was born evil, and would die the same. Evil was in her blood. It was in her DNA.

David lay there in disbelief. His tongue began to tingle. He moved it back and forth, but it felt heavy. His lips were dry. Parting them became an effort that he did not know how long he could control. He still didn't understand. What was happening to him? Why was Cat saying mean things when it was obvious he needed medical attention?

"I need a doctor," he rasped.

"I didn't let my first husband do it for free, why should I let you? He was a slovenly son of a bitch, too. Better looking, though." She arched her back and slapped his chest. "It felt so good killing him. He was so stupid, just like you." She looked down at him, and when she did, there was no love, just disgust on her face. "I got him to drink a lot that night. I slipped some barbiturates in his drink. I put a pillow over his face for several minutes. I dragged him to the car, pulled up to the stream, broke the windshield, and placed him on the hood. Aren't I ingenious? But, that mean cop got it right." She put her face right up to his. "Yes, the one you went to talk to. You think I didn't know? I put a GPS tracking device on your car. You should have listened to him, David."

She drew herself up to her knees and stroked her breasts, stomach, and hips. "I let the captain have me. Oh, he protected me against all those nasty, inquisitive investigators." She laughed, her teeth flashing. She looked down at David again. "He was grosser than you. I was eventually going to go back up there and kill him, but he died before I got the chance."

"Cat, please ..."

"Shhh. Be quiet and die." She glanced over at her clothes strewn about the room, and back into the living room. "Wait, just a second! Don't die yet." She hopped off and ran to the other room.

He heard cardboard tearing, paper rustling, and Cat humming a quiet tune. She returned quickly, wearing a low cut black dress. "See what I got you for your birthday? Do you like it?"

David remained speechless. Cat climbed back onto him. "Mmmm. I want to watch. I want to watch you die."

David's head spun. He could not believe his ears. He whispered, "Why? Why? I loved you."

"Money, my dear. You see, Donnie's money didn't last forever. I was so naïve when I killed him. I thought it would last forever, but I have expensive tastes. Beasley's money wouldn't have lasted a year.

At least I didn't have to kill her. And then there was you. You became so rich off stealing Haddie's story. And it was as much mine as yours. I did as much for her as you did."

She leaned over him. He felt her weight on his chest. His breathing was labored. It took all his energy to force oxygen into his lungs, and now Cat was bearing her weight on them, suffocating him. "Do you want to know what I poisoned you with?" She looked around the room as if unveiling a great secret. "Komodo dragon venom. From Indonesia. Did you know that scientists just figured out how those dragons kill their prey? They suspected poison, but only recently isolated it. But, did you also know that native shaman had secretly been using it in ancient rituals for thousands of years? I suspected you were going to be my next victim, and I wanted it to be special. For Haddie's sake."

She raised herself, and David felt his breathing become slightly less labored. He tried to form words in his mouth, but his tongue felt swollen, his jaw locking in place.

"It is a slow poison, but can be administered through the digestive tract. I got to use Haddie's method! Isn't that cool? I just didn't want you to eat too much, so I decided to kill you *before* lunch. Food can dilute the effects. No matter—" She inspected his eyes and throat like a doctor inspecting a patient during a physical exam. "You're coming along quite nicely."

She hopped off him. "You should have followed your gut, David. I even left you clues! I left my computer on for you to inspect. You found my filing cabinet after I dropped my keys in the park. I knew I couldn't wait at that point." She pointed a finger at him. "I was going to wait until fall. I wanted to really drive you crazy, so maybe I could show it was a suicide. You have had so many mental lapses, haven't you? But, you were just so inquisitive. You should have followed your head and not your heart. You deserve to die for being so stupid."

David's vision began to blur. Cat's body left trails as it glided around the room. She picked out a few clothes and placed them into a handbag.

"I'm glad I found you when I did. I'm still good looking, but the young men don't watch me like they used to. One called me "madam" the other day! I had to use my looks while I still could.

And you did nicely, especially considering how you treated poor Haddie. I have to leave for good, now. All this killing will catch up to me here in America. That's why I'm going to the Pacific. Tens of thousands of islands, many of them without extradition treaties to the United States! Your money's already there. Electronic transfers are a wonderful invention."

She walked over to him and sat on the bed, staring at his paralyzed body. "I want to make it clear to you before you die, David, that I never loved you. I *am* a good actress, aren't I?" She gave him her best "caring" look, her eyes turning soft, a small pout on her lips.

"Didn't you pity me, David?" She gave him a wicked smile.

David would have nodded if he could have moved his head. Instead, he stared at her blurred image.

"I've only loved once. Haddie was a beautiful woman who deserved more than you. After working for her for several years I tried to tell her that. But she never listened to me. And she always ignored my advances. Told me to find a good man. I told her they were all pigs." She looked down at her nails, and David had the distinct impression that she planned to have a manicure before hopping a flight to the other side of the world. "Can you believe that? She never would let me touch her. The only person in my life who wouldn't let me. It made me want her more. I swear if I hadn't been so important to her in her day to day business ... unlike you, she was very smart, she would've gotten rid of me. But, in the end, I knew it wasn't meant to be, though she wrote that book partially on our discussions. I had the poison idea, you know."

She leaned over him and reached out her hand, almost touching him, and then thought better of it. "Near the end I knew she was going to let me go. Things got way too tense. I hated killing her, but I had to."

David's eyes widened.

"I waited for her to leave her office. She was easy to spot with all that red hair." Cat looked off for a moment. "I'll never forget when she hit my bumper and flipped over my car, all that red hair flashing, and crashing into my windshield. She didn't have to die. She should have treated me better. I almost felt bad about spending the money she left me." She smiled at David. "Almost."

David felt tears well in his eyes. He tried to open his mouth to scream, but his muscles ignored him. He was shutting down, the image of Haddie's murderer fading. Justice! He wanted justice!

"What I can't figure out is how you wrote a second book. I know she didn't write a second one, because she had barely finished the first one when I killed her. And she would have told me if she was working on something else. She wrote that first book for me. I know she did." She ran her fingers through her blonde hair. "She loved me, but she didn't know how to tell me." Cat sighed. "But she couldn't have written a second book for you. She was dead. So, I've wondered how you could have done it." She shrugged. "Well, they say that if you put ten million monkeys in front of a computer and give them a thousand years to bang randomly on their keyboards, one will write a best seller."

Cat stood and flattened her black dress, looking at herself in the mirror. "I'll really enjoy your money, David. I'd like to stay, but on second thought I'd like to get to the airport before rush hour. It gets insane after four o'clock."

David's eyelids quivered. She came in and out of focus, as if he was alternately looking through a glass full of water. She no longer looked angry or disgusted. She looked relieved. She looked like she had taken a long journey along roads she never wanted to travel, searching for that reward that would allow her independence. Where she would have to rely on no one, where she would have to answer to no one. Ten million dollars would do that just fine.

And he hated her. As the lights gave out and he slipped away, he heard her mumble a few more words as she walked out of his life. She had killed the true love of his life. And he would take it to the grave. There was no stopping her. There would be no justice. She would live happily ever after on a tropical island. She was alone, but she seemed to have always been that way. And ten million dollars can buy her all the friends she wanted. In any make, model, or sex.

David blinked. He lifted his arms and stared at his hands as he rotated them. They moved freely, weightlessly. He looked around. He was no longer in his bedroom. This room was full of teak furniture and carpeted. A woman gasped. He lifted his head. It was Haddie.

"Oh my, David. What are you doing here?"

David's head spun. Moments ago he was lying catatonic in his bed, slipping into unconsciousness. Now, he was here with Haddie. This confused him. Since her death, whenever he dreamt of Haddie she had always come to him. So why was he dreaming that he was visiting her? Or, was it a dream at all?

"Oh shit. I'm dead, aren't I?"

"Well," Haddie said, "I've never seen you here before. You don't look like you got hit by a taxi. What happened?"

"Cat poisoned me. I must be dead."

Haddie sighed. "I tried to warn you. It came to me yesterday, or whatever time is measured in here. I suddenly had a vision of her. Actually, not her, but her car, as I was flipping head over heels when she ran me over." She sighed again. "She has been a lot of trouble to us. I am so sorry for ever hiring her."

"I treated her well. God, she said terrible things. She said she loved you. What was that all about? Why didn't you tell me?"

"She was my assistant, not yours. I'm not a homophobe, David. She was good at what she did. I never thought she'd kill me over it."

David shrugged. "I wasn't suspicious at all, at least at first. But everyone kept saying she was after my money, and that her first husband's death was odd. You even said she was cruel."

Haddie walked over and sat next to him. "Yes, I came to believe she was cold and manipulative. But, she was efficient. And there's a big difference between merely manipulative and being a cold-blooded killer."

"What a dope I am." David scratched his head. "So, am I really dead? Or am I just dreaming all this? Are you in my dream?"

"I don't think so. But, then again, if I was in your dream it wouldn't matter what I said, would it? I'd just be a manifestation of your thoughts."

"Well, are you?" David asked, sitting up and placing his hands on his knees.

"Isn't this a conundrum?" Haddie asked.

David had a vague idea what a conundrum was, but could have never used it correctly in a sentence, even in a dream. "Oh shit. I'm dead all right." Cat was going to be able to enjoy all his money, dance on his grave, and there wasn't anything he could do about it.

Haddie rubbed his back. "It's all my fault. I hired her, and kept her on long after I should have let her go. Maybe we wouldn't be dead now. I would have published my book under my name—"

She patted his knee. "No offense."

"I understand."

David understood pride of authorship. He felt that way about the second book, though as he sat there listening to Haddie discuss what might have been, he wondered how much of the second book he actually had written. He listened to Haddie as she finished the hopes she had if her book had been published while she was alive. A house on the park, time for vacations, establishing a foundation for the needy. He looked around the room. There was a window. It looked bright and sunny outside. "Well, I guess we have eternity together, now."

Haddie grimaced. "Oh."

"What's wrong?" David felt vulnerable. Cat had just killed him, which was the ultimate rejection, and now Haddie didn't want to spend eternity with him?

"Nothing, David," Haddie said quickly. "I just wasn't expecting you ... so soon." She forced a smile.

"That's comforting," David said.

"Now, don't be like that. I just wasn't expecting you."

"It really wasn't my choice. Sorry if I rained on your parade."

"Stop it, you're being mean." Haddie gave him her shark look.

"Yeah, well, I've had a hard day, being poisoned by Komodo dragon venom and all."

Haddie drew a sharp breath. "Oh! Really? Komodo dragon venom was my idea. I can't believe she stole my idea."

David stared at her. "You were going to poison me with Komodo dragon venom?"

"No, silly. Just the idea of using Komodo dragon venom. You know, in my book. I settled for cyanide because it was quick. I didn't want to have to write details about long, drawn out deaths. I just wanted Hannah in and out. Kiss him, kill him, and out the door."

David continued to stare. Her legs were long and fine, her jawline sharp, her eyes bright blue, and red hair cascading down her back. And he loved it when she spoke passionately about anything.

"David? David? You have that look, David."

He crawled forward toward her. "Yes. Are you glad to see me?"

Haddie sighed. "You *are* invading my space. I wasn't expecting you for a couple of decades."

David shrugged. "I've always been early to my appointments. And see? You get to have me while I'm still young and vigorous."

Haddie glanced at his paunch. "Lovely."

"I love you too."

He nuzzled his nose into her neck.

She giggled. "I guess I'm stuck with you. Even after death. So much for marital vows."

David kissed her and felt his body tingle. He first suspected it was because of her, but then he felt strange, as if he wanted to leap out of his body, to fall *upwards*. He looked down at his hands. "Something is happening, Haddie. I feel strange."

Haddie looked worried. "What is it, honey? What?"

David felt light-headed and the room began to swirl. He held Haddie tightly, afraid to let go, when it suddenly became clear. "I don't think I'm dead."

He looked at her and brushed his hand along her fine jaw. "I think I'm leaving you, Haddie."

She placed her hand on his head as he began to drift away. "I promise I'll be ready for you next time. Just don't surprise me like that."

David laughed. "Well, I'll do what I can."

As Haddie faded from view, he heard her final words.

"Make sure she pays for what she did!"

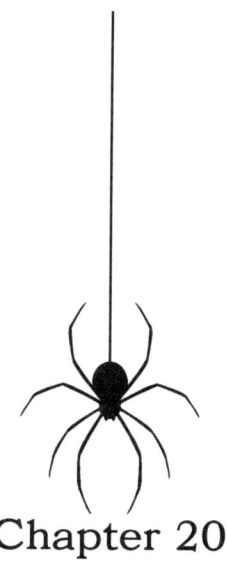

Chapter 20

"Yes, yes, you keep promising me, but I haven't seen a draft of anything, yet," Mary said.

David smiled into his cell phone. The maple leaves were bare outside his window, framed by the perpetual conifer green that dominated the Adirondack Mountains. The ground was covered by several inches of snow. Yes, he had promised Mary several times that a draft was coming along, not imminent by any stretch of the imagination, but coming along. That was not true. He had been preoccupied by Cat, and then the media circus surrounding her arrest. He could hardly escape the paparazzi, and when he did, he couldn't turn on the television, surf the Internet, listen to the radio, or even look outside his Manhattan window without being reminded of his near demise by the "Cat lady" as she was called. It was a mess.

Thank God she killed herself shortly after being taken into custody. David suspected it was because Cat had lost her anonymity. The police were investigating no fewer than eight murders based on the dossiers Cat kept in her file cabinet. How she got away with her murderous ways for so long was fodder for the talking heads, but David wasn't surprised. She certainly got her claws into him. And the doctors said it was only by the grace of the two chocolate éclairs that he didn't succumb to the Komodo dragon venom. All that chocolate and cream soaked up the poison, slowing its absorption into his circulatory system. The concentration remained just under the lethal dose threshold. He joked in a press conference that he would now eat two éclairs every day to foil anyone with evil plans to poison him in the future.

The media intensified for a short while after Cat's death, but then died out everywhere except for the most outlandish tabloids. One wrote that Cat had been abducted by aliens and swore vengeance on all of humankind.

So, no, he hadn't written a word of his next novel. But he really did know what he wanted to write about now. And he had a place to do it. He bought the Bear Lake Lodge and kept Mel and Kate on as caretakers. They worked hard and he adopted a lot of their ideas, like local potluck Saturday night barbecues and extra fish stockings of the lake. Local village people first came to the barbecues to gawk at the famous writer, but that died down quickly, and now he felt that a crowd showed up simply because they had a good time. They planned a fishing derby for the kids next spring. He wasn't going to get rich off the place, but he wasn't going to lose much money either, and he thought within a few years it would probably pay for itself. And he always had a clean place to write. He saw himself spending more and more time up here, and less and less down in the city.

"I'll have a clean draft in spring. I promise."

It sounded like she cleared a hairball from her throat. "Spring? Good Lord, David."

David briefly thought about inviting her up to the lodge. She had lost some weight and was more active. He saw her fast walking around Central Park several times, wearing her iPod and rocking out to Iggy Pop. She looked less matronly, and dressed ... younger was the best term, during their frequent lunches. But, it was too soon after his relationship with Cat to think about another woman.

"I promise, Mary. By spring."

There was silence. David knew Mary was jockeying for some sort of position. Spring was too far away! He was sure the publisher was leaning on Mary pretty hard. He could hear the man now. "Get him writing while the iron is hot! With all this media attention, a new David East book would sell like hotcakes! We would break records!"

"So, how far along are you?"

David stared at the computer screen. "Chapter 1" sat there, all alone on the page. "I've started, Mary."

There was silence again. Finally, "OK, OK. I'll stop bugging you. Are you doing OK?"

"Yes I am. And thanks for asking."

And he really was doing OK. As soon as the media died down, Cat quickly became a forgotten chapter in his life. He tried not to feel vengeful towards her. It wasn't that she wanted him only for his money or that she nearly killed him. She killed the only woman he ever loved. He may have been infatuated, mesmerized even, but he had never been truly in love with Cat. That was reserved for only one woman. And Cat had killed her.

But he tried not to dwell on those thoughts. He tried to keep the memory of Haddie alive inside him. He no longer had dreams about her. He missed them, but it was definitely in his best mental interest not to have them. He believed now that he would see her again, when he was all wrinkled like a prune and wearing adult diapers.

And he decided that if Cat was right, and Haddie had written her first book for her, and the second book for him, then this book was going to be written for Haddie.

A tale of love, mystery, and murder. A hint of the paranormal. Redemption. Shit, it had it all. How could he go wrong? He stared at the page, and began to type.

Andrei jumped from the taxi and raced to the hospital entrance as they pulled his wife out of the ambulance. Hannah stared up at him from the stretcher, her hand reaching for his, her flaming red hair matted with blood. He wondered how bad it was under that sheet.

"Hannah, you're going to be OK."

www.ingramcontent.com/pod-product-compliance
Lightning Source LLC
Chambersburg PA
CBHW071127170626
46809CB00002B/519